PRAISE FOR *1921*

"Llywelyn continues her magnificent multivolume saga chronicling the twentieth-century struggle for Irish independence. As in *1916*, she masterfully interweaves historical figures and events with fictional ones, providing both a panoramic and an intimate view of the Irish Civil War. . . . The lucid narrative and the compelling subject matter will enthrall both Irish history buffs and fans of sweeping historical fiction." —*Booklist*

"Morgan is unexcelled in her knowledge of Irish history and culture. For twenty years she has been my inspiration when it comes to meticulous research and respect for the people who lived her stories." —Lucia St. Clair Robson

"In sum *1921* is yet another of Morgan Llywelyn's epochal works breathing a soul into remarkable events of the past and doing so in a wonderfully warm, exciting and easy to read fashion." —John P. Flaherty, Chief Justice of the Supreme Court of Pennsylvania

"Morgan Llywelyn has written a masterpiece; I believe it is her best work yet. For Irish people born in the twentieth century, *1921* should be required reading." —Jean K. Bills, President of Celtic Women International, Ltd.

"That Llywelyn knows her Irish history, culture, language and ambience is unquestionable. . . . The account of the civil war is thorough and nuanced." —*Publishers Weekly*

PRAISE FOR *1916*

"The task of transforming the events of the 1916 Irish Rebellion into coherent fiction would terrify most writers. Llywelyn, however, has produced a thunderous, informative read that rises to the challenge. . . . Battle scenes are both accurate and compelling. The betrayals, slaughters and passions of the day are all splendidly depicted as Llywelyn delivers a blow-by-blow account of the rebellion and its immediate aftermath. The novel's abundant footnotes should satisfy history buffs; its easy, gripping style will enthrall casual readers with what is Llywelyn's best work yet."
—*Publishers Weekly* (Starred review)

"A timely and gripping novel. . . . The historical characters are woven into a masterful plot."　　　—*The Irish Times*

"The politics and factionalism behind the Rising are a tangled web indeed, but Llywelyn unravels them skillfully. Even those who know the story well will be surprised and rewarded by the way she brings back to life a group of brave men who went nobly to their deaths."
—*The Philadelphia Inquirer*

"In my judgement Morgan Llywelyn is a preeminent author of the twentieth century—and *the* preeminent in so far as I am concerned. *[1916]* is a GREAT historical novel."
—Senator Jesse Helms

"Llywelyn tells her tale with gusto and a respect for the facts."　　　　　　　　　　—*Kirkus Reviews*

"Llywelyn's *1916* is a work of true creative genius . . . will captivate those who love Ireland and are stirred by heroic virtue in the fight for human freedom."
—William M. Bulger, President of
the University of Massachussetts

"The reader is swept up in both the glory and the tragedy of the doomed battle for Irish independence. . . . First-rate historical fiction that will appeal to anyone with an interest in Ireland's tragic past."　　　　　—*Booklist*

DECLARATION OF INDEPENDENCE

WHEREAS the Irish people is by right a free people:

And whereas for seven hundred years the Irish people has never ceased to repudiate and has repeatedly protested in arms against foreign usurpation:

And whereas English rule in this country is, and always has been, based upon force and fraud and maintained by military occupation against the declared wish of the people:

And whereas the Irish Republic was proclaimed in Dublin on Easter Monday, 1916, by the Irish Republican Army, acting on behalf of the Irish people:

And whereas the Irish people is resolved to secure and maintain its complete independence in order to promote the common weal, to reestablish justice, to provide for future defence, to ensure peace at home and good will with all nations, and to constitute a national policy based upon the people's will, with equal right and equal opportunity for every citizen:

And whereas at the threshold of a new era in history the Irish electorate has in the General Election of December, 1918, seized the first occasion to declare by an overwhelming majority its firm allegiance to the Irish Republic:

Now, therefore, we the elected Representatives of the ancient Irish people in National Parliament assembled, do, in the name of the Irish nation, ratify the establishment of the Irish Republic and pledge ourselves and our people to make this declaration effective by every means at our command:

We ordain that the elected Representatives of the Irish people alone have power to make laws binding on the people of Ireland, and that the Irish Parliament is the only Parliament to which that people will give its allegiance:

We solemnly declare foreign government in Ireland to be an invasion of our national right which we will never tolerate, and we demand the evacuation of our country by the English Garrison:

We claim for our national independence the recognition and support of every free nation in the world, and we proclaim that independence to be a condition precedent to international peace hereafter:

In the name of the Irish people we humbly commit our destiny to Almighty God Who gave our fathers the courage and determination to persevere through long centuries of a ruthless tyranny, and strong in the justice of the cause which they have handed down to us, we ask His Divine blessing on this last stage of the struggle we have pledged ourselves to carry through to freedom.

BY MORGAN LLYWELYN
FROM TOM DOHERTY ASSOCIATES

1921

Morgan Llywelyn

FORGE®

A TOM DOHERTY ASSOCIATES BOOK
NEW YORK

This is a work of fiction. All the characters and events portrayed in this book are either products of the author's imagination or are used fictitiously.

1921

Copyright © 2001 by Morgan Llywelyn

A Forge Book
Published by Tom Doherty Associates, LLC
175 Fifth Avenue
New York, NY 10010

www.tor.com

Forge® is a registered trademark of Tom Doherty Associates, LLC.

ISBN: 0-812-57079-0
Library of Congress Catalog Card Number: 00-49021

First edition: March 2001
First mass market edition: March 2002

Printed in the United States of America

0 9 8 7 6 5 4 3 2 1

*For
Henry and Ella,
my grandparents*

Acknowledgments

The author wishes to express her gratitude to the numerous people who, in both a public and a private capacity, made this book possible. Family members of participants in the events of 1920–1923 gave generously of their time and memories, even allowing access to personal papers that may never be published. When they have asked that a relative not be mentioned by name in the narrative, their wishes have been respected.

A special thank-you goes to Alex Gogan for bringing me into the era of the Internet.

Last but certainly not least is Sonia Schorman. She is the first to read my books while still in draft form, and her comments and criticisms are invaluable.

This history came to me warm with living breath. Any errors in retelling it are my own.

No matter what the future may hold for the Irish nation, the seven years—1916 to 1923—must ever remain a period of absorbing interest.

Not for over two hundred years has there been such a period of intense and sustained effort to regain the national sovereignty and independence. Over the greater part of the period it was the effort of, one might say, the entire nation. An overwhelming majority of the people of this island combined voluntarily during these years in pursuit of a common purpose.

—EAMON DE VALERA

Frank Hardman: Ned's older brother.

Dramatis Personae

Fictional Characters

Henry Mooney: Born 1883 in County Clare, Ireland. Journalist.

Hannah Mooney: Henry's widowed mother.

Bernard (b. 1885) and **Noel** (b. 1891) **Mooney:** Henry's brothers.

Pauline "Polly" (b. 1895) and **Alice** (b. 1902) **Mooney:** Henry's sisters.

Louise Kearney: Henry's widowed cousin.

Edward Joseph Halloran (Ned): Born 1897 in County Clare. Member of the Irish Volunteers.

Síle Duffy Halloran: Born 1895 in County Clare. Married to Ned Halloran.

Ursula Jervis ("Precious"): Born approximately 1910 in Dublin. Abandoned during the Bachelor's Walk massacre in 1914. Informally adopted by Ned and Síle Halloran.

Matt Nugent: Dublin-based journalist specializing in international news.

Frank Halloran: Ned's older brother.

Norah Daly: Ned's aunt; his mother's sister.

Lucy and Eileen Halloran: Ned's younger sisters.

Ella Mansell Rutledge: Anglo-Irish widow. Older brother, Edwin Mansell, a solicitor, is married to Ava. Ella's younger sister is Madge Mansell.

Kathleen Halloran Campbell: Ned's older sister who lives in America.

Father Paul O'Shaughnessy: Former parish priest at Saint Xavier's in Manhattan.

Tilly Burgess: The Mansells' parlor maid.

Hester: The Mansells' cook.

The Walshe family: Friends of Louise Kearney.

Major Wallace Congreve: Ella's suitor.

Ernest and Winifred Mansell, Donald Baines, Ruth Mansell Moore, Ninian Speer: Ella's London cousins.

Hector Hamilton: Painless dentist.

Historical Characters

Ackerman, Carl: American reporter for the *Philadelphia Ledger* who secretly worked as an informant for the British government.

Aiken, Frank (1898–1983): Appointed chief of staff of the IRA following the death of Liam Lynch.

Ashe, Thomas (1885–1917): Kerry-born, a teacher in the Dublin National Schools and resident of Lusk in North County Dublin; commanded the Fifth Battalion, North County Dublin (the Fingal Volunteers), during Easter Week. Died while on hunger strike. Grand-uncle of film star Gregory Peck.

Asquith, Herbert Henry (1852–1928): Prime minister of the United Kingdom, 1908–1916.

Barrett, Richard: Republican executed, together with McKelvey, Mellows, and O'Connor, in retaliation for the murder of Seán Hales.

Barry, Kevin Gerard (1902–1920): Member of the Irish Volunteers; graduate of Belvedere; medical student.

Barry, Tom (1898–1980): Member of the Irish Volunteers; commander of the West Cork flying column.

Barton, Robert Childers (1881–1975): Cousin of Erskine Childers; commandant in the Volunteers; member of the Treaty delegation; elected Teachtai Dála (member of the Irish parliament, or Dáil Éireann) for Wicklow/Kildare.

Boland, Harry (1887–1922): Member of the Sinn Féin executive committee; member of IRB; assisted Michael Collins in organizing de Valera's escape from Lincoln Prison in February 1919; elected TD for South Roscommon 1919.

Breen, Dan (1894–1969): Born near Soloheadbeg, County Tipperary. Joined the Irish Volunteers in 1914; later served as quartermaster of the Third Tipperary Brigade. Co-planner of the Soloheadbeg Ambush and a member of Michael Collins' counterintelligence squad.

Breen, Honora Moore: Dan Breen's mother.

Brennan, Michael: FOC (first officer commanding), East Clare Brigade, Irish Volunteers; organizer of the first Clare flying column; later in charge of all three Clare Brigades of the IRA; commanded government troops in Limerick during the Civil War; became chief of staff of the Irish Army in the 1930s.

Brereton, Captain: British officer in Dublin during 1916.

Broy, Eamonn "Ned" (1887–1972): One of Michael Collins' most valuable "Castle Spies"; secretary to Collins during the Treaty negotiations; Garda commissioner, 1933–38.

Brugha, Cathal (1874–1922): Born Charles William St. John Burgess, in Dublin. Second in command under Eamonn Ceannt at the South Dublin Union during the Easter Rising; member of the Sinn Féin executive committee; chief of staff, Irish Volunteers, November 1917–April 1919; elected Member of Parliament for Waterford in 1918; presided at first Dáil Éireann and was appointed as its acting president.

Burke, Frank: Student at Saint Enda's who fought in the Rising. Later last headmaster of Saint Enda's.

Carson, Sir Edward (1854–1935): Leader of the Irish Unionist Party. In 1895 he was the Crown prosecutor at the trial that destroyed Oscar Wilde's career and, ultimately, his life.

Chamberlain, Austin: Leader of the British House of Commons and son of Joseph Chamberlain, a British politician who had been adamantly opposed to granting Home Rule to Ireland.

Childers, Robert Erskine (1870–1922): British-born, best-selling novelist (*The Riddle of the Sands*) and daring yachtsman. Mustered out of the Royal Air Force with the rank of major. Devoted to the cause of Irish freedom, Childers ran guns for the Volunteers before the 1916 Rising. With Desmond FitzGerald he managed the Republican Publicity Bureau and helped develop the *Irish Bulletin*. Teachtai Dála (member of the Irish parliament) for Wicklow; chief secretary to the Treaty delegation. Executed by the Irish Free State.

Childers, Molly: His wife.

Churchill, Winston Leonard Spencer (1874–1965): British secretary for war; later prime minister.

Clarke, Kathleen Daly (1878–1972): Widow of Thomas Clarke. Member of Sinn Féin executive committee; arrested May 17, 1918, and deported without trial; returned in the general amnesty; worked for Irish National Aid Association and Irish Volunteers' Dependants Fund; appointed a justice of the Republican Courts established in 1920. Later served as a senator, then in 1939 became the first female lord mayor of Dublin.

Clarke, Thomas James (1857–1916): Member of the executive committee of the Irish Republican Brotherhood; first signatory of the Proclamation; executed by the British May 3, 1916.

Cleary, Bridget: Tipperary woman burned to death by her husband in 1895.

Clemenceau, Georges (1841–1929): Premier of France, 1917–1920; president of the Peace Conference at Versailles.

Cohalan, Judge Daniel J.: Judge in the New York Supreme Court and head of the Friends of Irish Freedom, one of the most influential Irish-American organizations.

Collins, Michael (1890–1922): Born at Woodfield, Clonakilty, County Cork. Member and later president of the Irish Republican Brotherhood; aide-de-camp to Joseph Plunkett during the 1916 Rising; secretary of the Irish Volunteers' Dependants Fund; minister of home affairs, 1918; minister for finance, 1919–22; organizer of the Irish intelligence system; member of the Treaty delegation; chairman of the Provisional Government of the Irish Free State, 1922; commander in chief of Free State forces, 1922.

Connolly, James (1870–1916): Born in Edinburgh of County Monaghan parents, always considered himself an Ulsterman. Trade union organizer; dedicated Socialist; signatory of the Proclamation of the Irish Republic; commandant-general of the Dublin forces during the 1916 Rising; executed by the British on May 12, 1916.

Cosgrave, William Thomas (1880–1965): Won the Kilkenny seat for Sinn Féin in 1917. First president of the Irish Free State.

Craig, Sir James: Succeeded Edward Carson as leader of Ulster Unionist Party; subsequently named prime minister of Northern Ireland.

Dalton, James Emmet (1998–1978): Former major in the British Army; director of training for the IRA in 1921; aide and advisor to Michael Collins; in charge of the bombardment of the Four Courts; briefly clerk of Seanad Éireann; later, made a film career in Hollywood and London.

Deasy, Liam (1896–1974): Member of the IRA executive committee and commandant-general of the Southern Division under Liam Lynch.

de Valera, Eamon (1882–1975): Born in New York City to an Irish mother. Commanded the Third Dublin Battalion during the 1916 Rising; was the last commanding officer to surrender; elected as Member of Parliament for Clare in 1918; president of the first Dáil Éireann; named president of the Irish Republic in 1921; resigned from Dáil Éireann after the Treaty was signed; led the anti-Treaty resistance. Became president of the Irish Free State in 1932.

Dillon, John (1885–1927): Upon the death of John Redmond became leader of the Irish Parliamentary Party.

Duffy, George Gavan (1882–1951): Barrister; prepared the defense for Roger Casement; helped arrange the First Dáil and draft its Constitution; elected TD for South Dublin. Member of the Treaty delegation.

Duggan, Eamonn (1874–1936): Solicitor; commandant in the Volunteers; elected TD for South Meath 1918–1923; member of the Treaty delegation; became minister for home affairs in the Free State government and later secretary to the minister for defense.

FitzGerald, Desmond (1888–1947): Director of publicity for Dáil Éireann 1919–1921; cofounder of the *Irish Bulletin*; minister for external affairs in the Free State government. Father of future taoiseach Garrett Fitz-Gerald.

FitzGerald, Frank: Brother of Desmond FitzGerald.

Fitzgerald, Michael: Republican prisoner who died on hunger strike in Cork Jail.

Fitzsimons, Anna (later Kelly): Member of Sinn Féin office staff after 1916; worked on the *Irish Bulletin*.

French, John Denton Pinkstone: Commander in chief of the British Home Forces in 1916; appointed as lord-lieutenant of Ireland 1918–1921.

Fuller, Stephen: Member of the IRA; lone survivor of the blast at Ballyseedy; Fíanna Fail TD 1937–1942.

Gallagher, Frank (1898–1962): Cork-born journalist, cofounder of the *Irish Bulletin*; later first editor of the *Irish*

Press; director of the Government Information Bureau in the 1950s.

George V (1865–1936): King of the United Kingdom, 1910–1936.

Griffith, Arthur (1871–1922): Journalist, editor of the *United Irishman*; publisher of *Sinn Féin* and founder of the Sinn Féin political party in 1905.

Hales, Seán: Dáil delegate murdered by Republicans.

Harrington, George and Michael: Reporters for the *Cork Examiner*.

Harrington, Tim: Their brother, and editor of the *Irish Independent*.

Healy, John: Editor of the *Irish Times*.

Hitler Adolf (1889–1945): Born in Austria; served in German army during WWI; joined German Workers Party (later National Socialist, or Nazi party); appointed chancellor of Germany in 1933; when offices of chancellor and president were merged he assumed the title of Führer and became dictator of Germany.

Hogan, Seán: Member of the Irish Volunteers; took part in the Soloheadbeg Ambush; commanded the flying column of the 3rd Tipperary Brigade; took part in the ambush of Lord French.

Hyde, Douglas (1860–1949): Founder and first president of the Gaelic League. Later first president of the Republic of Ireland.

Hyland, Joe: Michael Collins' trusted taxi driver.

Joyce, Brian: Student at Saint Enda's; fought in the Rising.

Kearney, Peader (1883–1942): Composer of "A Soldier's Song," which became the Irish National Anthem. Also the uncle of writer Brendán Behan.

Kiernan, Kitty: Michael Collins' fiancée.

Larkin, James (1876–1947): Leader of the Irish trade union movement.

Larkin, Peter: Brother of James Larkin and cofounder of the Workers' Union of Ireland.

Lavery, Sir John (1856–1941), and his wife, **Hazel Lavery:** Sir John was a famous portrait painter whose wife was one of the acknowledged beauties of British society.

Lester, Seán (1888–1959): Journalist; editor of the *Freeman's Journal*; director of publicity for the Free State government; appointed high commissioner for Danzig by the League of Nations; appointed last secretary general of the League of Nations in 1940.

Lloyd George, David (1863–1945): British minister of munitions and secretary of state for war; prime minister 1916–1922.

Lynch, Liam (1893–1923): Member of the supreme council of the IRB; commandant of Cork No. 2 Brigade in 1919; divisional commandant 1921; chief of staff of the Irish Republican Army following the Treaty.

Lynch, Patrick: Former Crown prosecutor who opposed de Valera in East Clare by-election, 1917.

Macardle, Dorothy (1899–1958): Historian; novelist; drama critic; worked for the Republican Publicity Bureau; author of the *Irish Republic* (1937).

MacBride, Maud Gonne (1865–1953): Legendary beauty who inspired W. B. Yeats. Married Major John MacBride, who was executed following the 1916 Rising.

MacBride, Seán (1904–1988): Son of Maude Gonne and Major John MacBride. Journalist; chief of staff of the IRA 1936–38; barrister; founder of Clann na Poblachta in 1946; minister for external affairs 1948; founder-member of Amnesty International; won Nobel Peace Prize in 1976.

MacCann, Pierce: Member of Dáil Éireann who died of influenza in Gloucester Jail.

MacCurtáin, Tomás (1884–1920): Lord mayor of Cork; murdered in 1920 by British order.

MacDermott, Seán (1884–1916): IRB organizer; one of the executed leaders of the 1916 Rising.

MacDonagh, John: Photographer and brother of Thomas MacDonagh (1878–1916), one of the executed leaders of the 1916 Rising.

MacDonagh, Joseph: Brother of Thomas and John; first headmaster of Saint Enda's after Pearse's death.

MacDonagh, Muriel: Widow of Thomas MacDonagh.

MacEoin, Seán: Member of the Irish Volunteers; vice-commandant, Longford Brigade; elected TD for Longford/Westmenath; commanded Free State forces in the midlands in 1922.

MacGarry, Seán: President of the supreme council of the IRB in 1917; general secretary of the Volunteers.

MacGilligan, Kathleen: Worked on the staff of the *Irish Bulletin*.

McGuinness, Joseph: Sinn Féin member elected Member of Parliament for South Longford while in prison.

McKelvey, Joseph: IRA officer from County Tyrone who defended the nationalist minority during the Belfast pogroms in 1920. Appointed chief of staff by the Four Courts garrison.

McKenna, Kathleen: Secretary to Desmond FitzGerald and Erskine Childers in the Dáil Department of Publicity; member of *Irish Bulletin* staff; private secretary to Arthur Griffith with the Treaty delegation.

MacNeill, Eoin (1867–1945): Born in County Antrim. Cofounder of the Gaelic League; university lecturer and historian; first president and chief of staff of the Irish National Volunteer Corps.

Macready, Sir Neville: Commander in chief of British forces in Ireland.

MacSwiney, Mary: Sister of Terence MacSwiney; dedicated republican; became a Teachtai Dála in Dáil Eireann.

MacSwiney, Terence (1879–1920): Succeeded Tomás MacCurtáin as lord mayor of Cork in 1920; arrested by the British; died while on hunger strike in Brixton Prison.

Maguire, Josephine and **Sarsfield:** Publisher and editor, respectively, of the *Clare Champion.*

Markievicz, Constance (1868–1927): Born in London, daughter of Sir Henry Gore-Booth and Georgina nee Hill, granddaughter of the Earl of Scarborough. Raised in County Sligo. Married Count Casimir Markievicz; founded Na Fíanna Éireann; became an officer in the Citizen Army; fought in the 1916 Rising; was the first woman elected to the British Parliament; refused to take her seat at Westminster and instead became the first minister for labor in Ireland.

Maxwell, General Sir John: Commander in chief of the British forces in Ireland during the 1916 Rising.

Mellows, Liam (1892–1922): Quartermaster general, Irish Republican Army.

Milroy, Seán: Member of the Sinn Féin executive committee and organizer of elections.

Mulcahy, Mary Ryan "Min": She and her sister Phyllis were the last two civilians to see Seán MacDermott alive. Phyllis married Seán T. O'Kelly; Min married Richard Mulcahy.

Mulcahy, Richard (1886–1971): Second in command to Thomas Ashe during 1916 Rising; commandant, second Dublin Battalion; commandant, Dublin Brigade; chief of staff of the Irish Republican Army; commander of Free State military forces, 1922–23; elected Teachtai Dála for Dublin, 1922–43, and for Tipperary, 1944–61; minister of defense, 1923–24; senator, 1943–44; leader of Fine Gael Party, 1944–59; minister of education, 1948–51 and 1954–57.

Murphy, Joseph: Republican prisoner who died on hunger strike in Cork Jail.

Murphy, Sheila: Worked on the staff of the *Irish Bulletin*.

Murphy, William Martin (1844–1919): Businessman; owner of the *Irish Independent* newspaper, and chairman of Dublin United Tramways Company.

Nicholas II (1868–1918): Last tsar of Russia.

O'Brien, Nora Connolly: Daughter of James Connolly.

O'Callaghan, Michael: Lord mayor of Limerick, murdered by the Black and Tans. His wife subsequently became a Teachtai Dála in Dáil Éireann.

O'Connell, Kathleen: Eamon de Valera's secretary.

O'Connor, Rory (1883–1922): Member of the IRB; director of engineering, Irish Republican Army.

O'Daly, Major General Paddy: Member of Collins' assassination squad; led Free State assault on the Four Courts; general officer commanding, Kerry Command.

O'Duffy, General Eoin (1892–1944): Chief of staff, Free State Army, later commissioner of the Garda Síochána.

O'Dwyer, Rev. Dr. Edward Thomas: Bishop of Limerick, 1886–1917.

O'Flanagan, Father Michael: Vice-president of Sinn Féin.

O'Hegarty, Diarmuid: Member of the executive committee of the Irish Volunteers.

O'Higgins, Kevin (1892–1927): Elected in 1918 as Sinn Féin Member of Parliament for Laois; in 1919 was appointed assistant minister for local government in the first Dáil Éireann; in 1922 became minister for justice and external affairs in the Irish Free State. Established the Garda Siochána as an unarmed police force to replace the RIC. Assassinated in 1927.

O'Kelly, Seán T. (1881–1966): Member of the Irish Volunteers; fought in the Easter Rising; second president of the Republic of Ireland.

O' Máille, Pádraig: Deputy speaker of the Third Dáil.

O'Malley, Ernest (1898–1957): Member of the Irish Volunteers; took part in the Easter Rising; captain of headquarters staff, South Tipperary Brigade of the IRA in 1920; president of the first Republican Land Court in East Limerick; commander second Southern Division, Irish Republican Army, and member of the IRA army council in 1922.

O'Sullivan, Christopher: Proprietor and editor of the *Limerick Echo*.

Parnell, Charles Stewart (1846–1891): Leader of the Irish Parliamentary Party.

Pearse, Margaret Brady (1857–1932): Mother of Pádraic and Willie Pearse. Elected to Dáil Éireann; subsequently became a senator and a member of the Fíanna Fail executive committee.

Pearse, Pádraic (Patrick Henry Pearse) (1879–1916): Born in Dublin. Educationalist; poet; barrister; member of the Gaelic League; founder of Saint Enda's School in Rathfarnham; organizing director for the Irish National Volunteer Corps; member of the supreme council of Irish Republican Brotherhood; chief author and signatory of the Proclamation; commander in chief of the Republican forces in 1916; president of the Provisional Government of the Irish Republic; executed by the British on May 3, 1916.

Plunkett, George Noble: Made a papal count for services to the Catholic Church; appointed director of the National Museum of Science and Art in 1907; won North Roscommon by-election, 1917; appointed minister for foreign affairs, 1919; member of Irish delegation to the Paris Peace Conference; father of Joseph Mary Plunkett.

Plunkett, Grace Gifford (1888–1955): Widow of Joseph Mary Plunkett.

Plunkett, Joseph Mary (1887–1916): Cofounder of the Irish Theatre; editor of the *Irish Review*; member of the military council of the IRB; director of military operations for the 1916 Rising; chief of staff, Headquarters Company, in the GPO. Executed by the British on May 4, 1916.

Quinn, Ellen: Young mother in Galway who was murdered by the Black and Tans.

Redmond John (1856–1918): Leader of the Irish Parliamentary Party. Born of Catholic parents in County Wexford, Ireland. Died March 6, 1918, and was replaced as party leader by John Dillon.

Redmond, Major William: Brother of John Redmond; Member of Parliament for East Clare; killed at Messines.

Robinson, Séamus: Commanded the South Tipperary Brigade; participant in th Soloheadbeg Ambush.

Roosevelt, Franklin Delano (1882–1945): New York attorney; later became president of the United States.

Savage, Martin: Member of second Dublin Battalion, Irish Volunteers; fought in the GPO during the Easter Rising; shot during ambush on Lord French.

Shaw, George Bernard (1856–1950): Dublin-born playwright; literary critic; Socialist; winner of the Nobel Prize for Literature in 1925.

Smith, F. E., First Earl Birkenhead: Lord chancellor of Britain.

Smith, Patrick "The Dog": Detective with G Division, Dublin Castle.

Stack, Austin (1879–1929): Commandant of the Kerry Brigade; member of supreme council of the IRB; IRA deputy chief of staff; elected Teachtai Dála for Kerry; appointed as minister for home affairs in 1921; set up Sinn Féin courts and appointed judges.

Steele, John: Foreign correspondent for the *Chicago Tribune*.

Tobin, Liam: In charge of Michael Collins' intelligence office at Number 3 Crow Street.

Tone, Wolfe (1791–1828): Soldier, author, and revolutionary.

Traynor, Oscar (1886–1963): Commandant of Dublin No. 1 Brigade, IRA; commanded O'Connell Street fighting; elected Teachtai Dála for North Dublin, 1925–27 and 1932–61; appointed minister for posts and telegraphs 1936, minister for defense 1939, minister for justice 1957.

Treacy, Seán: Organizer of Volunteers in South Tipperary; second in command to Seámus Robinson of the South Tipperary Brigade; took part in the Soloheadbeg Ambush. Close friend of Dan Breen, and with him became a member of Michael Collins' squad. Shot dead in Talbot Street, October 14, 1920.

Wells, H. G. (1866–1946): British novelist; author of *The Outline of History*.

Wilson, Sir Henry Hughes (1864–1922): Chief of British imperial staff, 1918–22. Urged Irish conscription; recruited the "Cairo Gang"; became Unionist Member of Parliament for North Down and security advisor to the Northern Irish government in 1922. Executed by order of Michael Collins.

Wilson, Lee: District inspector, Royal Irish Constabulary.

Wilson, Thomas Woodrow (1856–1924): Twenty-eighth president of the United States.

Chapter One

GIFT-wrapped in a glistening membrane, the tips of two tiny hooves were barely visible within the old mare's birth canal. Her foal would be born headfirst like a diver plunging into life.

Before the slow seepage of years leached away her color the mare had been a lustrous gray, with shadowy dapples like black pearls seen through a mist. Now she was a dingy white, but her head was still beautiful. The huge eyes and tiny muzzle typical of Connemara ponies held a hint of Arab antecedents: a reminder of the ancient folkloric connection between Ireland and Egypt.

The cow byre that served as her stable smelled of musty straw. Icy rain spattered on the tin roof with a sound like fat sizzling in a skillet.

The little mare lay with her legs folded under her body. Her eyes were half-closed until her sides gave a violent heave. Flinging up her head, she turned to look anxiously at the man who knelt behind her on the straw.

Henry Mooney had taken off his coat and was working in his shirtsleeves as he tried to get a grip on the unborn foal. In spite of the cold he was sweating. "Be easy now, pet, be easy—you're doing grand," he murmured. His deep voice conveyed more confidence than he felt.

"What's taking so long?" a woman called from the doorway. "You're as slow as a wet wick. We et dinner without you and the afternoon's almost over."

Henry glanced up to see his mother silhouetted against spears of rain. "I'm doing my best, Mam . . . for a man who hasn't a blind notion what he's about," he added under his breath.

"Sorry? I can't hear you." Hannah Mooney picked her way toward him across the straw. A rustle of fabric, a smell of damp wool. She was scowling. She habitually scowled at her eldest son.

Nothing in Henry's appearance explained her displeasure. He kept his brown hair well brushed and was always clean-shaven. His was a kindly face, intelligent rather than handsome. A broad penthouse of forehead rose above a shelf of dark brows. Eyes of a clear deep blue were bracketed with laugh lines; a heavy jaw was redeemed by a generous mouth, shaped for smiling.

Henry was not smiling now. "I can hardly see what I'm doing with you blocking the light, Mam. Would you ever fetch me a lantern from the house?"

Ignoring him, she shrugged off her black woolen shawl to reveal a black flannel dress and jacket. No color, no ornamentation; not even a wisp of lace. The high collar reached her jawbone; the weighted hem swept the ground. For fifteen years Hannah Mooney had worn—some might say flaunted—widow's weeds in their most extreme form. In this somber attire she attended Mass twice daily, stays creaking as she paced down the center aisle to the front pew: a small woman with a large talent for dominating space.

Henry had once remarked that his mother sucked up all the air in a room.

Pursing her lips, she gave her shawl a vigorous shaking that showered man and pony. Then she slowly, deliberately, rearranged the shawl around her shoulders. At last she cleared her throat. As he knew he must, her son looked up. "A lantern, Mam?" he prompted.

She sniffed disdainfully. "There's enough light in here— no call to waste lamp oil. Besides, going back and forth in the rain hurts me rheumatics. I would be dry this minute if ye'd come to the house to tell me what's happening."

"I could hardly leave her like this; the poor pony's exhausted. I wish you'd sent for Bernard when I asked you to, Mam. He knows more about horses than I do."

"Why take your brother from work when you was here already?"

"My misfortune," Henry muttered.

"Sorry?"

He raised his voice. "I said it was Flossie's misfortune that you bred her to McGrath's stallion. He's a big horse and she's an old pony. McGrath should have warned you the foal might be too large for her to deliver."

"Mr. McGrath took pity on a poor widow in rags and jags and let me have the service for half-nothing," she replied smugly. "And where was you and your advice anyway? Who'd have thought me firstborn would run off to Dublin and abandon me?" Hannah Mooney pressed one hand dramatically to her bosom.

"You're hardly abandoned, Mam. The girls are still under your roof, and my brothers live within an ass's roar. If you—"

The mare rolled over on her side and scrabbled in the straw with her forelegs. A rivulet of blood pulsed from her vagina.

"Merciful hour!" gasped Hannah. "Do something!"

Henry braced the heel of one hand against the mare's haunch and worked his other hand into the birth canal. "You should have bought a new pony for the cart and let Flossie live out her old age in the orchard. Instead . . . unh, easy there . . . instead you may have killed her to save a few shillings."

"Don't be telling me how to care for animals. When your father, God a mercy on him, broke his back, me butter and egg money's what stood between this family and the workhouse. I suppose you've forgot that by now, though. Ye always was ungrateful, Henry." Her mind slipped into a comfortable groove, replaying familiar lines. "I give everything and ask for nothing, and nothing's what I get. And that's all I'm going to say about that."

The tremulous lip, the downcast eye: in her youth Hannah Mooney had been pretty, but she had become one of those compressed women of indeterminate age who practice a fearful tyranny on those around them.

She is my mother, so I should love her, Henry reminded himself as he tried to get some leverage on the unborn foal. *I should. Love her.*

The foal would not come out. When he gripped its slender fetlocks and leaned back, pulling, the mare moaned like a human.

"Please send one of the girls for Bernard, Mam. It's going to take the two of us if it's not too late already."

"I knew ye would fail me."

"Then why did you insist on my doing this?"

She did not answer.

WHEN Bernard arrived, Henry got to his feet. They had not seen each other for over a year.

Hannah Mooney's frown deepened. "Stand straight, Henry, and put your shoulders back. How many times do I have to tell you?"

The glance the brothers exchanged was layered with meaning. On the surface was mutual exasperation with their mother, but far below lay an antipathy neither would ever acknowledge. In their youth their father had pitted them against each other while Hannah made comparisons to the detriment of whichever boy was within hearing. Those scars ran deep.

Both men were of medium height, well proportioned and strongly built. There the resemblance ended. At thirty-four, Henry still had a flat belly and lean hips, though his shoulders were rounded from habitually hunching over a desk. Bernard was two years younger but looked older. He was sagging without a struggle into middle age. His belly hammocked on the waistband of his trousers.

"They don't like me leaving the plant early," he complained. "I'm after losing half a day's wages." He pulled off the thick woolen gansey his wife had knitted and rolled up his shirtsleeves. "We had best wrap her tail and get it out of our way."

"I told Henry you would know what to do," Hannah Mooney said triumphantly. "I wanted ye from the beginning, but he insisted he could manage." The glance she shot at Henry dared him to call her a liar.

Chapter Two

THAT evening Henry sat in the kitchen toying with a cold supper he could not eat. He had put his waistcoat and suit coat back on, a formality he clung to in his mother's house. A man's garments, to show he was not a child.

His sisters, Pauline and Alice, were keeping him company at table. Bernard had taken the newborn foal away and Mrs. Mooney had gone upstairs to bed, so the three had the kitchen to themselves. The room still smelled of bacon and cabbage. On the wall beside the black iron range, a calendar from the Capuchin Foreign Missions proclaimed the month to be March, the year 1917. A paraffin lamp glowed on the dresser; a brass clock ticked on the mantelpiece.

With a few exceptions, the west of Ireland was desperately poor. Thousands of country folk lived in hovels built of rough stones hewed out of the hills with primitive tools. The sagging roofs were turf; the uneven floors were mud. Sometimes the entire cabin was made of mud. The inhabitants struggled to coax a marginal existence from little strips of boggy or stony ground, and if they failed to pay rent for the land, they were evicted.

In spite of the poverty she affected, Hannah Mooney was far from destitute. The late John Mooney had been a successful blacksmith and a shrewd businessman. The poor of Limerick City lived in tumbledown shacks in fetid laneways, but Mooney had left his widow six acres of land on the outskirts of the town. The property included a stone-and-mortar cottage in good repair, a well-appointed farmyard, an orchard, and two fields rented to a neighbor. The workhouse had never been a danger.

"It's a pity about the pony," said Pauline. She was an angular woman in her twenties who wore her brown hair scraped back into an unbecoming knot. Even so, she might have attracted suitors if her mother had not constantly exhorted her to avoid making a show of herself.

"Flossie," Alice interjected. "The pony had a name and it was Flossie. We all learned to ride on her, and now she's been cut open like a butchered hog." The girl's voice teetered on the edge of hysteria.

"Stop going on about it, Alice," snapped Pauline. "You'll work yourself into a state."

"Flossie was dead by the time we finally took the foal from her," Henry said as gently as he could. "She didn't feel anything, I promise."

"You didn't . . . I mean, it wasn't you who . . ."

"It wasn't me—I couldn't. Bernard did what had to be done."

Rain wept down the windowpane. Pauline grabbed a cloth and began mopping up a puddle of condensation.

"Sit down and stop foostering, Polly," Henry said. "Can you never be still a minute?"

"I have too much to do, and there's no help to be had from that one." She nodded toward Alice. "If she as much as washes a cup she breaks it."

The girl seemed to shrink inside her clothes.

Henry stirred a third spoonful of sugar into his tea. "Be thankful that Bernard's wife keeps a milk goat," he commented, "otherwise the foal would die too. It may anyway, of course."

Pauline wrung out her cloth into the slop bucket and sat down, perching on the edge of her chair as if she were going to jump up again any minute. "Mam says you didn't save the pony when you could have, Henry."

"Nothing new there; no matter what I do it's not good enough. That's why I never come home if I can help it."

Alice hawked phlegm into a damp handkerchief, then

folded the fabric over and blew her nose. At fifteen she still wore her lank hair streaming down her back. Her father had died the year she was born. She worshiped his memory but was terrified of her mother, who dismissed her fits of melancholia as "Alice's spells."

In the autumn the girl would enter the convent. Sisters of Mercy.

RELIGION had been the bulwark of Ireland's poor down the long, hard centuries. The only art in the Mooney house consisted of Holy Pictures. The Sacred Heart of Jesus, bleeding luridly, had pride of place in the front room, together with a large crucifix and several rosaries prominently displayed. Every evening of their childhood the five little Mooneys, three boys and two girls, had knelt there to recite the decades of the rosary, then gone shivering to bed.

John and Hannah Mooney had buried four children who died in infancy. In conversation they were referred to by the generic title "the Ones Above." Little angels, endlessly mourned.

Life revolved around the Church. First Communion and Confirmation, Confession and Mass, Saints' Days and Holy Days of Obligation.

The Black Fast at Lent. One scant meal a day for forty days, with no eggs, milk, or meat. Two tiny "collations" of unbuttered bread and stewed tea without sugar.

Fish on Wednesdays and Fridays. A salt-rimed ling or cod drying hard as wood on a pole by the fireplace. Sufficient to put a person off eating fish forever.

The Last Rites. The Removal of the Remains: a somber communal march to the church behind the coffin. The Funeral: old women keening like banshees. Thirty days later, the Month's Mind. Frequent obligatory visits to the graveyard thereafter. Every anniversary of every death commemorated. Grief continually renewed while the joys of life were stifled.

On Sundays, even the rope-and-plank swings in the schoolyard were tied up to prevent any accidental pleasure.

Like all good Irish Catholic mothers, Hannah Mooney aspired to giving one or more sons to the priesthood. On the day of his birth in 1891, her third son, Noel, was chosen for this privilege. He was given the largest potato and the extra quilt for his bed, and exempted from the sibling rivalry encouraged between his older brothers. In spite of these advantages, Noel could not stay out of trouble. When the family moved to Limerick in 1899, every constable in the area soon knew him as "that wild Mooney lad." Bold words painted on fences and tin cans tied to dogs' tails were a specialty.

No one but his mother expected Noel to become a priest. Then, on his nineteenth birthday, a local carpenter's daughter informed him that he was about to become a father after all. "Not priestly, but biological," Henry had quipped.

Mrs. Mooney was not amused. "Why've ye done this to me?" she shrieked at her youngest son. In floods of tears she had retired to her room and locked the door. The house rang with her adjurations to God. The morning before the hasty wedding she had emerged to announce that little Alice would join the Sisters of Mercy as soon as she was old enough. "And that's all I'm going to say about that."

The child herself was not consulted.

Alice going into the convent meant Pauline would have to stay at home and take care of their mother until one of them died. Like generations before her, she was to be sacrificed on the pyre of duty. If Pauline had married, the sacrifice would have been demanded of Henry—but he had escaped. His mother unwittingly had driven him away.

DURING their childhood Hannah Mooney had regaled her brood with the story of their origins. "Mc Mam was only a few skips off the bog," she was fond of recalling, "and me Da was a mountainy man what could turn his hand to anything. He worked all the hours God sends. Everything we had he made for us, from the table we et on to the shoes on our feet, and to make a few shillings he mended carts and wagons as well.

"When I was near grown, Da was hired to do a job of work on a great lord's estate on the Shannon. A job with wages every week, it was, so we left Tipperary to live in Clare. One day Da took me with him to the blacksmith to have some carriage wheels bound in iron. That's where I first saw John Mooney. He come from the old stock and there was some Welsh in him, too. But he was only a smith's apprentice when I met him. Sure didn't he look like a young king, though, with the forge light on his face and the great arms of him? 'I'll have that,' says I. And I did. By the time we married he had a forge of his own and the respect of every man in the parish, including me da."

Hannah, who had fully expected her eldest son to follow in his father's footsteps, was dismayed when Henry showed no aptitude for smithing. He could not hammer iron to a shape no matter how he tried. Bernard was good with tools; Henry was interested in people. What Noel, the youngest, was interested in, no one knew.

When Henry left school, he had taken the first job he was offered, as a printer's devil with the *Limerick Leader* newspaper. He began work in the heavy country brogues, shabby serge trousers, and collarless shirt he had worn as a schoolboy. The brogues cramped his feet and the trousers were too short, but when he suggested new ones his mother said, "Wait till they wear out completely, same as your father did. There's no call for you to put on airs."

The official job of a printer's devil was to carry used lead type back to the hellbox to be melted down again. He also served as a dogsbody for everyone in the office. Henry fetched sandwiches and whiskey, cleaned muddy shoes, took letters to the post office, made excuses to wives when their husbands were working late and collected those same husbands from the pub when they needed collecting. Equipped with a battered bicycle, the ubiquitous form of transport for able-bodied Irishmen, he learned to wobble along with a drunken reporter precariously perched on the crossbar.

Henry's hours were long and his pay meager.

He was blissfully happy.

Compared to the stifling piety of his mother's house, the rough-and-ready camaraderie of the newspaper was like a window opened to the world. Newspapermen knew something about everything and loved showing off their stock of

information. To Henry's delight, they were also profane.
Good Irish Catholic boys were never profane—not within
earshot of their mothers.

"Christ on crooked crutches!" Henry began muttering on
occasion, or "Great God's garters!" Feeling daring and liberated. His expletives were extremely mild compared to
those he heard every day, but they were of his own devising.

Best of all, newspapermen talked about sex. Like Henry,
they had been raised according to the harsh Catholic moral-
ity that taught that sex was something vile, and rendered
many Irish men and women celibate even in marriage. But
the men at the *Leader* appeared to have thrown off this hand-
icap. From their conversation Henry gleaned tidbits of information that set his senses reeling.

On Saturdays his mother met him at the door with her
hand outstretched for his weekly pay packet. The money did
not overcome Hannah's reverse snobbery, however. "Them
newspaper people don't know what work is," she asserted.
"Not like me da or Mr. Mooney." When the *Limerick Leader*
promoted Henry to reporter, Hannah's response was, "No
good comes from getting above your station."

With his first promotion Henry began quietly saving a
little every week—without telling his mother. He discovered
that a man who could string simple declarative sentences
together coherently could find small jobs on the side. Book
reviews, fillers for periodicals, and advertising copy for local
stores brought in additional money—not much individually,
but they added up. As soon as he could afford to, he bought
a tweed suit. Coat, waistcoat, tailored trousers. A wing-
collared shirt. Shoes that fitted.

"You're all dressed up like the dog's dinner," his mother
said sarcastically.

"I refuse to look impoverished when I have a decent job,
Mam. It isn't honest."

"I could have put that money to better use. Ye have no
feeling for your own family, Henry."

After John Mooney died in 1902, Bernard had struggled
to keep the blacksmith business going. But he was little
more than a boy, and as shy as a stone under moss. He could
not ask people for the money they owed. Eventually the

forge was padlocked and Bernard went to work in Denny's bacon-curing plant. When he married, his wife urged him to work his way up to assistant supervisor, and there he was content to remain.

Noel was apprenticed to his new father-in-law as a carpenter. "At least he's following in our Lord's footsteps," had been Henry's wry comment to Bernard.

Hannah Mooney never spoke of Noel's wife. Nor did Hannah ever visit their house, even when the children were born, though Noel was expected to pay a duty call on his mother at least once a week. Both he and Bernard found modest homes not far from hers. Like Henry, they continued to contribute to the maintenance of their mother's household. This was a pattern repeated all over Ireland.

Henry had no intention of marrying. It was not a fear of sex but the possibility of spending a lifetime with a woman who might grow into another version of his mother that appalled him. One woman finding fault with him night and day was quite enough, thank you.

"It's for your own good, Henry," Hannah Mooney always insisted. "Ye should get down on your knees and thank the Sacred Heart of Jesus that you have your poor old mother trying to make a better man of you."

The quarrel that brought matters to a head was about John Mooney's watch. A fine pocket watch on a silver chain, it had been promised to his eldest son, but Hannah refused to pass it on. Instead she kept the watch in the bottom drawer of the chest in her room, where it lay tarnishing.

"You have no use for a pocket watch," Henry argued, "with a perfectly good clock on the mantel. I'm a working man and I have to keep appointments. That watch would be useful to me over and above its sentimental value."

These were justifications. The sentimental value was what mattered to Henry, but if he said so to his mother, she would never give him the watch. Hannah Mooney despised sentiment.

She did not give it to him anyway. "Watches is worth good money—we could buy another cow if times go against us," Hannah Mooney said. "And that's all I'm going to say about that."

One morning in the early autumn of 1912 Henry had packed a portmanteau while his mother and sisters were at Mass. He went to his mother's room, liberated the watch from beneath a tangle of thrice-mended black stockings that smelled of old woman, and left a note under the blue milk jug on the kitchen table. "Am taking the train to Dublin to look for work there. Will write and send money when I am settled. Henry."

Mrs. Mooney's door-slamming fury continued for a fortnight. In leaving her sphere of influence Henry had committed the ultimate rebellion. She would never forgive him.

He found Dublin to be bawdy, seedy, shabby, and gorgeous, rattling with British soldiers and frothing with the whores who serviced them. For a man interested in people, the capital was a fascinating kaleidoscope. Aristocrats and intellectuals, businessmen and laborers, poets and paupers and priests. Children singing skipping rhymes that parodied the politics of the day. Indigent gutties lounging on street corners, offering gratuitous advice to passersby.

Pungent smells of dark Guinness and the dirty river, of tar and abattoirs and venality and vice. And sometimes, like a stray lock of virtue blown across the pustuled face of sin, the smell of expensive perfume.

Henry loved Dublin from the beginning. But he suspected he would love any place that was more than fifty miles away from his mother.

In Dublin he had found a job with the *Irish Independent* and taken a room in a lodging house owned by a distant cousin, Louise Kearney. He unfailingly sent a portion of his weekly salary—"the Limerick tithe," he jokingly called it— to his mother. He was superstitious about the money. As long as he contributed to Hannah Mooney financially, she could not repossess his soul. In the five years since he left, he had made very few trips back to Limerick.

WE haven't seen you since before the Sinn Féin Rebellion," Pauline reproved him now, as they sat in the kitchen. "And that's a year ago."

"The British persist in calling it the Sinn Féin Rebellion,

Polly," her brother said, "but you should know better. Sinn Féin is a political party founded by a journalist called Arthur Griffith, who believes in using moral force rather than physical force. Sinn Féin had nothing to do with planning the insurrection. We prefer to call it the Easter Rising."

"We!" gasped Alice. "Are you a Republican rebel like Cousin Dan?"

He shook his head. "If you mean am I a member of the Irish Republican Army, I'm not. By 'we' I meant Irish nationalists in general."

"But you're talking like the rebels, and we know what happens to them." Alice's pale blue eyes leaked tears. "They get shot."

Henry tried to reassure her. "The closest I've ever come to danger was when I sneaked my wounded friend Ned Halloran out of Richmond Barracks after the Rising, before the British could deport him. Ned was a member of what you call the rebels—the Irish Volunteer Corps. He fought for Ireland's freedom in 1916, while I was merely an observer."

"You're a reporter," said Pauline, "so you're supposed to observe. That's what the *Irish Independent* pays you for."

"Not anymore."

"What do you mean?"

"I mean I don't work for the *Independent* anymore. I left them right after the Rising."

Pauline leaned forward, as avid as a sparrow watching a spider. "Then you don't have to stay in Dublin? You could come home?"

"I couldn't," Henry said hastily. "I'm working freelance now, so I need to be where the action is."

"Why did you leave the *Independent* in the first place?"

"Mmm . . . I was fired."

Pauline sank back in her chair. "Fired! Oh, lawney! Does Mam know?"

"She does *not* know, and I don't want either of you to tell her. She'd make a meal of it."

"What did you do to get yourself fired, Henry?" Like her mother, Pauline automatically ascribed blame to him without waiting for an explanation.

"The owner of the *Independent* is a man called William

Murphy, who considers trade unions an arm of Satan, and James Connolly was the union organizer who defied him. When the leaders of the Rising were being executed there was hope that Connolly might be spared because he was so badly injured. But in spite of the fact that the *Independent* had been supportive of nationalism, Murphy wrote blistering editorials that described the Rising as 'insane and criminal'[1] and practically demanded that Connolly be executed. I had a blazing row with Murphy and he fired me."

"You're a fool," Pauline said with undisguised contempt. "Imagine throwing away a good job for a silly reason like that. What did you tell Mam?"

"Just that I've come down to Limerick on business. And that's the truth, Polly. I'm writing an article on the mood of the country a year after the Rising and I want to interview the bishop of Limerick. I plan to begin the piece with a letter he wrote shortly after the executions. He delivered an almighty belt of the crozier to General Maxwell, who was in charge of the British forces in Ireland. Listen to this . . ."

Henry took out his reporter's notebook and flipped through the pages, then read aloud: "Dr. O'Dwyer wrote to Maxwell, 'You appeal to me to help you in the furtherance of your work as military dictator of Ireland. You took care that no plea for mercy should interpose on behalf of the poor young fellows who surrendered to you in Dublin. The first information we got of their fate was the announcement that they had been shot in cold blood. Personally I regard your action with horror, and I believe that it has outraged the conscience of the country.' "[2]

Pauline stifled a yawn. "Sure everyone in Limerick knows about Dr. O'Dwyer. He refused to dismiss two priests who were sympathetic with the rebels. I don't know why you're going over it all again."

"Because his letter was important for political reasons," her brother told her. Clearing his throat, he resumed reading. " 'Events have proved the bishop right. The British had provoked the long-suffering Irish to rebellion by repeatedly breaking faith with the people of this island. Even so, the vast majority did not stand beside Pearse and Connolly when the battle might have been won. The apathy bred from centuries of subservience paralyzed them. The heroes of Easter Week paid with their lives for that apathy.

" 'But in the smoke and flame of the Easter Rising, the Irish soul was reborn. For one week we had watched the flags of a sovereign Ireland flying over the General Post Office in Dublin; a sight unthinkable before 1916. We had read the Proclamation of the Republic asserting that this land belongs to its people. We had seen courageous men and women willing to lay down their lives for the sake of our independence. We had felt, however briefly, the self-respect of a proud nation.

" 'Afterward we pondered these things, and Ireland was forever changed.' "

Henry closed the notebook. "What do you think?"

Pauline shrugged. "You don't want my opinion. You just said I couldn't understand."

"I'm sorry, Polly. Please, I want to know how the article affected you."

She stood up and began clearing the table. "It didn't. Do you really think the Rising made any difference? It was just another failed rebellion, Henry, and you're wasting your time writing about it. A year from now no one will even remember."

But Alice, reading the expression in her brother's eyes, was dismayed. "Oh, Henry," she wailed, "you do want to fight!"

Chapter Three

In the room he had occupied as a boy, Henry Mooney was preparing for a new day.

Three of us lads growing up here with Mam standing guard over our immortal souls. Bursting into the room in the middle of the night. Whipping the cover off my bed because I was the oldest, and me half-asleep and not understanding. "I see what you're doing! Nasty! I'm going to tell the priest and he'll sort ye out!"

If we are made in God's image, how could our flesh be nasty?

How is it that I was the only one of us who asked that question?

Old ghosts clung to the faded wallpaper, waiting to be exorcised with the rituals of adulthood. Slivers of cocoa-butter soap whipped to lather in the shaving mug. Cheeks briskly slapped with bay rum. Braces securely fastened to hold up trousers, tie perfectly tied, shirt collar adjusted, waistcoat buttoned, watch chain draped in a precise curve, suitcoat brushed. Everything according to a personal standard with which he was never quite satisfied. The finishing touch, even here in the country, was a bowler hat.

As he started for the door he took a final glance in the looking glass—and stopped short, face to face with himself. *Perhaps I am jealous of Ned*, he admitted to the image gazing back at him.

Some people loved Ireland with the mawkish sentimentality that had characterized the Victorian era. Others could hardly wait to get on the first boat to anywhere else. When he was a child, Henry's feelings had fallen somewhere between the two.

As he grew older, his faith in the religion of his forefathers had waned. Increasingly resentful of the repressive effects of Catholicism, Henry concluded that while he believed in God, he did not believe in priests. To his mother's outrage he began attending Mass only once a week. He stood at the back of the church with his arms folded amid similar like-minded males, present but not participating, just in case God should be doing a head count.

Because he was Irish and had to be devoted to something, he replaced religion with a love of country. Mother Ireland instead of Mother Mary.

At seventeen Henry had joined the local branch of the Wolfe Tone Club, named after the famous revolutionary and founder of the United Irishmen. In the Fíanna Fail Hall off Barrington Street he had listened as accolades were heaped on dead rebels and failed uprisings were held to be the pinnacle of Irish achievement. There were a few exciting demonstrations of weaponry and some patriotic sing-songs, but eventually Henry lost interest. *Dead rebels. Failed risings. Nothing to show for it but songs that make grown men cry.* He stopped attending the meetings.

In his twenties he had taken an interest in politics but did not become actively involved. His experience with the Wolfe Tone Club had taught him he was not a joiner. He preferred to sit on the bank of a river and fish, or take long walks thinking. "Going for a little journey around the inside of my head," he called it. When he wanted to explore the thoughts of someone else, he visited his local pub.

Ireland's pubs had two conversational topics: sport and politics. In the early twentieth century, politics ranked higher. Men with no power vented their frustration by arguing about power. Someone might say, "I agree with Arthur Griffith—monarchy is the most stable system. He says we should have a dual monarchy with two kings, one for

Ireland and one for England. Like the government of Austro-Hungary."

"Home rule makes more sense to me," Henry would respond, leaning forward over his pint of porter. "We governed ourselves for two thousand years and we can do it again."

"You're right there, *avic*,"* agreed the man sitting next to him. "Local assemblies with representatives from every parish, that's the way. The wearer best knows where the shoe pinches."

The barman joined in. "I'd settle for an Irish parliament. Not made up of Protestant lords and landlords, but ordinary people like us."

"Working within the larger framework of the British Empire, of course," amended a thin man with the look of a schoolteacher about him. "That's what home rule means."

"Why within the empire?" asked a craggy-featured laborer in a cloth cap. "Yer so-called Great Britain's done shag-all fer me. We should be independent like the Americans."

An elderly man with a garrison accent said, "We're doing all right with the government as it is."

"How can you say that?" Henry challenged. "Anything we have that's worth having is taken from us. Our taxes are supporting a foreign monarchy and an army that's used against us. Besides, laws designed for English people fit us no better than someone else's shoes. Pass me one of those pickled eggs, will you? And I'll tell you something for nothing: This country will never prosper until it has control over its own resources. Home rule would give us that."

"Give us?" The man in the cap snorted. "Them English never gave us anything worth anything and never will. If we ever get home rule, all the blood and juice'll be drained out of it. Them politicians would see to that. Politics is behind everything, so it is," he muttered darkly into his glass.

Members of Parliament for Ireland belonged to either the Unionist Party or the Irish Parliamentary Party, usually just called the Irish Party. Although they represented a small

*Irish for "my son."

Protestant minority in Ireland, the Unionists wielded considerable power in the British Parliament. A delicate balance of power existed in the House of Commons. The Liberals were anticolonialist, and at least in part, pacifist. The Conservatives, familiarly known as the Tories, were committed to maintaining the status quo, the militaristic empire responsible for the prosperity of the upper classes. To this end the Conservatives relied heavily upon the voting strength of Ireland's Unionists.

Unionists emphatically rejected home rule, claiming it would threaten the Act of Union that had been forced upon Ireland after the failed Rising of 1798. Unionists' sense of identity depended upon being members of the ruling class. A democratically elected government in Ireland would give power to the huge Catholic majority. To Unionists this was unthinkable.

Not all Protestants were Unionists, however, or members of the privileged class. Many working-class Protestants considered themselves as Irish as any Catholic and loved their country just as much.

In opposition to the Unionists, the Irish Party claimed to represent the majority interest. Inheritors of Charles Stewart Parnell's dream of home rule, they unfortunately possessed no leader strong enough to challenge the Unionists. As a result they usually rubber-stamped British policy.

On the political fringes were parties such as Arthur Griffith's Sinn Féin.[1] *Sinn féin, sinn féin amháin*—Ourselves, ourselves alone—had been a battle cry of the Wild Geese, the exiled Irish fighting in the armies of Spain and France in the seventeenth and eighteenth centuries. Later it became a motto of the Gaelic League. A friend suggested the phrase to Griffith because it summed up his philosophy of national self-reliance.[2]

In 1905 Griffith began publishing a daily newspaper called *Sinn Féin*. In its pages he urged the diversification of the Irish economy and the achievement of social and economic reform through peaceful protest. His proposal for a dual monarchy was intended to accommodate both nationalist and unionist traditions.

A small political party formed around Griffith's philoso-

phy. Adopting the name Sinn Féin, they attracted little enthusiasm outside their own circle and had no seats in
Parliament.

But someone took notice of Sinn Féin.

In 1858 James Stephens, veteran of an aborted rebellion
ten years earlier, had met in Dublin with like-minded friends
to found a secret society sworn to bring about an independent Irish Republic through force of arms. At the same time
John O'Mahony in New York had organized an American
counterpart. The Irish Republican Brotherhood, commonly
known as the Fenians after the legendary army of Fionn mac
Cumhaill, was denounced by the Catholic Church and undermined by informers—usually paid spies in the service of
the British government. But the Brotherhood did not go
away.

After a century of unparalleled imperial expansion, in
1899 the British Empire declared war on the Boers of South
Africa—settlers of Dutch or Huguenot descent—in order to
seize their lands, diamonds, and gold. The Boers raised armies among the native South African population and fought
back. For a while it looked as if they might win. Britain
finally prevailed in 1902, leaving twenty-seven thousand
burnt-out farmhouses in the Transvaal and the Orange Free
State, thirty thousand Boer women and children dead of neglect in imperial concentration camps, and, although such
casualties were neither counted nor mentioned in the newspapers, innumerable black victims rotting in the African
sun.

The Boers' near-successful defiance of the world's mightiest military power gave the IRB hope. Britain was not
invincible. An Irish Republic might succeed where the Boer
republics had not.

With the formation of Sinn Féin, the IRB saw its opportunity for a political voice in Ireland. In the first decade of
the twentieth century there was a growing scent of nationalism in the Irish air.

To add to the brew bubbling in the cauldron, workers
were beginning to demand the decent pay and conditions
that had always been denied them. Labor and management
were headed for open conflict. In 1912 Henry had summed
up the situation in the last article he wrote while working

for the *Limerick Leader*: "Ireland has no strong voice to demand justice for her people in Westminster or anywhere else. Frustrated on every level, the ordinary Irish man and woman feels the pressure mounting inexorably. Living in this country is like watching a fatal accident about to happen."

The leader of the Ulster Unionist Party was Sir Edward Carson, who as a barrister had defended the Marquess of Queensberry in the famous trial that made public the homosexuality of Oscar Wilde—an avowed supporter of home rule—and resulted in Wilde's imprisonment. In 1913, just when it looked as if a home rule bill might pass, Carson created a militia called the Ulster Volunteer Force, whose avowed purpose was to resist home rule through force of arms.

"The UVF openly parade through the streets of Belfast with rifle and cannon," Henry wrote for his new editor at the *Independent*, "while their political leaders scream anti-Catholic slogans and give dire warning of the dangers of 'Rome Rule.' The drums bang and the Union flags wave and thousands of weapons gleam in the sun. The threat of physical force is as palpable as a clenched fist."

The threat succeeded. The home rule bill was deferred yet again. Unionists gloated. Nationalists learned.

The Irish Republican Brotherhood began quietly infiltrating Sinn Féin. Arthur Griffith's moral force was joined by the Fenian doctrine of physical force.

A home rule bill finally was placed on the statute books in 1914, but implementation was immediately postponed "for security reasons." The Irish were promised that home rule would go into effect when the Great War was over . . . or some time thereafter. "When pigs fly," Henry and his Dublin colleagues commented sourly to one another in the Oval Bar.

That same year the Irish Volunteer Corps was formed as a counterbalance to the UVF.

Henry Mooney had stood beside Ned Halloran on the Dublin quays as a troop of the new Volunteers marched past. Although they were ill equipped and improperly drilled, their faces shone with conviction. They were inspired and led by men who had lost faith in the "postdated check" of home rule. Men who wanted something more for Ireland.

Full independence.

Yes! Henry's heart had cried. But he saw the Volunteers as a symbol rather than a viable option. There was something faintly ludicrous about a mix-'em-gather-'em of office clerks and farm boys challenging the might of Great Britain.

Henry's colleagues at the *Independent* had taken a different view. Several had joined the Sinn Féin Party; others had joined the Volunteers. "If nationalists stick together, anything's possible," they enthused, "even a republic. But we'll have to get it the way the Americans got theirs—armed force, that's all the British respect."

Ned Halloran had enrolled in the Volunteers. When the Rising came, Henry Mooney had not shouldered a rifle and marched out to face death and glory with him. Henry agreed with Arthur Griffith: Irish nationalists would better serve their country through constructive political action.

But because he wanted to see Ireland free as much as any man, Henry had helped the rebels in every way he could short of fighting. To explain their position to those who called them cowards and traitors, he wrote: "It takes a great deal of courage to seek independence. The abused child, no matter how bullied and beaten, still clings to its mother's skirts.

"But we are not England's natural children. The Irish had a discrete identity and a rich, sophisticated culture long before English opportunists invaded this island. Not content with their land's resources, they seized upon ours. This is the pattern of imperialists; consider England's model and teacher, Rome. Beware of those who recognize no one's rights but their own. The time has come to separate ourselves from them and their influence."

In 1916 Henry had done more than write articles for newspapers. He had passed along information gleaned from his journalistic sources, and in the end he had rescued Ned Halloran with a large lie and a forged press pass.

• • •

KNOWLEDGE of those contributions did not ease the ache in his heart now—his heart, at war with his rational mind. His heart told him he had stood aside while better, braver men died for what he too believed in.

Meeting his eyes in the mirror, Henry Mooney knew he would be a happier man if he could count himself among the number who had marched out on Easter Monday to certain failure. In memory he watched the Volunteers stride past once more and did what he wished he had done on the day: He lifted his hat to them.

MAM'S keeping to her room until after the knackers come," Pauline told her brother when he entered the kitchen.

Hannah Mooney's children glanced toward the ceiling as if their mother's reproof were seeping through the plaster. Then Alice said to Henry, "Mam better not catch you wearing your hat in the house. You'll get us all in trouble. Or don't you care?"

"Stop whining," Pauline told her sister automatically. "Why are you wearing your hat, Henry?"

"I'm not very hungry this morning, so I'm going into town to see if the *Leader* will buy my 'One Year After the Rising' piece."

"And what about this breakfast I cooked you?" Pauline demanded to know. "Well . . . please yourself, but bring back a loaf of sugar when you come. I forgot how much you waste in your tea. Oh . . . your old bicycle's still in the shed, you know. A tire's gone flat—you'll need to patch it."

As Henry stepped out the door he saw the knacker's wagon coming up the road, pulled by a pair of draft horses who were oblivious to their cargo of livestock carcasses. Their vision was restricted by leather blinkers. They kept their eyes fixed on the road ahead.

The head of a horse hung over one side of the wagon, swinging on its slender neck like the clapper on a bell. *A fine saddle horse, once. Elegant head. Someone's pride and joy, no doubt*, Henry thought. Now black blood oozed in thick drops from its tongue.

Henry turned on his heel and went back inside. "Polly,

send the knacker away while I find some old clothes to put on. I'm going to bury Flossie in the orchard."

It was past noon before Henry finally went into town. There was no rain, but a chill wind was blowing off the Shannon estuary. Shards of ice rimed the edges of the ruts in the road, dangerous for a bicycle with a clumsily patched tire. He dismounted and walked, wheeling the bicycle beside him while he took a boyish delight in stepping on the frozen ruts and hearing them crunch.

The air was sweet with turf smoke. Pale banners billowed from every chimney. As Henry passed a mud-walled cabin with a thatched roof, a woman leaning on the half-door gave him a friendly nod. Farther along the road he met a gap-toothed farmer in a grimy suit and a cap. The man tilted his head in salute. "Desperate day."

"Desperate," Henry agreed, walking on.

Apart from Dublin, Ireland was rural; even towns like Limerick and Cork, which called themselves cities, revolved around a rural economy and were governed by seasonal rhythms. Weather was the common concern. To acknowledge atmospheric conditions was to acknowledge life itself.

The houses began to huddle closer together, staring at those across the road with tribal suspicion. Country gave way to town, thatched roofs to slate, rutted mud to cobbled paving. Gray buildings, gray skies, gray diffident faces. A garrison town with its back to the river, Limerick guarded its deprivations like treasures.

As he neared the center of town, Henry saw photographs of the bishop of Limerick displayed in flyspecked shop windows like a national hero.[3] The pictures were invariably framed with tricolor ribbon. The bright bit of color made a statement all its own.

The office of the *Limerick Leader* on O'Connell Street was comfortably familiar. Henry's eyes were drawn to one battered desk in particular, and a chair whose uneven legs he had cursed many a time. "I don't have time to talk about your article right now," the editor told him, pushing up his eyeshade, "because there's a big story coming over the telegraph. Can you call in tomorrow? We'll have a good ould natter then."

"What big story? Something to do with the war in Europe?"

"Not this time, at least not directly. Tsar Nicholas of Russia has abdicated. Gone like spit in the fire." He clapped his hands together for emphasis, and several of the men in the office glanced up.

Henry felt a moment of disorientation, as if he had slipped on the ice. The tsar claimed to rule through the direct authority of God. How in hell could he abdicate?

Could God abdicate? Could he wash his hands of the lot of us and walk away? I wouldn't blame him.

As he was leaving the newspaper offices, Henry saw a squad of British soldiers come marching up the street with rifles on their shoulders. Some of the soldiers looked very young.

The Irish Volunteers had been so very, very young.

THAT evening Henry went to his room to write a letter to Ned Halloran in Dublin. To avoid calling attention to Ned, he put Síle's maiden name on the envelope.

"The Russians are staging a revolution themselves," he wrote, "that seems every bit as muddled and confused as ours. It is expected that the tsar's cousin King George will grant Nicholas and his family sanctuary in England. I pray no harm will come to them in the meantime, and that the Russian revolutionaries prove as chivalrous as our own.

"I found a quote from a Captain Brereton of the British forces, who was captured and held prisoner in the Four Courts during the Rising. You will appreciate this, Ned. After his release, Brereton reported of the Irish Volunteers, 'They were not out for massacre, for burning or for loot. They observed all the rules of civilized warfare and fought clean. They treated their prisoners with the utmost courtesy and consideration; in fact they proved by their conduct that they were men of education incapable of acts of brutality.'[4]

"I hope we can hold to that, Ned. As long as we do, the world will support us. Then when the war in Europe is over, we can ask the peace conference to support the cause of Irish independence.

"In the meantime, you must take care of yourself. I understand how restless you are, but head wounds need a long time to heal and you cannot afford another relapse. Stay indoors as much as you can, and don't attract notice. Remember, you're not just a farmer's son from County Clare anymore. You were Pearse's personal courier in the General Post Office and privy to information the British still would like to get their hands on. But you have Síle and little Precious to consider now, so keep out of trouble for their sakes."

Henry folded the letter, then sat tapping it against his chin, wondering if he had wasted his words. Ned Halloran was not the same boy he had been before Easter Week. There was a simmering anger in him.

After the surrender, when many Volunteers might have slipped away through the Dublin streets and escaped, they had chosen to stay with their units and lay down their arms in the correct military manner. Pádraic Pearse had ordered them to behave as honorable men who would do credit to Ireland, and they did. Some even went home to wash and shave first, then returned to present themselves for arrest.[5]

Ned Halloran bitterly resented the wound that had kept him comatose and allowed Henry to rescue him. For him there had been no surrender.

Perhaps there never could be.

The door opened behind Henry, the floorboards creaked, and then his mother peered over his shoulder. She smelled like the old newspapers she used to line the shelves in the cupboards. "Who are you writing to?"

"Just a friend. Sheila Duffy."

Hannah picked up the envelope and rubbed it with her thumb to test the quality of the paper. Too heavy, said her frown of disapproval, Henry putting on airs again. "This is addressed to someone called S-í-l-e." She sounded out the name letter by letter.

"Síle, Mam. You know that's the Irish spelling for Sheila."

"The trouble is, I can't read your handwriting. I thought you was supposed to learn handwriting in school. Or is that why you never write me letters?"

Henry put both hands flat on the table he used as a writing desk and pressed down hard. His mother could barely read; she merely wanted the letters to show to the neighbors, proof of her absent son's devotion. "I do write you, Mam," he said in a voice flattened with the effort to control his anger. "As often as I can."

Chapter Four

Limerick ceased to exist for Henry by the time his train was halfway across Ireland. When he reached Dublin, he felt the relief of having once more outrun his past.

With electric trams, cinema houses, and an increasing number of public telephone callboxes, Dublin had a toehold in the twentieth century. The city held some of Europe's worst slums, but also the magnificent monumental architecture of James Gandon and street after street of eighteenth-century Georgian houses, which, though begrimed and neglected, still retained hints of their former elegance. Henry's pulse quickened. *It's good to be home.*

From the train station he walked home along the stone quays that contained the Liffey. Having grown up beside the Shannon, he was drawn to rivers. And Dublin was a city for walking. Henry had a bicycle that he kept in a shed at Louise Kearney's house, but he used it only when absolutely necessary. He hated what bicycle clips did to the legs of his trousers.

The damage from Easter Week was being replaced by new construction. Competing with the muddy stench of the Liffey was the smell of brick dust and freshly sawed planking. Yet ragged urchins still clambered over mountains of wreckage, searching out scraps of timber to burn for fuel. Roofless, windowless buildings stared blindly outward, waiting for rescue like shocked survivors of catastrophe.

James Connolly, that militant socialist, had believed the British would never destroy capitalist property.

He was wrong.

Although the British put all the blame on them afterward, it was not the rebels who had ruined Dublin. A massive pounding by British artillery and incendiary shells had reduced the heart of the thousand-year-old city to rubble in order to flush out a few hundred insurgents.

The walls still standing were covered with recruiting posters exhorting the young men of Ireland to enlist for the Great War. *The Great War*, Henry thought contemptuously. *Calling it "Great" to lend glory to a nasty stinking bloody horror. Telling our lads it's their duty to march off and die for England. Their privilege to be sacrificed to rampant imperialism and someone else's family feuds. All the Irish will get in return for their lives is a muddy grave in foreign soil.*

He could almost hear Ned Halloran saying, "Is it not better to fight under an Irish flag and win freedom for our own country?"

THE debris in Sackville Street—now more commonly called O'Connell Street—had long since been cleared away. The city's main thoroughfare was carrying its customary traffic. Shops and hotels, many of them new, were doing a brisk business. Men and women hurrying in and out, up and down, seeking, finding, buying, selling.

Above them loomed the burnt-out shell of the General Post Office like a specter at the feast. Some wanted it left as it was, a terrible warning of the consequences of rebellion. The men and women who had brought all their brightest hopes to the GPO on Easter Monday were gone, but the massive ruin was not empty. It was filled with a haunted silence.

Bullet holes pocked the Corinthian columns of the portico. Behind the portico was . . . nothing.

The flags that had floated so proudly above the GPO, proclaiming the Irish Republic for all to see, were gone too.

Henry slowed as he walked by, imagining Ned Halloran

in that hell on the last day while burning timbers crashed around him and machine-gun fire strafed the street outside.

THE first memoirs of the 1916 Rising had begun to appear in print—some from one side, some from the other. Henry read each as soon as it was published. In a book review for the *Dublin Evening Mail* he commented, "Oscar Wilde once said, 'Truth, in matters of religion, is simply the opinion that has survived.' The same may be said in relation to history. Facts are slippery. Already the truth of the Rising is escaping us. Soon all we will have left is the myth, so be warned: Myth may be rewritten to suit the purpose of the moment."

HALF a dozen uniformed British soldiers were standing in front of the GPO, smoking cigarettes and watching passersby. A man wearing the insignia of a captain met Henry's eyes. Abruptly the officer snapped his cigarette away with thumb and forefinger and strode toward him. "Your name and business here, sir?" he inquired politely. He had a square face and large ears crammed under the rim of his hat. A razor cut on his chin had bled recently.

"I was just walking past."

As soon as he heard Henry's Irish accent, the captain took an intimidating step closer to him. "Your name?" His tone was not so polite now.

"Henry Mooney. And as I said, I was just—"

"Your business?"

"I'm a newspaperman."

"Where do you live?"

"In lodgings in Middle Gardiner Street. I have rooms there." Henry was careful not to give the exact address.

"Rooms, plural?"

"Yes."

"So you have a wife and children?"

"I'm a bachelor."

"A bachelor with rooms, plural? Sounds as if you're doing all right for yourself."

"Things could be better."

"Things could be better," the captain mocked. "I daresay. Well, move along, Henry Mooney. There's nothing for you here. Those rebels are dead and gone to the hell they deserve. Most of them were certifiable lunatics anyway."

To his consternation, Henry spoke before he could stop himself. "That's the myth you want to peddle, is it?" He kept his hands at his sides but could not help knotting his fists.

The British officer glanced down, then raked his eyes back up the length of Henry's body. Slowly. Insultingly. "I wouldn't," he said.

Henry forced himself to turn and walk away.

The eyes that followed him dissolved the boundaries of his body, invading his inner space.

WHEN he first moved to Dublin, Henry naively had thought of the city as his; his chosen home, where he could be his own man at last.

The British had disabused him of the notion soon enough. Their attitude had made plain that Dublin was theirs as Ireland was theirs, by right of conquest. Unlike the officer Henry had just encountered, however, most of them individually were decent people. Among his friends he numbered several of the civil servants working in Dublin Castle, seat of the British bureaucracy in Ireland. The castle also housed the Dublin Metropolitan Police force and the main offices of the Royal Irish Constabulary, which policed the countryside. Both were under direct control of the British government, as was the educational system.

Most Irish people knew nothing of their history. The national schools taught English history exclusively and stressed that English superiority was the natural order of things. Only in private Catholic schools such as those run by the Christian Brothers, or through nationalistic periodicals such as *Ireland's Own*, the *Shamrock, Irish Nationality*, and *Sinn Féin*, could young minds discover a different truth.

Since the twelfth century the situation between Ireland and England had been that of a small country struggling against domination by a larger one. Step by step England's

control had tightened over not only Ireland, but the entire
area known as the British Isles.

Wales was forced to submit to the English crown in the
thirteenth century. During the seventeenth century, four-
fifths of the land of Ireland was forcibly confiscated by Protestant English and Scottish settlers.[1] In 1707 Scotland was
compelled to join England in a polity known as Great Britain, wherein the English parliament simply absorbed the
Scottish parliament. Then in 1800 Great Britain subsumed
Ireland through the Act of Union, abolishing the Irish parliament, and the United Kingdom of Britain and Ireland
came into being.

Eighty years later the British prime minister, William
Gladstone, had said of the Act of Union, "There is no
blacker or fouler transaction in the history of man. We use
the whole civil government of Ireland as an engine of wholesale corruption. We obtained that union against the sense of
every class of the community by wholesale bribery and un-
blushing intimidation."[2]

When Henry Mooney began writing political commentary, he sometimes took the Act of Union as a starting point.
"In spite of the words on that document," he told readers of
the *Independent* in 1915, "the Irish can no more cease being
Irish than the English could cease being English. The English have an advantage, however. In the United Kingdom
all real power lies with them. Their monarch wears the
crown—even though the English monarch is of German descent."

Henry understood why the Crown considered the Easter
Rising to be a stab in the back. Any rebellion in time of war
was treason. But he also appreciated that Irish nationalists
saw the Rising as a desperate bid for freedom at the most
opportune time, with Britain distracted by the Great War and
her troop strength in Ireland reduced.

"Two different viewpoints, two different truths," he had
written.

And of course, this being Ireland, there were complica-
tions. The Rising was funded largely by American sympathizers acting through the secret Irish Republican Brotherhood.
The rebels had compounded their crime in British eyes by

seeking aid from Germany as well. In spite of the blood ties between their royal houses, the two nations were making every effort to destroy one another on the battlefields of Europe.

Meanwhile America, against whom Britain had fought two wars, was being urged to enter the conflict on the British side.

Henry found the irony amusing.

In the months preceding the Rising, he had attempted through his writings to explain the Irish nationalists to the British government and vice versa. He often labored until late at night, striving to get exactly the right meaning for every word, every phrase. Understanding was crucial. His rational mind had insisted that with enough understanding on both sides, an accommodation could be reached. But the British remained unalterably convinced of their God-given right to rule, while the Irish remained equally convinced of their right to freedom from domination. The two viewpoints were irreconcilable.

The Easter Rising was the result.

The rebellion had been put down savagely and its leaders executed. Yet the struggle was far from over, Henry knew. Not while men like Ned Halloran lived with a passion simmering in them.

As he walked, the journalist noticed a poster advertising a film called *Ireland a Nation* at the O'Connell Street Picture House.[3] A paper ribbon had been pasted over the poster: CANCELLED BY ORDER OF HIS MAJESTY'S GOVERNMENT. Henry began framing a new article in his mind.

For a while he was unaware that the British officer was walking a few paces behind him.

Chapter Five

THE headache was agonizing today. Sitting on the edge of the bed, Ned whispered "please" to a God who did not seem to be listening.

A hand touched his shoulder. "Is it very bad?"

Ned looked up at Síle through slitted eyelids. Though it was past noon, her russet hair tumbled around the shoulders of her calico wrapper. In the privacy of their rooms, she let it fall free because Ned liked it that way. She had so many small ways of pleasing him: warming the sheets with her body before he got into bed, touching his shoulder for a moment when she passed behind his chair . . .

He forced a smile. "Not so bad."

"So you say. Why not lie back down?" Her voice caressed the sore places in his brain. "The washing is done and Precious is downstairs with Louise, so I can lie beside you for a while. You always say that eases your headaches." As she spoke, she was unbuttoning her shirtwaist.

He sat watching her. Sat naked, watching her. In their bed Ned was always naked for Síle.

The warmth of her. The fragrance of her. A glimpse of the soft down on the curve of her cheek, sweet as the down on a peach.

With a little moan he surrendered and let her press him back against the pillows.

She did not press her body against his, but kept a small

space between them; a space charged with desire. For the moment it was better than touching. In that tiny space the mingling of memory and anticipation became a passionate form of lovemaking all its own. Ned's senses rioted with heightened awareness and his headache receded, relegated to a distant pounding he could not separate from the pounding, rising tide of his blood.

When she shifted her weight ever so slightly, his flesh knew exactly how it would feel if she were moving against him. Her soft, full breasts dragging across his bare chest. The tingling of his nipples as she teased them with her own. The sweet, moist . . .

"Síle."

"Yes, love."

"Touch me."

"I will."

"Now."

"Where? Here?"

She held her hand palm down over him, maintaining a hair's breadth of space between them. Yet the heat of her hand scorched him.

"Or here?"

She moved her hand lower. The heat followed.

She shifted her weight again, bringing her hips fractionally closer to his. His erection leaped out to bridge the gulf between them, but without seeming to move she avoided him. "Not yet . . . not yet."

He closed his eyes. She entered into the darkness behind his eyelids and now they were touching, now her hands were moving sweetly down him, now her bare flesh was inviting his caresses, now her thighs were pressed against his thighs and then parting, parting sweetly, parting hungrily, and he was sliding into her, moist as he had known she would be, opening to him, sucking him into that secret, hidden mouth that was like a homecoming. The bliss became a knot at the base of his spine that moved out along all his nerves, gathering strength, and she with him, she with every movement, she inseparable from him, one flesh, one soul, one great long shuddering explosion of joy that rocked the world and filled the universe with a silent shout, and it was the two of them together, the two of them together always . . .

Then the slow, sweet shuddering, and the gentle drifting down, down . . . to find himself lying in Síle's arms and the pain gone, magically gone.

He never let himself think about how she had acquired the skills of which he was the beneficiary. She was Síle. There was nothing else.

NED stood up slowly, one section of himself at a time. "I have to get up. Henry's coming back today."

From the bed Síle said wistfully, "Everything's been so lovely with just the three of us up here under the eaves. Like having our own house, almost."

"It's thanks to Henry that we have a roof over our heads at all," Ned reminded her.

When Ned and Henry worked together at the *Independent* they had shared a room, second-story front, in Louise Kearney's lodging house for single men. There they dueled across a chessboard and became close friends. After the Easter Rising Henry had taken his cousin aside to explain, "Ned's been badly wounded, Louise. I have him well hidden until the repercussions die down, but it's only a temporary arrangement. I want to bring him back here so we can keep an eye on him while he convalesces."

Louise Kearney was a sturdy, middle-aged widow with a perpetual Celtic flush. Her jutting chin gave her the profile of a chest of drawers with the bottom drawer open. Yet a man had loved her once, and the warmth of that love would last her until the day she died. She had borne the late Mr. Kearney no children. "That was our cross to bear," she said simply.

When Henry told her about Ned, her reply was, "You go fetch that poor lad home right now. Sure, where else would he go?"

"Ah . . . there's a little more to it than that. You see, as soon as Ned's got his strength back, he wants to get married. So I'm asking you to bend your rules about men only."

She was going to refuse; Henry could read it in her face. He spoke first. "Looking forward to marrying his sweetheart has been the only thing that's kept Ned alive."

Louise drew a deep breath. "Well . . . I suppose rules are made to be broken."

"So they are. I knew you would understand. And . . . ah . . . there is one other thing. Ned and his wife will be needing a bit of privacy, and I should like to have an office at home myself, come to that. So I've been thinking . . ."

Louise had listened with amazement to what Henry was thinking. "Go on out of that! It's impossible, I could never afford it."

"Nonsense. You're a businesswoman, and this is a sound investment—it will increase the value of your property."

"I can't afford it," she had repeated less emphatically.

" 'There is no need like the lack of a friend,' " Henry said, quoting the old proverb. "Ned needs all his friends now, and that includes you, surely." He sensed victory; it only remained to deliver the coup de grâce. "Besides, I'll pay for half the work myself."

"You're a most persuasive man, Henry Mooney."

"It's my stock-in-trade."

The next day a pair of workmen had arrived at number 16 Middle Gardiner Street, where from disused maids' rooms and storerooms in the attic they created two new apartments. One consisted of a large bedroom with a bookshelf-lined alcove that Henry called his study, while the other apartment had two bedrooms and a small sitting room for Ned's family. Unlike the other lodgers, they took their meals with their landlady.

The arrangement seemed ideal; yet in spite of her gratitude Síle resented Henry's presence at the top of the house. The walls had been hastily erected and were thin. She tensed at the creak of his footstep on the floorboards, the rasp of his cough in the passageway, even his gentle chuckle when something amused him. Awareness of another man in their private space was like a splinter under Síle's fingernail, A painful reminder.

"I appreciate all that Henry's done for us," she assured Ned. "It's just that—"

"I know, I promised you a cottage on Howth." He paused; an Irishman did not discuss finances with his wife. Yet so-

ciety's rules never applied to Síle. "For now all the money
we have is what my brother sends me from the farm income," he said. "But Frank has our little sisters and our aunt
to take care of, and the farm's not making much these days.
If you and I didn't work around the house for Mrs. Kearney
to help earn our keep, we'd be totally skint. No one else
would employ me while my health's so uncertain."

"You were invited to teach at Saint Enda's," she pointed
out.

"Ah, Síle, imagine what would happen when I had one
of my dizzy spells and collapsed in front of the students.
They would be frightened and I would be humiliated. No,
teaching is out of the question. But when I sell my first novel
we'll buy that cottage. You'll see."

Ned was getting dressed as he spoke. He was tall, dark,
very thin, with intense green eyes fringed in heavy lashes.
Síle thought he was beautiful. Their marriage was the ful-
fillment of the only dream she had ever allowed herself.

Ned's dreams were more ambitious. At the *Independent*
he had been training to be a reporter, but he really wanted
to be a novelist. Pádraic Pearse had told him he had a talent
for creative writing, and to Ned, everything Pearse said was
gospel.

Abruptly Síle threw back the sheets and stood up, gathering her abundant mane in both hands and twisting it atop
her head. Proper married women put their hair up. She se-
cured her willful locks with the tortoiseshell combs Ned had
given her for Christmas, then busied herself dressing. She
kept her back turned to her husband so he could not see the
doubt in her eyes.

Sometimes Ned read aloud to her from the novel he was
trying to write. The words sounded fine and grand, strung
together so they danced on the tongue, but they did not relate
to any life Síle knew. She could not believe in a future built
upon fanciful adventures in faraway places. Castles in the
air.

In her experience reality had a harder edge.

* • *

MRS. Kearney met Ned at the foot of the stairs. "Is Síle coming down soon, Ned?" she asked as she dried her hands on her apron. "I need her in the scullery."

"She'll be here in a minute. She's tidying our rooms now."

Louise Kearney gestured with a nod. "Precious is inside, tidying the parlor."

Ned grinned. "Precious would tidy the world if we let her."

From the parlor doorway they observed a little girl enveloped in one of Louise's aprons. The garment went around her twice and was held in place by a wooden clothes peg. On the floor beside her was a basket containing a large tin of beeswax, a supply of rags, and a box of Keating's Powder, "Guaranteed to Kill Moths, Fleas, and Bugs."

Biting her lower lip in concentration, the child was polishing a tabletop. She swiped diligently, then squinted along the surface. When she found a tiny smear, she polished the entire table again.

Henry Mooney called her Little Business.

After the third time she found salt in her sugar jar, Louise Kearney had suggested a better nickname might be Mischief.

Strangers sometimes felt sorry for the child because she had not inherited her parents' good looks. Although Ned and Síle were both tall, Precious was small for her seven years, and plain. Her hair had darkened from an infant blond to a nondescript brown. But there was a good reason why she had neither Ned's crisp black curls nor Síle's dramatically slanted eyes. The little girl was a waif from the Dublin tenements. She literally had fallen into Ned's arms during the Bachelor's Walk Massacre in 1914, when British soldiers fired on Dublin civilians.

Ned had rescued the terrified child and taken her to the Charitable Infirmary on Jervis Street. When the nuns asked her name, all she could tell them was, "My mama calls me Precious." In the days that followed, no one claimed her. Dublin was teeming with tenement children; an abandoned one was not uncommon. Eventually Precious was consigned to an orphanage under the name of "Ursula Jervis." Thereafter, Ned visited her as often as he could.

When the center of Dublin was under bombardment during Easter Week, Ned's fiancée, Síle Duffy, had gone to the
orphanage to take Precious to safety. The matron had refused
until Síle brandished a pistol in her face. The terrified
woman surrendered the little girl at once.

Precious had been theirs ever since. Theirs by right of
love.

She called Henry "Uncle Henry" and Mrs. Kearney "Auntie
Louise," and would not go to bed without kissing them both
goodnight. At her recent First Communion, Henry and Louise had sat with Ned and Síle. The family.

"Precious?" Ned called softly.

The child's sudden smile lit candles in her blue eyes.
"Look, Ned-Ned, I'm doing housework."

"So I see."

"I'm helping earn our sub-sis-tence." She ostentatiously
returned to her dusting.

"You have another new word," Ned observed.

"Uncle Henry gave it to me."

Ned exchanged a knowing glance with Louise. Precious'
vocabulary was a source of amusement. As soon as the child
heard an unfamiliar word she seized upon it like a collector
and allowed the adults in the house no peace until one of
them told her its meaning.

"I didn't ask Precious to help with the housework," Louise
said. "It was her own idea."

"I know."

"I would keep the three of you for nothing if I could
afford to, Ned. It's small enough thanks for what you lads
tried to do."

"You've done more than enough for us. You even let us
get married in your parlor, when plenty of people in Dublin
wouldn't have allowed Síle through their front door."

"Whisht, go 'way out o' that!" Louise Kearney cast a
furtive glance toward Precious, who seemed absorbed in her
task. "You wouldn't want the child to be hearing such things
about her mother."

"Síle *has* become her mother, hasn't she? And myself her
father. Who's to know?"

"It's not that simple. Precious should be going to school,

and when she does there'll be questions asked. They'll be wanting a copy of her birth certificate from the Customs House."

"We've decided not to send her to school, Louise. The national schools have windows, but no light comes in. We're going to educate Precious at home."

"Can you?"

"Did I not have the best education in the world with Mr. Pearse at Saint Enda's? I can instruct her in Irish, Latin, Greek, history, literature, maths . . . and English grammar, of course. It's important that she speaks well. I don't want her labeled because of a Dublin tenement accent."

The front door opened, then closed gently, stealthily. Louise motioned to Ned to stay where he was and went out into the hall. "God between us and all harm!" Ned heard her exclaim. "Henry Mooney, why are you sneaking into my house like an early autumn? Come into the parlor this minute."

Henry immediately went to one of the tall front windows and peered out from behind the curtains.

Precious tugged at his sleeve. "I've been ever so anxious for you to come home, Uncle Henry! I want to ask you—do men with beards put them under the bedclothes when they sleep, or leave them outside?"

"I don't know; I don't have a beard," said Henry distractedly, keeping his eyes on the street.

"It's not like you to ignore one of her questions," Ned observed. "What's wrong?"

"I think a British officer followed me from the GPO."

Ned made shooing motions at Precious. "Run along upstairs, pet. Go to Síle."

"But I haven't finished doing the—"

"Shift!"

She trotted obediently from the parlor and halfway up the stairs, then crept back down to sit on the bottom step, straining to overhear their conversation.

Ned joined Henry at the window. Together they scrutinized the street. Red brick boardinghouses, their once elegant Georgian facades smoke-grimed and shabby. A Jack Russell terrier lifting his leg against an ornate iron lamppost.

A shawl-swathed woman with a shopping basket on her arm.

Louise Kearney went to the other window. "Just look at Dympna Dillon. Always late, that one. Pity her poor lodgers! I must remind her to do her shopping in the morning when everything's fresh. I don't see any soldiers, though. Perhaps you were imagining things, Henry."

"Or perhaps he recognized my name from my articles."

"If they were going to arrest you for sedition, they would have done it while we were still under martial law."

"What makes you think we're not now?" Ned snapped. "When Maxwell was recalled, it was supposed to be lifted, but I can't see much difference. They're still arresting people for singing rebel songs or insulting British soldiers. Do you realize that over two thousand were deported without any trial at all after the Rising? Including women? Many were innocent bystanders who just happened to be in the wrong place at the wrong time."

Henry said, "To be fair, at Christmas they did release the untried deportees. They only kept back the ones who'd been sentenced."

"They had no choice. So many angry Irishmen were turning British prisons into universities for revolutionaries," Ned countered.

Louise suggested, "If someone was following Henry, he may really have been after you, Ned."

"If they're going to start harassing my friends, I'll make it easy to find me." Ned thrust his jaw forward stubbornly; the inherited Halloran cleft stood out in sharp relief.

"I despair of you, lad," said Henry. "One would think you want to go to prison."

"Better men than me have done. Eamon de Valera, Michael Collins . . . even Madame."

Henry chuckled. "Countess Markievicz would be delighted to hear you classify her with the men. I hear she's furious because she wasn't executed with Pearse and the others. Next thing you know, Madame will have the suffragettes demanding she be allowed equal rights to face the firing squad."

"Perhaps we could arrange to be shot together," Ned suggested. "Is there someone you know in the Castle who could organize that for us?" Gazing toward the ceiling he drawled, in an excellent imitation of an upper-class English accent, "How impressed dear Mater would be if I died beside a countess. She would welcome me into heaven with the best tea service."

Henry laughed out loud, but Louise said angrily, "That isn't funny. I don't know how you can joke about such things. Tempting fate, that's what you are. I won't have you arrested and dragged out of this house, Ned Halloran!"

Ned sobered at once. "Perhaps I should leave under my own power, then. I don't want to bring trouble down on you, not after you've been so good to us."

Louise Kearney looked horrified. "Take that sweet innocent child out of here to God knows what? I won't hear of it."

Chapter Six

HENRY Mooney leaned back in his chair and rubbed his eyes, gritty with the residue of energy wasted. Soon the lamplighter would be making his rounds. Gaslight pouring down from the street lamps onto the cobblestones, painting the tired, tense, battered city with a deceptive romance.

Another day gone and nothing accomplished.

On the table in front of Henry was an article he could not sell. In the aftermath of the Rising, censorship had taken hold with a vengeance. Most newspapers sympathetic to the Republican cause had been suppressed. Arthur Griffith's weekly, *Young Ireland*, was still in business, but Henry's usual markets were drying up.

Before he went to Limerick he had offered his analysis of Lloyd George's recent speech in the House of Commons to several of the larger Dublin papers, only to have it refused. Upon returning to the capital he had expanded the article, polished it with the patience of a lapidary, and tried again.

No sale.

He sat staring down at his writing in a mood of dejection.

Maybe my work is simply not good enough. I don't have Ned's facility with words; I'm just a hack writer and that's all I ever will be.

A muscle worked in his jaw. *Stop feeling sorry for yourself, Mooney. This is important, damn it. These are things that have to be said and no one else is saying them.*

He put on his coat and went out in search of a stiff drink.

Henry's local was the Oval Bar on Abbey Street, a favorite haunt of journalists: dark paneling, a permanent haze of smoke, newspaper clippings pasted over the mirror behind the bar, ribald conversation on tap. He and Ned had spent many an hour together there. Before Síle.

Henry ordered a drink and found a vacant stool halfway down the bar, beside Matt Nugent, a red-faced, white-haired journalist with a beer belly and a whiskey voice. International news was Nugent's specialty. After a few minutes' conversation about the current state of the Irish newspaper business he remarked, "You're a decent skin, Henry, and I like you. But you'd better start conforming with the *Irish Times* point of view if you want to work in this town."

"The *Squirish Mimes*, you mean. They're too pro-British for me."

"Are you saying you're anti-British? That's not very smart these days, Henry—particularly not in Dublin. My round." Nugent lifted two fingers to signal the barman for refills before their glasses were empty.

Henry nodded thanks. "I'm not anti-British, I'm pro-Irish."

"Same thing, isn't it?"

"Not at all. That's just another way of using labels to set us at one another's throats. Unionist against Republican, loyalist against nationalist. It's a dangerous—"

Another newspaperman peered owlishly over Nugent's shoulder. "Don't you be encouraging Henry to write *Irish Times* material, Matt. There's too many of us doing that already. Let the man keep his own voice."

"You mean his integrity?" Nugent asked.

"If that's what you want to call it," the man replied.

Nugent turned back to Henry. "Pay him no mind—he just doesn't want competition. I don't worry about being shot by British soldiers, but I worry like hell about finding a knife stuck in my back by one of my colleagues."

"Listen here to me, Mooney," intoned a colleague on Henry's other side. A forest of empty glasses stood before him on the bar, and he spoke with the slow deliberation of a drunk imparting great wisdom. "Journalism today is about the subordination of truth to myth. People don't want to read the truth. They're afraid it won't agree with their own opinions. They want to read myths that confirm their prejudices." The inebriated philosopher wagged his finger at Henry. "Stop prattling about the decency and heroism of the Irish. We don't believe you. For centuries we've been told we're subhuman brutes. Criticize us and we will believe you. Or better yet, concentrate on the war. Write about brave Britain defying the forces of evil for the sake of small nations." He picked up the nearest glass and drained its last drops. "An inspiration to us all," he added sourly.

Henry said, "I happen to believe the truth's important whether people want to hear it or not."

Nugent snorted. "And you know what the truth is, do you?"

"It isn't what the *Irish Times* wrote during Easter Week. They dismissed the entire Rising as no more than 'a few evilly disposed persons disturbing the peace.' Those words are burned in my brain."

"When they were published in the *Times*, Henry, they became the official truth. You know that as well as I do."

"No newspaperman with any integrity should let statements like that go unchallenged."

"Maybe you can't, but I have to," interjected the philosopher. "I have a wife and family to feed. Barman? 'Nother pint of porter here. An' a round for my friends."

And that sums it up, Henry thought. *The British won and it's over, and people are doing what they must in order to get on with their lives. You can't blame them.*

He went back to the boardinghouse still sober. Wishing he were drunk.

The Hallorans had retired early, but a few male lodgers were still talking in front of the fireplace in the parlor. One of them beckoned Henry to join them. He smilingly refused and made his way upstairs. In the alcove he called his study, Henry turned up the gaslight and read his unsold article again.

Asquith, Britain's very English prime minister, had been forced to resign in December of 1916 in the aftermath of

the Easter Rising executions. He was replaced by David
Lloyd George, who formerly had held the posts of chancellor
of the exchequer, minister of munitions, and secretary of
state for war. The new prime minister found himself at the
helm of a Conservative-Liberal coalition. Managing this un-
easy alliance of opposed philosophies was a challenge even
for someone whose nickname was "the Welsh Wizard."

Strangely enough for a Celt, Lloyd George seemed more
inimical to the Irish than Asquith had ever been. But he was
clever; one had to give him that. On the seventh of March
he had proclaimed in the House of Commons: "Centuries of
brutal and often ruthless injustice—and, what is worse when
you are dealing with a high-spirited and sensitive people,
centuries of insolence and insult—have driven hatred of
British rule into the very marrow of the Irish race."[1]

With this expression of apparent sympathy, Lloyd George
hoped to placate Ireland's many friends in the United States.
Britain could not afford to antagonize America when a wartime alliance was desperately needed.

The new prime minister had then proceeded to cut the
ground from under any idea of an Irish nation, however. "In
the northeastern portion of Ireland," he said, "you have a
population as hostile to Irish rule as the rest of Ireland is to
British rule—as alien in blood, in religious faith, in
traditions, in outlook. To place them under national rule
would be as glaring an outrage on the principles of liberty
as the denial of self-government would be for the rest of
Ireland."

Lloyd George went on to say that his government was
perfectly willing to grant home rule "to that part of Ireland
that demands it." His meaning was obvious. If Ireland continued to insist on its own legislative assembly, the price
would be the separation of the Unionist-controlled province
of Ulster from the rest of the island.

After Lloyd George's speech, John Redmond led the Irish
Party out of the House of Commons in anger. The next day
they issued a formal protest against allowing a minority in
the northeastern corner of Ireland to have a veto over the
whole island's future.

Lloyd George undertook to mollify Redmond by promising that partition, should it ever occur, would be temporary. Furthermore, he repeated assurances that home rule would be Ireland's ultimate reward for encouraging her sons to fight and die for Britain.

"I don't believe a word the prime minister says," Henry had remarked to Ned. "Home rule's been waved in front of the Irish too many times before, like a carrot to tempt a donkey. But we never get the carrot. We get the stick every time."

He worded the end of his article more elegantly. "It would be a mistake to continue to anticipate home rule," he warned. "Now we must avoid any situation that might give Britain an excuse to dismember this country before nationhood can be achieved."

But who would print those words? Most of the papers sympathetic to nationalism were shut down, their doors boarded and padlocked.

A dead newspaper is like a dead person. All those hopes and dreams and ideas destroyed. All that potential lost.

Muffled sounds came through the wall from Ned and Síle's bedroom.

Henry went to the bedside locker where he kept his cigarettes. Only one, badly bent, remained in a crumpled packet. "Why do I never find a full packet when I need one?" he wondered aloud—then paused, realizing that like many people who live alone, he had begun talking to himself. He justified it by thinking, *Either you talk to God or you talk to yourself.*

And how do you know the difference?

IN the passage outside Ned's door Henry called, "I'm going out again. Can I bring you anything?"

"Nothing, thanks," Ned called back.

From Precious' room came a sleepy "Some boiled sweets?"

"You should be asleep," Síle told her sternly.

"Am asleep." Precious gave a credible imitation of snoring.

As Henry's steps receded, Síle asked, "Where do you suppose he's going at this hour?"

"Down to Monto for some female companionship," Ned answered without thinking. Too late he saw the expression that flickered across Síle's face.

Chapter Seven

April 6, 1917

UNITED STATES ENTERS WAR TO SAVE
DEMOCRACY

April 19, 1917

NATIONAL COUNCIL OF IRISH NATIONALIST
ORGANIZATIONS ESTABLISHED

EASTER Monday in 1917 was different from the preceding year. People openly wore armbands of tricolor ribbon. Defying the authorities, men and women pasted copies of the Republican Proclamation on every available wall.

In Dublin an even braver band succeeded in smuggling a tricolor flag to the ruined roof of the GPO and hoisting it at half-mast.[1] British soldiers struggled for hours to untie the cleverly knotted spiderweb of ropes that held the forbidden flag in place, while a large crowd jeered them from the street below.

Ned Halloran was out of the house all day. When he finally returned, his face was flushed and his eyes feverbright. Síle ran to meet him and kissed him, hard.

Dublin newspapers reported the flag-raising incident as

"regrettable," the act of "a few ill-advised criminal malcontents."

There was a fresh wave of arrests.

Until I was on my own," Henry remarked in Louise Kearney's parlor the next evening, "I didn't realize how much journalists depend on the office and the desk and having one another around. I miss all that. What I need is a newspaper that's not intimidated by the government—one that's willing to hire a moderate nationalist."

Ned said, "There's no such paper in Dublin. Nor a moderate nationalist, either."

"There's me." Henry folded the *Evening Herald* he had been reading and set it aside. "I'm a moderate nationalist. But Dublin's not my city right now. I'm thinking of trying my luck in the provinces for a while."

"Limerick?"

Alice whimpering, Pauline resenting, Mam like a black crow, cawing at him—Clawing at him. "Not Limerick. Meath, perhaps. The *Meath Chronicle* is hanging on—it just called for full independence for Ireland."

"Forget about Meath, Henry. We're west-of-Ireland men, you and I. The *Clare Champion* is still being published in Ennis—Frank sends me copies from time to time. Why not try them? If I could go home, I'd apply for a job at the *Champion* myself."

"If I could go home." As Ned spoke, his glance inadvertently flicked toward Síle, who was mending a shirtwaist by the light of the gas jet. If she heard him, she gave no sign.

But a spot of blood dropped onto her sewing from a pricked finger.

The next morning Henry made a little trip to the stationer's and purchased a dictionary. He carefully wrapped it in tissue paper, then presented it to Precious that night at the table.

"What's this for, Uncle Henry?"

"Next time you want to know what a word means, you can look it up instead of having to ask Ned."

"I can always ask you."

" 'Fraid not. I'm going to be away for a while—that's why I want you to have the dictionary to use. Until I come back," he added, dismayed by the grief-stricken expression on her face. "I shall always come back, I promise. Here now, what's this?" he asked as he took out his handkerchief and dabbed at her eyes.

"Paindrops."

"Paindrops?"

"You know, like raindrops. Only coming from people instead of from clouds."

"I don't think the child has any need for a dictionary," Louise remarked. "The words she makes up are better."

A few days later Henry was on his way to County Clare and a meeting with Josephine Maguire, sister of the paper's deceased founder, and her husband, Sarsfield Maguire, the editor.[2]

County Clare was beautiful in the spring. A froth of whitethorn in the hedgerows: lace petticoats hemming little green fields. Gentle hills singing with the lark and the cuckoo. Wild cliffs booming with the thunder of the surf. Narrow laneways clogged with cattle being moved from one pasture to another.

The county was deceptively peaceful.

The prevailing wind off the Atlantic was like the roar of a distant crowd.

Ned's brother, Frank Halloran, met Henry at the railway station with a pony and trap. "The pony's name is Tad," he explained as they drove away from the station. "The girls used to ride him, but they've outgrown the old fellow now." Henry grew mesmerized by the rhythmic movement of the rounded haunches in front of him as the pony trotted along the dirt road. The trap creaked; the wheels sang. The air smelled of growing things. He felt as if a clenched fist inside himself was gradually loosening. *I'm back in Ireland now. Dublin is Someplace Else.*

At first he stayed at the Halloran family farm. Since the death of Ned's parents in 1912, Mrs. Halloran's sister Norah Daly had kept house for Frank and his sisters. Frank Halloran did not look much like his brother Ned, though in his profile Henry caught glimpses of a familiar bone structure. The family farm was good land, but Frank had about as much talent for agriculture as Henry had for blacksmithing. He was weary and weatherbeaten, and the seat of his trousers drooped.

Norah Daly was a soft-spoken, self-effacing woman in her sixties. She punctuated her every movement with a little grunt, as if she were carrying an invisible burden. She seemed unaware of the habit, and no one else ever mentioned it.

Lucy and Eileen were the babies of the family, but older than Precious—girls on the brink of womanhood. After they got over their initial shyness with a stranger, they were friendly enough to Henry. They had no interest in the world beyond Clare, however; their conversation centered around pump and parish. An older sister, Kathleen, had escaped both. She was married and living in America.

The Hallorans refused to let Henry pay board. "You're Ned's friend. That's all that needs be said."

When Henry called in to the offices of the *Clare Champion*, Josephine Maguire told him, "We know your work, I've read a number of your columns." She was a brisk, nononsense person who dressed plainly and spoke in the same fashion. But there was warmth in her smile. Her husband—taller, thinner, grayer, but equally genial—added, "If you write as well for us as you did for the *Independent*, you have a job for as long as you like. We'll run your commentary on the Lloyd George speech in the next edition."

That night there was a celebratory dinner at the Halloran farm. Hearty country food: a heaping platter of chops and brown onions served with pitchers of cold buttermilk. Henry cleaned his plate and allowed Norah to fill it again. Although he was enjoying himself, he could sense a disturbed undercurrent. Something was troubling Frank and Norah.

After a couple of days Frank intercepted him as he was returning from using the earth closet out back. Embarrassed, but driven to ask, Frank said, "Why does Ned never come home and bring the wife for us to meet?"

"He took a nasty head wound during the Rising. He's not completely over it yet, Frank."

"Are you sure you're telling me everything?"

"What else could there be?"

"They didn't invite us up to Dublin for the wedding. Is Ned ashamed of us?"

"Not at all. When he speaks of his people in Clare he practically crows with pride."

"What is it then? Some problem about his wife? He's written hardly anything about her, except that she's red-haired and her maiden name was Duffy. Sure Ireland's chockablock with Duffys; that tells us nothing. You know her, Henry. What's she like?"

Henry hesitated before answering. *Tread carefully here.* "Síle doesn't have much education, but she's quite intelligent."

"Intelligent?" Frank looked as if a woman's intelligence was something he never considered.

"And attractive," Henry added. "She's very attractive."

"But?"

"There is no 'but,' Frank. I'm sorry you weren't invited to the wedding. You can blame me for that. Given the circumstances in Dublin these days, I advised Ned not to splash out and draw attention. It was a very small ceremony. Beside Ned and Síle there was only the priest—Ned's friend Father Paul—and myself and my cousin Louise for witnesses. And the little girl Ned rescued. You know about her, of course. She's their foster child now."

Frank appeared to accept the explanation, but later he told his aunt, "There's more to this than Henry's admitting. He pretends everything's grand, but that's bunkum. When I asked questions about Síle, his voice changed."

A smile seeped into the creases of Norah Daly's face like melted butter running through porridge. "Listen while I tell you. I think the poor man's in love with Ned's wife himself. That's why he's come away to Clare—to put distance between himself and a sweetheart he can never have. I could never do such a thing, but I admire him for it."

Frank clicked his tongue. "Ah, Norah, you're misreading the man entirely. He's simply here to do a job of work."

"I know what I know," his aunt insisted.

That night she took a cup of hot milk to Henry's room before he went to bed and offered to say the rosary with him.

Henry hated hot milk.

Next day he went in search of other lodgings. "I need to be closer to the newspaper office," he told the Hallorans. He soon found a room over the Ennis Town Hall adjacent to the Old Ground Hotel. The accommodation was plain, but he would not be there very much.

Ennis was the county seat and a market town: narrow, crooked streets rambling all unplanned, shabby shopfronts with cats dozing in windows, plainly dressed country people greeting a stranger with smiles and nods. Deep country quiet at night. The river Fergus murmuring through town like a satin ribbon, reed-fringed.

"You'll find everything you need within the reach of your arm," Henry's new landlord assured him. "And if it isn't here, you don't need it anyway."

"I suppose I'll need a bicycle."

"There's always one or two 'round the back. Help yourself."

Unlike the big Dublin newspapers, the *Champion* did not have subeditors or a separate commercial department. The small staff was expected to cover church, sporting, and social events as well as hard news, create fillers on the spur of the moment, and solicit and write advertising copy. "Suits me like my skin," Henry told the Maguires. "I've been doing those things for years anyway."

Away from the overheated atmosphere of Dublin, smoldering with bitterness on both sides, he felt as if a weight had been lifted from him. In rural Ireland many men were open about their nationalism. Henry met them everywhere, Volunteers who now proudly bore the name James Connolly had given the rebels of Easter Week: the Irish Republican Army. They felt an inchoate need to atone for not having been in the GPO during the Rising. The one thing they would not do was fight under a British flag.

British army recruitment in Clare had reached a peak following the sinking of the *Lusitania*, but the county's support

for the Great War had dwindled dramatically after the Easter
Rising. Yet Henry's feature articles for the *Champion* were
not blatant espousals of nationalism. He tried to strike a
balance.

He paid sincere tribute to the four thousand Clare men
who had marched off to fight under a British flag: "The
young men who join the Royal Munster Fusiliers and other
Irish regiments do so for understandable reasons. They are
escaping poverty or seeking adventure, they are responding
to the urging of their friends or the influence of their em-
ployers, they are defending Catholic Poland or fighting for
the freedom of small nations. This small nation, which is
not free, acknowledges the valor of these men—and mourns
the many who will sleep forever in foreign soil."[3]

Reading the copy, Sarsfield Maguire nodded in approval.
" 'This small nation, which is not free . . .' You're good,
Mooney. You're very good."

A change in public attitude was increasingly evident.
Many Irish—and even English—intellectuals and members
of the artistic community were beginning to express opinions
publicly that were in sharp disagreement with the view of
the British establishment.[4] They no longer accepted that the
leaders of the Easter Rising had been traitors. They called
them patriots.

In February there had been a by-election in County Roscommon. Sinn Féin had put forward a man whose son had
been shot against a wall in Kilmainham Jail by General
Maxwell. George Noble, Count Plunkett—the father of Joseph Plunkett—had won by an overwhelming majority, becoming the first member of Sinn Féin elected to Parliament.
Count Plunkett was a popular choice. A courteous, highly
educated man whose ebony walking stick and bushy white
beard were a familiar sight in Dublin's museums, he had
impressed everyone by his demeanor after the death of his
son. He did not cast blame; he did not collapse in grief.
Instead, Count and Mrs. Plunkett had set about championing
the cause for which Joe died.

When Count Plunkett won the election, Dublin Castle responded by arresting twenty-six prominent nationalists. Although in many cases there were no grounds for either

charging them or trying them, ten were promptly deported.

In May, South Longford, a stronghold of the Irish Party, held a by-election. As its candidate Sinn Féin nominated Joseph McGuinness, who was being held in Lewes Prison. The campaign slogan was "Put him in to get him out!"

When McGuinness unexpectedly defeated the candidate of the Irish Party, Henry wrote cautiously, "We may be seeing a trend."

The passion of his pen was reserved for the wave of diphtheria killing so many children in the west of Ireland: the little white coffins, the empty beds at home, the teachers recording deaths on the school rolls.

He attended cattle sales and cake sales, reported on births and deaths and marriages. Weather predictions were popular with his readers. "Farmers expect the coming summer to be very wet. Some herons have been observed leaving coastal areas and flying toward the mountains. The ash trees are already budding, and as you know, 'Ash before oak, in for a soak—oak before ash, in for a splash.' "

Every week—religiously—Henry sent the household tithe to Limerick. On most Sunday mornings, instead of going to Mass, he fished the clear water of the Fergus below the distillery. The Fergus meandered across the countryside, bristling with rushes for much of its journey as if ancient riverine monsters with raised hackles lurked beneath the surface. A blue heron claimed the stretch of river by the distillery. When Henry first arrived, it had glared with a cold eye at its human competition, but over time they established a grudging truce. Henry spent contented hours outsmarting silver salmon and fat brown trout, throwing some to the heron and trading the rest to the cook in the Old Ground for his Sunday dinner.

He began to feel at home. Almost.

Affable and gregarious by nature, Henry had learned early to guard his private core. An unspoken Irish commandment that Hannah Mooney's children had absorbed with their mother's milk was "Don't tell anyone your personal business." As he grew older, Henry had developed a shell of self-protection against his family as well. Ned Halloran was his first close friend.

In the five years they had known one another, Ned had learned to appreciate Henry's common sense and steadiness, bedrock qualities that had been missing in Ned's life since his parents died. Henry, on the other hand, admired Ned's fearless heart and reckless courage, his gift for passionate commitment. He was the younger brother Henry would have wished for.

When Síle and Precious joined Ned, Henry had accepted them too. They had added a new dimension to his life. Ned regaled Precious with imaginative tales of myth and magic, yet to Henry's surprise she preferred to sit at his feet listening while he read the daily newspapers aloud. In her curiosity about the world and its workings he saw his own youthful self reflected.

Now Precious was on the other side of the country. They were all on the other side of the country.

Sometimes Henry felt as if he were trapped in a glass bottle. He could see people and they could see him. He spoke and made gestures and they responded, but there was no touching. *We're born alone and we die alone. I accept that. But why, God, do we have to be alone in the middle?*

There was an option, of course.

A wife of his own. The chance to repeat his father's mistake.

After work Henry occasionally visited a ramshackle farmhouse half-hidden in a stand of trees off the Kilrush road, a house whose female occupants earned their living by comforting lonely men. As he rode his bicycle back to town, he saw oil lamps glowing in cottage windows. Little boys and girls running home up rutted laneways. A young wife waving a greeting to her husband from an open door.

Loneliness was a cold blue twilight.

FLOSSIE'S colt is still alive, much to our surprise," Pauline wrote from Limerick. "He is nearly black and will be much larger than his mother. Mam has not bought a new pony, so we cannot use the cart. Alice has a face on her longer than a wet winter. I do not know what ails the girl.

We need you at home, Henry. I do not understand why you persist in living elsewhere."

Ned's letter arrived in the same post. "When will you be coming back to Dublin? I miss our conversations about politics and writing and everything else on God's green earth. Precious chatters incessantly about her Uncle Henry, and of course Síle misses you too."

Henry stared at the page. *Does she? Does she indeed?*

One explanation sufficed for both letters. Henry replied, "Clare is the place for me right now. Major William Redmond, John Redmond's brother, was a member of Parliament for East Clare but has been killed in action at Messines. Sinn Féin plans to put forward a candidate for his seat. This particular by-election for a new MP could be crucial to the overall political scene, and I am lucky to be here."

Subsequently Henry wrote in the *Champion*, "By stubbornly and mistakenly referring to the Easter Rising as the Sinn Féin Rebellion, the British military has created a national image for Sinn Féin that the party never had before. A considerable amount of attention is now focused on the Sinn Féin candidacy of one Eamon de Valera, who is currently under life sentence in Lewes prison.

"The exotically named Mr. de Valera was born in America of a Spanish father and an Irish mother. Raised by relatives in Bruree, County Limerick, he attended Blackrock College in Dublin and became a teacher of mathematics. De Valera commanded the Third Dublin Battalion during the Easter Rising and has the further distinction of having been the last commandant to surrender."

Under considerable pressure from America, on the sixteenth of June the British government declared an amnesty for the remaining 120 Irish prisoners and sent them home. Among them were Eamon de Valera; Eoin MacNeill, who had been the first chief-of-staff of the Irish Volunteers; and Thomas Ashe, who had commanded the Fifth Battalion in North County Dublin. During Easter Week Ashe and his second-in-command, Richard Mulcahy, had overpowered the Royal Irish Constabulary at Ashbourne in the most successful military engagement of the Rising.

When the men reached Dublin, a hero's welcome was

waiting for them. Traffic was halted and all work suspended while they were driven in motorcars through throngs of cheering admirers. It was quite a different reception from the hostility Dubliners had shown the rebels immediately after the Rising. The mood of the people had changed.

Constance, Countess Markievicz, and Tom Clarke's widow Kathleen were also released from prison and arrived in Dublin later that same evening. Constance Markievicz in particular bore the marks of imprisonment. In her youth she had been considered a great beauty, with a tiny waist and a glowing complexion. Now she was as lean as a raw-boned boy. Her chiseled features were haggard, with great hollows beneath the high cheekbones. The clothes she wore could have come from a charity shop, and her gray-streaked hair was twisted into a careless knot. But she was indifferent to her appearance. A daughter of the Ascendancy, the so-called Rebel Countess had turned her back on a life of luxury to devote herself to the poor and downtrodden in Ireland. Not for one moment of her life would she regret it.

The women took the Dublin & South Eastern Railway from the port at Kingstown to the Westland Row train station, and from there were escorted through the city in an emotional torchlight procession. But there were no incidents. As their commander-in-chief, the late Pádraic Pearse had demanded that Republicans behave honorably. A year later, they continued to obey.

That night the hills of Ireland blazed with bonfires of celebration.

Chapter Eight

THE East Clare by-election campaign drew crowds of nationalists who were anxious to see the last commander to surrender during Easter Week, and equally passionate loyalists who still felt the tug of old ties with England. Most people expected some degree of violence. Irish politics was a blood sport. Arthur Griffith, founder of Sinn Féin, and Michael Collins, Joseph Plunkett's aide-de-camp during the Rising, had been released from prison in December. Together with Thomas Ashe, they were soon campaigning vigorously on behalf of Eamon de Valera. Relatives of men who had served in the British army took offense; in a few places shots were fired. De Valera's life was threatened if he showed his face in Clare.

Reactivated Irish Republican Army units were employed for protection at Sinn Féin rallies. Additional members of the Royal Irish Constabulary—known as the RIC—were brought in by Sinn Féin's opponents to keep the peace.

Against de Valera the Parliamentary Party pitted a man called Patrick Lynch, who was well known in close-knit, provincial Clare. The party assumed a local man could defeat any outsider. Lynch, however, was a former Crown prosecutor. As so often before, John Redmond's party misunderstood the feelings of the people.

De Valera traveled to Clare by way of Limerick, where he stopped off to meet with Bishop O'Dwyer. Henry Mooney was sent to Limerick to cover the first days of the campaign. He sketched a word picture of the Sinn Féin candidate for his readers: "At first glance, Mr. de Valera presents an austere, even awkward, appearance. He is exceptionally tall and angular, with a long nose and sloping shoulders. Gaunt and pallid, with his hair still cropped from prison, he looks like a man who has seen the farthermost reaches of hell. His physical presence is compelling, however. In public he wears the uniform of the outlawed IRA, and the aura of the Easter Rising thus invoked lends him an almost mythical quality.

"Mr. de Valera has a country man's slow voice that forces people to listen. Although he is no orator, his speech is characterized by a natural dignity, a gravitas, which makes it is easy to understand why he became the unquestioned leader of the Irish prisoners in Lewes."

Sinn Féin established its Clare campaign headquarters at the Old Ground Hotel. Henry wrote to Ned, "It's like having all my Christmases come at once. I need only go down one flight of stairs and through two doors and I'm at the heart of the action."

Soon he was a familiar sight at party gatherings; an amiable man in a gray suit and waistcoat and a bowler hat, chatting with everyone, interested in everything.

He informed readers of the *Champion,* "Highly respected figures such as Countess Markievicz are making speeches on de Valera's behalf. The candidate also keeps Eoin MacNeill beside him on the platform to heal the split in the organization between those who espouse the use of aggressive force to win independence and those like MacNeill, who think force should be limited to defense."

In his speeches, de Valera quoted from the Proclamation of the Republic. He reminded his listeners that the document had been ratified by the life's blood of its signatories. "My allegiance was given to the government of the new Republic in 1916, and my allegiance will remain with the spirit of that government," he repeatedly stated.

He was also a man of strong faith. Henry observed, "No matter how many engagements the Sinn Féin candidate has, he never misses Mass."

The campaign heated up. The voice of the sea wind came closer; the roar of the crowd.

Stones were thrown at both candidates. Broken glass was strewn along roads to damage the motorcars in which they were traveling. Fist fights broke out across the county.

On the twenty-fifth of June a group of Sinn Féin supporters gathered outside the Old Ground Hotel and sang rebel songs.[1] Henry leaned out his window to sing along. Seeing Sarsfield Maguire in the street below, he beckoned to him to come up and watch in comfort with a glass of whiskey in his hand.

At first the rally was a jolly, good-natured gathering. Townspeople joined in the fun. Small children played dodge-'em around the legs of the adults. When constables insisted on cordoning off the area, the Sinn Féiners laughed. But when one of de Valera's men began to make a speech, a swarm of women carrying British flags was allowed through the RIC cordon.

Maguire pointed toward them. "Did you see that, Henry? The police deliberately let those women in to make trouble." He was proved right immediately. They began waving the Union Jack and heckling the speaker. "Yez are all traitors, ye Fenian bastards!"

The mood in the streets of Ennis turned ugly. In Jail Street some young men broke through the cordon and marched toward O'Connell Square, shouting "Up Dev! Up the Republic!" The police attacked them with batons. A local girl's arm was broken, and a man was taken to the infirmary with a severe blow on the head.

LAMENTABLE AND UNNECESSARY VIOLENCE was the headline on Henry's report the next day.

As de Valera campaigned around the county, he continually stressed the importance of democracy. In Killaloe he said, "Let Ulster Unionists recognize the Sinn Féin position, which has behind it justice and right. It is supported by nine-tenths of the Irish people. Ulster is entitled to justice and she will have it, but she should not be petted and the interests of the majority sacrificed to her. Give Unionists a just and full share of representation, but no more than their share."[2]

Morning rallies, afternoon picnics, torchlight processions. Men shouting "Up Dev!" Women applauding; young lads throwing their caps in the air.

Someone gave the candidate a new nickname: "Jaysus, would you look at the Long Fellow—puts me in mind of Brian Bóru, towering head and shoulders over everybody!"

"The Long Fellow casts a long shadow," Henry told his readers.

The tumultuous campaign reached a climax in Ennis at the end of June. Even before dawn, great numbers were making their way to the town. A contingent from Newmarket-on-Fergus came marching in behind a brass and reed band, only to find the narrow streets already choked with pony traps and wagonettes and donkey carts, bicycles and saddle horses and one or two rare motorcars.

Late in the afternoon, a thousand supporters formed ranks outside the Old Ground to escort the Sinn Féin speakers to O'Connell Square. There they took turns addressing the crowd from a horse-drawn shooting brake. Henry was at the forefront of an audience that overflowed into every street and laneway, surging back and forth like the sea.

When it was de Valera's turn to speak, they fell silent. De Valera asked the voters of Clare to choose a man who had fought for Ireland's independence and whose goal was representation for Ireland at the peace conference when the war was over. There Ireland would present her case to be recognized as an independent republic. He also promised that if elected, he would not take his seat in any British parliament.

Henry reported every word.

On July sixth the Parliamentary Party's candidate publicly burned a copy of the *Clare Champion* in O'Connell Square.[3]

July tenth was polling day.[4] De Valera drew 5,010 votes to Lynch's 2,035. People who had never voted in their lives came down from lonely cabins in the hills to cast their votes for one of the heroes of the Easter Rising.

The next day Eamon de Valera was on his way back to Dublin to attend a funeral. Muriel MacDonagh, widow of Thomas MacDonagh, one of the executed leaders of the

Easter Rising, had drowned in a bathing accident at the seaside village of Skerries.

But the Sinn Féin Party was on the move. Victory bonfires blazed in Clare. Nationalists throughout Ireland were flying the forbidden tricolor. Arrests were numerous, and in County Kerry one man was shot dead by the police.

Chapter Nine

AFTER the tension of the campaign, Henry's column provided some light relief. "For those loyalists among you who complain that we do not give the monarchy enough coverage, I am happy to announce that as of yesterday, July 17, 1917, the British royal family has changed its dynastic name. The news was confirmed by telegraph this morning. King George V. formerly Saxe-Coburg-Gotha, has renounced his German name and German titles for himself and his descendants. Hereafter he and his progeny are to be known as the House of Windsor, after Windsor Castle.

"Obviously the change was undertaken to obliterate the king's German origins in the light of public opinion resulting from the Great War. A sensible move it was too, worthy of His Majesty's advisors. We loyally deny that they were influenced by Mr. H. G. Wells, who wrote a letter to the London *Times* describing the royal house of Saxe-Coburg-Gotha as 'an alien and uninspiring court.' We also thoroughly condemn the member of Parliament who recently referred to the king as 'a German pork butcher.' "

Henry's readers loved it.

Frank sent Ned copies of the *Champion* containing the election coverage. Síle read them over his shoulder. He liked her to do that, putting her arms around him from behind and pressing her breasts against his shoulders as he sat in his chair. The white lilac scent she wore filled his nostrils.

Sometimes he just closed his eyes and sat there. At peace. Being with Síle.

"What sort of man is de Valera, Ned?"

"I know him to speak to, but that's about all; I wasn't in his battalion. The men who know him well seem to have the highest regard for him, though."

Síle straightened up. "Are those the same men you meet after dark at Vaughan's Hotel?"

"Don't ask me about them. That way, if you're ever questioned by the authorities you won't have to lie for me. I know how you hate lying."

"And I know it's Michael Collins you're meeting, so don't deny it," Síle asserted. "You're as tight as a duck's arse with your secrets and I won't have it. I've been part of this from the beginning, remember? I was gathering information for Tom Clarke and the IRB before you ever enlisted in the Volunteers."

"Never say that where anyone might hear you."

"But it's the truth."

"That truth could get you arrested, and what would I do then?" Ned reached out and pulled her onto his lap, squeezing so tight she could hardly breathe. "Ah, Síle, *mo mhuirnín dílís*."*

"Tell me what's going on, please."

He did not answer, merely pressed his lips against her hair.

She was furious with him for trying to protect her. She did not want or need protection; she felt very well able to look after herself. But she desperately wanted to share. There was no arguing with Ned, however. His stubbornness was legendary.

A month after de Valera's victory in Clare, the editor of the *Kilkenny People* nominated a Sinn Féin candidate to run in an election in Kilkenny.[1] The newspaper was immediately suppressed by order of the government, but the candidate,

*My own true love in Irish.

William T. Cosgrave—a veteran of the Easter Rising whose death sentence had been commuted—won by a huge margin.

Raids on the homes of Republican sympathizers increased, as did arrests, most of them on spurious charges. Yet throughout the country men and women were flocking to join Sinn Féin clubs.

Newspapers in England reported with alarm that the party was sweeping Ireland like a tidal wave. Redmond's Irish Parliamentarians were in danger of being blotted out. One British paper, the *Morning Post*, suggested that the best response would be to enforce Irish conscription immediately.

"It is not only Irishmen who are against conscription," Henry informed his readers. "Since 1914 a number of English and Scottish conscientious objectors have fled to these shores. When caught, these 'conchies' are thown into Mountjoy Prison for refusing to kill their fellow man. Whose is the crime?"

NED wrote to Henry: "Did you know Thomas Ashe is in Mountjoy? In August he was rearrested for making speeches 'calculated to cause disaffection,' as the government put it. Republicans in Mountjoy are treated worse than common criminals, Henry. Their beds and shoes have been taken away, and we suspect they are being beaten. They have gone on hunger strike as the only form of protest left to them."

Soon meetings on behalf of the Mountjoy prisoners were being held throughout the country. Sinn Féin clubs besieged the authorities with letters protesting the treatment of men whose only crime was wanting a free Ireland.

No amount of protest saved Thomas Ashe. On the twenty-fifth of September he collapsed and died. According to witnesses at the inquest, his face and throat were covered with bruises. No one was willing to speculate on how he came by them. But he had been forced to lie on a cold floor for fifty hours, then force-fed, which in his weakened condition was sufficient to congest his lungs and stop his heart.

Ashe's body as it lay in the coffin was dressed in the IRA uniform. The shirt had been given him by Michael Collins. Thirty thousand people took part in Ashe's funeral procession. Richard Mulcahy, who now commanded the Second Dublin Battalion and had proved himself superb at organizing, was put in charge of the military arrangements.[2] Veterans of the Easter Rising came from all over the country to march in the cortege, which was led by Constance Markievicz with a revolver in her belt.[3] Crowds lined the streets along the way; many waved tricolor banners. There were so many the police dare not arrest them all, though names were taken down.

One of the honor guard chosen to fire three volleys over Ashe's grave was Edward Joseph Halloran.

While the echoes still rang, Michael Collins stepped forward.[4] He spoke in both English and Irish. "That volley we just heard is the only speech which is proper to make above the grave of a dead Fenian," he told the mourners. Then he melted into the crowd before anyone could take a photograph of him.

Ashe's death whipped up nationalist sentiment to a new high. In Dublin the Volunteer battalions were reorganized as the Dublin Brigade of the Irish Republican Army, with Richard Mulcahy as commandant.

In a gesture of atonement for Ashe's death, the British government granted political status to the other Republican prisoners it was holding. This was understood to guarantee them dignified and humane treatment.

1917 saw the various nationalist factions jockeying for power. Republicans who had been released from prison were busily recruiting more men and women into their ranks. In October the Sinn Féin Party held its tenth annual Árd Fheis, or National Convention, in Dublin.[5] By that time only a small percentage of party members still adhered to Arthur Griffith's philosophy of moral rather than physical resistance.

Henry Mooney traveled up from Clare to cover the Árd Fheis for the *Champion*. He thought about taking a motorcab from the train station to Louise Kearney's house—the *Champion* would pay for it—but decided to walk instead and set off across the city, watching for a shop where he

might buy a trinket for Precious. He turned a corner and—
  There she was.

  Or rather, there they were: three young women strolling along the pavement together, chatting, dressed in the height of fashion, with skirts that revealed trim, silken-clad ankles. One woman was small and dark. One was tall and stately.

  And one was a strawberry blonde wearing one of the new half-veils on her hat.

  Huge brown eyes met Henry's through a cobweb of silk.

Chapter Ten

H<small>ENRY</small> thought he walked on without missing a step. He did not look back.

Ned would say, "Her eyes are the color of sweet sherry," but that's not my style. Who, what, where, when, and why, that's me. Journalists aren't allowed flights of fancy.

As if it were a gramophone recording he replayed her voice with its Ascendancy accent in his head. Members of the Anglo-Irish Ascendancy spoke a pure English with little trace of Irish softness. They were Protestant, owned most of the land in Ireland, and sent their children to English schools.

Big House society. I doubt if she even knows any ordinary Irish people.

Was she married? No way of telling. Like any proper lady, she wore gloves on the street.

Proper lady. Wife-and-mother sort of lady. Henry Mooney walked blindly up the street. *What's the matter with me? I know plenty of women with beautiful eyes. I buy their company for the night and go my way in the morning.*

But he could not remember the faces of any of those women; not one. They were wiped from his mind as a slate is erased with a wet cloth.

I'll never see her again. Thank God. Yes; thank God. Forget about her. A momentary aberration.

He walked on.

• • •

AT number 16, Henry received a joyous welcome. Ned pounded him on the back several times, repeating, "Good on you! Time you came home." Then he hurried off to find a "drop o' the crayture" for celebrating.

When Henry leaned down to greet Precious, she almost strangled him with a mighty hug. "Uncle Henry, Uncle Henry!"

"Did you miss me, Little Business?"

"I missed you something dreadful, Uncle Henry! I have so many questions I've been saving up to ask you. Who was Edith Cavell, and where is Russia, and . . ."

Henry's eyes twinkled. "And were you good while I was gone? No butter on the banisters?"

"I don't do that anymore," she said with cool dignity. "I've outgrown that silliness, so I have." Then she whispered, "Now I put biscuit crumbs in the lodgers' beds."

Henry caught her under the arms and swung her around in a big circle that seriously endangered the parlor furniture. Precious squealed with delight.

When he put the child down, Louise kissed him on both cheeks, said, "It's about time you came home," then hurried out to the kitchen to prepare tea.

Síle simply held out her hand. She was always formal with him. He had a sense of walls erected around her, a barrier intended to keep out everyone but Ned. Henry understood about walls.

"We're glad you're back," she said.

"It's kind of you to say so."

"I mean it. You and Ned are such great friends, and he misses you more than he will admit."

He met her gaze squarely. "And what about you, Síle?"

With a smile that revealed nothing, she said, "It really is good to see you again."

"What's seldom is wonderful," Henry remarked dryly.

Precious stepped between them. "Let me carry your suitcase to your room, Uncle Henry!"

"Leave it—it's far too heavy for you."

Ignoring him, the child tugged at the handle and succeeded in lifting it briefly, then dropped it again, her face red with exertion. "I'll be able to carry it by Christmas," she announced with conviction.

Henry chuckled. "I expect you will, Little Business. I expect you will."

THAT evening Henry visited with his friends in their sitting room. Síle brought up a tea tray and a plate of sweet biscuits from the pantry, and after Precious went reluctantly to bed, Ned got out the chessboard. But Henry could not concentrate on the moves.

"You're not up to your usual standard, Henry. I never captured your queen before."

"I'm sorry, Ned. I suppose I'm thinking too much about tomorrow and the Árd Fheis."

"I'm going to be there too, you know."

"You didn't tell me you'd joined Sinn Féin."

"I haven't, at least not yet. I'm going to the convention as a representative of the Irish Republican Army."

"Don't try to talk him out of it," said Síle. "It won't do any good."

"Don't I know? No one could ever talk this lad out of anything. But why, Ned? I imagine the place will be watched—what if you're recognized?"

"I won't be. Besides, I want to be there to see the government proved wrong. Dublin Castle's only allowing the Sinn Féin convention because they think it will result in a final split among the nationalists, but it's going to have the opposite effect."

"How can you be sure?"

"Because de Valera's worked it out beforehand with the National Council. At first Arthur Griffith flatly refused to even consider a republican form of government. He was still talking about establishing a joint monarchy with England. On the other hand, Cathal Brugha threatened to resign from Sinn Féin altogether unless the party officially declared for an Irish Republic. Somehow de Valera managed to convince them both that the way forward meant securing international recognition for Ireland as an independent nation, then allow-

ing the people to choose their form of government themselves."

Henry gave a low whistle. "How do you know all this?
You're not on the National Council."

"I don't need to be." Ned glanced at Síle before adding,
"I've been doing some work for Mick Collins, and he knows
everything."

Michael Collins. Of course.

Chapter Eleven

OCTOBER twenty-fifth dawned cold and wet. "You'll all be destroyed with the damp," Louise said as she served fried bread and fried eggs for breakfast. "Síle, you put a piece of red flannel around that child's neck."

"My Mam," Henry remarked, "would say this weather is a bad omen for Sinn Féin."

Ned glanced up. "I've rarely heard you speak of your mother."

"I rarely do." Henry cut a bite-sized piece of bread and piled some egg on top.

From Pádraic Pearse, Ned had learned to teach by example. "Precious, did you know that Americans put down the knife after they've cut a bite, then transfer the fork to their right hand and use it like a shovel? Then they switch everything back again to cut the next bite. Here, I'll show you."

"Why do they eat the wrong way?" the little girl wondered.

"It's not the wrong way, any more than ours is the right way. The two are just different. Something can be different without being wrong."

Precious considered this, head cocked to one side. "Like Protestants?"

Louise choked on a bite of egg. Síle thumped her on the back.

Henry remarked, "I've rarely heard you speak of America, Ned."

"I rarely do." Ned had—almost—wiped his one trip to America from his mind. The ocean voyage in 1912 to attend his sister's wedding. The great ship sinking. His parents drowned. The return to Ireland, numb with grief.

America was like a black hole in Ned's memory.

He saw Henry regarding him sympathetically. "Sometimes things pop into our heads when we least expect them," the journalist commented.

A look of understanding passed between the two friends. Síle saw it—and felt a pang of envy.

ORIGINALLY a private home," Henry wrote in his notebook, "the Mansion House was purchased by the Dublin Corporation in 1715 as a residence for the city's lord mayor. In two hundred years its exterior appearance has changed dramatically. The red brick walls are now covered with painted plaster and embellished with frivolous cast-iron work and balustrades. The building resembles a Victorian wedding cake."

One small flight of fancy would do no harm.

Ned had gone to the Mansion House early to meet with members of his old company. By the time Henry arrived, the entrance hall was crowded with people. Hands waving, heads nodding, an occasional angry outburst, a less frequent placating murmur. The more thoughtful men chewed their mustaches or stroked their beards.

Henry recognized representatives of all the nationalist groups, including Cumann na mBan, the women's organization that had played an active role in the Rising. In the bleak days following the surrender it was the women, even more than the men, who had kept the Republican ideal alive. Wives and daughters, mothers and sisters, refusing to let the grave triumph. A few of the women were smoking the dainty scented cigarettes called My Darling's Cigarettes, which had become popular in recent years. Smoking in public was a small symbol of a larger emancipation.

With a nod here and a handshake there, Henry worked

his way through the crowd to the large assembly hall known as the Round Room.

"Mooney, reporting for the *Clare Champion*," he told the fresh-faced lad at the door.

"Clare, is it? You'd be a de Valera man, then."

"How many people are you expecting?"

"I'm told there are seventeen hundred official delegates, sir. Sinn Féin has over a hundred and fifty thousand members countrywide now. You'd best take a seat, we'll be starting soon."

Henry was directed to join the other newspaper reporters standing in the railed gallery that overlooked the floor of the hall. He peered down at the rows of seats below but could not find Ned among the delegates. He wondered which of the men in the room was Michael Collins.

Although Collins had worked for de Valera's Clare campaign, Henry had not met him personally nor seen any photographs of him. As befitted a member of the secretive Irish Republican Brotherhood, the man from County Cork kept a low profile. But his name was heard more and more frequently in nationalist circles, and Henry had been doing some quiet research on him.

During Easter Week Collins had played a minor role as Joseph Plunkett's aide-de-camp. He almost slipped through the net when members of the Irish Republican Army were being deported after the surrender. While imprisoned in Frongoch internment camp in North Wales—where the two main streets were called "Pearse" and "Connolly"—he formed a branch of the IRB under the very noses of the British. On the strength of this he was admitted to the Supreme Council of the Brotherhood.

The Royal Irish Constabulary office in Dublin Castle had a department known as Special Branch. About this time, Special Branch had begun expanding its file on Michael Collins.

After he returned to Ireland at Christmas, Collins had immersed himself in Republican causes. In February he became secretary to the Irish National Aid fund, which had been established by Tom Clarke's widow to help the dependants of dead or imprisoned Republicans.[1] Working out of offices

at 32 Bachelor's Walk in the heart of Dublin, Collins somehow also found time for the ladies. He was said to have "a
rag on every bush," meaning he courted many girls but proposed marriage to none. His engaging personality was much
sought-after by Dublin hostesses, and he rarely missed a
party or a dance.

All in all, a young man of impressive energy.

But which one is he? Henry leaned over the rail to scan
the hall.

Members of the Sinn Féin executive committee occupied
padded benches toward the front of the room. As Henry
leaned forward, one of them turned around to glance up at
the gallery. From beneath the brim of a plain navy blue hat,
Kathleen Clarke caught Henry's eye and waved. He
sketched a salute in return.

The British had executed her husband and her brother, but
Mrs. Clarke was not broken. Nothing could break her. Tom
Clarke had put his faith in his wife and she had never failed
him. Now like a buffer she was seated between Arthur Griffith and Cathal Brugha, men of diametrically opposed views.
As Henry watched, she cheerfully engaged them both in conversation.

Henry jotted down a few paragraphs for expansion later.
"Arthur Griffith is opposed to any form of violence, yet once
held membership in the IRB.[2] Simultaneously an idealist and
a realist, Griffith was one of the primary forces in stimulat-
ing the nationalist revival. He spent years developing detailed plans for reviving the Irish economy, eliminating
slums, and improving the entire social structure, plans he
hoped to bring to fruition through the political action of Sinn
Féin. To demonstrate another facet of his character, when
he was imprisoned by the British after the Rising, Griffith
chose to treat the whole thing as a paid holiday. He kept up
the morale of his fellow prisoners with his unfailing cheer-
fulness."

The pencil point was blunted. Henry paused long enough
to sharpen it with his penknife. *Smell of graphite, thin curl
of wood shavings: memories of school. Why are the remembered smells of childhood the strongest?*

He resumed writing. "During the Rising, Cathal Brugha

was second-in-command to Eamonn Ceannt at the South Dublin Union. The attack climaxed with a six-hour battle punctuated by bombs and grenades. Desperate men pursued one another through the building in a deadly game of hide-and-seek until the British advance was halted by Brugha, who was entrenched alone behind a strategic barricade. Although repeatedly wounded, he continued to defend his position for over two hours. His comrades assumed him dead and waited in despair to be overrun. Then they heard, faint but defiant, Brugha's hoarse voice singing 'God Save Ireland.' They rushed to his side and resumed the battle. That night the British called off the attack; the South Dublin Union remained in Republican hands until the surrender.

"In hospital, Brugha was found to have more than twenty-five bullet and shrapnel fragments in his body. He was considered as good as dead. The British did not even bother to bring charges against him. They misjudged his strength and spirit. Though permanently lame, Cathal Brugha is here today." Henry shook his head with admiration as he wrote the last sentence.

But where's Michael Collins?

"Here comes de Valera," said the reporter on Henry's left, gesturing to a towering figure in an old Volunteer uniform making his way through the crowd. People stepped back to make way for him. With the death of Thomas Ashe, de Valera had become the only surviving commandant from the Rising. He was regarded with awe.

They'll give Dev whatever he asks for, Henry told himself.

The convention opened with an address by Arthur Griffith. A sturdy, bespectacled figure with a square face and crisp mustache, Sinn Féin's founder radiated energy. When he walked, he bounced off the balls of his feet. "The position we dreamed of for so long has been achieved," he announced triumphantly. His voice was too high to make him an effective orator, but his message was welcome on its own. "Ireland has rejected the union with Britain. The Irish voters have pledged themselves to Sinn Féin and independence. Now we need a constituent assembly for the new Republic."

"A republic the world has yet to recognize," growled the man on Henry's left. "But they will. We'll make 'em."

When it was his turn to speak, Cathal Brugha received a standing ovation. He put aside his crutch and stood erect, like a soldier on parade. Brugha was slight and thin, with a long nose and wavy brown hair meticulously parted on the left side. The businesslike tweed suit he wore gave no hint of the character beneath. Lame he might be, but he was the toughest man in the hall, and everyone there knew it.

Staring modestly at the floor, Brugha waited until the noise died down. Then he proposed a new party constitution, which he read aloud. It would deny the right of any foreign government to make laws for Ireland. It also promised to use "any and every means available to render impotent the power of England to hold Ireland in subjugation by military force or otherwise."[3]

Cathal Brugha's words were met with a thunderous roar of approval. The constitution was passed unanimously.

"Here we go," said the man on Henry's left. "Up the Republic!"

There were numerous issues to be resolved. The decision was taken to put forward Republican candidates for every seat in the next general election. Sinn Féin would be in charge of organization and fundraising, with the understanding that the winners would refuse to take their seats in the British parliament. They would join instead in a new Irish national assembly. As Henry wrote, "From now on, Irish republicanism will operate under the banner of Sinn Féin, which is an ironic outcome considering that the British willfully misnamed the movement 'Sinn Féin' in the first place."

Eventually Henry's lower back began to ache from standing so long. He went outside to walk up and down for a few minutes. The rain had passed and a watery sun was shining. As he emerged from the Mansion House, he noticed that two women had set up easels on the pavement and were sketching the architectural wedding cake. One of the women unpinned her hat—a springlike confection of straw and flowers—and removed it to reveal billowing masses of reddish-gold hair piled atop her head. A few tendrils artlessly escaped to caress her temples.

Henry was down the steps before he knew it.

Why don't you go over and speak to her?" queried a voice behind him.

Henry whirled around. "Where did you come from? I didn't see you inside."

Ned replied with a wicked grin, "I was there, practicing a skill I've learned from Mick Collins—hiding in plain sight."

"And Collins, is he inside too?"

"Of course he is, he and Seán MacGarry are officially representing the IRB. Mick hopes to be elected to the Sinn Féin executive committee, and Mrs. Clarke will nominate him. But you're not interested in Mick right now, are you? You look positively smitten. As I said before, why don't you go over and speak to the lady?"

"She's obviously a lady, and we haven't been introduced, that's why."

"Is that all? Come on." Ned's posture underwent a dramatic change. Affecting a graceful insouciance, he sauntered toward the two women. When he was almost past them he paused, then doubled back. "I say, it is you, isn't it?" he asked the strawberry blonde. Any trace of his Clare accent had vanished. He spoke convincing Mayfair English.

"I beg your pardon?"

"We met ages ago and I don't expect you to remember me, but I could never forget you. It's just . . . you must forgive me. I have the most appalling memory for names," he drawled.

"Mrs. Rutledge."

She's married. Of course she's married. Thank God, Henry thought.

"Ella Rutledge," the woman elaborated. "And you are . . ."

"Edward Halloran, of course. I *knew* you'd remember. Topping to see you again." Ned turned toward Henry. "This is my friend Henry Mooney. Henry, I should like to introduce Mrs. Rutledge. Do you remember my singing her praises after the ball?"

At the mention of a ball Ella Rutledge looked mollified.

That's clever of Ned, thought Henry. *She must go to any number of balls and meet any number of men; she can't possibly remember them all.*

Mrs. Rutledge then introduced her sister, Madge Mansell—the small, dark one of the original trio. Madge had a heart-shaped face and a voluptuous little figure.

Henry barely noticed her.

Seen without a veil, Ella Rutledge had tiny lines in the delicate skin around her eyes. She was in her late twenties, with regal posture and a corseted waist still small enough for Henry to span with his two hands. Hers was a fine-boned beauty that would never surrender to age. She had removed her doeskin gloves for sketching. Henry could not help a surreptitious glance at the circlet of gold and diamonds on one slim finger.

They stood chatting on the pavement while pedestrians skirted around them. Ned was giving an excellent imitation of an Englishman. Ella Rutledge said to Henry, "From your accent I assume you are Irish?"

"I am Irish. From County Limerick."

She rewarded him with a warm smile. He discovered that she had dimples. A beguiling indentation in each cheek, just beyond the curve of her lips. *A dimple is the mark left by an angel's touch when it blesses a baby. Where did I hear that?* "I believe we have distant relatives in Limerick," she was saying. "They used to be in the banking business there."

Madge interjected, "Our sister-in-law Ava could tell you about them—she's very keen on genealogy. She's traced every drop of noble blood in our family tree."

Not our crowd at all, thought Henry.

Ned said, "Isn't it interesting that the first thing we in Ireland do is exchange pedigrees? I'm not sure I approve it's a bit like comparing livestock at a fair." He turned to Madge. "Living people are much more interesting than dead ancestors, don't you agree, Miss Mansell?"

Ned proceeded to draw out the ladies with a combination of flattering charm and pretended knowledge. Thus Henry learned that their mother was born in Belfast and that their Dublin-born father had been an officer in the British army. Both parents were now deceased. The women had one brother, Edwin, whose wife, Ava, was the third of the trio Henry had seen. They all lived together in Dublin.

"Ava's the family beauty," Ella Rutledge said laughingly. "My late husband used to call us the Three Graces."

"I'm sorry," Ned murmured. "I was unaware of your bereavement."

The light went out of her face. "He was an officer in the Royal Navy. He was killed at the Battle of Jutland."

A year and a half, Henry calculated swiftly. *She's been a widow for a year and a half.*

THAT evening as the two men walked back to the boardinghouse, Henry alluded only once to their recent encounter. "I remember when you were shy. Now you're a positive genius when it comes to talking to women."

Ned shrugged. "It's easy to talk to women when you know that the only one in the world for you is waiting at home."

"Ah."

After a time Ned thought he heard Henry say under his breath, "Sweet sherry."

"Sorry?"

An embarrassed chuckle. "Guess I was thinking out loud again. It's a bad habit I've got into."

"Comes from living alone," Ned commented.

Autumn night. Footsteps echoing in half-deserted streets. Fitful wind stirring rubbish in the gutters.

Sudden rectangle of yellow light as a shop door was opened; mouth-watering smell of salty hot grease.

Henry stopped abruptly. "Are you hungry, Ned? The chipper's still open."

"Síle's waiting for me."

"We can take some home with us. You know Little Business loves fish and chips."

Still Ned hesitated. "I'm a family man; I never have any money. Remember what they say: 'From the day you marry your heart will be in your mouth and your hand in your pocket.' "

"Come on then, family man. I'm buying."

Ned grinned. "You're a brick."

Huge slabs of batter-fried cod and thick fingers of potato were served in cones of newspaper translucent with grease. Ned and Henry stood shoulder to shoulder at the counter, sprinkling the piping hot food with salt and lashings of malt vinegar.

As they were leaving, Ned remarked, "You're right, you know. Her eyes are the color of sweet sherry."

Chapter Twelve

October 26, .1917

DE VALERA ELECTED PRESIDENT OF SINN FÉIN AT PARTY ÁRD FHEIS

FATHER MICHAEL 'O FLANAGAN TO BE VICE-PRESIDENT

THAT night Henry went over his notes before joining the others in the dining room. Something was bothering him, a warning flag at the back of his brain.

Arthur Griffith had been the president of Sinn Féin since its founding. Its original inspiration had come from him. Yet he had just stepped aside and accepted the vice-presidency of the party to make way for de Valera, who was a very different sort of man. In two days Sinn Féin had been utterly transformed.

Early in his acceptance speech, de Valera had placated Griffith by saying, "We do not wish to bind the people to any form of government." A few minutes later, however, he reassured Republicans with equal sincerity. "It is necessary for us to be united now to the flag we are going to fight for, that of the Irish Republic. We have nailed the flag to the mast and we shall never lower it."[1]

The double standard thus adopted united the moderates and the militants by allowing each to think they would get what they wanted through the newly enlarged Sinn Féin. But it made Henry uncomfortable. It was not the first ambiguous speech he had heard Eamon de Valera give.

That night at the table he remarked to Ned, "Dev's a bit of a slippery character. He may be a politician now, but he was a warrior first, and he still wears the Volunteer uniform. At the Árd Fheis he suggested that every Sinn Féin club buy a rifle so its members could learn how to use one.[2] With that sort of thinking, I don't hold out much hope for a negotiated settlement between us and Britain."

Ned's eyes flashed. "What good is political negotiation when one side has all the power?"

Following the Sinn Féin Árd Fheis, the Irish Republican Army held a secret convention of its own. When he returned to number 16 afterward, Ned found Henry in the parlor reading to Precious. The little girl had pulled a footstool close to his armchair and was listening enthralled to an account of pony races in County Meath.

"Oh, Uncle Henry, I would so love a pony!"

"Easy to say if you've never had to care for one. I'm not over-fond of shoveling muck, myself."

"I wouldn't mind that. There's lots that's dirtier than horse muck."

"Horses can be dangerous, Little Business. One panicked while my father was shoeing it and broke his back."

"I'm not going to shoe my pony," she replied with irrefutable logic. "I'm too little. I'm just going to ride it."

Ned said, "If she's talking about 'my pony,' Henry, she's already determined to have one. I don't thank you for putting the idea in her head. You know it's impossible."

Henry winked at Precious. "You never know what the future holds." He turned to Ned. "How was the meeting?"

"We elected de Valera as president of the executive committee.[3] Seán MacGarry is general secretary, Cathal Brugha is chief of staff, Richard Mulcahy is director of training, and Michael Collins is director of organization. He's also drawn up a new constitution for us, just as he's done for the IRB."

Michael Collins again. And the IRB. "Can I print any of that?"

"Of course not."

"So now Dev's heading up both a constitutional political party and an outlawed militia," Henry observed. "It'll be interesting to see how the Long Fellow manages to wear the two hats at the same time. And speaking of time . . ." He took his pocket watch from his waistcoat and flicked open the case. "If I want to make the last train I had best be going, Ned. I've already said my goodbyes to Louise and your wife—I was just waiting for you."

"You're leaving now? We hoped you would spend more time with us."

"I have a job, you know. I really wish I could stay a few days longer, but . . ."

Ned clapped him on the shoulder. "Don't look so glum, old fellow. I'll find out her Dublin address for you. Then I know you'll come back sooner rather than later."

HENRY commented in the *Champion*: "The recent Sinn Féin Árd Fheis successfully united the two major strands of nationalism: those who believe physical force is necessary to win our independence, and those like Arthur Griffith who favor moral resistance. Now they speak with one voice."

Yet that warning flag still fluttered at the back of his mind.

He had more than Irish politics to write about. Bad news from the battle fronts of Europe was a constant. At the end of October, the Italian front collapsed. The Germans were using poison gas, followed by heavy artillery, and Italian casualties were enormous.

"The Great War has changed my writing style," Henry commented in a letter to Ned. Letters kept alive the tradition of thoughtful conversation the two men had long enjoyed. "Death and horror require a stark, stripped-down language. Refined phraseology has no place; this is not a boating party on the Shannon but trench warfare. Yet I wonder, Ned—is the way we newspapermen describe this thing trivializing its appalling nature? Will so many uncushioned facts piled upon one another eventually erect an emotional wall between the event and the observer, so that people no longer feel an individual responsibility?

"Men like Pádraic Pearse felt that responsibility, but they subscribed to the romantic nationalism of an earlier era. They truly believed that mankind had a higher nature and right would prevail. Things are changing rapidly now. Those ideals seem old-fashioned, gone the way of knights in armor. How can they be sustained in the face of millions of corpses piled high on bloody battlefields?

"But Ned—if we lose our idealism, what the hell will we become? I don't know how I feel about any of this. I only know that I feel."

Ignoring the advice of the Irish Party, the British government redistributed parliamentary representation for Ireland. The Ulster Unionists were to receive seven or eight new seats. The power of the minority was thus hugely increased. A despairing John Redmond commented, "Our position in this House is made futile, we are never listened to."[4]

In November, the Bolsheviks overthrew the provisional government in Petrograd. It was Russia's second revolution in eight months.

Chapter Thirteen

THE New Year, 1918, brought rationing to Britain and an explosion of military activity to County Clare.

"Maneuvers have become an everyday occurrence," Henry reported in the *Champion*. "Companies of Volunteers, now proudly styling themselves the Irish Republican Army, are drilling on every sports field and country road."

The authorities grew alarmed. Fights broke out between the IRA and the RIC. A Republican squad was arrested and jailed in Limerick, where the men promptly went on hunger strike. When they were brought before the magistrate, a number of their comrades packed the courtroom and reduced order to chaos, shouting and waving to one another, singing rebel songs, leaving their seats to create a milling eddy that surged back and forth across the courtroom. While the police had their hands full trying to reestablish control, the prisoners seized their opportunity and escaped. Embedded in a crush of bodies, the RIC men could only watch helplessly.

The humiliation of the police was duly reported the next day in the *Champion*. "Our merry-hearted lads know how to have a good time even in court," Henry commented.

On the twenty-seventh of February, he had just arrived at the newspaper office when a constable came in carrying a folder. Henry knew the man; Ennis was a small town. "Who's in charge here?" the constable asked with stiff formality. His tone was strangely at odds with his facial expression, which was almost apologetic. He looked at the walls, the floor—anywhere but at Henry.

"I expect you want Sarsfield, but he hasn't come in yet. He'll be here any moment if you care to wait. Is there anything I can do for you in the meantime, John?"

The constable took a sheet of paper from the folder. "Here, you can print this on the front page of the *Champion*. In a box. Bold type. There'll be announcements posted all over town as well." For the first time the constable's eyes met Henry's. "I'm sorry about this, you know. It's none of my doing."

As the constable left the office Henry was reading the notice.

"The County of Clare is hereby proclaimed a Military Area from this date. The County is to be Garrisoned. Weapons of All Types are Prohibited to Civilians. The Authorities will assume Censorship for the Protection and Peace of Mind of the Populace."

"Jumping Judas!" Henry crushed the notice in his fist and hurled it as far as he could. "Great jumping Judas *Iscariot!*"

The door opened; Sarsfield Maguire entered on a blast of cold air. "The weather's desperate today and I—" He stopped when he saw the look on Henry's face. "What's wrong?"

Henry retrieved the crumpled ball of paper and wordlessly handed it to him.

Maguire smoothed it out on a desktop and read through it once, then again. "Not this paper," he vowed through gritted teeth. "They're not going to censor the *Champion* while there's breath in my body."

AT the beginning of March, the Bolsheviks signed a humiliating peace treaty with Germany for which they were excoriated by the Allies.

In Ireland one word was on everyone's lips: conscription.

The Allies in Europe were in desperate need of reinforcements. The Russians had withdrawn and the Americans had not yet arrived. The Parliamentary Party vehemently opposed conscription for Ireland, warning that it could precipitate another rebellion. They were aware that some two hundred thousand young Irish men were organizing resistance to British rule in their own country.

The military establishment, however, pressed for a policy of seizing all Irish men of fighting age, scattering them among the English regiments, and if they would not fight for Britain, shooting them.[1] A proposed military services act enforcing conscription was seen as the most efficient method of ridding Ireland of revolutionaries.

By now Ireland was full of revolutionaries.

On the sixth of March, Henry wrote an obituary. "Died today after a brief illness, John Redmond, leader of the Irish Parliamentary Party. Redmond worked to the end of his life in hopes of gaining home rule for this country."

When he put the obituary on Sarsfield Maguire's desk, Henry said, "I'm sorry poor old Redmond's gone, even if he was a fool for believing the government every time they promised him home rule was just around the corner. Naïveté is a common Irish trait, God knows. I think he tried to do the right thing as he saw it, though."

"Most people do, Henry."

"You believe that?"

Maguire nodded. "I have to, and so should you. Where's your idealism?"

"I left it in my other suit," Henry said without smiling.

In April, Lloyd George said that the coalition government at last was prepared to implement a limited degree of home rule for Ireland—under certain conditions.

The Irish would have to agree to conscription first.

Henry was furious. "It's the carrot and stick all right, but the stick's a rifle held to our heads unless we're willing to take it in our hands and kill strangers for King George."

Lights burned late in the offices of the *Champion*. Sarsfield Maguire sent his reporters to cover every anticonscription speech and rally in the county. "Our people are outraged at the idea of being forced to fight for Austria and Belgium," Henry commented, "when decent Irish men were shot at Kilmainham for fighting for this country."

His words were printed in a box on the front page. Within days there was a response.

Dear Ned," Henry wrote, "A government flunky came to the offices of the *Champion* yesterday to tell the Maguires they could continue to publish only upon their guarantee that they would print no more subversive articles.[2] 'We simply cannot have newspapers undermining Dublin Castle,' the little maggot said. 'You must support your government in time of war.'

"Ned, I wish you could have seen Josephine Maguire's face. She threw her head back and stared him down until the man shriveled like a rasher in a hot skillet. 'I am supporting my government,' she told him. 'I'm just not supporting yours. My late brother Tom Galvin founded this paper and it's his monument. We won't surrender a single word of it to the likes of you.' She was Caitlín ní Houlihan in that play of Yeats'; she was one of the great warrior queens from the ancient time. I think for a moment every man in the office was in love with her.

"Sarsfield showed the government man to the door and bowed him out with the most icy courtesy I've ever seen. Then this morning a detachment of the military entered our printing plant and took away critical sections of the machinery. They left the presses gutted.

"The *Clare Champion* is suppressed for six months. The action was not unexpected, we had practically dared the government to shut us down. Yet the shock was enormous just the same. I have a sense of personal grief, almost as if they killed a child of mine, and I don't even own the paper. I cannot imagine what the Maguires are going through."

By the time he finished penning the letter, Henry's hand was shaking. He went out to pace the streets of Ennis and work off his rage.

That's the word for it. Rage. I never felt it before, even during the Rising and the executions. But now. But now.

He wanted to hit someone. He wanted to drive his fist into a human face and feel bone crunch.

He was astonished at himself.

• • •

WE'LL wait them out and publish again in September,"
Josephine Maguire assured Henry. "There's no way we'll let
them close us down permanently, and when the presses are
rolling we'll want you back."

In the meantime, Henry had to make a living. There was
not enough work in Clare, under the current circumstances,
to support him as a freelance journalist, so Henry decided
to return to Dublin. "Surely I can scrape up something
there," he told Sarsfield Maguire. He had to eat and the
Limerick tithe had to be paid. Besides, Dublin had something else to offer. In his wallet was Ella Rutledge's Dublin
address. "She and Madge live with their brother and his
wife," Ned had explained in a letter. "Ella and her late husband had no children. When he was killed, she returned to
her own family rather than stay with his. The Mansells are
devoted to one another."

A close family. What do you suppose that's like?

When he packed his things Henry was surprised at how
much he had accumulated in a few months. He had to store
a small Turkish carpet, a good armchair, and a tea chest full
of books with the Maguires. It was as if he had intended to
stay permanently and had been gathering bits and pieces for
a home in Clare.

Once going to Dublin had been a moral victory; now it
seemed a defeat. Henry sat gloomily staring out the window
while the train lurched and rattled eastward. As it began to
slow for Limerick Junction he briefly glimpsed, alongside
the track, a face he recognized.

When the train stopped, Henry collected his suitcase and
got off.

Newspaperman's hunch.

He walked back along the track to the maintenance shed
of the Great Southern and Western Railway: tar paper peeling off the roof, door sagging open on rusty hinges. Henry
rapped with his knuckles, then thrust his head inside to be
greeted by the scent of machine oil, strong coffee, and cheap
cigarettes. Woodbines, by the smell of them.

"Anyone here?" he called into the gloom.

"Depends on who you're looking for," came a truculent answer from the rear of the shed.

"A linesman called Dan Breen. Thought I saw him out on the track a few minutes ago." Henry did not add that Dan was his cousin, because strictly speaking that was not true. Dan Breen was related to the Mooneys only through the lifelong friendship of his mother, the former Honora Moore, and Henry's mother. The two had grown up as neighbors in the parish of Doon, southwest of the peak of Gortnageragh. Marital circumstance had separated them, but the tie of a shared townland could be as strong as kinship.

"Well, you didn't see him because he's not here. And we never heard of him anyway," stated the disembodied voice with finality.

"My eyes must be going bad on me. If you ever do run into a fella called Breen, would you tell him Henry Mooney's looking for him?" He turned as if to walk away.

"Hold on there, Cousin Henry!" A figure emerged from the shadows, wiping his hands on a greasy rag. He was no more than twenty-two or-three but looked older: short and sturdy, a hammer of a man with a broad, coarse-featured face and swarthy complexion.

"Hiding out, are you?" Henry inquired casually.

Dan Breen gestured toward a nearby bench where a huge enameled pot sat on a gas ring, surrounded by tin cups. "Let me offer you some of our coffee. It's mostly grounds, but the cup's clean. Or was yesterday."

Henry accepted a battered cup and took a tentative taste. The sugarless brew was scorched and tasted of machine oil. He put the cup down with a shudder. "Saint Patrick on skates! What is that, the drainings of a tar barrel? Would you not drink tea like the rest of us?"

Breen hooted with laughter. He resembled a sulky bulldog until something amused him; then his features were transformed by a merry grin. "The mother raised me to be very particular about the way tea was brewed," he explained. "But you can treat coffee any old way, and we do. It's reheated a dozen times a day."

"You have any stomach lining left?"

"Never looked. But sure, isn't it nice of you to stop and

inquire after me health—or did you have some other reason?"

"Curiosity," Henry admitted. "I haven't seen you for donkey's years and a lot's happened. Last I heard, you were helping reorganize the Republicans in Tipperary town. Are you still?"

"Too right! I'm commanding the South Tipperary Brigade these days."

"Are you really up to brigade strength in Tip?"

"We have plenty of men," Breen assured him, "and we're getting them armed—mostly by raiding the houses of the local loyalists.[3] A nationalist is arrested for having a rusty shotgun in the barn to shoot rats, but anyone who sympathizes with the British is allowed to keep all manner of rifles and revolvers. They're mostly willing to hand them over to us with a little persuasion, so we've never had to get rough, thank God.

"We're acquiring a nice little arsenal of our own, and not a moment too soon, with conscription hanging over our heads. Not that everyone's happy about what we're doing. Some of the more conservative Sinn Féiners in town think we should have no stronger weapons than resolutions. They want everything discussed at party meetings and put to a vote, but you don't get anywhere that way."

"Be careful you don't get yourself arrested," Henry warned.

"Hazards of the job. My best friend's been in and out of prison for months. Seán Treacy. He was originally supposed to command the brigade, but after he was jailed the post was given to me instead. Then when Seán went on a hunger strike in Dundalk, a band of us decided we had to do something drastic before he went the way of Thomas Ashe . . . Say, are you planning to print any of this?"

"Of course not. You should know me better than that. I told you, I was just curious. What about Seán Treacy?"

"We planned to capture a Peeler," Breen said, using the pejorative term for a policeman, "and hold him as a hostage for Seán's safety. A band of police usually go on night patrol around Limerick Junction, so we brought in forty of the brigade to kidnap one and hold him in the mountains. Then the police found out about it and kept the men confined to barracks."

"Do you think someone informed on you?"

Breen's heavy eyebrows drew together. "Wouldn't be the first time. Sure, since the bloody English started bribing the Irish to inform on each other hundreds of years ago, informers have been the curse of this country, worse than the drink. Seán's off the hunger strike now, thank God, and he's due to be released in the autumn. Then we'll see some action. Say, you wouldn't be interested in joining the South Tipperary Brigade, would you? We could give you an address at the mother's house."

For half a heartbeat Henry was tempted. *Hit someone. Drive a fist into a human face and feel bone crunch.*

With an effort he blotted out the image. "I appreciate the offer, Dan, but I try to stay within the law. It's a peculiarity of mine, like believing it's better to talk than fight."

"Maybe it is—if you can get the other fella to talk. If he's a Brit, though, you can't trust a word he says. Not to an Irishman."

"I'd hate to believe that's true."

"Prove to me it isn't, Henry. Until you can, I'll go on arming my Republicans."

"The Irish Republican Army is an illegal organization now."

Dan Breen retorted, "And the British army's in our country illegally. But not for much longer."

Chapter Fourteen

WHILE Henry was on his way to Dublin, the Military Services Act came up for a vote in Parliament.

The first newspaper Henry saw when he got off the train carried a banner headline: CONSCRIPTION PASSES—ENFORCEMENT EXPECTED SOON.

Although the entire Irish Party had voted against it, the bill had passed by 301 votes to 103. John Dillon, the new leader of the party, immediately left the House of Commons in protest and returned to Ireland to organize resistance against conscription.

NED Halloran was on hand to welcome Henry back. "I'm afraid we won't see much of each other," he apologized in advance. "No long talks or chess games. I'm doing all the maintenance work here, plus trying to work on that book of mine. It's an adventure novel like Erskine Childers' *Riddle of the Sands*, only set in the Far East."

"Why not choose something you know more about? The Easter Rising, for example."

"That's what I told him myself," said Louise.

"Och, there'll be lots of historians writing about the Rising."

"I'm not talking about nonfiction, Ned. History tells what happened; literature tells what it felt like."

Ned's focus changed; he stared into shadows. A faint
shudder ran through his body. "Maybe I'm still too close to
it. In the future, perhaps . . . Anyway, my time is pretty
scarce. I'm out of the house most nights on military business."

"How's your health?"

"Grand," said Ned.

"Dreadful," Louise contradicted. "I soak brown paper in
vinegar and try to make him put it on his head for the pain.
It's a great pity we've no holy wells nearby, I know the
saints would heal him. I tell him and I tell him, but . . ."

Precious was tugging at Henry's hand. "Uncle Henry, before you unpack come and see my collection."

She had driven a number of large nails into the walls of
the scullery. From them hung a motley assortment of iron-
mongery and leather. "What class of collection do you call
this, Little Business?"

"It's horse tackle, can't you tell? I pick them up off the
street, or from rubbish skips. Here's a bridle bit—it was
rusted and bent, but I've cleaned it up and straightened it—
and a curb chain, and a tool for picking stones out of hooves,
and a broken rein I've mended . . . and this was part of a
leather headcollar. I'm going to use it to contrapt a bridle."

"Contrapt?"

"You know, make a contraption. Like you construct
something to make a construction. I looked in the dictionary
you gave me, but 'contrapt' isn't in there."

"It should be," Henry said. "I must contrapt a dozen things
a week myself."

Because his former apartment in the attic was rented to
someone else, Louise Kearney gave Henry a room off the
first-floor landing and her promise that he could move "back
home" as soon as the current tenant left. Two days later he
was offered a job writing advertising copy with a firm that
counted Dublin's largest stores among its clients. It was not
journalism, but the hours were regular and he would be able
to pay his bills. Yet he felt strangely cut adrift, marking time
between the irretrievable past and the unknowable future.

Several times he took Ella Rutledge's address out of his
wallet and looked at it . . . then put it back.

* * *

On the twenty-third of April, all work was suspended as a nationwide protest against conscription. Shops did not open, trains did not run. A Sinn Féin rally in Dublin drew men and women from the entire spectrum of nationalism to hear conscription condemned as a declaration of war on the Irish people. Ned and other members of the Dublin Brigade served as security officers at the rally.

The atmosphere in the city was highly charged. An exceptional number of policemen were patrolling the streets. Members of the Dublin Metropolitan Police—known as the DMP—were chosen for their size; not one stood less than six feet. In their dark blue uniforms and spiked helmets they could look menacing, and on this occasion they did. Henry refused to let them intimidate him. When one looked at him particularly hard, he reminded himself that the telegraph address of the DMP was DAMP, DUBLIN.[1]

They're Irish, same as me; right down to the sense of humor. He smiled, relaxed. The policeman's attention turned elsewhere.

When Henry reached number 16, he found Síle waiting in the parlor. "Did you go to the rally? Did you see Ned?" she asked before he had his coat off.

"I've been working all day—how could I? Is he not home yet?"

"He's not home, and I'm worried about him, Henry."

"When you married a revolutionary you knew what you were getting into."

"I did; I was a revolutionary myself. We were young and strong and the cause was just," she said with conviction, "and we were caught up in the adventure of it all. Secret messages and marches and maneuvers. Then Easter Week and the guns, and us ready to die for something more important than ourselves." The light of those days still shone in her face. Passionate woman, steadfast as stone, intense as flame.

"Funnily enough, I never really thought I might be killed," Síle went on. "When Ned found me and we were running

across Dublin and the soldiers were shooting at us, I felt
so . . ."

"Exhilarated?"

She gave a reluctant nod. "That was how I felt, even
though I knew people were being killed. Does that make me
an awful person, Henry?"

Her uncharacteristic question surprised him. "Of course
not, Síle. You know the old saying: 'The nature of the rain
is the same everywhere, yet it produces thorns in the hedgerows and flowers in the garden.' You were experiencing the
flowers. The thorns came after."

"So they did, for all of us. But that doesn't stop Ned; he's
more determined than ever. And . . . I have the strangest
feeling, Henry. This time . . ." Síle looked past him, her
slanted, catlike eyes focusing on something beyond mortal
vision. "This time we won't all survive."

Henry wanted to gather her into his arms and comfort her.
The impulse was unexpected and overpowering.

Ned entered the parlor.

Henry took an involuntary step backward. Ned looked at
him curiously. "What's the matter?"

Before Henry could answer, Síle slipped past him to nestle
against her husband's chest. "I was worried about you. I'm
so glad you're back."

Ned pressed his lips to her bright hair.

Henry ceased to exist for them. He waited uncertainly,
then went out into the hall. Precious in her nightdress was
sitting on the stairs, obviously eavesdropping. He swooped
down on her, pretending to be angry. "Don't you know that
earwigging is bad manners?"

She was unabashed. "That's how I learn things."

"If you have questions, just ask one of us. I've never
noticed you having any trouble asking questions."

"But I don't always get answers," she told him. "Grown-
ups tell me what they want me to know, not what I need to
know."

"I'll answer your questions honestly, Little Business.
What do you think you need to know?"

"Is there going to be more fighting?"

Henry believed in protecting the innocence of children

and sustaining their sense of security, but Precious already knew that security was a myth. Her eyes as she looked up at him were the eyes of an adult asking an adult question. He crouched down so his face was on a level with hers. "In the heel of the hunt, there will be more fighting, Little Business."

"When?"

"I don't know."

"Will it ever be over?"

"I don't know that either. But I don't want you to be afraid. Being fearful only makes things worse."

Precious considered his words for a few moments, then stood up and brushed off the back of her flannel nightdress. "I understand," she said gravely. "Thank you, Uncle Henry." She held up her arms. "It's past my bedtime. Will you carry me pickaback and tuck me in, please?"

As Henry carried Precious upstairs on his shoulders, he thought his heart would break. Her weight was too slight, too sweet. Too mortal.

Protect her, God. Whatever you do to the rest of us . . . protect this one.

HENRY bought a new notebook and began carrying it everywhere with him, jotting down events and his impressions. There was in him an urgency to record the world as it flew past him. He could not have explained the impulse, and he could not justify it by calling it reporting. He was an ad writer now.

But still . . .

JOHN Dillon and the Parliamentary Party were organizing their constituents to resist conscription. A National Defense Fund was opened and people throughout Ireland contributed wholeheartedly. From their annual meeting at Maynooth, the Catholic bishops issued a manifesto proclaiming. "We consider that conscription forced in this way upon Ireland is an oppressive and inhuman law which the Irish people have a right to resist by every means that are consonant with the law of God." Eamon de Valera declared: "It is in direct violation of the rights of small nationalities to self-determination, which even the prime minister of England—now preparing to employ naked militarism and force his Act upon Ireland—himself officially announced as an essential condition for peace at the peace congress."[2]

Backed into an indefensible corner, the British government took action.

ONE night in May when Ned returned late to number 16, instead of going straight upstairs to Síle he knocked softly at Henry's door. "Are you awake?"

"I am now. Come in."

Henry propped himself on one elbow and hunted for a match on the locker beside his bed. When the little oil lamp which he kept close by him flared into life, he took a good look at Ned's face. "What's wrong?"

"I've just come from an IRA briefing. Mick Collins told us that a couple of months ago he recruited a fellow called Eamonn Broy who works out of Dublin Castle and—"[3]

Henry sat bolt upright. "You mean Ned Broy? Isn't he the top detective in G Division?"

"That's right, Henry. The political division of the Dublin Metropolitan Police. G-men are stationed at every harbor and railway station these days, spying on Republican movements."

"Sweet merciful hour! How ever did Collins persuade a G-man to—"

"Never mind about that. Broy said the Castle is planning wholesale arrests of Sinn Féin party members. Mick has corroboration from his other Castle sources, and it's definite."

"His other Castle sources? Jesus, Mary, and Joseph—how many does he have?"

"Listen to me, Henry!" Ned cried in exasperation. "We haven't time to go into all that now!"

"But I've never heard anything about this."

"Of course not—Mick's a genius at secrecy. Will you pay attention! I'm trying to tell you we're in danger of being arrested!"

Henry blinked. "I don't belong to Sinn Féin, and the last time I asked, you said you didn't either."

Ned gave a harsh laugh. "Things change, don't they? And it's not just Sinn Féiners they're after—they have one of their damned lists. They're likely to drag in every nationalist they can lay their hands on."

"When?"

"It could be as soon as tonight. Mick warned us not to even go home, but I wanted to get you all out of here before—"

The house reverberated to a thunderous knock on the front door. Ned swore fiercely.

"Go get your women," said Henry in a quick, tight voice. "I'll keep the police here while you take Síle and Precious down the back stairs and out through the scullery. Hurry around to number 33 and knock at the back door of the confectioner's shop. Mrs. Gill will take you in."

"I hate running from those bastards," Ned said through gritted teeth.

"I know, lad, but you don't want them arresting Síle, either."

While Ned raced up to the attic, Henry pulled on the first pair of trousers he could find and put on his suitcoat over his nightshirt. Then he stepped out onto the landing. He could hear loud voices in the front hall. Louise Kearney was remonstrating with someone, but it did no good; within moments half a dozen men hurried up the stairs: four members of the DMP and two men in British army uniforms.

Henry stood waiting for them on the landing, deliberately blocking further upward progress. "What's all the ree-raw about?" he asked with a composure he did not feel. "Working men are trying to sleep here, you know."

"We have orders to search this house," replied an army officer whose face looked vaguely familiar.

"Whose orders?"

"That's none of your business, Mooney," the man snapped, meeting his eyes.

Henry noticed and remembered eyes.

The British captain who had followed him from the GPO produced a piece of paper from his pocket. He glanced at it far too briefly to read anything, though he said, "Just as I thought—your name's on here. You're to come with us."

"On what charge?"

"Conspiring with enemies of the Crown."

"You can't be serious."

"I assure you I am." The captain rattled off by rote, " 'Certain subjects of His Majesty the King, domiciled in Ireland, have entered into treasonable communication with the German enemy. Therefore such persons are to be taken into custody immediately under the Defense of the Realm Act.' That includes you, Mooney."

"This is ridiculous," Henry protested, shifting to the right. "I don't even know any Germans." He moved again, attempting with his body's bulk to divert the man's attention from proceeding farther up the stairs.

"Take this one and tie his hands to the stair rail, then search every room and . . . why do you keep dodging around like that, Mooney? What are you trying to . . . Edwards!" the captain bellowed abruptly to someone in the hall below. "Take a party around to the back! The servants' stairs! Hurry!"

Running feet, shouts. Lodgers began emerging from their rooms in various states of undress, complaining vehemently. The sight of uniforms subdued them. The captain began questioning each in turn, checking names against his piece of paper.

Louise stomped up the stairs. "I'll have you know I'm a respectable woman," she announced with her hands on her hips, "and this is a respectable house! How dare you bleedin' Tommies come in here and disturb my lodgers!"

"Ladies," the captain reproved, "don't say 'bleedin.' "

"Then I guess I ain't your kind of lady, you wretched streak of misery!"

The stairwell was cold, but Henry was sweating under his nightshirt. *How long will it take them to get to Mrs. Gill's?* When he heard the front door open again, he peered over the banister. More policemen entered the hall below, shoving Ned and Síle ahead of them. Ned's hands were fastened behind his back. Síle was carrying Precious.

"We've caught Halloran," one of the policemen called.

The captain leaned over the stair rail. "Well done. Now let's get this lot out of here and into some nice safe cells, eh?" Straightening, he flicked a disdainful gaze over Henry. "Not as nice as your *rooms*, of course," he added sarcastically.

"You have a long memory."

"Long enough," the captain agreed. He untied Henry's wrists, then hit him in the back with the flat of his hand to urge him down the stairs. When they reached the group waiting at the bottom, the captain wanted to know, "Who's the woman?"

Ned said, "Just my wife, she doesn't know anything."

"Being a Shinner's wife is crime enough. What do you papists call that? Original sin?" The captain smirked; the two soldiers laughed. "Handcuff her and bring her along."

When a policeman tried to take Precious out of Síle's arms, she whirled away from him with an agility that caught him unprepared. In a single movement, she set the child down and produced a Luger pistol from under her skirt. "Don't you dare lay your hands on my little girl!" Síle aimed the weapon unwaveringly at the nearest British uniform.

For a moment the tableau was frozen. Then Ned cried, "No, Síle, we've been warned—they want to make the IRA fire first!"

"Who told you that?" asked a startled policeman with a thick Dublin accent.

Before Ned could answer, the captain shouted, "Just get them out of here! Now!"

Chapter Fifteen

As soon as they were out of the house, Henry was separated from Ned and Síle and hustled into one of several closed motorcars waiting at the curb. Precious was left behind with Louise Kearney.

Henry was taken to Store Street Police Station. There was no sign of Ned and Síle there, but Matt Nugent was leaning across the desk, chatting with the duty sergeant. When the white-haired reporter saw Henry enter between two policemen, he hurried over. "What in God's name is happening tonight? Don't tell me you've been arrested."

"It's a mistake," Henry replied.

"It's always a mistake. Here, you," Nugent addressed one of the policemen, "what've you done this fellow for?"

The man nodded toward the British captain. "Ask him."

The captain said truculently, "What business is it of yours?"

"I'm on an assignment," Nugent told him, flashing his *Irish Times* press card, "and I happen to know Henry Mooney because he's a colleague of mine."

The captain glowered. "This doesn't involve the press."

"It does if you've arrested this man. He's no criminal; didn't you know he's a reporter at the *Times*? They love him down there," Nugent elaborated with a glint in his eye. "Why in God's name have you put handcuffs on him? I can just see the headline tomorrow. '*Irish Times* Reporter Manhandled.' They'll have heart attacks in the Castle."

"Here now, there'll be none of that," the captain said, but he freed Henry's hands. "Don't you try anything," he warned. "Stand right where you are while I go and book you. What's your full name?"

"Henry Price Mooney."

"Sixteen Lower Gardiner Street?"

"You know that already."

"Occupation?"

"Journalist!" Matt Nugent almost shouted.

While the captain was busy at the desk Henry rubbed his wrists, then took his ubiquitous notebook from his pocket. *Thank God I brought this coat.* He scribbled a few words like any reporter taking notes. The policemen watched but made no move to stop him. Henry paused, chewed thoughtfully on his pencil, then tore the sheet out of the notebook and wadded it up as if he had changed his mind. When he was led away he let the little ball of paper drop from his fingers. No one paid any attention—except Matt Nugent.

Henry was taken to a small holding cell that already contained three men. Their faces were unfamiliar. Everything seemed unfamiliar: iron door slamming behind him, bleak sound echoing down the passageway; other iron doors clanging elsewhere in the building; dingy gray walls; pervasive smell of stale urine from a tin bucket in the corner; chill draft at ankle height sweeping across the floor.

The occupants of the cell stared silently at the newcomer, but one gave a sharp nod of his head to indicate someone might be listening outside. Henry looked around for a place to sit down. There were neither stools nor bunks. The other men were sitting on the bare cement floor with their backs against the wall.

Henry willed himself to stay calm, but it was surprising what latent feelings of paranoia were brought to the surface by being arrested. A small voice deep inside—a voice that sounded remarkably like his mother's—suggested he was getting what he deserved for the sins of a lifetime.

"Your braces are hanging below your coat," one of his cellmates remarked. "It's a wonder your trousers don't fall down."

"I came away in rather a hurry."

"Didn't we all, boyo. Didn't we all."

Another silence ensued. One of the men began gnawing at his hangnails. Henry sat down on the floor and tried to make himself comfortable for what remained of the night. Eventually he stretched out on his side with his head pillowed on the crook of his arm.

THERE was in Henry's mind a flat eerie echoing place as sinister as a murder scene and giving off the same chill. When his family still lived in Clare, the old folk had gathered to tell tales around the hearth on winter nights. The small boy who was Henry sat on a stool in the chimney corner, eagerly absorbing every detail: battles and massacres and streams clotted with gore; a desolate field where people lay dying of the famine; a blackened church in which people were burnt alive for their religion.

"Nothing's too awful for that one," his father had boasted to the neighbors. "He's a little man, so he is."

Although during the day Henry appeared undisturbed by tales of violence, the tortured landscape of the past became the backdrop of his childhood nightmares. He was simultaneously frightened and . . . fascinated. He became convinced he was dreaming of his own future.

When Henry became a reporter, one of his first assignments had been to cover the Limerick morgue. He had been shown the charred victims of a house fire, twisted into grotesque configurations. A baby drowned in a sack like unwanted kittens. The half-decomposed bodies of a couple shredded by the blast of a shotgun. "Hunting accident," the morgue attendant remarked cynically. "Her husband thought they was deer."

For hours Henry had gazed at human wreckage, trying to probe the secrets locked in dead minds. These unfortunates had entered the dark realm of Henry's nightmares. They knew what he had yet to discover.

Then, all at once, he had had enough. He was disgusted by the darkness in himself; the fatal attraction of violence.

"I don't want to cover the morgue anymore," he told his

editor. "Being a reporter's a great job for someone who's interested in people, and that's me. But I'm interested in live people. You can assign somebody else to the dead ones."

In the holding cell at Store Street Station, the old fascinating terrors came flooding back again.

If there is a hell, he thought as he lay on the gritty cement floor with his head pillowed on one arm, *for me it will be like this. A desolate place where any sort of outrage may happen, and myself at its center, victim or perpetrator, waiting.*

Victim or perpetrator—which was worse?

Sometime during the night he fell into a troubled sleep.

Henry awoke achingly cold and stiff. The gloom of the cell was permanent; he could not tell if it was night or day. A voice was shouting his name.

"Here!" he called groggily. A warder appeared and ushered him from the cell while the other three watched impassively. Henry was taken to a small room containing a plain table and two chairs and told to wait. After an interminable time the door opened. The man who entered was as powerfully built as a professional boxer, yet dressed like a company director in an immaculate suit. Although he stood a little under six feet, he gave the impression of being much bigger. Lustrous gray eyes were set wide apart in a broad, fresh-complexioned face. Full cheeks, a wide mouth, and wavy, dark brown hair that sprang thickly from his scalp. Henry guessed him to be in his late twenties.

The stranger sat down at the table and held out a pack of cigarettes. "D'ye want a fag?" he asked in a lilting Cork accent.

"I do indeed, I'm all out. Thank you."

The stranger produced a box of matches and handed them to him with the cigarettes, saying, "Keep the pack. I borrowed them off your guard anyway." He flashed a sudden, totally irresistible grin. Boyish, reckless, full of high good humor. Henry could not help grinning back.

When Henry had lit a cigarette and drawn the smoke deep into his lungs, the other man remarked in a conversational voice, "I assume you'd like to get out of here?"

Henry exhaled in an explosive cough. "I would of course!"

"Then we should leave now. I've your signed release slip, but it would be a good idea to be out of the building before the new duty sergeant comes on."

"Do I *know* you?"

That irresistible grin again. "You know me well enough to send a message to me."

Michael Collins. Of course!

Collins sprang to his feet. "So now that you've had a smoke, are you ready to leave? Or had you rather stay for breakfast?"

"I think I'll forgo any more police hospitality, thank you. Let 'em save my breakfast for the next fellow—it'll prob'ly taste like old shoes anyway."

They emerged from the police station into a dismal drizzle. "This country must be God's urinal," Collins remarked as he turned up his collar. He collected a bicycle leaning against the side of the building but did not ride it. Instead, he set off down Store Street wheeling the machine beside him, and gesturing to Henry to walk with him.

The drizzle became rain, soaking rain that penetrated Henry's suitcoat and nightshirt. He felt damp to the soul.

"No one's likely to come looking for you," Collins said as they walked. "In spite of what you were told, your name wasn't on the list to be picked up. If ye've a nervous disposition you might want to avoid your own place for a while, though. A pal of mine called Harry Boland who fought in Fairview during the Rising has a tailoring shop in Middle Abbey Street. Call in to him and tell him I sent you. He has a room at the back where you could stay and no one would be the wiser."

"I know Boland—pleasant young fellow with a high forehead and a great talent for fitting suits and waistcoats. But I'd rather go home, if it's all the same to you. Which reminds me—what about my friends? Did you understand my note?"

"I've deciphered far more cryptic notes than yours. 'Halloran and wife arrested. Can you help them. H. Mooney. Store Street.' A schoolboy would have understood. What surprises me is that you didn't ask for help for yourself."

"Ned's my best friend," Henry said simply.

"Ah."

"He was Pearse's personal courier, so I worry about what the British might do to him. Successful rebels are patriots, but failed rebels are criminals."

"We haven't failed, Mooney. We're not going to."

"Answer me one question: How did you get me out?"

"Knew who to ask, that's all. The police are still Irish lads underneath, in spite of the indoctrination the British give them, and some of them help me from time to time."

"How far up does that go?"

"You don't need to know, Mooney."

"IRB secrecy, eh?"

Collins shrugged his broad shoulders.

"What about Ned? Did you get him and Síle out already?"

"They weren't taken to Store Street. When I got there I found your name on the arrest log, but not theirs. I was told she's being held at Kevin Street Barracks and he's in the police depot in the Phoenix Park." Abruptly Collins turned into a narrow, litter-strewn laneway where they would not be overheard. Henry followed him. As he maneuvered his bicycle across rain-slick cobbles Collins asked, "How much do you know about what's going on?"

"Ned didn't have time to tell me much of anything before we were arrested."

"Our dear Lord-Lieutenant French decided he was going to 'put the fear of God' into Irish nationalists,"[1] Collins said, "so he requested a massive new supply of bombs and machine guns from British Ordnance."

"How do you know that?"

Collins' teeth flashed in a jaunty grin. "A cousin of mine who works in Dublin Castle's been put in charge of handling the most secret coded messages because the British want to be sure they're in safe hands. She puts 'em in safe hands, all right—mine. Makes you wonder how in the name of Jaysus those people ever got an empire."

Henry laughed.

"Anyway," Collins went on, "the Castle's decided they need an excuse for all this new weaponry, so they're accusing Sinn Féin of being in league with Germany against Britain."

"The Volunteers were eager enough to buy German weapons during the Rising," Henry reminded him.

"I know, but this is a different situation. Last month the police arrested a man on an island off the coast of Galway. He'd been sent on a German submarine to communicate with the leaders of the 'Irish resistance movement.' It was the Germans' own idea; the Sinn Féin executive didn't instigate it and didn't know anything about it. A link with Germany would do us no good in the international community now.

"The incident was unfortunate, to say the least. It's allowed the Castle to concoct a whole new conspiracy to justify arresting prominent Republicans."

"Apparently that doesn't include you," Henry remarked.

"That's because I know how the authorities think. To them we're all Paddies fresh off the bog, so I'm careful not to conform to their image. Joe Plunkett always said, 'If you don't think of yourself as being on the run, you aren't a fugitive,'[2] and it's true. Special Branch and the G-men would both like to get their hands on me, but dressed like a businessman I can go anywhere in Dublin and the police tip their hats to me." Slipping into an even broader West Cork accent, he added, "And other times, sure I'm just a shadow in the rain."

"You're damned near invisible as far as I can tell," Henry said admiringly. "But you still haven't told me if you can get the Hallorans released."

"It may be possible to help her—though I understand she threatened a British officer with a pistol, which complicates matters somewhat. But I don't want Ned released just now."

Henry caught hold of Collins' arm. "Why ever not? He's clever, resourceful . . ."

"Exactly. Ned Halloran will be a lot more use to me in prison than out of it." Beneath the sleeve of Collins' coat Henry felt the tensing of iron muscles. "Understand this,

Mooney. From now on we're going to fight the government with their own weapons—spies, informers, a whole network of contacts infiltrating every level of their damned bureaucracy, and that includes the prison camps in Britain. A number of our people are going to be there in a matter of days, if not hours, and I need Halloran and a few more like him as conduits for communication."

"But," Henry protested, "he has a family."

"Most men in Ireland have families—who d'ye think we're doing this for? I don't have any children yet, but when I do, I don't want them growing up with King Georgie's foot on their necks. Come on, I need to be ten other places in the next five minutes."

At the mouth of the laneway Collins stopped and cast a swift glance up and down the street. "I must leave you here, Mooney, but I'm glad we met—I've been impressed with your articles. Why haven't I seen any of them lately?"

"I'm afraid I'm not working as a journalist these days. The Dublin papers aren't exactly clamoring for my stories. And call me Henry, please."

Collins rubbed his jaw with his thumb. "You know, Arthur Griffith says we should make the most of our natural resources. I don't agree with him about a lot of things, but on that subject I do. It seems to me you're one of our resources. Tell you what—I'll see that you have inside information from time to time, if you make good use of it. Understand me?"

"I think I do."

"Good on ye." Collins clapped Henry on the shoulder, then stepped on the pedal of his bicycle and wheeled off down the street. After a few yards he called back over his shoulder, "Oh, by the way—you will look after our friend's family until he comes home, won't you?"

Chapter Sixteen

LOUISE Kearney greeted Henry with a gasp of relief. Precious flung herself into his arms, but Louise pulled her away. "I'm putting more kettles on, and not just for tea. You get those clothes off right now, Henry Mooney, and give yourself a good scrubbing. I won't have prison lice in my house."

After he had bathed, Henry put on fresh clothes and stretched out on his bed. It felt good to have a mattress under his spine again, but he could not rest. In a few minutes he was up and peering out the window, hoping against hope he would see Síle and Ned coming up the street.

Louise Kearney tried to keep herself busy. With the exception of Henry all of her lodgers had gone to work, and there were rooms to sweep and linen to change. She started each chore with a flurry of determination that soon faded. Only baking offered relief; she pummeled the dough unmercifully, for once not caring if her bread was tough.

Eventually Henry went looking for Precious. He found the child in her parents' sitting room. Instead of playing she was seated in Síle's customary chair, with her back ramrod-straight and her hands folded in her lap. Her dangling feet did not reach the floor.

"What are you doing in here all alone, Little Business?"

"I'm not alone," the little girl replied matter-of-factly. "I'm being with myself."

"Is that not the same as being alone?"

Precious shook her head. "Alone is when nobody's with you. When I'm being with myself I have company."

"What do you mean?"

"Oh, Uncle Henry, I'm lots of different people. So are you. You're a little boy who used to ride in a pony cart, and a grown-up who talks to me like a grown-up too, and my papa's best friend who laughs a lot, and a lonely man who looks sad sometimes when he thinks no one is watching."

Henry was taken aback. "Who told you all this?"

"Nobody. I just pay attention."

"What about you? Who are you right now?"

"Well . . . I'm being an adult because adults are braver than children are. Ursula Jervis Halloran, that's my grown-up name."

"Is Precious gone for good, then?"

"Course not," the little girl said firmly. "I don't want to lose any of my bits."

Henry went down the stairs shaking his head. *Fey, fanciful child! Old people down the country might suspect she was a changeling, a fairy exchanged for a mortal. They still believe in fairies as surely I believe in electric light.*

William Butler Yeats and Lady Gregory had presented a romanticized image of the fairies of Ireland, but their whimsical tales overlaid something quite different. Even Christian zeal had not quite destroyed the last remnants of an older, darker faith.

In 1910, one of the stories Henry had covered for the *Limerick Leader* was the release from prison of Michael Cleary. Fifteen years earlier, a young Tipperary woman called Bridget Cleary had been tortured over the grate of her own kitchen fireplace, soaked with paraffin oil and burned alive. Her husband, Michael, her father, and nine other men and women had taken part in the murder because they were convinced she was a changeling.[1]

Children in Tipperary still sang a skipping song that went, "Are you a witch or are you a fairy, Or are you the wife of Michael Cleary?"

The deed was committed not in some isolated rural backwater, but on the outskirts of the large town of Clonmel, fourteen years after electric cables were laid in Dublin. The overlap of past and future had an eerie resonance for Henry Mooney.

THE rain continued throughout the day. The streetlamps were lit by the time Síle returned. Louise was in the kitchen, polishing the range with Zebra Black Lead, while Henry was trying to distract himself by reading newspapers in the parlor. Precious was keeping a vigil at an upstairs window. They heard her come racing down the front stairs, shouting, "Mama, Mama, Mama!"

Ursula Jervis Halloran, adult, was forgotten.

Accompanying Síle was a man in a nondescript Crombie coat. Once she was safely inside the house, he touched the brim of his hat and left without speaking.

Síle's clothes were rumpled and she looked very tired. "You come inside and sit down close to the fire," Louise said.

"Don't fuss over me, please; I'm fine," Síle replied.

"What you need is a cup of tea with a drop of something in it. And beef tea, and some nice cheese-and-onion sandwiches. Drag the couch close to the fireplace, Henry, and fetch some blankets. Would you ever listen to the cough on her? I'm going to make a mustard plaster for her chest."

Soon Síle, half-smothered beneath layers of wool, was reclining on the black horsehair couch in front of a blazing fire. Undeterred by the fumes of the mustard, Precious snuggled into the curve of her arm. Every time Síle moved, the little girl pressed closer.

"Was it very bad so?" Louise asked solicitously. "Drink your tea now, while it's hot."

"Just unpleasant. They shouted at me and demanded I tell them everything I knew, but I pretended to be too stupid to understand. Finally they decided I was nobody important. 'She's just some ignorant whore off the streets,' one of them said."

If she weren't so tired, Henry thought, *Síle never would have repeated that with Precious in the room.* "Did anyone tell you why you were being released?"

"They just said a man had come to take me home. That was him at the door. He's IRB, I know that much, but he wasn't much of a talker. May I have more milk in this, Louise?"

"What about Ned?"

"I never saw him after we left here. I was hoping he would be back by the time I got home."

Louise said indignantly, "They can't hold people forever on trumped-up charges."

Henry and Síle exchanged a long look. "I hope you're right," said Henry.

USING the mythical German plot as pretext, the authorities arrested leading Republicans as a "preventive measure."[2] Every Sinn Féin member who had been elected to Parliament, with the exception of one man who was visiting in America, was consigned to prison for an indefinite time without charge or trial. Officers of the Republican Army were taken in the dragnet as well. Henry, who had the list of names before any other reporter in Ireland, took it to The *Irish Times*.

"The Castle hasn't released these names yet," the editor, John Healy, said in surprise. "Where did you get them?"

"I have my sources."

"You know we can't give you a byline on this."

"I do know, John. Just remember who brought it to you."

In its next edition, the *Times* scooped all other newspapers by reporting that seventy-three individuals had been deported to Britain, including Eamon de Valera, Arthur Griffith, Count Plunkett, W. T. Cosgrave, Seán MacGarry, Countess Markievicz, Kathleen Clarke, and Ned Halloran. Michael Collins and Cathal Brugha were not on the list.

There would be demands from many quarters for the government to produce hard evidence of the alleged German plot, but none was ever forthcoming.

THE days became weeks—weeks in which Henry did his best to be a second father to Precious. Every time someone came to the front door the child's face lit briefly in a way that broke his heart.

Without any formal agreement, in Ned's absence the others took over the schooling of Precious. Henry, who wrote a fine copperplate hand, somehow found extra time to instruct her in penmanship and grammar. Louise taught her the practicalities of weights and measures, pounds, shillings, and pence. And Síle, though her own formal schooling had been scanty, revealed an unsuspected gift for maths and drilled the little girl relentlessly. Schooling was conducted throughout the day, knitted in and around the business of living.

Henry halfway expected to be arrested again, but it never happened. "I was a minor minnow caught in their net," he told Louise, "and they don't care that I slipped away. Perhaps I should be insulted, but I'm just thankful."

Síle was holding herself under iron control. Her drawn face and hollow cheeks testified to the strain she was feeling, but she never spoke of it. Outwardly she was the same as ever. Henry found himself thinking of all those other courageous women who had lost sons and husbands to the dream of Irish freedom. They too went on washing clothes and baking bread and going to Mass and caring for children and sometimes arranging a bunch of flowers in a jam pot for the table.

How do they do it? The waiting is the worst; I never realized. How do women do it?

Henry wrote to Ned's brother Frank, explaining the situation to him, and Frank promised to keep sending Ned's share of the farm income for Síle and Precious. "Although," as Henry told Louise, "I could apply to the Irish National Aid fund on their behalf. Michael Collins would take care of it, he's the secretary there now."

Louise peered at him over her new wire-rimmed spectacles, which she wore perched on the end of her nose. "Is that man running everything?"

"Just about," Henry said. "He keeps opening more offices."

He thought of writing to Ned's sister in America and telling her of his arrest, but there was nothing she could do.

Besides, Henry had never met Kathleen ní Halloran Campbell. All he knew from Ned was that she was very pretty, an ardent supporter of the Republican cause, and had left her husband. The last was, in Henry's experience, almost unprecedented behavior for an Irish Catholic woman. *What does one say to a woman in those circumstances? How does one even address her?*

He decided it was best not to write to her at all.

When his former quarters in the attic became vacant, Louise assumed he would reclaim them, and was surprised when he demurred. "It wouldn't be proper for me to be up there with Síle, unchaperoned."

"Oh, Henry, if she can't trust you, who can she trust?"

But he was adamant. He stayed on the first floor.

He was beginning to hate writing advertising copy, persuading people to buy things they did not need instead of helping them understand the forces affecting their lives. When his pocket notebook was filled, he bought a new one. Every night after work he assiduously recorded the day's political events.

On the fifteenth of June, the cities of Cork and Limerick and a number of counties suspected of harboring too many Republicans were designated proclaimed districts, meaning anyone arrested there could be tried elsewhere at the government's convenience. "The Castle wants to keep them in its own pocket," Henry wrote in his notebook.

On the twenty-first of June, a by-election took place in Cavan. Henry recorded afterward: "Although John Dillon did his best to secure the seat for his party, Sinn Féin nominated Arthur Griffith. Griffith, who is still in prison, won by twelve hundred votes."

On the fourth of July the Sinn Féin Party, Cumann na mBan, and the Gaelic League were proscribed, and their meetings declared illegal. Their members ignored the ban. "The Fourth of July is also Independence Day in America," Henry observed in his notebook.

The Royal Irish Constabulary undertook a new recruitment drive. More police barracks were opened, studding the country. It was impossible to travel from Dublin to Swords, a distance of seven miles, without passing three RIC stations and being stopped and questioned at each of them.

Arrests continued throughout the summer. The police even broke up sporting events—if those events were considered of a seditious nature, such as Gaelic football or Gaelic hurling matches.

When Henry saw Michael Collins in the street he made a point of never calling attention to him, but Collins always gave Henry a cheery nod. From time to time a sealed note addressed to "HM" was pushed through the letter box at number 16. The notes did not come by way of the postal service. Catching a glimpse of the delivery boy one day as he sped away on his bicycle, Henry thought, *It's astonishing the Castle hasn't picked him up by now. They don't seem to have any idea who he is.*

Letters from Lincoln Jail addressed to Mrs. Halloran also bypassed the government post office. Síle would run upstairs with the sealed envelope and reappear later, glowing, to report, "Ned's all right. He sends his love." She never said more than that to Henry and Louise. Ned's letters were too tender to share. They were written in pencil, sometimes on sheets of toilet paper, and Síle slept with them beneath her pillow.

In September the ban against the *Clare Champion* expired. Sarsfield Maguire immediately sent a letter to Henry. "The presses are rolling again," he wrote. "Come back to us."

Chapter Seventeen

T HAT evening, Henry sat at the dining table with Maguire's letter burning a hole in his pocket.

"You're not eating, Henry," Síle remarked. "I made that bread sauce myself—Louise taught me. Is something wrong?"

"Not at all—the sauce is grand. Sometimes I just go off my feed. Like a horse," he added with a wink at Precious.

"Will my horse go off its feed, Uncle Henry?"

"You needn't worry about that, Little Business—you don't have a horse."

"I don't," the child agreed. "But Ursula Jervis Halloran will."

Louise sputtered in her tea. Síle raised her eyebrows. Louise made a negligible gesture with her hand, the signal by which one woman says to another, "I'll tell you later."

There was something more pressing on Síle's mind, however. When Henry went to his room later, he found her waiting for him outside the door. "May I speak with you in private?"

"I don't—"

"Please."

He opened the door and stood aside for her to enter, then left the door conspicuously ajar.

Thank God I have two chairs, so neither of us must sit on the bed.

Síle perched stiffly on the edge of her chair, as aware as he was that this was the first time they had been alone in a bedroom together. She went straight to the point. "If something's happened to Ned, you have to tell me, Henry. You do me no favors by keeping things from me. I always want to know the truth, no matter what."

So that's where Precious gets it from. "I give you my oath, Síle, there's no bad news of Ned. If there ever is, I promise I'll tell you straightaway."

"I'll rely on that. And thank you." She stood up and started for the door. He stood too . . . just as she swayed and almost fell.

With one long stride he caught her in his arms. When she sagged against him, he could smell the white lilac scent Ned had given her at Christmas.

"It's all right, Síle," he murmured, awkwardly patting her back. "Everything will be all right."

"Oh, Henry, nothing's all right."

"I was afraid you were going to faint. Are you ill?"

She tried to push away from him, but the strength had gone out of her. "Just ill with worry over Ned. The British abuse our lads, everyone knows that, and he's not well anyway. I go to bed terrified for him and I don't sleep and I get up still terrified for him. The mornings are worse than the nights. He always kissed me awake in the morning." A dry sob burst from her throat.

I should not be hearing this. "Here, sit back down," Henry urged.

He watched helplessly while she buried her face in her hands. None of the phrases that came to his mind were of any use. She reminded him of a bird huddled on a branch in a rainstorm. When she finally took her hands away and looked up at him, her eyes were dry but naked with pain, and she spoke as if the words were being dragged out of her. "Ned didn't have to marry me, you know. But he loves me. Truly loves me. Can you understand what that means? What I was . . . what I did . . . doesn't matter to him."

I wonder if that's true, Henry thought. "Ned's a good man."

Síle swallowed hard. "The only decent man I've ever known."

There's me. I try to be decent. "Do you need my handkerchief?"

"I don't, but thank you. I never cry, Henry. If you cry, they can break you."

"Can I get you anything else then? A glass of water? Or . . . there's an old saying in Limerick: 'What butter or whiskey does not cure cannot be cured.' I've a bottle of Jamesons in my locker. You're welcome to some if you can drink it from a tooth glass."

"I could lick it off the floor," Síle assured him gratefully.

He poured half a tumblerful and watched while she tossed it back like a man. Women did not drink whiskey. But this was Síle, and as Ned had so often said of her, none of the rules applied.

Her breathing steadied. "I'm sorry, Henry, I didn't mean to lose the run of myself like that." As she handed him the empty glass her eyes became guarded. She had re-erected the wall behind which no one was allowed but Ned.

"Don't apologize for being human," Henry told her. "Do you feel any better now?"

"I suppose I do."

"That's good then. Go on up to Precious, I'm sure she's waiting for you."

At the door she turned and looked back at him. "I know another old saying: 'It is a lonely washing that has no man's shirt in it.' "

I'M afraid I cannot come back to Clare right now," Henry wrote to Sarsfield Maguire. "I am needed here. But I should be happy to function as a sort of roving correspondent for the *Champion* and send you material from here. I would not expect full salary, of course. You can pay me by the piece."

When Maguire agreed, Henry contacted other newspapers and periodicals and established enough freelance arrangements to make him confident he could support himself and maintain the Limerick tithe. The mood in the country had indeed changed; both his straight news stories and his feature articles now had a market. With a sense of relief he gave up the advertising business.

Aside from Irish politics, there was a lot to write about that autumn. In America fourteen million men had registered for the draft. An influenza epidemic sweeping across Europe was killing tens of thousands. In the Irish Sea more than five hundred civilians died when the Germans torpedoed the mailboat *Leinster*. The dead were brought back to Kingstown, where they lay in long rows under tarpaulins, waiting to be identified. As the sinking of the *Lusitania* had been to America, so was the destruction of the *Leinster* to Ireland. The mailboats were sacrosanct; the Irish would never forgive this act of treachery. People had felt a certain sympathy with the Germans because they were fighting Ireland's ancient enemy England, but that sympathy was blown away with the *Leinster*. New angers were born.

It seemed the Great War would never end.

At her insistence, Henry read newspaper accounts of the conflict to Precious and discussed them with her afterward. They disturbed and repelled her, but nothing could dampen her need to know, her effort to try to understand the world around her.

"Why, Uncle Henry? Why do so many men have to die?"

"They don't have to, Little Business. They could be safely home with their families if it weren't for the kings and kaisers who command them to fight."

"What reason do the kings and kaisers have?"

He hesitated a long moment before answering. "They invent any number of reasons. But in truth, there is an element in men . . . in some men . . . that requires a battle. Combat is how they define themselves, and when such men rise to leadership they can indulge their passion. If they didn't have this war, they would manufacture another one. Do you understand what I'm saying at all?"

She nodded. "I think so. I've seen dogs fighting in the street just for the sake of fighting. It seems stupid, though."

"Don't mistake stupid behavior for stupidity. The other day I saw a copy of a letter that a very intelligent man called Winston Churchill wrote in 1915. He told a friend, and I can quote it exactly, 'I think a curse should rest on me—

because I *love* this war. I know it's smashing and shattering the lives of thousands every moment—and yet—I can't help it—I enjoy every second of it.' "[1]

THEN, as if between one day and the next, the tide of war turned in favor of the Allies. There was a general lifting of spirits among the journalistic fraternity. "Even the darkest cloud must blow away sometime," Henry wrote in *Young Ireland*. "The world is awaiting a new dawn that may see better things for us all."

ON the second of November, Lloyd George stated that Britain had the right to solve "the Irish question" by partition, giving control of six northeastern counties to the Unionists.

Henry did not go to bed that night. He sat hunched over his writing table until morning light streamed through the windows, then proofread the final draft of a feature article he hoped to sell to the *Enniscorthy Echo*.

"Partition, if implemented, will divide us where there was no division before," his article concluded. "Catholic or Protestant, the inhabitants of this country have always had one thing in common: an Irish identity. Some of Ireland's greatest patriots have been Protestant. In the Rising of 1798, Scots Presbyterian and Roman Catholic fought together against English injustice. This is such a small island. We have always seen our destinies as intertwined.

"If Ireland is partitioned, two discrete identities will develop. Two fragments of a mutilated country will face one another across an artificial border, with mistrust and hatred encouraged between them by politicians seeking to manipulate the situation to their own advantage."

The next morning Henry posted the article to Enniscorthy from the temporary GPO at number 14 O'Connell Street.[2] Then he went for a solitary walk through a city dense with history. Dust bins clanging; bullet holes in shopfronts. Grubby corner-boys shouting at one another; a memory of machine-gun fire rattling through the streets.

A Catholic church on one corner and a Protestant church

on the other, their working-class congregations lifelong friends.

An occasional motorcar in spite of wartime shortages, but many more horse-drawn vehicles. Dung steaming on the cobblestones; men in rags scooping it up to dry and sell for fuel in the tenements. Dog feces provided another source of income. Known as "pure," the substance was sold to tanners for darkening leather.

Eventually Henry made his way to the Liffey. He strolled along the quays, staring down at the murky water.

The river Lifé, in Irish. Carrier of life and death. Fecund mud and stinking sewage.

Irish soldiers dead in the trenches of Europe. Rotting into a soil not theirs.

Henry made himself look at the sky instead.

Above the Liffey, gulls were wind-planing on currents of air. Free sky. No borders.

Chapter Eighteen

November 11, 1918

VICTORY! GERMANY SIGNS THE ARMISTICE!

THE Kaiser fled Germany. France was saved, Belgium was liberated.

Rudyard Kipling, whose son John had died on the first day of his first battle, wrote of the Great War:

If any ask why we died,
Tell them,
Because our fathers lied.

The ruin of the sprawling empire of the Hapsburgs, constructed through war and marriage over a thousand years, was carved into new polities: Austria, Hungary, and Czecho-Slovakia. In a reverse action, a Serbo-Croatian kingdom was established by amalgamating a number of formerly separate kingdoms and territories. Born from the womb of opportunity, these new nations were gifted with independence.

Forty-nine thousand Irishmen had died while serving with the British army in the Great War. Not one drop of their sacrificed blood had won independence for Ireland.

Dublin celebrated the Armistice with near hysteria. The city was over a thousand years old and had seen many wars and many truces, but this had been the War to End All Wars. It was a hell of an excuse for a party.

"You can't sit around the house on an occasion like this," Henry told Síle the morning after Armistice was announced. "I'm going to take the day off. Put on your best frock and let's go celebrate."

"I don't feel like celebrating, not without Ned. You and Louise go, and take Precious with you. She's busy upstairs now, cutting out the newspaper headlines for her scrapbook. Ned would say an event like this is part of her education, and I refuse to spoil it for her by being a damp squib. I'll stay here and," she smiled faintly, "keep the home fires burning."

There was no arguing with Síle. She was like Ned in that respect.

The streets of Dublin were thronged with revelers holding a festival at every crossroads, but Henry feared the crowds might bring back memories of the Bachelor's Walk Massacre for Precious. He decided they would go to one of the hotels instead. To make the occasion even more memorable, he chose Dublin's grandest, the Shelbourne, though he did not tell the others. He wanted to surprise them with a special treat.

Because there were no motorcabs to be hired at any price, he ordered a brougham to transport his little party through the riotous streets in the afternoon. Louise agonized over her limited wardrobe, trying on different dresses and bonnets while Precious ran up and down the stairs, trailing ribbons. "Mama said we could plait green ones into my hair, but I want these blue ones too. Or the gold ones . . . or maybe red? What do you think, Uncle Henry?"

He solemnly adjudicated; they finally settled on green and gold. For himself Henry selected his best suit and waistcoat, with a boiled shirt and a collar so stiffly starched it rubbed his neck. His looking-glass assured him he looked very dapper.

Síle bade them goodbye at the door.

The horse, a mettlesome bay gelding, shouldered through

milling crowds while Precious leaned out the window and bombarded the driver with questions about the animal. As they clattered onto O'Connell Bridge, Louise said rather nervously, "You didn't tell me we were going across the river, Henry."

"Thought you'd enjoy a change of scenery."

"But it's so . . . posh."

He laughed. "Hardly. Different, yes—every part of Dublin is different from every other part. But south of the river isn't all posh by any means. There are people here no better off than you are, and a lot who are much poorer."

Circling around the front of Trinity College, the brougham headed up Grafton Street with its expensive shops. Jubilant crowds were even thicker here: voices shouting, hats tossed in the air, banners waving, total strangers throwing their arms around one another. All of Saint Stephen's Green was one vast party, and someone was setting off fireworks. At the first loud bang, the horse shied and Precious flinched. Then she looked at Henry and made herself laugh.

When the brougham pulled up in front of the ornate Victorian porch of the Shelbourne, Louise let out a gasp and pressed back against the seat. "I can't go in there, Henry."

"You can, of course."

"But the gentry stay at the Shelbourne. *Protestants*," she added in a whisper.

"Aren't you just as good as any of them? Ireland's going to be a republic, Louise, just as Pearse wanted. A nonsectarian republic that treats everybody equally. Might as well start now!" Without giving her a chance to refuse he maneuvered her out of the carriage, then lifted Precious down. "You both look grand entirely. In you go now. Heads high!"

The doorman in his tall silk hat winked at Precious as he ushered her through the double doors. "You're very welcome, Miss."

She beamed back at him. "I'm going to stay here when I'm grown," she confided.

Louise was plainly uncomfortable, but Precious, child of the slums, swept into the Shelbourne Hotel as if she owned the place.

In spite of the hour, electrified chandeliers were blazing

in the entrance hall.[1] Their diamantine brilliance added to the air of festivity. Accustomed to the gentler gaslight of number 16, Precious asked in a stage whisper, "Uncle Henry, does the same electricity that runs the trams run those lights?"

"It does, Little Business."

"Is electricity only for trams and hotels?"

"Not at all. Electricity's a form of power, and power's like water, it can go anywhere. The first cables were laid in Dublin in 1881,"[2] Henry elaborated, happy to display a newspaperman's general knowledge. "Most large commercial firms here use electricity these days."

"Then why don't we have electric lights at home?"

"There simply is not enough power available."

"Do they use electricity down the country?"

"A couple of towns have it on a very limited basis, but nothing like here."

Precious cocked her head to one side. "Why? Is Dublin better than the rest of Ireland?"

Their conversation was overheard by a tall woman swathed in a coat of Mongolian blue fox. She interjected, "Of course it is, my dear. Dublin is the second capital of the empire."

"What empire?"

"Why, the British Empire."

Precious stared up into the woman's face, which was concealed from Henry by the deep brim of her hat. "We're not part of any old empire," the little girl asserted. "We're a republic and that's a lot better. My Uncle Henry said so."

Louise caught the child's arm and hurried her into the formal room beyond the lobby. Biting the inside of his cheek to keep from laughing, Henry followed.

The room faced south, offering drapery-framed views of Saint Stephen's Green. Within the Green deciduous trees stood leafless, but around their skeletal forms clustered the evergreens that made the park luxuriant in every season— though some of these were still recovering from the damage done by fusillades of bullets during Easter Week 1916.

Pale sunlight streamed through tall windows, revealing a slightly dusty elegance. Hospitality was more important than

housekeeping at the Shelbourne. A certain artless dishevel-
ment made the Anglo-Irish gentry feel more at home, while
visitors from England considered it local color. The room
was crowded with celebrants. Class distinctions were set
aside in the general euphoria. Some of the hotel staff had so
forgot themselves they were mingling with the guests, but
no one seemed to mind.

Henry wedged his womenfolk onto a tufted-velvet ban-
quette whose prior occupants moved over without interrupt-
ing their own conversation. From a nearby table he borrowed
a chair for himself. Coal fires were roaring in the marble
fireplaces at either end of the room. "That's terrible waste-
ful," Louise commented. "So many people in this room, they
don't need any fire at all."

"Would you like a cup of tea?"

"Isn't it frightful dear here?"

Henry chuckled. "Don't worry about that today. There's
going to be no expense spared where my ladies are concerned—you can even have a meal if you want." He stood
up to look for a waiter, but they all seemed busy with other
patrons.

Henry's eyes met those of a woman just entering the
room.

Eyes the color of sweet sherry.

Ella Rutledge's arm was linked with the arm of the
woman in the blue fox coat. When she saw Henry, she nodded in recognition and guided her companion across the
crowded room toward him. There was an exchange of introductions during which Henry referred to Precious as Ursula.
The child promptly stood taller, growing into the name. Louise was flustered to be presented to "such grand ladies," as
she afterward described the sisters, for the tall woman in the
fox coat was none other than Ava Mansell.

She held out her hand to Precious with slightly mocking
formality. "We've already met, Ursula. You are the Littlest
Republican."

Precious knew she was being patronized. She shook hands
but broke contact first.

"We were just about to order tea," Henry said to Ella.

"We should like it very much if you and your sister-in-law would join us."

"Thank you, that's very kind. Does the invitation extend to Edwin as well? He should be here any minute." When she smiled, her dimples winked at him.

"By all means," Henry replied. *What a wonderful day this is!*

"My husband is a solicitor," remarked Ava Mansell, "but he's currently serving as a captain in the army."

Henry's stomach knotted. *Please God, no. Not a captain. Not that captain. Don't do this to me. Please.*

The headwaiter himself materialized beside them without being summoned: striped waistcoat, immaculate morning coat, and beaming deference. "Would you prefer to go into the coffee room, Mrs. Mansell? It's less crowded there."

"This will be fine, thank you. We require tea, and we shall sit by the windows." Within moments a table was cleared in front of one of the great windows, then laden with fresh starched linen, a silver tea service and a decanter of sherry, a tray of meatless savories, sweet biscuits, and a pitcher of milk for Precious.

The little girl eyed the savories with suspicion.

"Meatless days have been compulsory for hotels and restaurants because of the war rationing," Ella said to Precious, "but if you would like some meat, we bring our own when we come to the hotel. I'm sure the chef would be happy to prepare something for you."[3]

If Henry expected Precious to be overawed, he was mistaken. Without missing a beat the little girl replied, "I should like some roast chicken, please, and thank you." She laid one hand confidingly on Ella's arm. "I'm most awfully fond of roast chicken."

Conversation flowed while Ava Mansell poured the tea. Only Louise did not take part. She sat rigid on her chair, a woman very much in charge at number 16 but intimidated in the Shelbourne. Precious had no such problem. She chattered away to Ella as if they were old friends.

Ava remarked to Henry, "Your daughter is quite a little chatterbox, isn't she?" In polite society, her tone implied, children were seen but not heard.

"She isn't my daughter. Her father is my friend Ned Halloran."

"I remember Mr. Halloran very well," said Ella. "We met him with you at the Mansion House. That explains Ursula's accent, of course."

Henry was puzzled. "What accent?"

"Why, she sounds so educated. Not that you don't, Mr. Mooney," Ella said hastily, a delicate blush creeping into her cheeks. "But your accent is Irish, whereas I recall Mr. Halloran speaking like someone educated in England."

Henry could hardly admit that Ned had been employing his gift for mimicry in order to impress Ella Rutledge. He was rescued when Ava leaned forward to beckon to someone in the doorway. "There's Edwin now."

Ella beamed. "Brother mine!" she called softly.

Henry dreaded turning around, certain he would see the captain who had arrested him. Instead, Edwin Mansell was a fine-boned, hollow-cheeked stranger with a black patch over one eye. In his relief Henry pumped the other man's hand effusively. "You're very welcome, so you are. Here, let's get another chair for you. And a whiskey? Waiter!"

Precious was trying not to stare at the eyepatch but could not help herself. Edwin did not take offense. "I was wounded in the war," he explained to the child.

"Oh, I am sorry. Does it hurt very much?"

"Not now," he told her gently.

Ava cut in. "We're hopeful of a new treatment that may restore Edwin's sight. After Christmas we shall go to London for it."

"I'll pray every night for you to get better," Precious promised Edwin.

Watching Ella Rutledge, Henry saw the way her face melted. "And will you also pray for our Edwin, Mr. Mooney?" she asked him.

"I shall, of course. If you'll call me Henry."

She blushed again. "Henry."

Conversation flowed back and forth across the table. Henry engaged Ava on the subject of genealogy. "My husband is descended from Sir Rhys Mansell," she announced proudly. "The family name originally was Maunsell, Norman nobles who arrived in England with William the Conqueror. They intermarried with the Welsh nobility, which is where Sir Rhys got his Welsh Christian name. He was knighted by Henry the Eighth and sent to Ireland to help surpress a rebellion by the Earl of Kildare. The family has been here ever since."

"Oh, my," said Henry, trying to sounding suitably impressed. He saw Precious looking at him across the table and winked at her. *Imagine trying to impress Republicans with crowns and titles.*

Understanding perfectly, Precious winked back at him.

She was enjoying herself until Ava asked a question about her father. Precious nonchalantly replied, "Oh, Papa's away at the moment. My mama's in Dublin, but she didn't feel like celebrating without him, so she stayed home."

Ella nodded. "I would feel the same myself."

But Ava would not leave it at that. "Where is your father, Ursula?"

The child's face tightened. Looking Ava straight in the eye, she said, "He's in prison in Britain. My papa fought in the Easter Rising. He's a hero."

There was an awkward silence. Then Edwin cleared his throat. "You must be very proud of him. I think we should be proud of all brave men, don't you?" He swept his gaze around the table, demanding concurrence.

"Well, I'm sure that's true," drawled Ava, "but the fact remains, the Sinn Féin Rebellion was a great inconvenience. Our cook couldn't get to the shops because of the barricades, so we had no fresh food for days."

Ella said, "Oh, Ava, that sounds so petty. Men dying and you complaining about eating leftovers! I agree with Edwin—courage is to be admired, and the Republicans certainly had courage. They also believed they had right on their side, we must not forget that."

"I daresay the Germans believed they had right on their side too. But it may have cost my husband his eye."

"Must you always reduce everything to the personal?"

"War is personal," Edwin interjected. "To every man who fights on whatever side, in whatever battle, it's intensely personal. Only you who sit safe at home are afforded the luxury of distance. Let me tell you a little story . . ."

Precious leaned forward eagerly. "Is it true? I like true stories best."

He smiled at her. "This is true, I assure you. It happened in December 1914, and I was there. My company had just been ordered to Messines, on the front lines. Casualties had been enormous, and we men from Ireland were the replacements. We were welcomed with rain, mud, snow, and sleet, sometimes all at once. I have never been more frightened or confused in my life. All I could be certain of were the fellows on either side of me. We spent hours knee-deep in icy water, trying to improve a position that could not be improved short of a hot August. It wasn't the danger that depressed us so much as overfatigue and appalling conditions.

"Between us and the Germans lay No-Man's-Land, twenty to seventy yards across and flanked on either side with barbed wire. The only living things were a few shell-splintered trees, and I doubt they were actually living anymore. For a man to attempt to cross that space under the guns of both armies was almost certain death. Our ears were constantly assaulted with cannon fire, rifle fire, officers shouting, occasionally an artillery horse screaming when it was hit. War is a hellishly noisy business . . . Forgive me, ladies."

"There's nothing to forgive," Ella said. She reached across the table and touched her brother's hand. "Go on, Edwin."

"On the afternoon of Christmas Eve, a Scottish major got a group of us together to sing Christmas carols. It was as much to drown out the other noise as anything else. To our amazement, the Germans joined in. We could hear them clearly across No-Man's-Land. And as we sang together, one by one the guns fell silent. Farther along the trenches we could hear other men begin to sing. At first their officers ordered them to keep on firing, but they ignored the order.

"For a stretch of four or five miles along the front lines, as we learned afterward, the firing ceased that Christmas Eve. We kept on singing; the other side kept on singing. The same hymns in different languages. At last a German who had the most pure, perfect tenor I've ever heard began 'Silent Night.' Everyone else stopped to listen. Some of us were crying. Lying there in the mud on bags of sand, we were crying. But not for ourselves. We were crying for the beauty of it.

"When he finished the carol, several of us scrambled up out of the trench. We fashioned a white flag and held it over the barbed wire just as a similar flag was raised on the other side. We crawled over the barbed wire and went out into No-Man's-Land to meet the Germans in the middle. We were wary at first; then a man from one side held out his hand and said 'Happy Christmas,' and a man on the other side shook the hand and repeated the greeting. After that, everything was all right. Some of us had a bit of German; many of them spoke English. But we all spoke Christmas.

"We swapped cigarettes for wine and showed one another photographs from home. I had somehow obtained a bar of American chocolate that I gave to a young German boy. In return he gave me a linen handkerchief, beautifully monogrammed with a 'C' in Gothic script by some loving hand at home. I have it still.

"But the astonishing thing is . . . the war stopped. Simply stopped. We helped the Germans carry away their wounded and they helped us fortify our trenches. The ordinary fighting men did that, the men to whom war is personal."

Henry, deeply moved, glanced at Ella Rutledge. Her eyes were moist.

"What happened then?" Precious wanted to know.

"Some deuced general—German or English, I never knew which, but someone miles from the trenches and very safe— heard about the Christmas truce and ordered the war to resume." Edwin Mansell dropped his voice so low they could hardly hear him. "Later I came across the dead body of the German boy who had given me his handkerchief. I've always been afraid mine was the bullet that killed him."

Chapter Nineteen

Síle was furious. "How could you do such a thing!" she shouted at Henry. "When I was in Stephen's Green with Madame Markievicz, the British fired on us from the Shelbourne. They were shooting at us like ducks on a pond—we could hear them laughing and encouraging each other. They killed a girl who was fighting right beside me. I never knew her name, but that's her pistol they took away from me when they arrested Ned. Yet you took my child to the Shelbourne just as if—"

"We need to put that behind us, Síle. We mustn't drag the past into the future like a stinking corpse."

But she would not listen. Not with Ned in a British prison and the unfinished revolution all around them.

With the war over, the British prime minister turned his attention to domestic matters. Within days he reiterated that self-government for Ireland would not be possible without first partitioning the island.

"This has been Lloyd George's intention from the beginning," Henry wrote in an article for the *Freeman's Journal*, "the method by which he means to divide and conquer the Irish permanently. That word 'permanently' is important. Lloyd George assured the late John Redmond that any partition of Ireland would be temporary. However, this reporter has learned that as far back as May of 1916, Lloyd George, while still secretary of state for war, sent a private letter to Sir Edward Carson of the Ulster Unionists in which he wrote, 'We must make it clear that at the end of the provisional period Ulster does not, whether she wills it or not, merge in the rest of Ireland.' "[1]

When the editor asked where he had obtained his information, he replied, "You know I can't tell you that." The *Journal* printed the piece anyway.

People read Henry's words over the breakfast table or in the barber's chair or on the tram, but they read them.

"Partition is a price we cannot afford to pay," Henry insisted in the *Evening Herald*. "Partition would leave a large Catholic minority stranded in northern Ireland, effectively deserted by the rest of the country in the effort to achieve independence for twenty-six counties. Similarly, the Protestants in the south would find themselves separated from those who share their heritage. In founding Sinn Féin Arthur Griffith envisioned one Ireland large enough in heart to encompass all traditions, Catholic and Protestant, nationalist and loyalist. That is the vision to which we must aspire."

In December of 1918, the British government declared a general election. The Sinn Féin Party made the Irish electorate two promises: they would establish a native government functioning independently of Britain, and they would appeal to the International Peace Conference to recognize the Republic of Ireland.

Sinn Féin won 73 of the 105 Irish seats in Parliament, an astonishing achievement. Most of the newly elected had been asked to run for office simply because they were being held in British prisons. All vowed never to take the seats they had won.

One of their number, Constance Markievicz, was the first woman ever elected to Parliament. Precious cut out every newspaper article about the countess and gave them pride of place in her scrapbook. "My papa knows Countess Markievicz personally," she boasted to Henry. "I think she's wonderful and I want to be just like her when I grow up."

"I don't think anyone could be quite like the countess," he replied rather absently. He was wondering, *When did Precious begin calling Síle "Mama" and Ned "Papa"?* He could not pinpoint the exact time, yet it seemed important, a milestone.

In an article about Sinn Féin's victory, Henry wrote, "These are people who fought for Irish freedom, but for the most part they have had no training in politics. Never having been allowed to run their own country, they have not developed the arts of compromise and manipulation. But they will learn. With the 1918 election the struggle for independence has become not only military but democratic."

There was a fever in the air in Ireland now; a sense of gathering forces.

The government in Dublin Castle grew increasingly edgy. The number of raids and house searches accelerated dramatically. Meetings were suppressed; men and even women were thrown into prison on the slightest pretext if they were suspected of Republican sympathies; and baton charges against crowds became a familiar part of the urban scene.

DURING December, Henry Mooney received two personal letters on the same Saturday afternoon. The first was a note from Ella Rutledge, hand-carried by one of the urchins who made a precarious living by delivering such messages—boys who lived in Dublin Corporation housing and cleaned their teeth with chimney soot. While the messenger waited, shifting from one foot to the other and whistling tunelessly, Henry opened the envelope and took out a formal calling card that bore her name in embossed copperplate script, and a single folded sheet of creamy notepaper. "Dear Henry," she had written in a clear hand, "Please do call on us during the holidays. We are 'at home' from two to five on Thursday afternoons."

Dear Henry.

Henry dug into his pocket and handed the boy a coin. The lad gaped. "Jaysus, misthur, I don't have change for a shilling! People usually give me a ha'penny, or a penny for somethin' special."

"This is something very special, and I don't want change. Just wait while I write an answer, then carry it straight back to Mrs. Rutledge."

"I'll wait for ye till the Divvil goes to Mass," the lad assured him.

The second letter was hand-delivered by a man Henry did not recognize. On a scrap of brown paper Ned had written, "I have no money at present, but if you will select a nice Christmas present for Síle for me, I shall repay you when I can. Which may be soon."

ELLA Rutledge lived in Herbert Place, in the Ballsbridge area of south Dublin. The imposing house, which stood on a large corner site, possessed four storys over a ground floor. Beside the front door was an oval brass plate simply inscribed MANSELL. A parlor maid in a starched apron and cap answered Henry's knock, took his bowler and his topcoat, and showed him into a room aglow with peach-colored moiré wallpaper. From a ceiling of rococo plasterwork hung a crystal chandelier. A French-polished table was crowded with silver-framed photographs of family and friends. Embossed invitations were prominently displayed on the Italian marble mantelpiece, including hunt balls in the country and receptions at Dublin Castle.

Definitely not our crowd.

Ella swept into the room with her dimples dancing and her hands extended in welcome. "I'm so glad you could come. I hope you won't think me forward in inviting you, but I was delighted to find someone who enjoys good conversation as much as my family does."

"I was afraid I might have bored you that afternoon at the Shelbourne."

"Far from it. Most men don't talk to a woman as if she had any intelligence, but you do."

"I've always found intelligence attractive."

For much of the afternoon they had the house to themselves. Edwin was at his law office. Ava and Madge chatted vivaciously while a maid served refreshments, then excused themselves to go shopping.

When they were alone, Ella and Henry began the conversational exploration of two people getting to know one another. She spoke of art and the theater, and visits to relatives in Belfast and London. Henry learned that the Mansells also owned property in County Roscommon. Ella described their country house, Beech Park, as "a sprawling pile with bats in the top story. If you're partial to dry rot and damp wallpaper, it's a grand place."

"Is it haunted?"

"Edwin's thinking of charging the ghosts rent. He hardly ever goes down—Dublin is his life. But Madge and I love Beech Park. She's a member of the local hunt, and we both fish."

"Do you now?" Henry said delightedly. "I'm something of an angler myself." He told her his favorite fishing stories, then expanded to describe his life in the west of Ireland, though he mentioned his siblings only casually and his mother hardly at all. Next he dredged his memory for anecdotes about the journalist's trade, which led Ella to remark, "I read all the papers. I have to be quick, though, before Madge puts them in the bottom of her cages. This month she's a canary breeder, you see. Last month she was going to be an opera singer."

Henry lost all sense of time and was astonished to hear the clock strike five. He found one final excuse to linger. "Before I go, I wonder if you would give me the benefit of your advice on a rather delicate matter?"

"If I can."

"My friend Ned has asked me to buy a Christmas present in his name for his wife. I confess I have no idea what to look for. Nothing too intimate, since I must be the one who selects it."

Ella nodded understandingly. "Tell me about her; what sort of person is she?"

I should have prepared some sort of answer to that question long ago. How can I possibly describe Síle to this woman? A lady like Ella could never understand a girl who was a whore in Monto before Ned married her. But without giving that background, how can I explain how far Síle's

*come? How can I convey how valiant she is, how spirited
. . . how—*

"Is Mr. Halloran's wife very feminine?" Ella prompted.

Henry said the first thing that popped into his head. "She
can shoot as well as a man."

"Really? She hunts, too, I suppose?"

"Hunts?"

"Rides to hounds. Perhaps Mrs. Halloran would appreciate new leather gloves and a riding crop."

The image struck Henry as irresistibly funny. "No sane
man would put a riding crop in Síle Halloran's hand," he
told a mystified Ella Rutledge. "Think of something else."

"Well . . . Spanish lace mantillas are becoming popular,
and they're always flattering. Might one of those suit?"

"The very thing! And if she really likes it, I'll take you
to dinner in the best restaurant in Dublin."

Two days before Christmas Henry received a letter from
London in Michael Collins' handwriting. "Myself and three
colleagues have hopes of meeting the American president,
Woodrow Wilson, here. He is due in London for a short
visit before attending the peace conference in Paris. What a
propaganda coup it will be if we win Wilson's pledge of
support in advance. Don't write anything about it yet, but if
we are successful, I promise you an exclusive account when
we return. M. C."[2]

On Christmas Eve everyone at number 16, even Henry,
went to Mass, then came back to the house to celebrate with
punch and hot mince pies and open their presents. Precious
was thrilled with a kaleidoscope from Síle and Ned. Henry
gave her a pair of leather gloves. "A friend of mine gave
me the idea for these, Little Business. They're too big for
you now, but save them until you're older. They're for horse
riding."

"Oh, Uncle Henry!" The child buried her face in the soft
leather and took a deep sniff. "Don't they smell gorgeous?"

Lifting a pale gray lace mantilla from its box, Síle held it
up for all to admire. From Henry's point of view, it covered
her face with a silken cobweb. *Like Ella's veil.* "This is

lovely, Henry. I've never had anything like it."

"It's from Ned," he said quickly.

The third of January brought another note from Collins, who was back in Ireland. "Forget that story about Wilson. He refused to see us. I even suggested kidnapping him, but no one took me seriously, which is probably just as well. I have asked the Lord Mayor of Dublin to grant him the Freedom of the City in hopes that it will give him some feeling of connection with Ireland. P.S. You'll be glad to hear that the British have just released Count Plunkett."

LATE at night on the seventh of January yet another note from Collins was thrust through the letter box at number 16. "Tonight there was an important meeting of the Sinn Féin executive, or at least as many of us as are not in prison. We have decided to convene an independent constituent assembly for the Irish nation. The new body is to meet in the Round Room of the Mansion House at three-thirty in the afternoon on the twenty-first of this month.[3] It will be open to every elected representative of the Irish people, no matter what their party. You are invited to attend as my personal guest."

As Henry held the paper in his hand, a thrill ran through him. *Our own parliament—a chance to build a new nation and get it right, without all the old colonial baggage!*

On the tenth of January, the British appointed Winston Churchill as secretary of state for war.

That same night Henry called at Herbert Place to take Ella Rutledge to the best restaurant in Dublin, her promised reward for suggesting the lace mantilla. As he waited for her in the front hall he remarked to the parlor maid, "Did I not hear Mrs. Rutledge call you Tilly?"

The girl dropped her eyes modestly. "You did, sir."

"Tilly what?"

"Burgess, sir."

"That's not an Irish accent."

She cast him a swift glance, then looked down again. "No, sir. Leeds. Me family comes from Leeds. Mister Edwin brought me mum over to cook for him. The rest o' the staff here's Oirish, but we're Henglish."

"Your mother's name is?"

"Mrs. Hester Burgess, sir."

"And do you like living in Ireland?"

The girl was so shocked at having a guest inquire about the feelings of a servant that she forgot to keep her eyes lowered. "Oh, I do, sir! 'Deed I do. We've made ever so many friends, and—" She stopped in confusion.

"That's all right, Tilly. I'm glad to hear you've made friends here. I hope you'll consider me one of them."

Henry took Ella to Jammet's, at the corner of Andrew Street and Church Lane, which advertised as "Dublin's Only French Restaurant." The main dining room contained famous allegorical paintings of the Four Seasons. Henry showed off by introducing Ella to several of the well-known artists and writers who patronized the place. She acknowledged each politely, but as the evening wore on he realized that she was unimpressed by fame. "I don't think life should be a competition to see who can make the biggest name for themselves," she told him. "I try to paint myself, but I think the people who appreciate art—or books, or music—are every bit as valuable as the artists. I think that's why God made man—to appreciate his creation."

Late in the evening Henry excused himself and went to the toilet. He came back to find her sitting, as she often did, with her chin propped on her left hand and her index finger tucked behind the curve of her jawbone. Seen thus, pensive, with dreaming eyes, she struck him as inexpressibly beautiful.

On the eighteenth, the first formal session of the International Peace Conference was convened at Versailles.

On the twenty-first of January, 1919, Dáil Éireann—the Assembly of Ireland—met in inaugural session. A large crowd gathered outside the Mansion House. Some were well-dressed businessmen or fashionable ladies drawn by curiosity to interrupt their day's shopping, but the majority of the spectators belonged to the shabby working class of Dublin. They were keyed up and tense, but behaved impeccably. Thrilled by the solemnity of the occasion, they matched it with their own dignity. A squad of the DMP in capes and spiked helmets stood at the gates but made no effort to interfere.

In the gallery of the Round Room, journalists and observers from several European countries rubbed elbows with an overflow of spectators.[4] Although most had to stand, a few chairs were provided at the front for women. The usher who escorted Henry to the gallery gestured to one of these. "Please be seated, sir. Mr. Collins expressly ordered that a seat be saved for you."

Henry shook his head firmly. "Not at all. Not while there's a lady who doesn't have a chair." He joined his standing colleagues. Soon he was explaining to a Spanish reporter the differences between the assembly and the British parliament. "Even the titles are new. Assembly members are to be called Dáil deputies rather than members of parliament. That's *Teachtai Dála* in Irish, so we'll have TDs rather than MPs. It's a small thing but it matters . . . In the heel of the hunt, everything matters."

The opening prayer was read in Irish by Father O'Flanagan, and then the roll call began. All of Ireland's elected representatives had been invited to take part.[5] Those belonging to the Unionist Party and the Irish Party chose not to attend, however. Their names—including that of Sir Edward Carson—were called out with the others. After a suitable pause, the clerk of the day marked each man *As lathair*—absent. Many of the Sinn Féin representatives were absent as well. Of the seventy-three Republicans who had been elected, thirty-six were in jail. For each of them a colleague cried out, *"Fé ghlas ag Gallaibh"*—imprisoned by the foreign enemy.

Someone else also answered for Michael Collins, to Henry's surprise. *Imagine him not being here today of all days. What could be more important than this?*

The assembly, with Cathal Brugha presiding, was conducted in Irish. For centuries the policy of the British government had been to eradicate the culture of the conquered country, so few if any of the participants had been born into a household where Irish was the first language. They were for the most part members of the Gaelic League founded by Douglas Hyde, and had learned their native tongue in adulthood. Therefore they spoke carefully and to the point.

Henry was embarrassed that he only understood a few words. *God, I wish Ned was here. Pádraic Pearse made certain his students were fluent in Irish, and he was right, too. The language is the heart of any people, and they stole ours from us: stole the hot poetic Gaelic heart from us. Damn them. Damn them.*

The session lasted only until five-thirty in the afternoon, but during those two hours the Dáil adopted an Irish Declaration of Independence, ratified the 1916 Proclamation of the Irish Republic, and elected Eamon de Valera president— *Príomh-Aire*—of Dáil Éireann. In de Valera's absence, Cathal Brugha was appointed acting president.

"There is a feeling in this room today unlike any I have ever experienced," Henry wrote in his notebook, more for himself than for publication. "De Valera has brought physical-force Republicans and nonviolent Griffith monarchists together in one fold. No matter how divergent their political philosophies, they have one point of agreement: Ireland. A sense of kinship fills the hall. It is evident in the exchange of warm smiles between old adversaries. All present share a deep and radiant joy, knowing themselves privileged to attend a momentous birth."

A provisional constitution for the Dáil passed unanimously. Three men were appointed as delegates to the International Peace Conference once Ireland was admitted: Count Plunkett, Arthur Griffith, and Eamon de Valera—the latter two still in British jails. A democratic program proposed by the new Dáil was read, and the assembly was adjourned to thunderous applause.

Before they left the building, journalists were given copies in English of the Declaration of Independence, the Constitution, and the Democratic Program. Henry asked for a second set, one he would fold away and cherish with the copy of the Proclamation he had taken from a wall during Easter Week, 1916. *Treasures for my grandchildren.* It was the first time he consciously had thought of grandchildren.

Henry had persuaded John Healy to print his report of the session in the *Irish Times*—"As long as you don't say anything too blatantly nationalistic, Mooney." Coverage of the new Dáil by the *Times* would amount to a tacit recognition of the Irish Republic by Ireland's most imperial newspaper—a victory won by the pen rather than the sword.

From the Mansion House Henry hurried straight to the *Times* offices on D'Olier Street—which is how he happened to be on hand when a far different story came over the telegraph. John Healy read aloud to the newsroom: " 'Soloheadbeg, County Tipperary. Today Dan Breen, Seán Treacy, and several other Republicans ambushed and killed two RIC constables. They seized a cartload of gelignite the constables were guarding.' "

"Fuckin' hell!" cried one of the reporters. "That crowd's going to make bombs!"

With the founding documents of the new nation in his hand, Henry tried to absorb the news. Dan Breen . . . bombs: the thrill of the Dáil was replaced by a chill of apprehension.

The next day he went to the Bleeding Horse Pub on Camden Street, a favorite meeting place for Republicans. The events of the twenty-first were on everyone's lips. Henry sat in a corner unobtrusively taking notes. "I guess Dan Breen showed the bloody Brits!" exclaimed a round-faced youth, pounding his fist on the bar. "Sinn Féin isn't going to do anything—politicians never do anything but feather their own nests. It's up to the Republican Army to prove the people of this country won't lie down and roll over for the bloody Crown anymore."

"We showed the British something, all right," commented someone else. He had a laborer's hands and an alcoholic's complexion, but he spoke like an educated man. "Yesterday while our new parliament convened in Dublin we were behaving like outlaws down the country. Which speaks for Ireland?"

A tall man with deep-set eyes said, "The Republicans speak for Ireland."

"Which Republicans? Those in the Dáil or those in Breen's Tipperary Brigade?"

Henry closed his notebook.

*One war barely over, and now this. Through the peace
conference we'll get the Republic internationally recognized
without bloodshed; we just have to be patient a little longer.
Dan's an intelligent man. Maybe I can reason with him and
persuade him to reason with the others.*

But Dan Breen had become a will-o'-the-wisp, constantly
on the run between safe houses. A reward of a thousand
pounds was being offered for his capture. No one admitted
to knowing where he was. Hannah Mooney and Honora
Breen were close friends; that link should be sufficient to
put Henry in touch with Breen. Yet he could not bring himself to pick up his pen and ask a favor of his mother.

The new Dáil sent Seán T. O'Kelly to Paris as an envoy
to secure admission to the peace conference for the three
Irish delegates—which would put pressure on Britain to release de Valera and Griffith from prison. "Ireland's very first
diplomat is on his way to the City of Light," Henry exulted
in the *Evening Herald*. "If America upholds our claim at the
conference, the other nations are bound to be swayed in our
favor."

When they met in the Oval Bar the night the story was
published, Matt Nugent cautioned, "Don't pin too many
hopes on America, Henry. After the Rising there was a huge
wave of pro-Irish sentiment among the people. Our revolution reminded them of their own. But Britain's been bombarding the Americans with anti-Irish propaganda lately, and
some of it's bound to stick. The influence of the printed
word   you know."

Henry nodded.

Nugent went on, "I've been covering the international
news for a long time now, and that includes the States. So
I happen to know that one of our most influential supporters
over there is a member of the Supreme Court of New York,
a man called Daniel Cohalan. Cohalan has a lot of friends
in the IRB. He was also an exceedingly vocal opponent of
Woodrow Wilson's nomination for president. Anything Cohalan's for—such as independence for Ireland—is likely to
get a cold shoulder from Wilson. Added to that, since the
Armistice Paris has been awash with British delegations, and
you can bet tuppence ha'penny they're whispering against

us in every ear. I tell you, there's a fierce lot of political maneuvering going on behind the scenes."

"As always," Henry sighed.

SEÁN O'Kelly sent letters to Georges Clemenceau, the president of the International Peace Conference, and to every delegate, asking that they support the democratically expressed desire of the Irish people for independence. Paris was swarming with journalists clamoring for information about the new Irish Republic. For the first time since the Act of Union, the Irish benches in Britain's House of Commons were almost empty.

In Ireland, postwar gaiety was reaching a climax. Dublin heard the first wild, free notes of the Jazz Age. Among those who could afford to do so, it became almost an obligation to forget care and plunge into pleasure. Stores thronged with shoppers. Hemlines crept upward. An endless round of dances, parties, race meetings. New motorcars raced down narrow country lanes, terrifying sheep and cattle.

Together with the officers of the British regiments stationed in Ireland, the Ascendancy partied as if there were no tomorrow.

Chapter Twenty

March 4, 1919

OVER PRESIDENT WILSON'S OBJECTIONS U.S.
HOUSE OF REPRESENTATIVES VOTES 216–45 TO
REQUEST PARIS PEACE CONFERENCE ACCEPT
IRELAND'S CLAIM TO SELF-DETERMINATION

UNITED STATES SENATE PASSES SIMILAR
MOTION

Dateline: Paris

RECOGNITION FOR IRELAND DENIED

I feel like I've been personally betrayed," Henry told Síle. Since the night she visited him in his room some of her walls were down. There was still a distance between them that he dared not overstep, but she seemed more comfortable with him. Sometimes, as now, she invited him up to the attic apartment to read to Precious before bedtime. Afterward she lingered talking with him in the sitting room.

"What do you mean, 'betrayed'?" she asked.

"I've always maintained that we could achieve independence through political negotiation, even if it took years. Anything was preferable to violence. Ned and I used to argue about that, you know; he is so much a physical-force man. I believed the peace conference would be my vindication. Surely the other nations would understand that Ireland has as much right to exist as the small countries the war was supposed to be fought for! We need only present our case through the proper channels. But there aren't any proper channels, not for us. The door's been slammed in our faces."

"Why, Henry? I don't understand."

"I'm beginning to. Woodrow Wilson's dream is to establish a League of Nations to prevent global war. He's been working in Paris during the peace conference to ratify a covenant for the league. The support of the Allies is essential, of course. I've been doing some investigating, and it looks like the price of British support for the League of Nations is to be the Irish Republic. According to Article 10 of the league's covenant, Ireland is an appendage of the British Crown. So much for going the political route, Síle. Maybe your husband was right all along."

THE twin cancers of anger and frustration ate at Henry Mooney. He knew the members of Sinn Féin were trying to work out a new political strategy, but there was another element in the equation: men like Dan Breen—tough, gritty physical-force men. Whatever chance might have existed to persuade them to peaceful means was lost now. The price on Dan's head had been raised; he and those like him were fighting back, all across the country.

"We'll see some action," Dan had said. "Say, you wouldn't be interested in joining the South Tipperary Brigade, would you?"

Henry took up his pen instead.

"In 1914 Prime Minister Asquith justified Britain's entry into the war on the grounds it was to defend the neutrality of Belgium against German aggression," he wrote for the *Clare Champion*. "Asquith said, 'it is impossible for people of our blood and history to stand by while a big bully sets to work to thrash and trample to the ground a victim who has given him no provocation.'[1] Yet for eight centuries his

people have relentlessly bullied ours, and now they have
used their strength against us yet again. They would argue
that the cause is just. The most degrading attribute of hu-
mankind is not callousness or greed or even violence, but
the ability to justify all three."

Writing helped release some of the tension Henry felt, but
not enough. He spent sleepless nights pacing the floor of his
room, smoking cigarette after cigarette and then opening the
window to let the smoke out. The rush of cool, damp air on
his face did not ease his fever.

*Ireland's nationhood has been bartered for other men's
dreams*.

Other men's . . .

Síle, upstairs. Another man's dream.

Ella Rutledge on the other side of town. A woman to put
on a pedestal.

The whores of Monto only a short walk away. Ready and
willing.

But Henry did not visit Monto anymore.

The decision had not been a conscious one. A seismic
shift had taken place within him; the easy relief of Monto
was no longer enough. He spent his evenings at home with
Síle and Precious, wrapped in an emotional contentment that
did not satisfy physical desire but fed a deeper need.

IMMEDIATELY following its inauguration, the Dáil had
set about putting new government structures in place. In voting for independence the Irish people had voted to govern
themselves, so on both national and local levels men and
women were being recruited to serve a new nation. There
was no shortage of willing, if inexperienced, workers.

The response of the entrenched power was predictable.
Dáil members were watched and harassed, forced to meet in
secret. People began referring to them as "the Underground
Parliament." A favorite rendezvous was the Wicklow Grill,
where they conducted the Republic's business in whispers
over steak-and-kidney pie.

British agents were searching for Michael Collins with
arrest warrants in hand. They still did not know what he

looked like, but were increasingly aware of his importance. He lived a life on the run, sometimes sheltering in the house of a friend or sympathizer, sometimes spending nights in the open, sometimes sharing a bed with a comrade such as Harry Boland, each of them sleeping with a gun by his pillow. Once, when Vaughan's Hotel was raided, Collins got out just in time and found shelter crouched behind the stone buttress of a nearby church while heavily armed British soldiers paced back and forth just a few yards away.

When under pressure Collins became irascible and profane, even cruel. At such times his friends walked carefully around him. Then, in the blink of an eye, he would return to the merry fellow no one could resist and be forgiven everything.

Colorful stories about Collins were proliferating. Henry Mooney was not the only journalist who wrote down every one he heard. "There's a book in the Big Fellow one of these days," Matt Nugent prophesied.

"Ah, sure," said Henry, "there's a book in all of us. But I'd rather mine remained unread."

THE spring weather was bitterly cold. The air of central Dublin was so thick with coal smoke that a perpetual twilight hung over the city. The twin horrors of influenza and consumption stalked the streets.

Henry emerged from number 16 later than usual to find Ned Halloran coming up the front steps.

Ned laughed out loud at the expression on his face. "Going to work, Henry? Surely you can spare an hour or two. It isn't every day a friend escapes a British prison. Come inside with me and let's tell the women." He clapped one hand on the astonished Henry's shoulder and steered him back into the house.

"I'm home!" Ned shouted at the foot of the stairs. He drew a deep breath, then repeated softly, as if to reassure himself, "I'm home."

There was shriek, then a clatter of running feet from various parts of the house. Síle arrived first, hair flying as she tore it free from its hairpins. Everything she felt was in her

eyes. Henry could not bear to look at them. Their message
was for Ned alone.

Precious flung herself at Ned. "Papa, Papa, Papa! I knew
you were coming home today! I knew it, I knew it!"

He lifted her to cover her face with kisses. "My, you're
getting heavy. How did you know I was coming home, Precious?"

"The birds told me," she said seriously. "The birds under
the eaves. I listen to them and they tell me things."

Ned laughed again. "There are spy networks everywhere,"
he said.

Louise Kearney's way of expressing herself was to prepare a celebratory meal they were too excited to eat. As they
sat around the table with the food congealing on their plates,
Ned spoke offhandedly of his imprisonment. "It wasn't so
bad. We had a roof over our heads and walls to keep out
the wind, and something they claimed was decent food. Matter of opinion, of course. We were watched, but there's nothing new about that. Besides, they couldn't watch us all at
the same time."

"Obviously not," said Henry. "How did you get away?"

Ned put his hand over Síle's. "It's a long story and I'm
knackered. Do you suppose we could save it till later?"

As if she had been waiting for the clue, Síle shepherded
her returned hero upstairs. "He needs a good long sleep in
his own bed," she announced firmly.

"That means you stay down here with us and let him rest,"
Louise said in an aside to Precious.

"But Mama's going with him, so why can't I—"

Henry interrupted. "You come into the parlor with me and
I'll read to you. Anything you like."

The little girl's expression brightened. "Something about
ponies?"

NED did not reappear until late that night. When he came
downstairs he found Henry alone in the parlor, slumped in
a chair and gazing at the dying flames on the hearth. Ned
ran his fingers through his tousled hair before sauntering into

the room. "Want some company, Henry? A good talk, like old times?"

Henry started from a deep reverie. "Where's Síle?"

"Asleep. She put Precious to bed hours ago, and now they're both asleep."

"So should you be at this hour."

Abruptly Ned coughed, a deep, racking expulsion from the bottom of his lungs. "I don't think that chimney's drawing properly," he said in response to Henry's glance of concern. "I'll have a look at it in a day or two."

"There's nothing wrong with the chimney. I wish I could say the same for you."

"You're as bad as my wife. I'm all right, truly I am. Just overtired." Ned's boyish grin resurfaced. "I've had something of an adventure."

"I'm sure you have," Henry said with a touch of envy. "Do you feel up to talking about it now?"

"I suppose so. I keep going over our escape in my head anyway; that's why I can't sleep."

" 'Our' escape? Who else did you bring out with you?"

"It was the other way around, Henry. He brought me out with him. De Valera."

Henry sat bolt upright in his chair. "I think you'd better tell me."

Ned was too restless to sit. He paced the room as he talked, occasionally pausing to lean against the mantelpiece with his arms folded. Henry was struck by his physical beauty: the elegant, attenuated line and careless grace of the man.

How easy it is to take our friends for granted until we almost lose them.

"We thought the British might release us sooner rather than later," Ned began, "because some had already been sent home. But we couldn't be sure how strongly the government was still regarding the 'German plot.' Besides, Dev wanted to give our lads the morale boost of a dramatic escape. He said it was our duty to resist the British every way we could.

"From the beginning of our imprisonment, Dev had used coded messages to communicate with Mick Collins. Some of the messages were in Irish and others in Latin. Translation was my specialty, so I worked closely with Dev, but I wasn't the only one. There was an elaborate Republican network inside the prison, and Mick was setting up a similar network outside. Since the start of the year he's been our director of intelligence, as I'm sure you know.

"When we first arrived at Lincoln, Dev had insisted we were not to receive any food parcels. He said it was up to the British government to feed us. Then he changed his mind. The food was dreadful and they kept cutting back our rations, but that wasn't the reason. Dev and Mick had a plan, you see.

"Dev was serving as an altar boy and had gained the trust of the prison chaplain. So he was able to sneak into the sacristy during Mass and use candle wax to take an impression of the chaplain's master key. Then Seán Milroy made a very precise drawing of the impression, and we smuggled it out of the prison as part of the design on a Christmas card.

"Using that drawing as a template, Mick's people on the outside had a key made that they smuggled back into the prison inside a cake. The guards never checked our food parcels for contraband. They thought the Irish were too stupid for clever plots.

"So we got the key in with no problem. But unfortunately it didn't work in our locks. Neither did the next one Mick's people sent in another cake. At last, in desperation, they sent us a blank key of the right size and the tools, and we cut it ourselves. Fortunately Mr. Pearse had made us boys learn craftwork at Saint Enda's.

"Meanwhile, Mick was in England making the final arrangements for the escape. He wanted to be in Dublin for the first Dáil, but even he couldn't be in two places at once."

If Collins was in England at the time, Henry thought, *at least he wasn't killing RIC men in Tipperary.*

Ned continued, "When the key was ready I gave it to Dev. He sent word to Mick, and one night in February Mick and Harry Boland cut a hole in the barbed wire around the prison. Everything was timed to the last minute. They hid in a field close by and flashed a signal with an electric torch at 7:40 precisely, and we were watching for it."

"You and de Valera?"

"And Seán MacGarry and Seán Milroy."

"Why them in particular when there were so many of you?"

"Only a few could possibly get out at one time without alerting the guards. MacGarry's the president of the supreme council of the IRB as well as being the secretary of the IRA, and Seán Milroy's on the Sinn Féin executive committee. As for me—and promise you won't tell this to my wife—I'd been having a lot of dizzy spells, and Dev was worried about me. He thought if I didn't get out soon . . ."

Henry nodded. There was no need to finish the thought. "Go on about the escape."

"When we saw the signal, Milroy answered it from his cell window. But he accidentally set a whole box of matches alight in the process. The poor sod was having a run of desperate bad luck that night. Dev let us out of our cells with his key, but then the sole of one of Milroy's shoes came loose, and it kept flapping on the stone floor while we were trying to sneak out."[2]

Henry chuckled. Ned said, "It's easy to laugh now, but it didn't seem so funny then. A jail at night echoes something fierce. Luckily we made our way to a side gate without arousing the guards, and Mick and Harry met us there. Mick had brought a duplicate key made from our drawing, and he was so impatient that he tried to use it before we could use ours. When he turned his key in the lock the damned thing broke off.

"I'd never heard Dev swear before, but he did that night. He kept his head, though. He used his own key to push the broken one out of the lock, and when the gate swung open we all ran like the hammers of hell."

"Holy God," Henry breathed.

"God had nothing to do with it. Ourselves alone, that's who pulled it off. And it wasn't over yet. When we got to the road we saw several courting couples out walking together, nurses and soldiers from the local military hospital. Dev was unusual-looking enough to attract notice, so Harry whipped off the heavy fur coat he was wearing and wrapped it around Dev. Dev turned up the collar to hide his face, then linked Harry's arm and they strolled off together like another pair of lovers. The 'woman' in the fur coat was uncommonly tall and gawky, but the genuine lovers didn't pay a blind bit of notice, even when Dev and Harry said 'goodnight' to them in their deep voices. The courting lads and lassies had other things on their minds."

Henry was shaking his head. "Still, I marvel at the neck of you—the sheer brass neck of the lot of you!"

"Nothing succeeds like effrontery," Ned laughed. "We walked to Lincoln town as cool as you please, although I had to sit down by the side of the road once and put my head down for a few minutes. Mick had one of his men waiting at a pub with a motorcab. Mick and Harry went to Worksop to catch the train for London; then a different cab took the rest of us to Sheffield and we changed cars again. Another of Mick's men drove us on to Manchester. A safe house had been arranged for us there, but Dev was put up at the local presbytery. Mick had told the priest he would arrive by midnight, and he actually walked in the door at 12:05."

Henry said, "Leave it to de Valera to go to a priest's house."

"Actually, it wasn't such a great idea. The British police started watching the presbytery, so Dev had to move again. The rest of us were all right where we were, though; we only had to stay out of sight and wait. Mick had us smuggled out of England one at a time. I came back to Ireland on the mailboat with false whiskers and a false identity Mick had borrowed for me from the postal employees register. It really was quite an adventure. I'm almost sorry to see it end," he added, stifling a yawn.

"Is de Valera in Dublin now?" Henry asked eagerly. "I'm writing for the newspapers again, thanks to your Mick Collins, and if de Valera would give me an interview . . ."

"I know he made it back to Ireland without being picked up, but I don't know where he is at the moment. I'm just back myself, remember? He might be with his wife and children in Greystones, or he might have thought it safer for them if he stayed away. I'm sure Mick can tell you, though. I have to report to him in the morning. You come with me, then maybe I'll go with you to de Valera. I'd like to see the Chief again myself."

"The Chief?"

"That's what we began calling Dev in prison. *Taoiseach* in Irish. There was no other name for him. I wish you could have seen him, Henry. He organized sports days at Lincoln to make us keep fit, then won the mile himself and the weight throwing, too. He made sure all the Irish prisoners went to Mass, he held classes in Irish and mathematics—he even read Machiavelli and discussed some of his ideas with us."

Henry raised his eyebrows. "Dev was reading *The Prince* in prison?"

"Indeed. The Chief admires Machiavelli's work immensely.[3] He quoted us that bit about the ideal state being a republic, and he said the concept of a citizen army could safeguard our republic's future. He was always planning for the future—he even had a typewriter sent in and taught himself to type. He was so resolute that he simply carried us along with him, like warriors of old marching behind their chieftain."

In Ned's eyes Henry saw the light that once shone when he spoke of Pádraic Pearse.

Ned's found himself a new demigod, Henry thought later, lying sleepless in his bed. *We Irish need a hero, and we have an inborn reverence for teachers. But I wonder if Ned ever recognizes any flaws in his idols. Or do they always appear to him as perfect and whole?* With a weary sigh, he turned over to pound his pillow.

THE next morning Ned took Henry to the intelligence office Michael Collins had set up on Crow Street—two hundred yards from Dublin Castle.[4] The sign over the door read THE IRISH PRODUCTS CO. In charge was a bony, deceptively listless individual called Liam Tobin. When they asked for Collins he told them, "The Big Fellow hardly ever comes here." The words were hardly out of his mouth when Mick bounded through the door, bareheaded, shaking the rain from his hair. "It's all right, Liam, I know these men." He greeted Henry with a broad smile and a hearty handshake. "Great to see you! Don't suppose you have a fag you can spare, do you? . . . Thanks! Now if you'll just wait a few minutes while I debrief your friend, Liam here will entertain you."

Collins ushered Ned into a back room. They were gone for half an hour. Liam Tobin was not an entertaining conversationalist. There was only so much one could say about the weather, and he said it in the first five minutes. After that Henry read the newspaper clippings on the walls— many of them written by himself—pared his fingernails with his pocketknife, then stood staring out the window with his thumbs hooked under his braces. Collins had taken his last cigarette.

At last the two men returned. "I have no objection to your seeing Dev," Collins told Henry. "In fact, an interview with him about the escape is the very thing I want. Great propaganda value." He shrugged his meaty shoulders. "But it's up to him, of course."

"Is de Valera in Dublin?"

"He is. I got him out of England disguised as a priest and arranged for him to stow away in the second mate's cabin on the *Cambria*. He's had several hiding places since he got back. Right now he's at the archbishop's palace in Drumcondra."

Henry caught Ned's eye and winked. *The archbishop's palace. Naturally.*

As they made their way across the city to Drumcondra, Henry remarked to Ned, "Collins seemed a bit stiff when he spoke of de Valera. Have they quarreled?"

"Of course not. Mick's loyalty to the Chief is total. But . . ."

"But what?"

"Well, there is a difference of opinion. As you know, from the executions in 1916 until the founding of the Dáil, the Irish government was in the hands of the IRB. They considered the president of their supreme council to be the president of the Republic. Mick says the IRB has now voluntarily ceded all its powers to the Dáil except one—the presidency. That remains with the supreme council. The Chief doesn't agree. He says the Dáil's constitution makes its president the president of the Republic as well."

Henry gave a low whistle. "I wouldn't call that a mere 'difference of opinion.' "

"Och, they'll sort it out, Henry. They're friends; they're not going to fall out over the simple politics of who bears the title of president."

"Politics," Henry told his friend, "is never simple."

DE Valera was not in the archbishop's stately residence, but in the gatelodge. The archbishop was supposedly unaware of his presence. When Henry knocked at the door of the lodge a muffled voice asked his name and business. He gave both, plus the password Collins had supplied, and after a few moments the door was opened by de Valera himself.

Henry's initial impression of the man was that repeated imprisonments were taking their toll. His face was deeply seamed and his lips had narrowed perceptibly. Any lingering joy of life had been burned away from him as if in a crucible. Having just come from seeing Michael Collins, Henry could not help comparing the two. De Valera's grave demeanor was in marked contrast to Collins' joyous vitality.

Ducking his head under a low ceiling, de Valera led Henry and Ned down a passageway to a small sitting room. An unmade cot stood against one wall; the windows were tightly curtained. There were only two armchairs, which de Valera insisted his guests take. He folded himself onto a straight chair that was too small for him and sat with his knees jutting out while he and Ned briefly reminisced about their recent escape. De Valera was not good at small talk. He soon turned to Henry and said, "If you want an interview we had best do it now. I won't be here much longer."

"Is Collins shifting you again?"

The thin lips tightened. "My movements are my own decision."

"Of course," said Henry quickly, taking out his pencil and notebook.

De Valera answered his questions but volunteered nothing. If Henry wanted more, he had to ask. In this manner he learned that Cathal Brugha had visited de Valera in England after the prison escape and persuaded him to come back to Ireland.

"Why do you say he persuaded you? Were you not planning to come home?"

"It was my intention to go straight to America," de Valera replied.

Henry's pencil halted in mid-flight. "America? Whatever for?"

"For the sake of the Republic, of course. We have to have support from America; she is the only country strong enough at the moment to stand up to Britain. I shall be going there in a few weeks in any case. I hope to meet with President Wilson and ask him to reconsider his position vis-à-vis the peace conference."

"That's a mission for a head of state," said Henry, watching de Valera's eyes.

The man whom Ned called the Chief gazed back at him impassively. But something glowed, far down.

Aha.

"What will you do if Wilson won't see you?"

"Go over his head and appeal to the people. We have great support among the members of the Irish-American community, you know."

"My own sister, for one," Ned interjected. "I'll give you her address. I'm sure she would be delighted to help any way she can." He held out his hand and Henry passed him the pencil and a sheet of paper from his notebook. Ned scribbled down Kathleen's address and gave it to de Valera.

As he went over his notes that night in preparation for writing the article, Henry jotted down a possible opening line. "In spite of his worn appearance, Eamon de Valera remains unbroken and unbending."

Chapter Twenty-one

DE Valera's escape and the subsequent explosion of publicity thrilled the Irish. Every newspaper containing "Dev" stories was snapped up as soon as it appeared on the streets. The people were starved for good news. Influenza was sweeping the country and times, as always, were hard.

Influenza was also rampant in the British prisons. When Pierce MacCann, a member of Dáil Éireann, died in Gloucester Jail, the House of Commons decided to release the remaining Irish prisoners to avoid more unfavorable international publicity. The hunt for the Lincoln escapees was called off.

Now that it was considered safe for de Valera to appear in public, Collins wanted Dublin to honor him with a huge civic welcome and the keys to the city. When preparations were well underway, Dublin Castle banned all public gatherings and brought additional soldiers into the city. Collins was unperturbed, but at de Valera's request the ceremony was cancelled to prevent violence.

De Valera did attend the second sitting of the Dáil, which was held in secret. Henry Mooney was flattered to be invited as the only representative of the press. De Valera was re-elected *Príomh-Aire*. Michael Collins was appointed minister for finance.[1] Arthur Griffith became minister for home affairs; Count Plunkett, foreign affairs; Cathal Brugha, defense; Eoin MacNeill, industry; and W. T. Cosgrave, local government. Constance Markievicz was named the minister for labor, the first woman in the British Isles ever to hold a ministerial post.

Henry chuckled as he wrote down her name, deciding the rebel countess would get an additional newspaper column for herself.

For your scrapbook, Little Business.

In further appointments Seán T. O'Kelly became speaker of the Dáil and Richard Mulcahy was made the chief of staff of the Republican Army. The Dáil also certified the issuance of Irish government bonds in the amount of £250,000, to be known informally as the Dáil Loan, and entrusted Collins with their sale.

That night as he sat at the table in number 16, Henry remarked, "I've never seen a man able to do as many jobs as Collins. My mam used to boast that her father could do everything, but he was only in the ha'penny place compared to the Big Fellow. Collins is doing everything but running the army."

"My papa can do everything," Precious said with confidence.

Henry met Ned's eyes across the table. "I envy you," he said.

"You know I can't do everything."

"That wasn't what I meant. I envy you a love that believes you can."

ON the eighth of April, Sinn Féin held a public Árd Fheis. Arthur Griffith proposed the name of Eamon de Valera for re-election as the president of Sinn Féin and he was voted in unanimously. De Valera spent the next several weeks catching up with his family and handling various political matters. This included signing, together with Arthur Griffith and Count Plunkett, a letter to Georges Clemenceau repudiating Britain's claim to speak for Ireland.[2] And as always, there were factions among the Republicans that had to be placated and held together. But he was more determined than ever to go to America.

"When the time comes, Mick will make de Valera's travel

arrangements," Ned told Henry. Ned was ill again, dizzy and pale and spending the day in bed under Síle's watchful eye. Henry had come up after work to keep him company for an hour or so.

"Detectives from G Division are watching the Chief in four-hour shifts," Ned went on, "so the plan is to snatch him away during a shift change. I wish I could go with him, but Síle won't hear of it. Besides, Mick has Harry Boland in the States already and he can look after him." Ned's sunken eyes took on a faint gleam. "I was at Vaughan's Hotel with some of the boys the night before Harry left. A grand night it was, too. The last thing I remember is Mick and Harry and me standing on a table with our arms around each other's shoulders while we sang, 'Oh, the fighting races won't die out if they seldom die in bed.' "

Henry could well imagine the scene, but the reporter in him was intrigued by something else. "How does Collins know about the four-hour shifts?"

Ned managed a grin. "Recently Ned Broy smuggled Mick into Detective Headquarters in Brunswick Street and he spent the whole night going through their files. When he left he took the detectives' day book with him as a souvenir. He knows more about what the police are up to, minute by minute, than Dublin Castle does."

DE Valera set off from Greystones on the first of June, taking the boat from Kingstown to Holyhead. When he reached Liverpool, Collins' men smuggled him aboard a liner bound for America. Most of his voyage was spent hidden away in the lamplighter's cabin and fighting seasickness.

While de Valera was at sea, Woodrow Wilson was at Versailles. In private he expressed sympathy with the plight of Ireland, but he was still unwilling to antagonize the British. On the eleventh of June he summoned the Irish contingent to inform them that after due study and consultation he still would not support their claim. Not only would Article 10 of the League of Nations stand; it was part of the peace treaty being drafted by the international conference.

"Just wait till the Chief gets to America," Ned told Henry. "He'll turn things around, you'll see."

Henry murmured, " 'And bloody Faith, the foulest birth of time.' "

"Shelley. From *Feelings of a Republican*. I didn't know you read poetry, Henry."

"I have plenty of time to read in my room at night."

Alone in my room at night. While life goes on elsewhere. I must be a fool.

ONE June evening Henry returned to number 16 to find Precious lying on her stomach on the floor of the parlor. She was propped on her elbows and poring over the *Irish Times*. When she looked up, her face was suffused with excitement. "Uncle Henry, you'll never guess what's happened."

"I suspect you're going to tell me. But should you not be sitting in a chair before someone comes in and sees you?"

She snorted contemptuously. Without changing position, she read aloud, 'The first nonstop aeroplane flight across the Atlantic has been successfully completed. Today Captain John Alcock from Britain and Lieutenant Arthur Whitten Brown from the United States landed in a bog on the Irish coast at Clifden. Their Rolls-Royce–powered biplane was fitted with long-range fuel tanks and made the 1,900-mile flight from Newfoundland in sixteen hours, twelve minutes. Sustained during the flight by coffee, beer, sandwiches, and chocolate, the men flew through fog and sleet storms.' Can you imagine, Uncle Henry? Flying all the way across the ocean in an aeroplane?"

"I can't imagine," Henry said honestly. "It must have been terrible."

"Oh, no. It must have been wonderful!"

WITHIN weeks of de Valera's departure, Michael Collins replaced Seán MacGarry as the president of the supreme council of the IRB.

•   •   •

NED knocked on the door of Henry's room and entered without waiting for a reply. "Are you doing anything?"

With a sigh, Henry put down his pencil. "Nothing at all. Just trying to write."

"I've been trying to write too; I need to work on my novel. But my eyes . . . Anyway, I thought you'd like some good news. I just received this from my sister Kathleen." Ned held up a letter. "She belongs to an organization called the Friends of Irish Freedom and they gave the Chief a huge reception at the Waldorf-Astoria. Afterward he held a press conference attended by all the major newspapers.

"And listen to this, Henry. A reporter asked de Valera if he was an American citizen and he said, 'I am an *Irish* citizen.' When they insisted on knowing if he had renounced his American citizenship he said, and I quote, 'I ceased to be an American when I became a soldier of the Irish Republic.'"[3]

That's a revealing answer, Henry told himself. *De Valera won't officially relinquish his American citizenship, because it gives him a degree of protection from the British and an emotional toehold in the States. He's very clever. Bold gestures on the surface, deeply conservative underneath.*

I wonder if he took his copy of Machiavelli to America with him.

HENRY Mooney had become a frequent visitor to Herbert Place. The affection the Mansells felt for one another permeated the atmosphere; their warmth extended to envelop him from the moment he entered the door. He had become a Friend of the Family. "Everybody likes you," Madge Mansell confided, "because your visits always cheer my sister. She's been so lonely since her husband . . . you know."

When Ella Rutledge offered Henry one of her sketches, he had it framed and hung it over his bed where his mother would have hung a crucifix. But they did not have an "understanding." They had not even exchanged caresses. Henry was Catholic and Ella was Protestant. An intimate relationship would face daunting obstacles.

Yet Henry felt waves of almost overpowering desire for

Ella, a passion that, he realized, owed much of its intensity to the fact that it could not be consummated. It fed in the dark spaces of his being, growing honeyed and heavy, a suffocating pressure at the back of his throat, a maddening distraction when he was trying to concentrate on something else.

At Herbert Place Henry enjoyed a quality of life he had never experienced before. Hester Burgess was an excellent cook, though her repertoire was limited to English menus such as clear turtle soup, turbot with lobster sauce, roast mutton, pheasants and port jelly. The paneled library was redolent of leather bindings and fine cigars. Most of the volumes were English rather than by or about the Irish, because Edwin Mansell was an unabashed admirer of all things English. But as Henry sank into the depths of a comfortable armchair with a copy of Dryden's literary criticisms and a glass of vintage port, he could not complain.

Leisurely pursuits amidst gracious surroundings. A private telephone and an extensive wine cellar. A fireplace in every room and, on chill days, a fire in every fireplace. A way of life sustainable almost without reference to the outside world. No one seemed to worry about how the bills would be paid. The money was simply there; it always had been.

How seductive it is, Henry admitted to himself. *How can we condemn the beneficiaries of the empire for wanting to hold on to what they have?*

SNUG in their haven, the Mansells were confident of their future. But beyond the sheltering walls of Herbert Place the winds of change were blowing.

Sinn Féin, through the Dáil, was putting in place the basic bureaucratic structures required by a new nation. Courts were being set up and a consular service organized. Departments were being established to address the problems of farmers and fishermen. A commission of inquiry had begun looking into industrial resources.

Faced with the obstinate determination of the Irish to govern themselves, Dublin Castle's reaction was draconian. Respectable citizens were stopped and searched in the street for no reason, and with no apology given. Motorists had to carry passes and were halted outside the larger towns. Sometimes they were kept waiting for hours at gunpoint, even after they had proved they were traveling on legitimate business.

Foreign journalists sent to cover an increasingly explosive situation reported to readers abroad: "Soldiers with fixed bayonets parade the streets of Dublin, restraining crowds of angry civilians. A machine-gun post has been set up facing Liberty Hall. Whole districts of the Irish capital are surrounded by military cordons. The quays are so choked with troops and armored vehicles that the port could be mistaken for the base of a formidable expeditionary force."[4]

The violence was not all on one side. G Division was the lynchpin of the British intelligence service in Ireland. Within two days of Michael Collins' midnight visit to the files of G Division, political detectives bringing charges against Republicans began receiving warnings to back off. Sometimes the warning came from a civilian whispering in a doorway, sometimes from a party of Republicans paying a visit to his house. One G-man was simply told the time of the next boat leaving Ireland.

At first the penalty for ignoring a warning was relatively harmless. An unfortunate detective was gagged and chained to the railings of the Brunswick Street police station, to his own humiliation and the great amusement of local street urchins.

Then matters grew more serious. A detective called Patrick Smith arrested a leading Republican on the grounds of a dossier forged in Dublin Castle. In spite of several warnings, Smith refused to be intimidated into dropping charges. He was shot—shot suddenly and unexpectedly, by a mysterious team who knew exactly where to find their man. Other shootings followed, including that of Lee Wilson, now an RIC district inspector in Gorey, who had publicly stripped and humiliated Tom Clarke the night of the surrender. Another who met the same fate was the detective who had picked out Seán MacDermott for the firing squad.

One Sunday afternoon Ella remarked, "I just cannot see how it's to end, Henry. Imagine the working classes trying to take government into their own hands. It's so . . . precipitate."

This was the closest they had come to discussing politics, and he answered before he thought. "Precipitate? We've been trying for over seven centuries to get our freedom back."

"Well, impetuous then. And foolish besides. Consider all the benefits accruing to Ireland as a result of being part of the empire. The English have brought civilization to an ignorant, uncouth people who were little more than barbarians."

"Is that what you really believe?"

"It's the truth."

"Who told you it was the truth?"

"Really, Henry. We learned it in school, of course."

"A British school. Ella, don't you know that history is always taught by the conquerors?" That said, Henry quickly changed the subject. He felt they were on dangerous ground.

THE Mansells were a close-knit family, devoted to one another. It was no wonder Ella had chosen to return to them after her husband's death. Ava was a self-absorbed bird of paradise, but aside from her snobbery there was no harm in her. "She and Edwin haven't had children yet because she's afraid they would ruin her figure," Madge once confided to Henry. A talented pianist, Ava often invited family and guests to gather around while she played and sang polite ballads such as "Speak to Me, Flora."

Madge, nineteen, was the youngest of the family. Although she loved foxhunting, she brought home an endless succession of injured stray animals and birds fallen from nests and nursed them back to health. Her contralto voice blended well with Henry's bass-baritone when they gathered around the piano, but sometimes she sang naughty music-hall lyrics from London under her breath, making it impossible for him to keep a straight face.

The longer Henry knew Edwin Mansell, the better he liked him. A confirmed Anglophile, Edwin possessed the best qualities of the race he admired. He was dignified and unfailingly courteous, as befitted a man certain of his place in the world. But Ella privately told Henry, "My brother's not so self-assured when he goes to England. He resents the fact that over there, they consider him an Irishman."

"That's all they know," Henry said. "Edwin doesn't bemoan and begrudge enough to be Irish."

When Edwin returned from London after his eye treatment Henry was his first visitor. Edwin was still wearing an eyepatch. "I have some sight restored, but not much. The eye needs to be shielded from the light as much as possible, so I shall continue to look like a bloody pirate. No harm, really. It rather puts the clients in awe of me."

"You intend to keep working as a solicitor?"

"Of course, old chap—with the added benefit that I shan't be expected to enlist in the next war."

"You think there will be a next war?"

For once Edwin's optimism failed. "Surely you've read the published text of the Treaty of Versailles. It has a war guilt clause intended to punish the German people by demanding enormous reparations that will bankrupt the country. Germany won't accept that for long; no great nation would. The Allies haven't guaranteed peace with the treaty. The War to End All Wars will simply be the cause of another war."

"You may be right," Henry agreed, thinking of another, smaller nation that would suffer at least indirectly because of the Versailles Treaty.

"I am right—though God knows I wish I weren't. No sane man wants war. Oh, I grant you the idea of the noble warrior is glamorous. When the war first broke out, my friends and I rushed to enlist. After all, I was a Mansell, heir to a family tradition of military service, et cetera, et cetera. Looking back, I realize the only reason we were so enthusiastic is because none of us had any battlefield experience. We had no concept of what we were getting into. Neither did the girls we knew. They cheered us on like spectators at a sports day."

Henry said thoughtfully, "I suppose if a man knew he was immortal, he might actually enjoy a war."

"We thought we were immortal," Edwin replied, "right up

until the moment we faced the guns and the gas. God, the gas! And the grenades. You can't imagine what grenades do to human bodies. Yet I actually saw men taking photographs of the corpses for souvenirs. They were absolutely fascinated by them—the more ghastly, the better. What makes anyone want to look at such things?"

"The fatal attraction of violence," said Henry.

Henry applied to several newspapers for an assignment to cover de Valera in America. *Maybe even get to meet Ned's beautiful sister, Kathleen.* The Long Fellow's progression across the United States was a triumph. In New York's Madison Square Garden he had addressed fifty thousand people, and seventy thousand people had gathered at Boston's Fenway Park to hear him speak about the Irish Republic. Such events, Henry argued, certainly should be covered by a reporter from home. But "Sorry, we don't have enough money to send you" was always the answer.

In a way Henry was relieved. He was increasingly dissatisfied with the role of observer. In his secret heart, he craved action.

He was not the only one. Without Dáil sanction, but with the full knowledge and approval of Michael Collins as well as the head of the army, Richard Mulcahy, rural Republicans were waging a campaign against what they called "the army of occupation." In August a number of RIC barracks were attacked and their supplies commandeered. Constables who surrendered were released unharmed, but if they fought to protect their weapons, the Republicans fought back.

In September the Second Cork Brigade, commanded by Liam Lynch, encountered a company of British soldiers on the road to Fermoy. Angry words were exchanged. During the skirmish that followed a soldier was killed. Next day two hundred British soldiers were turned loose on the little town of Fermoy. They looted and sacked the shops and terrorized the citizenry for hours—yet received no reprimand from their superiors.

"There was a time," Henry Mooney wrote in white heat for the *Freeman's Journal*, "when these bully-boy tactics would have worked; when we Irish were cowed and submissive. But no more. We fought for our freedom in 1916 and we shall again. And again and again until it is won."

Ned Halloran was blunt in his appraisal. "This is more than political commentary; it's a naked threat. If you're not careful, they'll come after you."

Chapter Twenty-two

In September Dáil Éireann was proscribed by the British government. Dublin Castle called it "a parliament of felons." Warrants were issued for the arrest of TDs.

It was a declaration of war.

Within days the DMP raided Sinn Féin headquarters in Harcourt Street and arrested two prominent party members. Michael Collins was working upstairs in the finance office. After a jovial exchange with one of the arresting officers—who failed to recognize him—he sauntered down the passageway and escaped out a skylight.

Newspaper censorship returned. Henry started soliciting book reviews and fillers again to take up the slack in his income.

Military aggression against civilians increased alarmingly. More private houses were raided, more people arrested on the flimsiest grounds or none at all, more innocent social gatherings dispersed at gunpoint. Markets were forbidden to advertise "Irish" produce. Farmers' meetings were suppressed by soldiers with armored vehicles.[1]

Nationalists responded with a grim exhilaration. "If they want a fight, we'll give it to them!" was the oft-repeated slogan, not only in pubs and on street corners but even in the vestibules of churches.

An English journalist voiced alarm: "Fears are being expressed that we may see a repeat of the Amritsar Massacre in Ireland." The reference was to an event that had taken place in India on the thirteenth of April, when British government troops fired on a gathering of Indian protesters and killed 379.

In October Sinn Féin held its autumn Árd Fheis in secret—after midnight. Once again it was covered by Henry Mooney. "I'm worried about the split that's developing," he said to Ned afterwards. "There's little doubt that Collins and Mulcahy want an all-out war to finish what was started in 1916, while the majority of the Sinn Féin executive is following de Valera's lead: less militant and more political."

"Like you," Ned remarked.

Henry frowned. "I wouldn't say that. No."

A sealed note delivered on a frosty autumn evening summoned Henry to Vaughan's Hotel. After giving the password at the desk he was shown to a back room. Tightly closed curtains, air thick with cigarette smoke. Secrets soaked like patterns into the wallpaper.

Michael Collins was deep in conversation with two other men, both of whom Henry knew. One was Desmond Fitz-Gerald, who had been the officer in charge of the canteen in the GPO during the Rising. He was now the director of publicity for the Dáil. The other man, Frank Gallagher, was a journalist from Cork who had covered the home rule debates in Westminster while still in his teens. He also had been a Volunteer, and he and Erskine Childers were running the Republican Publicity Bureau.

Collins greeted Henry with "We have a job for you if you want it."

"Can I take off my hat first?"

"I'm serious. Now that the commercial Republican papers are banned again, the Dáil wants to circulate a newsletter to tell the truth about what's going on. Arthur Griffith's very enthusiastic about the idea. The intention is to publish reports and commentaries from prominent nationalists like Erskine Childers, and I suggested you'd be a valuable addition to the staff, Henry."

"Who do you have on board so far?"

Indicating Gallagher, Desmond FitzGerald said, "Gally here will be the chief compiler, and I'll serve as editor. My secretary, Kathleen McKenna, will do our typing, and Anna Fitzsimons, who works at Sinn Féin headquarters, will glean additional news items for us from the daily press. We've recruited one of the Fíanna boys to be office boy and general factotum."

"Dogsbody," Henry muttered, making a mental note to be kind to him. "Where's the office going to be?"

"That's a good question," Gallagher replied. A slim man with raven-wing hair and an engaging personality, he was well liked in the journalistic community. "We'll start off at Sinn Féin headquarters in Harcourt Street, but since the Castle will probably outlaw us after the first issue, that may not be a permanent address. And there's one other thing—we won't be able to pay you. We'll have to operate on a voluntary basis."

"With an inducement like that, how can I refuse?"

Collins gave him a hearty thump on the back. "Good on ye, boyo. Say, do you happen to have a smoke you can spare?"

That night at number 16 Ned warned, "Mick's itching for a fight, and this newsletter idea sounds like it will hot things up considerably. But you're not a fighter, Henry. So take my advice and steer clear."

Not a fighter. A muscle jumped in Henry's jaw. "Advice is only advice if it's asked for, Ned. Otherwise it's interference."

THE first issue of the new *Irish Bulletin* was dated November 11, 1919. Printed on a multigraph, the folded newsletter measured barely five by seven inches. The office boy addressed envelopes for the initial subscribers, a mailing list of around thirty, and then he and Henry took copies around to the other Dublin newspapers and to the hotels where foreign correspondents usually stayed.

Henry could not resist sending a *Bulletin* to Limerick. "I'm working for this publication now," he wrote to his mother, "and we feel that what we're doing is very important."

By return post he received a painfully scrawled one-line note from Hannah Mooney. "Do it pay good?"

At Henry's request Ned sent copies of the *Bulletin* to his sister, Kathleen, in New York to distribute to the American press. She wrote back, "Your friend is a great success over here. He is being introduced everywhere as Eamon de Valera, president of the Irish Republic."

One evening Henry dropped into Phil Shanahan's public house, another favorite haunt of Republicans. Sitting by the door was Peadar Kearney, author of "A Soldier's Song," the unofficial republican anthem.[2] Henry was about to stop for a chat when a familiar face emerged from the shadows at the end of the bar.

"Cousin Henry!" cried Dan Breen.

Henry's jaw dropped. "What the hell are you doing here? Don't you know there's a price on your head?"

"And going up all the time," Breen added proudly. "It's my shout; what are you drinking?"

They took their pints to a tiny table at the back of the pub. "How long have you been in Dublin?" was Henry's first question, followed immediately by "Why did you not look me up?"

"Och, I knew we'd run across each other sooner rather than later. Dublin's just a small town stretched out, though it took me a while to realize that. But once me and Seán got acclimatized . . ."

"Seán who?"

"Treacy. Pal of mine. We've been up here a while now. It got too hot for us down the country, so the Big Fellow reeled us in."

"You mean Michael Collins?"

"I do of course. We're in his counterintelligence squad now. He thought our talents could be—how did he put it?— better employed under his supervision."

"You said it was too hot for you down the country. What's been happening? The last I heard of you was Soloheadbeg."

"Soloheadbeg." Breen shook his head. "That went badly

wrong. We had expected half a dozen RIC men, so we brought enough of our lads to overpower them. But there were only two constables on guard, and when they saw they were outnumbered they panicked. Afterward we took the horse and cart and buried the gelignite in a safe place, but unfortunately the frost got to it and spoilt it, so it was never used."

"Whose orders were you acting on? Sinn Féin's?"

Breen glowered under his heavy eyebrows. "Those stuffed shirts in the Dáil want us to sit with our hands folded and take whatever shite the Brits dump on us. They knew nothing about Soloheadbeg; it was strictly army business. Anyway, we'd put the cat among the pigeons for sure, so we decided if we were going to be outlaws we'd be outlaws for Ireland. We devoted ourselves to tracking down spies and informers in Tipperary and giving them what they deserved. There's more of them than you'd think. The British are spending money like water to crush the Republican movement. We saw terrible things, Henry—things being done to our people. There's lots goes on in the dark in this country that will never see the light of day.

"The country people were wonderful to us, though. They appreciated what we were doing. Many's the night some patriot family gave us their warm beds so we could have a rest while we were on the run. Then one of our lads, Seán Hogan, was caught as he was leaving a dance. Now they're shooting Republican prisoners 'for trying to escape,' but when they took Seán the practice had not yet begun. They hustled him off under guard to Thurles Barracks. They meant to hang him, because some informer told them he was with us at Soloheadbeg. Hang a boy not yet eighteen years old," Breen said bitterly. He paused and took a deep drink.

"We knew we couldn't break him out of the army barracks; it's a fortress. So we waited until they had him on a train bound for the prison in Cork. Eight of us intercepted them at Knocklong. It was a battle from the moment we boarded the train, Henry. We meant to get Seán Hogan or die trying. One of the constables handcuffed to Seán put his revolver to Seán's head when we burst into their compartment. He was about to pull the trigger, but we shot first. In the finish-up one constable was dead and another dying. But we hadn't hurt any passengers, and we rescued Hogan."

It was Henry's turn to take a long drink. "What happened then?"

"There was an inquest and the local jury refused to bring in a verdict of murder. They blamed the government for exposing policemen to danger and demanded self-determination for Ireland. But we were on the run for sure, after that. What with arrests and illness and one thing and another, eventually there were just the four of us: me and Seán Treacy and Séamus Robinson and Seán Hogan. People helped us, fed us, hid us. We had more close escapes than you've had hot dinners. British soldiers scouring the countryside for us. Bluffed our way past 'em, several times. Some of the Irish police recognized us but let us go. Their hearts were with us, whatever about their heads.

"Things got pretty difficult for us after a while. Walking through the mountains at night, with our shoes so worn out there was only a bit of sole and the laces left. Stumbling into bogs. Sleeping in barns and ditches. Trying to keep each other's spirits up. Sometimes it felt like we were the only ones fighting for Ireland."

"You weren't," Henry assured him. "There've been plenty of incidents all across the country."

"Maybe we were just the coldest and hungriest. Anyway, we finally made contact with the Big Fellow and had a frank talk with him. He brought us up to Dublin and here we are, as busy as a fiddler's elbow."

DURING the second week in December Sinn Féin party headquarters in Harcourt Street was again raided. A number of members of Dáil Éireann were arrested. Kathleen and the office boy managed to sneak the *Bulletin*'s files and equipment out and took them to the Farm Produce Shop in Baggot Street for the night. Next day the newsletter office was transferred to the basement of a house in Rathmines.

On the nineteenth of December Lord-Lieutenant French was ambushed at Ashtown. He escaped uninjured, but one of his armed escort shot dead a young Republican.

Michael Collins exploded into the basement office. Henry looked up from the table where he and Anna Fitzsimons were assembling the next day's newsletter by lamplight. "Leave the hinges on the door, will you?"

Collins was in no mood for humor. "Martin Savage was my friend—we were in the GPO together Easter Week. Now those bastards have killed him." He slammed his fist against the wall. "We'd been planning that ambush for weeks; it should have run like clockwork."

"By 'we,' I assume you mean your assassination team?"

Collins favored Henry with a ferocious scowl. "You disapprove of my counterintelligence squad?"

"I was just inquiring."

"I told you a long time ago we were going to fight the enemy with their own weapons. Look how many of our people they've killed."

"Those weren't assassinations, Mick."

"No? An assassination is a political murder. Think back, Henry. When the Proclamation was signed, the signatories formed a provisional government with Tom Clarke as its president because he'd been the first to sign.[3] But Clarke was an old IRB man who preferred to work in the background. So they made Pádraic Pearse the president of the Irish Republic in addition to being the commander-in-chief. When the British shot Pearse, they were shooting a head of state. That's why they killed him first. Then they shot Clarke and the other signatories. I don't know what you could call that but assassination on a large scale."

"In our case," said Henry, "the British called it execution. For treason."

"Well then, we intended to execute the lord-lieutenant of Ireland. For tyranny."

"Is that what you want us to write in the *Bulletin*?" Henry asked innocently. Anna Fitzsimons covered her mouth with her hand to stifle a laugh.

Collins' scowl dissolved into a grin. "You might tone it down a bit—make it more palatable for people to digest with their tea and biscuits."

"Can murder ever be made palatable?"

"I'm not going to get into that old does-the-end-justify-the-means argument with you, Henry. We're just paying the British back in their own coin. I'm not bloodthirsty, though, and I won't allow my men to be. They're only sent after selected military targets, such as spies in the pay of Dublin Castle. Spies don't have the soldier mentality. When we shoot one down, there's not another marching up behind him like a good little soldier to fill his shoes. And even if a replacement is found, he doesn't have the dead man's knowledge, so valuable information is lost forever. The squad's mission is to make the British intelligence service deaf and blind. And it's working, mark my words. Dublin Castle's going to panic. When they hit back at us, which they will, they'll just be recruiting more men for our cause."

Henry wanted to retain the high moral ground of indignation, but that would be hypocritical, would mean denying the secret fierce joy he felt at seeing his own people outmaneuvering the ancient enemy.

THE *Bulletin* moved again, barely staying ahead of the authorities.

DAN Breen had been wounded in the attack on Lord French and was in hospital under an alias. When Henry visited him, he found Breen reading a copy of the *Irish Independent*. "This rag's calling young Savage a wanton murderer, Henry. I won't have a dead comrade insulted that way. When I get out of here, we're going to shut the *Independent* down."

Henry held up one hand. "Whoa there! Suppressing the news is what the British do—we don't want to fall into that trap. Besides, during the Rising some of the *Independent* staff were Volunteers."

But recalling his own parting from Murphy's newspaper, Henry thought to himself, *I hope you do shut them down. Serve them right. They forget that their readers voted for the establishment of the Republic.*

The actions of Collins' squad were having a paralyzing effect on the intelligence service. Pressured by an opponent as invisible and relentless as a swarm of gnats, the government became more repressive than ever. The authorities hit back blindly out of pride. This in turn generated more support for the Republicans, as Collins had predicted. New IRA recruiting offices were opened to meet the demand.

"Mick has what country people call 'an eye for the gap'— he knows how to exploit a weakness," Henry remarked to Ned one morning as they left number 16 together. Henry was on his way to the *Bulletin* office; Ned was going to buy some nails and putty. At the bottom of the steps Ned turned to wave back at Síle and Precious, who, as always, were watching from the window.

Henry did not allow himself to look back.

"You've become a Collins man in spite of my warning," Ned said as they walked down the street together.

"I'm not anyone's man but my own," Henry assured him. "But I can't help liking Mick. Everyone does. In some ways he's like a cocky little boy thumbing his nose at the teacher and in other ways he's the shrewdest man I've ever met. In spite of working thirty-six hours a day, he's very methodical and precise about details." Henry added with a chuckle, "You might say the Big Fellow's a painstaking man. He takes pains and gives them to others."

"You could hardly call him an idealist like the Chief, though."

"Idealism got us as far as 1916, Ned, but it didn't win the war. Mick Collins is a realist, and that's what we need now. I used to agree with Griffith's philosophy, but I'm beginning to think politics is just a more subtle form of violence—a way for those who have power to exercise it over those who don't."

How do you explain, Henry wondered to himself, *the process by which you come to a different way of thinking? It takes place below the surface; the mind follows an imperceptible pathway marked by invisible signposts.*

To many Erskine Childers was an enigmatic figure. Born in London to an Ascendancy family, he had been mustered out of the Royal Air Force with the rank of major and had served for a time as a committee clerk in the House of Com-

mons. A small, spare man with a permanent limp resulting
from sciatica and a permanent thirst for adventure nothing
could quell, Childers was a best-selling novelist, daring
yachtsman, and motorcycle enthusiast . . . and had become a
dedicated Irish nationalist.

He continued to maintain a number of English connections, however—though his wife, Molly, was a confirmed
Anglophobe. Childers frequently wrote for the London papers and had been commissioned by the *Daily News* to write
eight articles explaining, for the average English reader,
what was going on in Ireland. Childers introduced Henry to
his British journalistic contacts, and soon he also was selling
articles there. The pay was very welcome, but Henry was
careful to keep the content of his writing as objective as
possible.

In the *Bulletin* he could say what he really felt.

ON the twenty-third of December the *Bulletin* reported, "As
a Christmas present to the people of Ireland, yesterday Lloyd
George introduced a Government of Ireland Bill with one
parliament for the six northeastern counties in Ulster and
another for the remaining twenty-six. Under this bill Ireland
would, de facto, be partitioned. The powers of both Irish
parliaments would be severely restricted and the supremacy
of the British parliament maintained."

Lloyd George then attempted to influence American opinion by comparing Ireland's fight for freedom with the secession of the Southern states during the American Civil
War. Countering the analogy, Erskine Childers wrote in the
Bulletin: "We do not attempt secession. Nations cannot se-
cede from a rule they have never accepted. We have never
accepted yours and never will. Lincoln's reputation is safe
from your comparison. He fought to abolish slavery, you
fight to maintain it. You own a third of the earth by conquest; you have great armies, a navy so powerful it can
starve a whole continent. You wield the greatest aggregate
of material force ever concentrated in the hands of one
power; and, while canting about your championship of small
nations, you use it to crush out liberty in ours. We are a

small people with a population dwindling without cessation under your rule. Nevertheless, we accept your challenge and will fight you with the same determination, with the same resolve, as the American States, north and south, put into their fight for freedom against your empire."[4]

Ned sent thirty copies of this issue of the *Bulletin* to his sister in America to distribute.

"I have put the *Bulletin* into President de Valera's hands personally," she wrote back.

De Valera's American tour had been a spectacular success. He had received pages of newspaper coverage in New York, Chicago, Boston, and San Francisco. Great crowds had attended his speeches. His appearance at Madison Square Garden had broken all records.[5] The only time he was booed was when he made an attempt to conciliate Woodrow Wilson by approving of the League of Nations. The League was not popular. In the wake of the Great War, Americans were increasingly isolationist.

De Valera had begun as a warrior, but he was getting a crash course in politics. He learned fast. His subsequent rhetoric was couched in ambiguous phrases that did not offend anyone. With deft skill he maneuvered among the various contentious Irish-American factions, courting the support of each without offending the others. Instead of coming home when originally planned, he decided to stay on in America for some months more. The Dáil, which was kept informed of his activities with frequent telegrams, named Arthur Griffith to serve as its new acting president until his return.

In his desperate clawing struggle to plant Ireland's flag, de Valera called upon "the scattered children of the Gael" to help build the new nation with support both political and financial. To circumvent laws that could stop the Irish from selling Dáil bonds in the United States, de Valera hired a sharp young lawyer who had recently left Wilson's administration. His name was Franklin Delano Roosevelt.[6]

In Ireland Michael Collins was consolidating his own support.

• • •

EARLY in the new year the *Bulletin* relocated yet again, this time to a flat on the upper floor of a private house in Upper Mount Street. Here the little newsletter received a number of important visitors, Maud Gonne MacBride among them.

Henry tried not to stare at the tall, stately woman in black who had inspired William Butler Yeats. Yeats had never made any secret of his unrequited passion for Maud Gonne. Everything in life was grist to his mill. He had even agonized in print over whether poetry of his had been responsible for sending the patriots to their deaths in 1916. *The incredible arrogance of someone who thinks the entire world revolves around him!* Henry had thought at the time.

"Maud Gonne's still the greatest beauty in Ireland," Kathleen McKenna whispered to Henry under her breath. "What do you suppose it's like, being worshipped by men?"

Henry chuckled. "Don't you know?" Kathleen was something of a beauty herself, with tiny hands and feet and a glossy mane the rich sable color of bog oak. Desmond Fitz-Gerald was fond of teasing her by saying, "When Kathleen washes her hair there's enough ink in the water for the next day's *Bulletin*."[7]

MUNICIPAL and urban elections were to be held throughout Ireland. By this means the government sought to take the reins of control firmly back into its own hands. Two weeks ahead of time, martial law was declared in the counties of Waterford, Wexford, and Kilkenny. Sinn Féin posters were torn down and speeches by Republican candidates suppressed. A Sinn Féin campaign manager found with election materials was charged with possession of seditious documents and jailed for three months.

Simultaneously Collins added three more men to his assassination squad, bringing it to an even dozen. All in their early twenties, they soon were being called "the Twelve Apostles"—although not in Collins' hearing. He was strict with the squad, demanding that no one was to be shot except under orders. "Any man who has revenge in his heart is not fit to be a Republican," he told them. But they were ruthless in seeking out approved targets. Hard men, forged in fire.

The resolve of the police force faltered. Even plainclothes detectives suddenly found urgent reasons for requesting transfers to a different division. Dublin Castle was unable to learn the whereabouts of Sinn Féin candidates in time to prevent their making speeches.

On the fifteenth of January, 1920, Ireland went to the polls. Two days later the *Bulletin* announced: "Republican candidates have won a momentous victory. Of the twelve cities and boroughs on this island, eleven have declared for the Republic. Only Belfast voted Unionist, and even there the majority was reduced. In spite of protests of Unionist solidarity, two of the six north-eastern counties which Lloyd George wants cut off from the rest of us voted solidly for Sinn Féin. Out of two hundred and six local councils elected throughout Ireland, one hundred and seventy-two have a Republican majority. Ireland has once again voted for independence. How long can Britain ignore the democratically expressed will of the people?"[8]

The *Bulletin* was not alone in celebrating Sinn Féin's victory. Nervously but with increasing optimism, newsagents were welcoming Republican newspapers back to the stands.

MICHAEL Collins peered round the door of the flat in Upper Mount Street and caught Henry's eye. His own eyes held a gleam of mischief. "D'ye want to come along and see me have my picture taken?"

Kathleen McKenna stopped typing. Henry put down the page he was proofreading. "Are you serious?"

"Too right I am. Dev's over there in America talking to bankers and businessmen, raising money for the Dáil Loan and taking all the credit. *I'm* the finance minister. We're going to make a little propaganda film ourselves, so get your hat, Henry. I have Joe Hyland waiting with his taxi to take us to Rathfarnham. Kathleen, you'll hold the fort, won't you?"

"I always do," she answered with a martyred sigh.

The two men were no sooner settled in the cab than Collins asked Henry for a cigarette.

"Don't you ever buy your own?"

Collins gave Henry a wide-eyed stare. "And where would I be findin' the time to buy fags? I have a nation to run." As if a thought had just occurred to him, he reached into his jacket pocket and took out a notebook similar to the one Henry always carried. He wrote, "Commission Frank Fitz-Gerald to source arms in America for the defense of Catholics in the north of Ireland."

Peering over his shoulder, Henry asked, "Are you serious?"

"I am of course. We can't be abandoning those people up there."

Collins' film was to be made at Saint Enda's College, the school founded by Pádraic Pearse. The photographer was John MacDonagh, a brother of the late Thomas MacDonagh. He met their motorcab at the school gates and rode up the curving drive while standing on the running board. "Since the light's good, we're going to set up a table on the lawn," MacDonagh explained to Henry through the open cab window. "We're going to photograph Mick and Diarmuid signing National Loan bonds for the ladies right here where it all started."

The ladies he referred to were Pearse's mother, Tom Clarke's widow, and James Connolly's daughter. On the broad front steps of the house they stood chatting with Diarmuid O'Hegarty, a member of the army executive committee. As soon as Margaret Pearse saw Henry emerge from the cab, she excused herself and came to greet him.

She was a graying, matronly widow with fine features and an elegantly straight nose. Before her sons, Pádraic and Willie, were executed, she had been plump. Her clothes were loose on her now. Like Hannah Mooney, Mrs. Pearse always wore black; but unlike Hannah Mooney, she exuded a genuine warmth that put people at ease. From the first time he had met her in Ned Halloran's company (*God, was it only 1913! It seems a thousand years ago*), Henry had envied the Pearse brothers their mother.

Margaret Pearse had been elected to Dáil Éireann as the

highest honor the new nation could bestow. Although she protested that she was only a simple woman with little understanding of politics, her credentials were impeccable. She had been the mother of two men; now she was mother to the Republic.

"How nice that you could come, Mr. Mooney." She took both his hands in hers and squeezed them. Her skin was dry and papery, with calluses on the palms; those hands had known a lifetime of work. "It's been far too long since we saw you last," she said. "And you brought the sunshine with you just when we need it."

"I wouldn't miss the chance to see Mick Collins sit for his photograph. I can hardly believe he's doing something so reckless."

Mrs. Pearse said gently, " 'Reckless' is a term one might apply to any courageous act, Mr. Mooney. My Pat and Willie were reckless, but without risk there is no chance of success. Mr. Collins believes this film can sell a lot of bonds for the Republic, and so it is worth doing."

Katty Clarke was the next to greet Henry. She had a long, rather somber face and a no-nonsense mouth, but her bright blue eyes were dancing as she said, "Imagine us all being film stars, Mr. Mooney!"

"You have a lovely setting for it," Henry observed, indicating the sweeping lawns leading up to the handsome house once known as the Hermitage. Pearse had almost bankrupted himself leasing the Hermitage and turning it into a school that would provide Irish boys as fine an education as any of their English contemporaries. "I'm surprised Madame Markievicz isn't here, though. I understood she was staying with you these days."

Katty's eyes clouded. "Haven't you heard yet? Con was arrested again. Last night. She went with her back straight and her chin up, spitting defiance at them."

In a flash Henry had his notebook out and was conducting an interview.

When the filming was concluded, Mrs. Pearse provided refreshments. No liquor was served. MacDonagh fiddled with his cameras while Collins and O'Hegarty talked earnestly in low voices. Balancing a cup of tea in one hand and a plate of sandwiches in the other, Henry ambled over to Mrs. Pearse. "I've been wanting to tell you how much I admire you for keeping Saint Enda's going."

"Thank you, Mr. Mooney, but I deserve no praise. I had no choice; it was what Pat would have wanted. For a little while after my boys were shot I nearly lost my mind. General Maxwell would not even let me have their bodies back. Then people began urging us to reopen the school as a monument to Pat's memory. I must confess, it was a relief to have something to do. Joseph MacDonagh was our headmaster until he was arrested in 1917, and when they were released from prison Frank Burke and Brian Joyce came back to us as teachers." She lowered her voice. "The authorities don't make it easy for us, you know."

"I'm sure they don't. I think you are very courageous."

"Or reckless?" she smiled, a worn, sweet smile. Scores of tiny lines radiated from her lips like the cracks in a riverbed parched by drought.

"Courageous," Henry repeated firmly.

"Oh, there are always money troubles, but people send contributions," she told him. "Everything from pence to pounds. The pence mean the most, because they come from those who can't afford even that much. Katty Clarke has arranged additional support through the Dependants' Fund, and the Americans, bless them, have organized a Save Saint Enda's Committee and are fund-raising for us out there. We are hopeful of being able to buy this property outright soon. But—" she laid one hand on his arm—"between you and me, Mr. Mooney, I'm afraid the school is no longer up to Pat's standard. He *was* Saint Enda's. We do our best, but . . ."

"I'm sure your best is good enough," he told her gallantly.

When the cab arrived to take them back to Dublin, Henry was reluctant to leave. He lingered talking with Mrs. Pearse until Collins called sharply for the second time.

"I had best go," Henry sighed. "Where did you put my hat?"

She brushed the dome of his bowler with her palm before handing it to him. "Would you not think of wearing a soft hat, Mr. Mooney? Orangemen wear bowlers."

"As do half the Catholic men in Dublin," he assured her.

That night he surveyed himself searchingly in the looking glass. *Not a cap*, he decided. *I'm not a cap sort of man. Perhaps a trilby? Smart narrow brim, indented crown— rather dashing. That's it, dashing.* He did not buy a new hat immediately, however. Such a serious decision must be weighed and pondered.

Dozens of copies of Collins' brief film clip were made. Republicans visited cinema houses and burst into projection booths with metal canisters under their arms. They demanded that the film be shown, then fled before the police could arrive, taking the film with them. Almost overnight Michael Collins' name and face, largely unknown to the public until then, were famous. People loved his audacity. Dublin Castle proclaimed him the Most Wanted Man in Ireland, but were still unable to catch him. Strangely, even policemen who had seen the propaganda film seemed incapable of recognizing Collins in the street.

Copies of the film were sent to America to stamp the Collins image firmly on the bond drive there. Harry Boland wrote Collins, "Gee, boy, you are some movie actor! No one could resist buying a bond and we having such a handsome minister for finance."[9]

When Henry mentioned the letter to Ned, his friend remarked, "They're both in love with the same woman, you know. Harry and Mick, I mean."

"Fancy that," Henry said tonelessly.

"It's difficult, them being such good friends."

"Difficult," Henry echoed.

"She's a Longford girl called Kitty Kiernan," Ned went on, "a real charmer by all accounts. Harry's quite convinced she will marry him, but I don't think so. Harry's a decent fellow, everybody likes him, but Mick is bold and dashing, and that's what women go for every time."

"Every time," Henry said.

I was thinking of buying myself a trilby, Ella. What do you think?"

"I can't imagine you in anything other than a bowler.

Besides, a trilby wouldn't balance your jaw."

"What's wrong with my jaw?"

She gave a fond laugh and patted his cheek with her fingertips. "Oh, Henry. Nothing's wrong with your jaw. Nothing's wrong with you at all."

The gesture went straight to his heart. Catching her fine-boned wrist, Henry turned her hand palm-up and kissed the soft flesh. It seemed to him she tasted of apples. "Would you be willing to give up all this?" he blurted. "This house, the servants, everything?"

Her eyes widened. "Why should I?"

"Suppose I asked you to. Suppose I asked you to walk away with me tonight and never look back. Share my life just as it is and . . ." His words faltered as the enormity of what he was asking swept over him.

He released her and took half a step backward. "I don't know what came over me, Ella. It was a wild impulse, a foolish, selfish . . . I have too much on my mind and . . . I must go now, I'm really very late for an appointment. Please forgive me!"

He bolted for the door.

Chapter Twenty-three

WHAT do you mean, you're giving up your room? You can't do that, Henry Mooney. This is your home!" Louise Kearney stood with her hands on her hips and her feet firmly planted: a tree blocking his road.

"It's because of my work," he explained. "The campaign against the British is heating up, and the *Bulletin* is sending me down the country to cover it. Since I'll be away from Dublin for weeks at a time, it's foolish for my room to stand empty. I insist you let it to someone else."

"But what about your bits and bobs? You're like a nesting bird, Henry, always bringing things home. Your writing table, those bookcases—what shall I do with them?"

He gave a rueful chuckle. "At the rate I'm going, I'll have possessions strewn over half of Ireland before long. Tell you what—store them away for me, and if anything should happen to me, sell them and put the money aside for Precious."

"What's likely to happen to you?"

"Nothing at all—don't look so worried. I won't be in any more danger than a salesman on the road."

He did not tell her how hard he had fought for the assignment. "The *Bulletin*'s only a newsletter," Desmond Fitz-Gerald had protested, "and newsletters don't have war correspondents, Henry."

But for once events had conspired in Henry's favor. As the police system crumbled under Collins' relentless assault,

Dublin Castle was forced to rely more and more on the military. At the end of January an RIC officer known to be a government spy had been tracked down and shot by members of Collins' squad in Thurles, County Tipperary. In retaliation British soldiers attacked the town in the middle of the night, smashing windows, throwing hand grenades, and firing their weapons into civilian houses while women and children cowered under their beds. Within days the Sinn Féin members of the county council were arrested. They were deported without trial and thrown into Wormwood Scrubs prison. The young son of one councilor was dying. The man appealed to be allowed to return to Ireland for the boy's funeral, but his request was denied.

Newspapers roundly condemned the shooting of the constable but made no mention of the military reprisals. The councilors who had been arrested were described as supporters of a rampaging Republican murder gang. When the young lad in Tipperary was buried without his father at graveside, no reporters covered the story.

"There's going to be a lot more of this before it's over," Frank Gallagher predicted. "Henry, I like your war correspondent idea and I've said as much to Desmond. I persuaded him to ask the Dáil to pay your expenses."

"Will they?"

"They will—as long as you don't inflate your expense account. He pointed out that the Castle's undertaking a hate campaign aimed at convincing people that the Irish are a race of congenital murderers. It's the same old thing we've heard before. We're unfit to govern ourselves, our leaders are madmen, the rules of civilized warfare can't be applied to us, etcetera. We need to give the real picture."

"I'll do my best, Gally. But I hope the Dáil understands we can't compete with the circulation of the pro-British newspapers."

"We can't compete with the might of the British Empire, either. Not militarily. But we're going to beat 'em, Henry. We're going to beat 'em."

Ned was envious of the assignment. "I'd like to go down the country myself," he told his friend. "I'd sign up with Michael Brennan and the West Clare Brigade."[1]

"Brennan was just hauled over the coals by Dick Mulcahy for 'unauthorized militarism,' " Henry told him. "You're needed more here; you have a wife and child to take care of." In truth, Henry felt that it was Ned who needed Síle. He was notoriously careless of his health. Síle tended him constantly without allowing him to feel she was hovering over him. She kept him fed and rested and held the dizzy spells at bay through the sheer force of an indomitable will.

HENRY sent a note to Ella, apologizing for his recent impetuosity and bad manners.

"Neither is typical of me, I assure you," he told her. "I hope you know that I would not, for the earth, do anything to hurt you. The only excuse for my behavior is overwork, the sort that brings on a brainstorm when a man least expects it. Unfortunately I am going away for a while on assignment and shall be even busier. When I have an opportunity I promise to write you a good long letter, though. In the meantime, please do not think too harshly of

"Your devoted friend,

"Henry Mooney."

AT number 5 Mespil Road, one of the many offices he used, Michael Collins sat working at a desk. Lace curtains on the windows concealed the interior from passersby. A stack of documents was piled on the desk with a revolver used as a paperweight. Collins often cycled around Dublin with a price on his head and top-secret documents stuffed into his socks.

He greeted Henry with a wave of the hand. "You're about to be off, then?"

"Tomorrow."

"Good. I have something for you here someplace. Ah sure, there they are." Lifting the revolver, he took two pieces of paper from beneath. "This is a note in my handwriting," he said as he handed the first to Henry, "identifying you and requesting that you be given every possible cooperation. Be careful who you show it to."

Henry observed that Collins had not signed his own name to the note.

The second piece of paper was a list of contacts. "Memorize these names and then burn the paper. If you're arrested, we don't want any names found on you."

"Seems a mighty short list, Mick."

"We keep each cell small, so if we do have an informer, he can't identify more than a few people."

"Have you had any informers yet?"

Collins bared his teeth in an expression that was not a smile. "Not yet."

The first person on Henry's list was Terence MacSwiney, which Collins spelled "MacSweeney," the way it was pronounced. MacSwiney was an instructor and lecturer in business methods in Cork City, co-founder of the Cork Celtic and Literary Society, a respected playwright, and had been a frequent contributor to the suppressed weekly, *Irish Freedom.* Elected to the Dáil in 1919, MacSwiney served on the foreign affairs committee and was also active in matters relating to trade, commerce, and forestry development. His business acumen was invaluable to Collins, who had put him in charge of raising money for the Dáil Loan in Cork.

"Terry's one of those romantic Republicans who writes his letters in Irish," Collins told Henry. "He was in Lincoln the same as Dev, and Dick Mulcahy was the best man at his wedding. Terry's under a lot of pressure right now. He expects the RIC to lift him at any excuse; he just barely avoided a British raiding party that burst in on a Dáil Loan meeting. Go talk to him and get a feeling for what's happening down there. Give us a word picture of the spirit of the people in Cork these days. Say, do you have a gun to take with you?"

"I don't want a gun. If I had a gun, somebody might get shot."

"That's the purpose of 'em," Collins said cheerfully. "This is a war of independence even if the British won't admit it. But in your case, a gun would be for self-protection."

"That's as maybe, but I still don't want one. I'll protect myself with my wits."

Collins said with a laugh, "Mind you're not half-armed."

"The old jokes are the best, aren't they?" Henry retorted.

WHEN Precious peered around the open door of Henry's room, she found him standing beside his bed, smoking a cigarette. A half-packed suitcase lay open before him. "I don't think I can get everything in, Little Business," he said ruefully. "Didn't realize I'd bought so many clothes."

"You bought them to wear when you go to visit Mrs. Rutledge."

Henry took an exceptionally deep drag on his cigarette and exhaled a cloud of smoke. Precious waved a hand in the air. "Do you have to do that, Uncle Henry?"

"Do what? Visit Mrs. Rutledge?"

"I meant, do you have to smoke cigarettes. They remind me of the way Dublin smelled after Easter Week, when so many buildings burned. They make me cough."

Henry took the cigarette from his mouth and held it between thumb and forefinger, examining it as if he had never seen one before. "You know something, Little Business? They make me cough too." Giving her a wink, he ground out the cigarette in a tin dish on the windowsill. "Is that better?"

She nodded. "Could I ask you something else?"

"You can ask me anything, you know that."

"Do you really have to go?"

"I do, Little Business. For a while."

She sat down on the bed beside the open suitcase and began refolding and repacking Henry's clothes. "Why do things have to keep changing all the time?"

"Because that's the way life is. You were someone else once, but now you're Ursula Halloran and you have a home and a family that loves you. Would you not agree that was a good change? Well, going away for a little while is a good change for me right now. I shall come back though, just as your papa did."

She cocked her head to one side and looked up at him. "Is that the truth?"

"I would never lie to you."

"Mama says truth is very important."

"Your mama's right."

Precious gave a deep sigh. "But she isn't my mama, not really. Yet Papa said I must believe they're my parents, or the authorities might take me away."

"He's right, I'm afraid. You don't understand, but—"

"Of course I understand. I'm ten years old. That's not a baby anymore. I understand perfectly well that you should always tell the truth—except when you need to tell a lie. I just don't understand *why* that is. Can a person hold the truth and a lie in their head at the same time and believe them both?"

"Some people can," Henry told her. "They're called politicians."

THE velvet shadows of early morning lay like dust in the corners of number 16. Henry had set his overpacked suitcase down beside the front door and was giving Louise last-minute instructions about forwarding his mail. Lodgers streamed past them on their way to work.

Unnoticed on the stair landing above, Síle Halloran was drawing a last comfort from the familiar rumble of Henry's voice. As long as Henry was in the house they were all safe. Superstition, perhaps; but she had come to believe it. Strange, now, to recall how she had resented him at first.

"Where will you be staying down the country?" Louise was asking.

"Hotels, or with friends."

"Country hotels indeed! Damp, dreary places. Fleas in the beds. Bad food. What about when you come up to Dublin?"

"I should like to think you'd find a spare bed for me, or let me sleep on a couch."

"Let you sleep on the floor more like, you maggot," Louise said fondly. "Do you have everything now?"

"I think so. I'll take a last look through my room before I go, and I want to say goodbye to Precious."

"You've been putting that off," Louise told him.

"I have."

He had not yet said goodbye to Síle, either.

When he started up the stairs, he saw her above him on the landing.

"It's today, then?" she asked.

"It is today."

"Is there nothing I could do to persuade you to stay in Dublin with us?"

For a moment Henry closed his eyes. His knuckles went white on the stair rail. "Nothing," he said crisply, opening his eyes and smiling at her. "Nothing at all."

WHEN Henry had gone, Síle thought the house seemed strangely empty. A dozen lodgers. Ned and Precious and Louise. But no Henry Mooney. No reliable rock to lean upon. No reassuring gaze meeting hers across the table when Ned was ill and she was too worried to eat. Together the three of them had formed a unit more solid than a couple. Without Henry, she and Ned seemed somehow diminished.

She could not settle to anything. Finally she went to the kitchen to peel potatoes, that unfailing distraction of troubled Irish women. Her eyes were drawn to the advertising calendar for Robert Roberts Teas & Coffees hanging on the scullery door: March 17, 1920.

THE train to Cork carried a company of British soldiers who, ten days before, had shot up the little town of Thurles yet again. A few were loudly reliving the incident to the discomfiture of the civilian passengers. The rest slumped in their seats and gazed out the window. Some of them looked depressed, Henry thought. Homesick, maybe.

He ostentatiously unfolded the latest edition of the *Irish Times* and disappeared behind its camouflage.

CORK City was beautifully sited along a wide river valley between lofty hills. Henry's first impression, in the golden light of late afternoon, was of numerous bridges spanning the tranquil Lee, and numerous spires lifted toward heaven like praying hands. The city owed its commercial prosperity to nearby Cork Harbor, and boasted a university, an opera house, some fine late-Victorian bow-fronted residences, a Grand Parade—and electric trams. Henry made a mental note to tell Precious about them.

As soon as he checked into the Imperial Hotel, which Collins had recommended as "honest Republican digs," he left his suitcase in his room and set off on a stroll. It was only a few steps from his hotel to the stone quays bordering the Lee, a river as pungent as the Liffey. Henry drew a deep breath. The marshes, or *corcaigh*, that gave the area its name had gradually been reclaimed and built over as the town expanded, but the air retained a semitropical dampness spiced with a tang of salt from the harbor.

Above the river small houses climbed steep hills shoulder to shoulder. Henry wandered at random up one street and down another. He stopped to chat with anyone who would talk to him, and most would. Corkonians were responsive where Dubliners would have been suspicious. The lilting musicality of the Cork accent gave an impression of light-heartedness which was, perhaps, misleading.

Tidy terraced houses soon gave way to dilapidated hovels cobwebbed by sagging lines of faded laundry. The fragrance of bakeries mingled with the stench of slaughterhouses. Henry paused to write in his notebook: "An old Irish proverb says, 'It is not a matter of upper or lower class but of being up a while and down a while.'"

When he returned to the Imperial Henry planned to have a good dinner and an early night. First he must unpack and hang his clothes in the wardrobe to let the wrinkles fall out. As he unfolded a pair of gray serge trousers from the bottom of the bag, something fell out and hit the floor with a clunk.

Henry stared down at the dull black gleam of a pistol.

BEFORE he left his room next morning he stood lost in thought, the pistol in his hand. Then he scooped up the cartridges he had found in a twist of paper at the bottom of the suitcase, and thrust them, together with the pistol, far under his mattress.

Henry's first call of the day was to the offices of the *Cork*

Examiner in Patrick Street to buy a morning edition fresh off the presses. He wanted the feel of newspaper stock in his hands; the smell of newspaper ink in his nostrils. Even more than the river, they would give him a sense of home.

George and Michael Harrington, whose brother Tim was the editor of the *Irish Independent*, were working at the *Examiner*. They offered to give Henry a tour of the offices.

"Do you ever see Mick Collins up in Dublin?" Michael Harrington asked.

"From time to time."

"What do you think of him?"

"He's . . . mmm . . . a very clever man."

Harrington grinned. "What we in Cork call a cute whoor. Too crafty by half, which is just what we need. It'll take a Cork man to outsmart the British."

"You should move down here, Henry," George Harrington suggested. "The Southern Capital's a grand place to live."

"That's as maybe. I heard that some houses were wrecked by soldiers the other day."

"I'm afraid they were," said Michael. "And now there's more troops in town, so I suppose we can expect a repeat performance. The British are trying to intimidate our lord mayor, but he's a Cork man too, and hard to intimidate."

"Tomás MacCurtáin," Henry said, referring to the second name on his list.

"The very one. He's also the commandant of the Cork Brigade of the IRA."

"I understand he's been receiving death threats?"

George nodded. "You're well informed. The prominent Republicans here have been getting death threats. Some are living more or less on the run, but the lord mayor's a married man with five children; he can't desert them and go live in a hedge. Say, are you here to do a story on him?"

Henry rocked back on his heels and sucked the inside of his cheek, wishing he had a cigarette. "Might be. Might not. But I would appreciate a map of the city and environs if you have one—and any other useful information you would care to pass along."

George grinned. His teeth were yellow and his features

asymmetrical, but he had the same jauntiness as Michael Collins. "Let us have an advance copy of your story and it's a deal."

Michael Harrington added, "And come back anytime— you're among friends here. We're not as intimidated by the *Sasanach** as our brother in the Big Smoke."

TERENCE MacSwiney was married to Muriel Murphy, a daughter of the distillers who produced Paddy's whiskey and Murphy's stout. The Murphy family were amongst Cork's wealthiest Catholics, and according to Henry's information, Muriel and Terence occupied a handsome residence in the Douglas Road. When Henry went to that address, the house-maid who answered his knock said bluntly, "There's no one here of that name."

He was taken aback. "Are you certain?" Beyond the maid he could see a shadowy figure in the room. He cupped his hands around his eyes and peered in. "Mrs. MacSwiney?"

The woman who stepped forward was in her late twenties and very pretty. In her arms was a toddler, who instantly won Henry's heart with a huge smile and two pearly teeth.

"Are you sure you're not Mrs. MacSwiney?" Henry asked the mother.

Her reply was evasive. "I know who I am."

"But you don't know who I am. My name is Henry Moo-ney, and Mick sent me."

She glanced past Henry, looking up and down the road, then in a low voice asked, "Are you referring to the man from Clonakilty?"

"Indeed. I have a note from him identifying me. It's un-signed of course, but perhaps you'd recognize his handwrit-ing?"

She shifted the baby to her other hip. "You'd best come inside."

When she was satisfied as to his bona fides, Muriel MacSwiney gave Henry tea and scones and let him hold

*Irish word for "the English."

baby Máire. "Before she was born we called her Terry, because we both wanted a boy. But she's our little angel and we wouldn't trade her for a hundred boys now. Mind there, she's pulling on your watch chain, Mr. Mooney. Do you want me to take her?"

Henry chuckled. "She's just playing—leave her be. I don't get to hold a little one very often."

"Máire was born while my husband was in prison in Belfast. I took her there to visit him when she was only two months old, and one of the guards said—"

With a crow of triumph, little Máire pulled the watch from Henry's waistcoat pocket and popped it into her mouth. The watch was swiftly rescued and patted dry, but its silver case would carry the marks of two small front teeth forever.

Muriel MacSwiney gave Henry directions to a safe house in the village of Glanmire. As he left the MacSwiney home, he noticed a member of the RIC standing across the road with his arms folded across his chest—not doing anything, just standing there. *I've never had my photograph taken, so he can't identify me. Anyway, I have a right to go anywhere I want, damn it!*

Henry walked a quarter-mile or so until he found a horse-drawn cab without a fare. He gave the driver directions to take him to the suburb of Sunday's Well, and they set off at a brisk trot. After a few minutes Henry knocked on the back of the driver's seat. "I've changed my mind—I want to go to Glanmire."

"But that's in the opposite direction," the man protested.

"I know. Just take me there, please. I'll pay for the extra distance."

Eventually he arrived at an unoccupied Georgian country house that had fallen into disrepair. Behind it was an ivy-mantled carriage house that looked equally deserted. From the dovecote came the music of pigeons cooing. As Henry walked around the side of the house a black-and-white sheepdog slunk forward on its belly, sniffed his shoes, then offered a tentative tail wag.

Terence MacSwiney answered Henry's coded knock on the door of the carriage house. They had met before only briefly at the Dáil the year before, and Henry was flattered that MacSwiney recognized him. MacSwiney was equally recognizable: tall, slim, very dark, with a lock of jet-black hair falling over his forehead and intense blue-gray eyes with hooded lids. While he talked, he nervously paced the floor with short, surprisingly awkward strides. *He's not an athlete like so many Cork men,* Henry thought to himself. *But he sure burns hot just the same.*

"The situation here is pretty bad," MacSwiney admitted, "but we've laid our lines carefully. If anything happens to one of us, the others will carry on the work. We've set up five Dáil Loan subexecutive committees, and we're also establishing more Sinn Féin clubs in some of the more isolated areas of the county. There's more work to be done than a thousand men could do, but with the help of God we'll do it."

"Do you not find it difficult to be separated from your wife and baby?"

"I do of course, but it's necessary for their safety."

"I saw a constable outside your house this morning, Terry."

"They won't bother Muriel as long as I'm not there. The RIC are Irish after all—they won't hurt a woman."

"It's not much of a life for either of you, though . . . like this."

"Few men are given the chance to help build a new nation, Henry."

"What about your family?"

"You've seen my little Máire—would you want her to spend her life enslaved by a foreign power?"

"Ah, now, I'm not sure that 'enslaved' is the right—"

"Subjugated, then." MacSwiney stopped pacing. In a voice that vibrated with feeling he said, "We're subjugated in our own country by an imperialist nation that has no scruples about seizing our land or taking the food out of our mouths or shipping us off to be cannon fodder in their wars. We're just a commodity to Britain, something to be used up. That's why I decided to put the cause of Irish independence above family considerations. It's a sacrifice some of us *must* be willing to make if things are ever to get any better. What greater gift could I bequeath my children than a free Ireland?"

There it is again, that wild light that burns in only a few. Pearse, Connolly, Countess Markievicz . . . Síle. What must it be like to feel such passion?

Even as he asked himself the question, Henry knew the answer. Deep inside him, suppressed, controlled, reined in, the passion was waiting. For a cause. Or a woman.

He spent the afternoon with MacSwiney but did not write down anything he was told. It was stored safely in his memory, in the dark vault of the skull, beyond the reach of prying eyes.

By the time Henry returned to his hotel the March night was closing in. The desk clerk looked up as he entered the lobby. "You going out again, Mr. Mooney?"

"I don't know. Why?"

"A policeman was shot earlier. There may be trouble, so we're recommending that our guests stay off the streets tonight." He smiled apologetically. "We'd hate to lose you."

Henry went to his room and knelt down beside the bed. At first his groping fingers found nothing under the mattress, and he experienced a brief panic. *They've searched the room, they found . . .* Then there it was. Cold. Heavy. Deadly.

He took the weapon out and looked at it again. A Mauser semiautomatic. His mind ran back to Limerick and the Wolfe Tone Club in Barrington Street. One evening a senior member had brought in a new-model Mauser similar to this and passed it around amid great excitement. Henry had been as fascinated as anyone, seduced not so much by the deadly purpose of the pistol as by its engineering. He had asked a number of questions and paid close attention to the answers.

Holding a Mauser again brought them flooding back, as if memory were a tactile function.

The pistol was fitted with an external hammer and a fixed magazine in front of the trigger. On firing, the barrel and breechlock, which were joined by heavy lugs, recoiled together. After a few millimeters the lugs fell, the barrel was halted, and the bolt continued to the rear to extract and eject the spent case and cock the hammer. Then it was ready to fire again.

I know how to use this. I could shoot someone if I had to.

This time he hid the weapon by rolling back part of the rug and putting the gun underneath. He pulled the bed over it and threw damp towels and yesterday's underwear under the bed, then went downstairs for a meal in the dining room. Afterward he stood beneath the Imperial's shallow neoclassical portico, a traveling businessman innocently taking the air. He was wearing his good suit. His hands were casually thrust into his trouser pockets, drawing his coat aside so his watch chain glinted. His shoes were polished to a high shine. No one bothered him, although there was a large police presence in the South Mall. Henry observed both men and women being stopped at random and roughly questioned. If they protested, they were marched away.

Henry went back inside and ordered a large whiskey in the bar. A stout man in a seedy overcoat was trying hard to strike up a conversation with a bored-looking woman. Another man was downing one drink after another, like someone trying to put out a fire. At last Henry went to his room and wrote a long, rambling letter to Ella Rutledge on hotel stationery. He read it through twice, crossed out some lines, rewrote others, tore the whole thing up, wrote another, more ardent, which he also discarded, fell into bed, and finally succumbed to a troubled sleep.

He awoke to the sound of distant shouting. Dim gray morning light filled the room. Raising the window, Henry looked down into the street. A newsboy in a cap was waving a copy of the *Examiner* and shouting, "Lord mayor murdered!"

Henry pulled his trousers over his pajamas and ran down into the street without a coat. He carried his newspaper back into the hotel and read its lead story in the lobby, oblivious to those around him.

Shortly after midnight a cordon of soldiers and police had isolated the area surrounding Tomás MacCurtáin's house. Mrs. MacCurtáin was awakened by a ferocious pounding on the front door. When she looked out the window, she saw a number of men with soot-blackened faces. Before the startled woman could respond, they broke down the door and rushed in. They shot MacCurtáin in the doorway of his bedroom. He died within a quarter of an hour while his killers were still searching his house and smashing his furniture.

Chapter Twenty-four

Two days after MacCurtáin's murder, British soldiers in Dublin shot and killed a young man and a girl, both civilians. An elderly man was shot in the back by police in Thurles as he was leaving a pub, and the next night another man was murdered in his bed by members of the RIC in County Tipperary.

"Police show excessive zeal," commented the *Irish Times*.

Henry tried to send a telegram to Desmond FitzGerald's house at 6 Upper Pembroke Street, Dublin: "Coroner's jury finds lord mayor of Cork City was murdered under circumstances of most callous brutality. Further finds assassination was carried out by members of Royal Irish Constabulary under direction of British government. Verdict of willful murder returned against Prime Minister Lloyd George, Lord-Lieutenant French, and senior officers of Cork police force."[1]

The clerk in the telegraph office was dismayed. "I can't send that—it would be worth my job."

"But it's the truth."

"Sometimes," said the telegraph operator, "you have to forget you know the truth."

Henry Mooney wrote out two copies of his report and sent them in separate envelopes to Desmond FitzGerald and Frank Gallagher. They were not entrusted to the regular mail service but were smuggled to Dublin by railway employees, part of the secret network that was reliably delivering IRA communications throughout the country.

Almost by return he received a note from Kathleen McKenna. "We have been raided!!! They carried away our typewriters and multigraph and the mailing list for *Bulletin* subscribers. According to one of Michael Collins' contacts in Dublin Castle, they are going to print forged copies of the *Bulletin* cleverly worded to turn people against the IRA.[2] But we will be back in business just as soon as we can get another typewriter and some sort of printing machine. We're determined not to miss a single issue. We shall tell our readers how to spot forgeries."

On the twenty-fifth of March Frank Gallagher was arrested. Anna Fitzsimons gave Henry the news by telephone while he stood in the editor's office of the *Cork Examiner*, listening to faraway Dublin crackling down the line. "They've put him in Mountjoy," she said, "as a political prisoner."

"Do you want me to come back?"

"Desmond says no; it's better that you're at large where they can't get at you. Wait a minute—there's someone here who wants to speak to you." There was a pause, during which Henry was afraid the line had gone down; then he heard Erskine Childers' clipped English accent. "I say, Henry, are you there?"

"Ready and waiting. I'm damned sorry to hear about Gally."

"He may not be in prison for long. The other political prisoners in the Joy have been talking about going on hunger strike to try and force the authorities to release them. Since Thomas Ashe's death garnered so much bad press for the British, they may be amenable to that sort of persuasion."

"Or they may not," said Henry. "It's hard to predict how they'll react to anything now."

INDIFFERENT to the charge of murder laid at his door—if he even knew of it—Lloyd George was preparing for a partitioned Ireland with two parliaments. This included making a number of personnel changes. Sir Nevil Macready was appointed commander in chief of His Majesty's forces in Ireland. Formerly the commissioner of the metropolitan police in London, Macready had a reputation for ruthlessness.

The British also were introducing a new weapon to use against the Irish Republican Army.

Crown forces stationed in Ireland were not trained for counterinsurgency. Many of the regular army still subscribed to the code of chivalry that for all practical purposes had breathed its last gasp in the trenches during the Great War. As for the Royal Irish Constabulary, it was becoming increasingly unreliable under the combined weight of public opinion and IRA onslaught.

Therefore a third force had been created.

After the Great War a certain type of soldier, often with a low mentality and limited prospects, no longer had a legitimate outlet for the violence they had learned to enjoy. Many of these were English, others had belonged to Irish battalions, but all had one thing in common: once demobilized, such men ran wild.

Lloyd George's government considered them perfect for Ireland.

They were recruited through advertisements promising "a rough and dangerous task," in return for which they would be receive ten shillings a day and unlimited access to firearms. Although they would comprise a military force of irregulars, they were funded out of police funds rather than through the War Office.

When the first of them arrived in Ireland at the end of March, they were given a memorable nickname. They became known as the Black and Tans.

The name was bestowed by Christopher O'Sullivan, proprietor of the *Limerick Echo*.[3] In his paper he remarked on a belligerent individual he had just encountered on the train to Limerick City. The man was wearing an oddly mixed uniform consisting of a slouched black cap, a dark green RIC tunic, and the khaki trousers of a British soldier. "Judging by his strange attire," O'Sullivan wrote, "this creature resembled something one would associate with the Scarteen Hunt." His reference was to a foxhunt, the Scarteen Black and Tans, whose hounds were well known for savagery to their prey. O'Sullivan's readers understood the allusion.

The Black and Tans had orders to make Ireland a hell for rebels to live in.

HENRY Mooney took the next train to Limerick. From there he reported to the *Bulletin*: "Yesterday a string of military lorries entered this city. The Black and Tans proceeded to swarm over the place like rats over corn. They have been having indiscriminate target practice, which includes shooting up one of Limerick's landmarks, Tate's Clock. They fired on the clock tower in relays for some time, then forced their way into the bar of the Glentworth Hotel and demanded drink for which they did not pay. Even the RIC is giving these newcomers a wide berth."

Henry would have preferred to stay at the Glentworth, but went to his mother's house instead. He did not like the idea of the women being alone there at night.

Hannah Mooney met him at the cottage door with a string of complaints that would not wait until he took off his coat. "Have you heard what's happening? Another army, God between us and all harm! Shooting up the town, so they are, and everyone in it. We'll be slaughtered in our beds while you swan around Dublin not caring."

"I'm not in Dublin. I'm right here."

"Ye've come home where you belong then, and not before time."

"Ah . . . not exactly, Mam. I'm here on assignment, so to speak. I may not stay long, I have to go wherever—"

"That's just like you. Unreliable, always was." As Henry shrugged out of his coat, Hannah eyed his suit. "That's new, that is."

"I bought it last year."

"Fancy goods," she said contemptuously, fingering the fabric. "Ye'll make a holy show of yourself. And that's all I'm going to say about that."

By now Alice was ensconced with the Sisters of Mercy, so Pauline and Hannah had only each other to chew upon, day after day. Henry provided a welcome diversion. They both attacked him. After a miserable evening during which his undigested dinner sat in his stomach like a cannonball, he put on his hat and fled the house on the pretext of visiting his brothers.

He went to Noel rather than Bernard. Henry's youngest brother had freckled skin, muscular arms, and a lumpy nose resulting from youthful fistfights. He could still give a good account of himself in a brawl on payday. He also had an unexpected talent for cabinetry and had considerably increased his father-in-law's business, but one would never know it by looking at his own house. Noel shunned any signs of prosperity. Success brought begrudgery. A man who visibly had done better than others would be ostracized in the pub.

Noel's wife, whom Henry recalled as a blooming girl with a trim figure, had ripened into a flaccid matron. Like many Irish wives, she had acquired a peculiar anonymity. She was simply Her Inside. Public appearances limited to Mass, weddings, and funerals.

As soon as she had served whiskey to the men, Noel's wife vanished into the back of the house.

Henry's eyes followed her. *A baby in her arms and another hanging onto her skirts. Year after year after year. She will live and die a sinner in the eyes of the Church, and invisible as far as my mother is concerned. And for what? For loving my fool brother more than he deserved.*

Noel eyed Henry over the rim of his glass. "What are you up to at all?"

"Just visiting. Can I not visit my own brother?"

"Don't get shirty. I'm after doing all I can for Mam, if that's why you're here."

"All I'm asking is that you keep an eye on herself and Polly. Take a quarter-hour every night to walk over to the cottage—at different times every evening, if possible—and ask Bernard to do the same. I also suggest you fit a lock to the door."

"A lock on the door!" Noel set down his glass abruptly. "Where do you think this is, London?"

•   •   •

ON the thirtieth of March Tomás MacCurtáin was replaced as lord mayor by his second-in-command in the Cork Brigade—Terence MacSwiney.

No attempt was being made by the British authorities to bring MacCurtáin's killers to justice.

HENRY went out to the orchard to have a look at Flossie's colt. Now three years old, the animal had grown too tall to be called a pony. His coat was a steel gray so dark it appeared almost black, and he had his mother's beautiful head. When he saw Henry, he came trotting over with his ears pricked. His friendly nicker brought a smile to Henry's face. For some minutes he stood stroking the velvet nose and the silken neck. "There now," he murmured. "There now."

When he left the orchard the young horse followed him all the way to the gate.

"That's a fine animal," Henry remarked to his mother. "Gentle, even though I notice you haven't gelded him."

"Bernard says he might be worth something if we leave him entire. Alice made a pet of him, that's why he's so soppy."

"Is he broken in yet?"

"Bernard's going to do it when he has time."

Henry studied his fingernails. "Was there not a friend of my father's who broke horses in very gently, so they were safe for anyone to handle?"

"He charges money." Hannah drew her lips together as tight as purse strings.

"I'll tell you what, Mam," Henry said, glancing up. "Why don't you sell the colt to me? I'll give you enough to buy a pony who's already trained to the cart."

Hannah looked at her son as if he had lost his mind. "And what would you be doing with a horse? You don't even like horses."

"I never said that. Will you sell him to me or not?"

A cunning glint crept into her eyes. "Have ye as much money as all that?"

"I do not have much money, but I think it would be good investment," he replied, swiftly calculating his finances.

Hannah Mooney was a shrewd dealer, and never more than when dealing with her family. Henry spent the better part of the morning arguing with her. At the end of the negotiations both felt sure they had been cheated and there were hard feelings, but the colt belonged to Henry.

He posted a letter to number 16 in the ordinary way, from the Limerick post office. In it he wrote, "Ask Precious if she can suggest a good name for a horse."

ON Easter Monday Frank Gallagher was one of sixty political prisoners in Mountjoy who went on hunger strike. They claimed they were being illegally incarcerated and demanded pardons.

Meanwhile General Macready, anticipating an anniversary repeat of the 1916 Rising on that date, had positioned troops and police on the main roads between Cork, Limerick, and Dublin. The rising did not come. The vacated barracks, however, were mysteriously burned. Simultaneously Republicans entered local revenue offices throughout Ireland, soaked the tax records with paraffin oil, and set them afire.

In County Limerick the situation was similar to that throughout the south and west. The Republicans knew the territory and had the support of the majority of the people. Under an IRA brigade structure they operated in small, mobile companies known as flying columns, which consisted of between fifteen and thirty men. They could appear suddenly, strike a target, then disappear before the British could mobilize against them. For this new sort of warfare they had no uniforms. Dressed in soft hats and trench coats, they overpowered garrisons and seized the weapons. Initially policemen who tried to stop them were bound hand and foot and left, cursing but generally unharmed, at the side of the road.

Crown forces had no idea when or where a flying column might strike. There was a sudden dearth of informers to provide this information.

There were not as many Republicans in the field as the British were made to think; prisons in both Ireland and Britain were packed to the rafters with men who would swell their ranks if only they could get out. But clever marshalling of its resources was enabling the IRA to confuse and demoralize a much larger force.

This was the arena into which the Black and Tans were pouring.

In the *Bulletin* Henry commented, "This band of brigands is being allowed to maraud and murder with impunity. Their targets are not limited to Republicans. Anyone Irish is fair game. The Black and Tans are not nearly as civilized as the hounds for which they are named."

Dublin Castle retaliated by claiming that the victims of the Black and Tans actually were being murdered by "Republican extremists." A similar claim was made concerning the death of Tomás MacCurtáin. The new lord mayor of Cork rejected this story outright. Terence MacSwiney publicly laid the blame for MacCurtáin's death on the British government and the blame for the lie on Dublin Castle.

National newspapers were covering the hunger strike in Mountjoy with almost fevered intensity. Too many men were involved to ignore. Every day saw larger public demonstrations outside the prison. The first international journalists, including John Steele for the *Chicago Tribune*, arrived to cover the story. Rumors abounded. The men were being released; they were being paroled; they had refused parole and were holding out for complete pardon.

ON the fourteenth of April the hunger strikers were released from Mountjoy Prison. Beds were waiting in the Mater Hospital for those who were too ill to go home. A steady rain fell all that day. The streets leading away from the prison were lined with cheering crowds waiting under umbrellas to see the taxicabs pass by.

After Frank Gallagher had been home for two days, the *Bulletin* staff went to visit him. They found him propped up in a chair in his own room, with a fire burning brightly on the hearth and a vase of fresh flowers on the table. He greeted them each by name with a wan but cheery smile.

Gallagher's time in prison had left him with a straggly auburn beard that contrasted startlingly with his black hair.

He was even more emaciated than Henry had expected. The cords on his neck stood out like vines on a tree; his Adam's apple protruded like the stump of a sawn-off limb.

Kathleen McKenna had to turn away from the horror that lingered in his eyes.

A journalist to the bone, in spite of his weakness Gallagher insisted on relating his experiences to his colleagues: "At the start I was intensely happy. That may sound strange, but we all were. The fight had begun; something that must be done in the name of liberty and the rights of men. The last bowl of porridge we were willing to accept tasted so good.

"We told one another it was no different from fasting at Lent, and we thanked God we had the strength to do it. Then the headaches began. The cramping in the belly. The first days are the hardest. One is so used to have the day in prison divided by mealtimes. Eventually you think you're getting used to it. You feel clammy and weak, but determined; you even make jokes. Though never about food. You daren't talk about food.

"Reading. Reading is a godsend. In the exercise yard you look at the other men and see how sharp their features are becoming and how feverish their eyes. And you know the same mark is on you, too: that curious slouching gait that comes from having no energy and a dizzy head. Emotions start to run riot. Anger, despair, sometimes a marvelous ecstasy like that of the ancient saints. In my cell I talked to Jesus quite a lot, I think.

"The guards were vicious to us, they wanted to break us. They let our families visit just to torment us with thoughts of leaving them forever. Officials came and made offers and promises we knew they did not mean to keep. Oh, they had so many ways to torture us. There is a cruelty that lurks in some men's souls which is only released when they have other men in their power.

"One of their tortures was to tempt us with food. Another was to prevent us from sleeping. I began to have waking nightmares about a coffin, about all of us in one coffin together. I knew I was raving and I prayed God to let me hold onto my sanity and not die some broken mad creature.

"But there was a paradox in all this. The weaker we became, the stronger we proved ourselves to be. After a while we knew nothing could break us. We had won then. No matter what else happened, we had won.

"Sometimes I was peaceful and sometimes I was desperately afraid. I began to believe that all the others were dying, or dead, and I should be the only one left. I was frantic with fear; fear of surviving when all my comrades were gone. You know how it is with our boys, that grand sense of camaraderie we've shared from the beginning. To be the last one alive . . . it was the worst torture of all.

"And then, when I thought I could endure no more, the warder came to say a release had been agreed on. My dear friends weren't dead after all. We were going home."[4] Gallagher paused, then turned his face toward the open window. "Listen," he said in a rapt voice. "I can hear a blackbird sing."

THE British government announced that the category of political prisoner was being revoked. In future, Republicans would be treated as common criminals.

Winston Churchill, Britain's secretary of state for war, had yet another idea for bringing the Irish to heel. His concept was the recruitment of a band of ex-army officers to be known as the Cadet Auxiliaries. Ostensibly attached to the police, they were in actuality another force of military irregulars. Calling them cadets was a cynical ploy to make it sound as if they were fresh-cheeked young lads rather than experienced fighting men. The Auxiliaries were paid an extravagant pound a day and were answerable only to themselves. Their instructions were the same as the Black and Tans'.

Terrorize.

Within days the irrepressible Irish had new nicknames for both organizations. The Black and Tans were the "roughs"; the Auxiliaries were the "toughs."

The regular members of the RIC were torn between loyalty to British paymasters and empathy for fellow Irishmen. A number of constables resigned. Others hardened themselves and joined the hunt for "Shinners," meaning any Republican who could be brought within gunsights.

The IRA extended its campaign to shooting policemen.

EVENTUALLY Ella responded to Henry's written apology with a note in which she assured him there was nothing to forgive. The rest of the brief letter was formal, almost impersonal. "I am well, though Madge is recovering from a cold. The weather in Dublin is hopeless. We may go to Beech Park for a few days."

"I am well also, though very busy," Henry wrote back in the same tone. "Roscommon will be a pleasant change for you. I know the hunting season is long over, but Madge will enjoy the fishing. Please give my regards to your family."

The letters were less satisfying than no communication at all. It was obvious a rupture had taken place in the relationship, but he could hardly repair the damage by post. *Perhaps it's better to leave things as they are. I have nothing to offer to compare with what she has.*

IN England one hundred and thirty Irish Republicans began a hunger strike in Wormwood Scrubs Prison. They demanded to be treated as prisoners of war.

In May the Irish Transport Workers Union declared a strike. If either soldiers or members of the Black and Tans boarded a train, the engineer would refuse to start.

The Dáil Loan, the *Bulletin* reported, was oversubscribed. The original goal had been £250,000. The total had reached £357,000 in spite of repeated efforts by British agents to seize the money.[5]

By decree of the Dáil, the Irish Volunteers, the Citizen Army, and the Irish Republican Brotherhood officially were amalgamated into the army of the nation.[6]

HENRY Mooney traveled up and down the west interviewing people and documenting events. He wrote: "Wherever I go I hear stories of tragedy and anger—and optimism. For

Irish nationalists, centuries of oppression are culminating in a flare of hope."

Because he was Henry he also interviewed loyalists. He wrote: "These are men and women who genuinely love their monarch and are baffled that anyone would want to live under any other system. Like children threatened with being orphaned, they are frightened and resentful. The new Republic must offer them at least as much as they are losing."

Henry's personal commentaries appeared in many issues of the *Bulletin*. "We cannot print enough copies of the newsletter to meet the demand," an elated Kathleen McKenna informed him. "Desmond's duties as a member of the Dáil are keeping him increasingly busy and Erskine has been wonderful about taking on the editing chores. All is well here, but we miss you."

One day Henry received a personal letter addressed in a childish hand. Holding it close to the lamp in his mother's kitchen, he read: "Dear Uncle Henry, I think a good name would be an Irish word my Papa taught me. Saoirse. It makes me think of a horse running wild and free, with the wind blowing its mane."

Hannah Mooney bustled over. "What's that word?" she demanded to know, stabbing the paper with her finger.

"Sayr-sha," Henry enunciated phonetically. "That's the colt's new name: Saoirse. The Irish word for freedom."

As birds sang their summer songs in the hedgerows, the activities of the Black and Tans increased: a reign of terror unlike anything Ireland had seen since Cromwell. Civilians were used as target practice from army lorries. Republican prisoners were shot in the back on the pretext they had been trying to escape. When the authorities could not find a Republican marked for extinction, they had his mother or father shot.

In faraway India on the twenty-eighth of June, 250 members of the First Battalion of Connaught Rangers laid down their arms in protest against what was being done by the

British government in Ireland. Sixty-two were court-martialed for mutiny.

IRELAND had become a very dangerous place. Any road might lead British troops into a Republican Army ambush, although Cathal Brugha was against ambushing, preferring what he called "straight fights." His vision of the best way to fight the British was diametrically opposed to that of Mulcahy and Collins.

"The wrongdoing is no longer limited to the Crown forces," Henry reported regretfully. "Violence infects the very air. The plain people of Ireland, who once would do 'anything for a quiet life,' are like a nest of hornets disturbed."

Erskine Childers wrote, "It is impossible to escape from the subtle demoralization which comes to a people bludgeoned into silence by the law, driven underground to preserve its national organization and forced under intolerable provocation into desperate reprisals."[7]

The coarsening of the Irish was evidenced in a number of ways. Henry noticed that the everyday language of the streets was becoming more vulgar, liberally sprinkled with profanities which would have been unthinkable only a few years earlier. His own mild expletives began to seem quaint.

"If we are not careful," he warned, "we will turn into the brutes our enemies picture us."

The *Bulletin* informed readers that frightened bureaucrats had begun moving themselves and their families behind the protective walls of Dublin Castle. They slept on office furniture and sent out for meals.

From his office in Dublin Castle, surrounded by police who thought they were protecting him from the Republicans, Ned Broy actually was providing a base for penetrating the deepest secrets of the British government. He made two carbon copies of every report he typed: one for his bosses and one for Michael Collins.

Collins' intelligence network now included Belfast as well as England. Constantly on the move, he covered Dublin by bicycle and the rest of the country in friends' motorcars. He

had offices and safe houses everywhere and was said to carry
a hundred keys. One thing was certain: he held a hundred
Republican strings firmly in his hands.

By the time Eamon de Valera had been in America a year
the most popular games among Dublin children were ambush games.

The Dáil was aware of every aspect of IRA activity but
did not comment officially and gave no approval. By June
arbitration courts had been set up in twenty-eight of Ireland's thirty-two counties. Through these courts, plaintiffs
were appealing to the Dáil to enforce law and order—an
enforcement the British could no longer guarantee.

In the June elections Sinn Féin candidates enjoyed a land-
slide. "We're away in a hack!" a jubilant Arthur Griffith
announced at a party held to celebrate in the Gresham Hotel.

At the end of the month the Dáil set up Land Courts that
considered over three hundred cases. A number of loyalists,
finding themselves landowners in a new republic not under
their control, were desperate to sell their property. The Land
Courts guaranteed that they received a fair price and were
treated with every courtesy.

"The Republic of Ireland exists," Henry wrote, "whether
Britain and the world choose to recognize it or not. The
people have brought their nation into being through the bal-
lot box, and continue to support it with their devotion."

The Republicans also were establishing their own police
force. Dublin Castle was outraged anew. In a land with a
British administration and almost fifty thousand armed men
under British orders, the audacity of the Irish in trying to
police themselves was unforgivable.

Erskine Childers told readers of the *Bulletin*, "Daring daylight raids on government buildings are taking place in
Dublin. Documents and even arms have been seized by Republicans without having to resort to gunplay."

In July the IRA appropriated Dublin Castle's mail at the
General Post Office. When Lord-Lieutenant French received
his next postal delivery, he was astonished to find the packet
marked PASSED BY CENSOR, IRISH REPUBLICAN ARMY.

The Black and Tans and the Auxiliaries began burning
the homes of civilians whose greatest crime was living in

the vicinity of a Republican ambush. They also burned down the creameries upon which the support of many rural people depended, leaving farm families destitute.

The IRA retaliated by burning some of the great country houses belonging to British loyalists. Many of these houses were very beautiful, an irreplaceable part of Ireland's architectural heritage. They were also hated symbols of the conqueror: the Haves flaunting their triumph over the Have Nots.

Edward Carson was furious about the results of the election and made a real rabble-rousing speech on the twelfth," Desmond FitzGerald told Henry by phone. "It was plainly intended to incite violence against the Catholics. Get yourself up there—you know the train connections—and send us a description of the situation. Mick Collins gave me the name of an inexpensive hotel just off Victoria Street, not far from the Ulster Hall. He has an agent on the staff who'll look after you."

I have arrived on 19 July, in the middle of the Marching Season," Henry wrote in his notebook as soon as he had unpacked his bag in Belfast. He wanted to set out the historical context before exploring the city and recording his impressions. "Those who do not live in the northeastern corner of this island may not fully appreciate what the Marching Season represents. The Orange Order is a Protestant organization founded in County Armagh in 1795. The Order began as a secret society committed to imposing its will by physical force. Its name was taken from William of Orange, the Protestant king who defeated the Catholic King James in the Battle of the Boyne in 1690. The Order grew out of earlier sectarian groups such as the 'Peep O' Day Boys,' which had kept Armagh, Tyrone and Down in a state of turmoil for years. These self-appointed vigilantes visited Catholic peasants by night, threw them out of their homes and destroyed their property.

"At the end of the eighteenth century a concerted effort

was being made to ban northern Catholics from employment in the thriving linen industry, and Protestant businessmen flocked to join the new Orange Order. The Order also spread to America. In the 1870s violent Orange Riots rocked New York City as Protestants staged triumphalist marches through Catholic neighborhoods. Irish, Spanish, and Italians were targeted. Almost seventy people were killed before the city government banned any further marches.[8]

"In 1913 Sir Edward Carson, leader of the Ulster Unionists, looked to the Orange Order for support when founding the Ulster Volunteer Force. Carson encouraged naked sectarian hatred to keep himself in power. This resulted in the founding of the Irish Volunteers as a countering force, which in turn led to the Easter Rising and the current situation.

"There are many decent members of the Protestant community who do not agree with the politics of the Orange Order. But as so often before in Ireland, bullying and intimidation triumph. Every July the Orangemen celebrate the Battle of the Boyne by parading throughout the northeast, beating huge drums, shouting antipapist slogans, and physically assaulting any Catholic foolish enough to come within reach. The Marching Season is a terrifying time."

When Henry had completed his article, he set out for the railway station to give it to a safe courier.

The streets of Belfast were gaily decorated with arches of red, white, and blue bunting, the colors of the British flag. Surmounting these were brilliantly colored panels depicting King William on his white horse; an open Bible; a black servant kneeling submissively at the feet of Queen Victoria. On a piece of waste ground between two shops Henry saw the smoldering remains of a huge festive bonfire. A few hundred yards farther on, he encountered an Orange parade.

The drums announced it first; the awesome Lambeg drums whose menacing thunder drowned out thought.

Crowds lined the street waiting, craning their necks. Excited, happy; a holiday atmosphere. Men and women eating ice cream. Children with balloons on strings. When a little lad of five or six gave Henry a gap-toothed grin, he found himself grinning back.

The parade, he had to admit, was a stirring sight no matter

what one's persuasion. A flute-and-pipe band ecstatically playing "The Sash My Father Wore"; brilliant banners tossing in the wind; burly drummers beating the immense Lambeg drums with such energy the blood ran down their wrists. Unconsciously Henry began tapping his foot to the infectious beat of the drums.

Behind the band marched the Orangemen themselves in their unofficial uniform of dark serge suit and bowler hat. The Orange sash was prominently displayed. They walked with stiff dignity, their faces set in grim lines that belied the festival atmosphere. But when someone in the crowd shouted, "Burn all the papists and bugger the pope!," many of the marchers grinned.

Henry—who had thought himself antithetical to the religion of his birth—turned and went back to the hotel. In his room he took off his bowler hat and stamped the hard crown flat with his foot. He put the ruined hat in the bottom of his suitcase with his revolver, then went out into the streets again to soak up more local color.

He never heard the shot that hit him.

Chapter Twenty-five

An unreliable sun played tag among the clouds over Dublin. Ned had gone to a meeting. Síle was boiling sheets in the big copper boiler in the yard behind number 16 when Louise came stumbling out of the house. "Sweet Mother Mary," she gasped, wringing her hands. "Curse them terrible Proddys!"

Síle looked up. "What are you talking about?"

"The Prods have shot our Henry."

Síle dropped the wooden stirring pole and ran into the house.

Four men in the somber black of undertaker's assistants had deposited a coffin in the middle of the parlor. As Síle burst into the room they were just unscrewing the lid. She stood transfixed while a hundred images of Henry flooded her mind, tumbling over one another like pebbles on the bed of a rushing river. All so alive. She could not picture him dead. Perhaps it was not Henry after all, she thought desperately. Perhaps there had been some dreadful mistake of identity.

She forced herself to approach the coffin and look down as the lid was removed.

Henry Mooney lay inside.

A moan was wrung from Síle.

Henry's eyes opened.

She staggered back with her hand to her mouth.

"It's all right," a familiar deep voice said. "I'm not a ghost, though I might have been if these lads had made the airholes in the side of this contraption any smaller."

The "undertaker's assistants" carried him to the best bedroom in the house, while Louise arbitrarily dumped the belongings of its usual tenant into a smaller room. Within half an hour of his arrival Henry was resting on clean sheets. His cousin was busying herself in the kitchen, preparing food he did not want. Síle had assigned herself to be his nurse. Precious was in charge of fetching and carrying, though every few minutes she trotted into Henry's room to reassure herself that he was still alive.

"It's really not serious," Henry assured Síle. "A wound in the hip, but the bullet went clean through. A freak shot, perhaps even a ricochet. It nicked the bone but didn't break it, and missed all the vital organs."

"Any bullet wound is serious."

"Well, Mick's man didn't seem to think this one was. Thank God he was on duty when they brought me into the hotel. He found a doctor to patch me up and pronounce me dead, all in the one visit. Then he arranged for . . . er, undertakers, to bring me back to Dublin. All I need now is a few days to recover."

"You'll need more than that," Síle told him. "We'll have to keep the wound clean and those dressings changed, for one thing."

"Louise can send for that doctor of Ned's."

Síle bristled. She had decided the man was a quack, and said so. "I can tend a wound as well as any doctor. Didn't I learn first aid for the Rising?"

Henry felt his neck redden with embarrassment. "It's a hip wound, Síle. I really don't think—"

"And haven't I seen any number of naked men and their private parts?" she snapped.

Henry's mouth fell open.

"I'll tend you myself, Henry Mooney, and no arguing. The fewer people who know about this, the safer for us all."

By the time Ned came home Henry was sound asleep. Síle, Louise, and Precious took turns telling Ned the story, or as much of it as they knew. Two days later Michael Collins told him the rest.

Collins arrived shortly after Síle carried a breakfast tray to Henry's room. He stood filling up the doorway, grinning in at the patient. "How's she cuttin'?"

"Don't use your Cork slang on me," Henry said. "I'm not able for it this morning."

"He's feeling better," Síle interpreted. "That's why he's so narcky."

"I am not! Narcky, I mean. What have I to grouch about? I spent half a day in beautiful Belfast and saw shag-all of it, got shot in a painful place, came home in a coffin, and am lying here with no privacy and no peace while women fuss over me and feed me beef tea. Which I hate."

Síle lifted her eyebrows at Collins. "See what I mean?"

"I do indeed. Leave me with him for a few minutes, will you?"

Síle Duffy Halloran was one person who did not jump when Michael Collins issued an order. She merely looked at Henry, who nodded. "It's all right, Síle. If I need you I'll give a shout."

"So that's Ned's wife," Collins said when he judged her out of earshot. "Somehow she's not what I expected."

Henry chuckled. "Síle's not what anyone expects."

"She's a fair lass," Collins added.

"Have you not met her before?" *Given her a gun, perhaps, to sneak into my suitcase?*

"I have not; I'd remember her surely." His expression was guileless, but by now Henry knew him too well. It could be the complete truth or a total lie.

Collins abruptly changed the subject. "We got you out of Belfast just in time, Henry. The same day you were shot, armed mobs attacked the Catholic areas, burning and looting.[1] The riot's still going on. More than fifty people have been wounded and nineteen killed so far, but the police are making no effort to intervene. And we don't have enough armed men up there to protect our people, damn it.

"Oh, by the way, at least there's some good news. Erskine and Molly Childers have bought a new house."

"Really? Where?"

"Bushy Park Road in Terenure. Erskine's working on the *Bulletin* at home now."

When Collins had gone, Síle came in to change Henry's dressings. As she turned down the bedcovers he closed his eyes. He could not watch her face while his body lay exposed to her. Her fingers were cool; competent. Stripping away the old dressing, she gently bathed the wound with carbolic and tepid water. "There's an artery that runs down through the groin," she remarked, tracing its route with her fingertip. "If the bullet had gone an inch to the left you could be dead now."

"Lucky me," said Henry. His eyes were so tightly shut he could feel the lids crinkle at the corners.

Síle bent down to examine the wound more closely, looking for any hint of infection. He could feel her warm breath on his bare skin.

Does she know what she does to me? Of course she does; she's an experienced woman if ever there was one. Dear God . . . something's stirring down there, and it's not just the hair on my belly.

He lay in an agony of embarrassment, but she made no comment. She dressed the wound with professional expertise, then said briskly, "There, that's you done and dusted." When she had pulled the sheet over him and tucked the blanket in, Henry finally opened his eyes. Síle rewarded him with a smile. "I didn't hurt you too much, did I?"

"No. You didn't hurt me too much."

DEAR Ella,

"I am back in Dublin for a while, although currently indisposed. As soon as I am up and about again I hope you will allow me the pleasure of calling upon yourself and your family.

"As ever,

"Henry Mooney."

IT was the first week of August before Síle and Louise would allow Henry to leave the house. His hip was very

sore, and he was not certain he wanted to entrust himself to
a bicycle just yet, so he began building up his strength by
walking around the neighborhood. What he saw made him
resolve to keep his revolver with him at all times.

Regular army men patrolled the streets of Dublin carrying
rifles with bayonets fixed. In addition to their traditional
batons, the Dublin Metropolitan Police force was now
equipped with handguns. Plainclothes members of G Division loitered around known Republican meeting places.
They tried to appear inconspicuous but sometimes gave
themselves away by looking nervous.

And everywhere, swaggering like beings beyond the
moral restraint of gods or men, strode the Black and Tans.

Dubliners were living in a state of siege. A residence or
commercial premises could be raided at any time without
warning. Looted articles were displayed like trophies. At
night searchlights played on the fronts of houses while military transports rumbled incessantly through the streets.

On the ninth of August the Restoration of Order in Ireland
Bill received the royal assent. Trial by jury was virtually
abolished. The military forces were relieved of almost all
restraints under law.

Henry immediately wrote an angry denunciation of the
bill and took it to Terenure by tramcar. In spite of his emotions, he was careful to make certain he quoted the bill precisely. Erskine Childers was a meticulous editor. Every
detail of every story had to be checked and double-
checked—a finickiness that was turning Arthur Griffith's initial admiration for the Englishman to sharp dislike.

Childers read Henry's article twice, checked it against the
bill himself, and promised to publish it in the next *Bulletin*.
Henry Mooney was back at work.

His next article, he decided, would focus on the mass
hunger strike that had just begun in Cork Jail. Sixty Republicans—many of them being held without charge—were demanding that the category of political prisoner be reinstated.

"The British government has decided to risk their deaths
rather than accede to what is, after all, a reasonable request,"
Henry wrote. "Other countries recognize political prisoner
status. It is meant to guarantee humane treatment; nothing

more sinister than that. Yet this is being denied in Ireland."

As he was walking to the tram stop on the thirteenth of August he passed a newsagency and the headline of the *Cork Examiner* leaped out at him. He bought a copy and read incredulously: "Yesterday evening Lord Mayor Terence MacSwiney was arrested in City Hall while attending a meeting of the Sinn Féin Arbitration Court. Also arrested were several ranking officers of the Cork Brigade, including Liam Lynch. The lord mayor was transported under military escort to Victoria Barracks. There he was charged with taking part in illegal activities and possession of a police cipher code. When the authorities demanded that he remove his chain of office MacSwiney refused. Instead he has gone on hunger strike."

Dublin trams were always either ahead of schedule or behind. This morning the tram was late. Henry had time to read the article again before it arrived. On the ride to Terenure he sat staring blankly at an advertisement for White's Delicious Crystal Jellies over the window opposite his seat.

Erskine Childers had a copy of the *Examiner* lying open on his mahogany desk. On this morning his eyes were sparking fire. "Those bloody swine!" he exclaimed as Henry entered his study. "Terry, of all people. How *dare* they attack him after what they did to Tomás?"

"Do you want me to ask them?" Henry inquired, fighting to keep his own anger under control. "I'm on my way down there."

"Are you sure you feel up to it? I don't like the idea of you traveling when—"

"There's a train to Cork this afternoon and I'll be on it," Henry said determinedly. "I'll have the story back to you as soon as I can."

"Michael Collins was here only a few minutes ago. He left this for you." Childers handed Henry one of Collins' familiar contact lists. "He was that certain you'd be going to Cork."

"Where was he going?"

Erskine Childers, who loved adventure but had an intense dislike of violence, said through tight lips, "Mick's going to order the squad to shoot the first half-dozen G-men they see leaving Dublin Castle."

SPENDING six hours on a jolting train was agony. Henry endured it with gritted teeth, cursing the British, the Great Southern Railway, the weather, and life in general.

He was not allowed to interview MacSwiney. Nor was the lord mayor's wife allowed to visit her husband until the day his trial—a court martial—began on the sixteenth of August. There was already considerable interest from the foreign press. "The county of Cork is a hotbed of IRA rebellion," an English reporter had written. "In July the rebels murdered the divisional commander of the Royal Irish Constabulary, claiming he had attempted to incite his policemen into violent acts against the populace. This is of course scurrilous and defamatory."

As he sat among the other journalists at the trial Henry wrote in his notebook: "Lord Mayor MacSwiney appears pale but composed. He has been without food for four days. He is standing trial alone because the IRA officers arrested with him were released by mistake. According to rather embarrassed testimony this morning, the authorities had employed British soldiers who did not fully realize the importance of their captives. The use of soldiers was an attempt to distance the operation from the murder of Tomás MacCurtáin by policemen."

During the interval Henry made his way to Muriel MacSwiney. "I'm so sorry about this," he told her.

"Why? It's not your fault."

"Is there anything I can do?"

"Thank you, but no. Isn't it strange that people always ask that? There's nothing anyone can do, yet they ask."

"Is someone minding the baby?"

"My sister-in-law's taking care of her. She'll be all right. It's Terry I'm worried about. He must be so hungry. I would give anything if only I could cook him a proper meal. But what about yourself, Mr. Mooney? Why, you're limping." Her brow creased with concern.

"It's nothing—a minor injury, I assure you. Didn't take a

feather out of me." Henry was touched that in spite of all her troubles, Muriel MacSwiney took time to notice his.

The military prosecutor brought several charges against MacSwiney based on papers found during an unauthorized search of his office and "likely to cause disaffection to His Majesty." MacSwiney's speech following Tomás MacCurtáin's murder, when he had expressed the determination of Cork Corporation not to be intimidated by official acts of terror, was also used against him.

The tribunal deliberated for no more than fifteen minutes. During this time MacSwiney and his wife talked together in Irish. When the president of the tribunal returned, he announced that MacSwiney had been found guilty on three of four charges. He was sentenced to two years' imprisonment.

Terence MacSwiney then made the final statement allowed him. "You have got to realize that the Irish Republic is really existing," he told the court. "The gravest offense that can be committed is against the head of state. The offence is only relatively less great when committed against the head of a city."

Under the laws of the Republic of Ireland, MacSwiney insisted, the British government had no right to try him. He concluded by saying, "I wish to state that I will put a limit to any term of imprisonment you may impose. I have taken no food since Thursday. I shall be free, alive or dead, in a month."

What sort of men and women have we in Ireland? I thought valor died with Pearse and Plunkett and MacDonagh; I was afraid that integrity was a casualty of war.

I was wrong.

That same night Terence MacSwiney was sent to Brixton Prison in England, putting him at a safe distance from the other Cork hunger strikers. There was nothing more Henry could do for him in Cork. But there were other stories to be told.

The first name and address on the list Collins had given him was Tom Barry, Bandon, West Cork.

Henry hitched a ride with a grocery suppliers' van headed southwest from the city. He rode in the front with the driver while the bicycle he had borrowed from Michael Harrington rode in the back, wedged between stacked cartons of Oxo and Germolene. The lush, fertile area through which they drove gave little hint of the general West Cork landscape: bogland and wasteland and rugged mountains. Poor land and impoverished people.

The valley of the Bandon was Big House country. Secure behind the high walls of extensive demesnes, British loyalists hunted game on their private lands, fished their private streams, and entertained members of their own class through the efforts of retinues of servants—servants whose ancestors had once owned these same lands.

Henry sat watching the scene unfold past the van window.

"Have you people in Bandon town?" the van driver asked conversationally.

"My father's mother was a Cork woman, but she's been dead for many years."

"Godamercyonher," responded the driver.

"I'm not looking for relatives. I'm . . . ah . . . interested in the military."

"Plenty of British soldiers around Bandon," the driver said darkly. He spat out the window. "One of 'em has a nasty accident every now and again."

"I'm looking for the Republican Army."

The man turned to Henry with a gap-toothed grin. "Why dint you say so? It's the First Battalion, West Cork Brigade you want then. I've two brothers with the IRA myself. You don't look much like a recruit, though," he added, eyeing Henry's good suit.

"You never can tell," said Henry.

The van driver let him out at the last crossroads before Bandon town. "You don't want to ask a lot of questions in the town, because there's an army barracks there," he warned. "They wouldn't be friendly. Just last month an RIC sergeant, the chief intelligence officer for the British forces in West Cork, was shot dead on the steps of the church. It was the one place he thought he was safe. He went everywhere else with an escort of Black and Tans. The lads who did him just walked away; no one tried to stop them." The driver grinned again. "If you want to find the First Battalion HQ, follow that road off to the left for a mile or so. Go straight until you come to another crossroads. Turn left, then right, then left again, maybe three more miles. You can't miss it," he assured Henry. "A sentry will have seen you coming."

The road was far from straight: twisty and winding and deeply rutted, barely navigable for a man on a bicycle with a healing bullet wound in his hip. When he came to the crossroads, Henry had to stop. He leaned his bicycle against a tumbled-down stone wall while he caught his breath, then stepped to the center of the crossroads.

He stood in the middle of a vast emptiness.

Four roads going four ways and no traffic. No people. Not even an ass and cart.

Henry listened to the tides of blood beating in his ears.

At length he remounted the bicycle and pedaled on.

Like most Irish directions, the van driver's were a marvel of imprecision. When Henry felt sure he had gone at least ten miles, the last five in considerable pain, he dismounted again and eased himself into a sitting position at the side of the road.

Amid the blazing yellow blossom of a furze bush a small bird sang. A gentle wind blew in from the sea, shivering the grass. Henry closed his eyes for a moment.

"D'you have any weapons on you?" a mild voice inquired.

THE sentry, who had been watching Henry from concealment for the last half-mile, was a lad of twenty-two or-three. He was brandishing a pitchfork like a bayonet.

"I have a revolver in my coat pocket," Henry told him.

"Give it over."

"I could shoot you with it instead."

"You could," the sentry agreed. "But the noise would bring fifty men down on you at once and you'd never leave here alive. Give me your gun, please, and come with me."

Please. Henry handed him the weapon.

It was beginning to rain.

They wheeled the bicycle between them across an expanse of boggy field. When Henry paused to bend down and remove his bicycle clips from his trousers, the sentry watched with fascination. "Where'd ye get them things?"

"Dublin."

"Ah," the young man said in a tone reserved for addressing wonders and marvels. Obviously Dublin belonged in the mythical realms of Camelot and Xanadu. "And what d'you do there?"

"I'm a journalist. My name's Henry Mooney." He held out his hand.

The young man took the proffered hand and gave it a vigorous shake. "A newspaperman? Say, I have an inclination that way myself. I'm thinking of applying to the *Cork Examiner* for a job. D'you happen to know anyone there?"

"I do."

"Would you put in a good word for me?"

"Consider it done."

The rain fell harder. On the far side of the field they came to a cut bank, below which the ground fell away sharply. Snugged into the lee of the bank, and well hidden until one was almost upon them, were three tents. The sentry whistled; four men emerged from one of the tents and trotted toward them. "Who've you got there, Ellis?"

"A journalist from Dublin. Says he's looking for Tom Barry."

"He's found him," called a voice from the largest tent. "Bring him in to me."

Henry was escorted into an old British army tent that sagged from its tent pole with the weight of the rain. Tom Barry was sitting on a packing case, eating a sandwich. He was in his early twenties, with tousled brown hair, a square face, and a short upper lip. Instead of a uniform he wore a tightly belted trenchcoat, but when he stood up to greet Henry he carried himself with military bearing.

"I have a note," said Henry, "which will identify me. It's in my sock. May I show you?"

Barry gave Henry's suit the same look the van driver had. "Wait a minute." He unfolded a newspaper—the *Examiner*, Henry observed—and spread it on the packing case. "Here, sit on this. You must be perished with the cold. Bring him a wee drop of whiskey, somebody."

Henry lowered himself with difficulty. He was getting stiff. He removed his shoe and sock and handed Collins' note to Barry, who read it through twice. "So the *Bulletin* readers want to know what we're getting up to in West Cork," he said. "It's about time."

"What's your strength in manpower? We won't print that, you understand; it's just for my own information."

"We have seven battalions organized around the major towns," Barry replied.[2] His manner was calm and confident, that of a man already accustomed to command. "The Bandon battalion's the largest; thirteen companies. We're all volunteers; no one draws pay. And we're dreadfully underequipped. Right now the whole Cork Brigade has only about thirty-five serviceable rifles and slightly fewer pistols and revolvers. But what we lack in arms, we make up in the spirit of the men. They've already proved they're willing to endure empty bellies and sleep in hayfields and, most important of all, to accept strict military discipline. I say without fear of contradiction—and this you can print—that nine out of ten of these fellows are prepared to give their lives for the Republic.[3]

"As the brigade training officer, I'm in charge of setting up real training camps for them, starting next month. There will be five camps for both officers and men, and the good women of Cumann na mBan are going to see to feeding us. When training's completed each camp will become a flying column. Every brigade is more or less autonomous, and we intend to make West Cork Brigade the best in the whole Irish Republican Army."

"Did you have any prior military experience?" Henry asked.

Tom Barry smiled. "The best or the worst, depending on your point of view. I'm Cork born and bred, but I enlisted in the British army on my seventeenth birthday.[4] There wasn't anything exciting happening for a young lad in Cork in those days. That's why a lot of us enlisted. Not for king or empire; we just had an itch and we needed to scratch it.

"I was assigned to the Mesopotamian Expeditionary Force, so I saw a lot of action. Learned a lot from what I saw, too. In May of '16 we were trying to break through and rescue General Townsend at Kut-al-Imara, where the Germans and the Turks had him pinned down. One evening when I went to the orderly tent someone had posted a commuiqué from home. 'Rebellion in Dublin,' it said. That was the first time I ever heard any mention of the idea of an Irish republic. In my school days I could name you every king and queen of England but was taught nothing of Irish history.

"The rebellion got me thinking about my own country. I set myself to learning everything I could about our relationship with England. Didn't take me long to realize that a war for Irish independence was infinitely more worthwhile than supporting British imperialism. So as soon as the Great War was over, I came home and joined the IRA.

"For our new recruits, I sum up what I've learned in one sentence. 'You need caution and courage in equal measure,' I tell them, 'and in that order, not the other way around.'"

As Tom Barry spoke, Henry forgot how young he was. The strong bones of his mature character showed through his youthful flesh like the bare winter tree glimpsed through summer's foliage. "Do you remember when the police murdered Tomás MacCurtáin?" he asked.

"I do remember," the journalist replied. "As a matter of fact I was in Cork when it happened."

"A man called Swanzy was the RIC district inspector for MacCurtáin's area. He'd hounded MacCurtáin for years and finally got him. After the jury brought a verdict against the police Swanzy was transferred, but some of the lads have found him in County Antrim. We're sending a squad of Cork men up there to do him; every one of them volunteered for the job."[5]

Henry shifted on his packing crate. The pain in his hip had become a drumbeat. "What can you do about Terence MacSwiney?"

"I don't know . . . yet. He was arrested and deported so fast we couldn't organize to break him out."

"He's threatened to starve himself to death, you know."

"If he does," said Barry grimly, "Cork will rise to avenge him."

Henry spent the night in a leaking tent talking with Tom

Barry. Sometime during the long hours his wound and its circumstances are mentioned; he tried to be offhand about it. "I'll have a scar but no lasting damage—not like a friend of mine who'll probably suffer from a head wound for the rest of his life."

"Still, being shot is no fun. Did it put the frighteners on you?"

"It made me want to shoot back. Which reminds me . . . your sentry took a revolver off me. Would you like to keep it, since you have so few weapons?"

"That's very tempting," said Barry, "but you may need it yourself one of these days. You're not afraid to use it, are you?"

"No," said Henry.

"Good. Once a man knows the meaning of fear, he has no business fighting."

WHEN Henry returned to Dublin, he barely noticed the welcome he received from number 16. The work he had to do was in the forefront of his mind, crowding everything else out—except Precious, whom he gave a mighty hug, a pocketful of boiled sweets, and an old snaffle bit he had seen hanging in a shop window.

Then he went to his room and began to write.

First he described the trial in angry but measured tones. Then he wrote a glowing tribute to the spirit and determination of the West Cork Brigade. He did not reveal any sensitive information with the exception of one item, which he had first cleared with Tom Barry. "Tell them," Barry had insisted. "We want people to know what we're up against."

Henry wrote: "Following the shooting of the head of British intelligence in Cork a number of Republicans were hunted down at random. Two of these were Tom Hales and Pat Harte. They were captured at Laragh and ordered to reveal the names of those involved in the shooting. When they refused they were tortured in front of witnesses, as if this were a Roman spectacle.

"According to signed affidavits, Hales and Harte were stripped naked and brutally beaten.[6] Then they were bound hand and foot and a charge of gun-cotton was strapped to their backs. The officer in charge vowed to 'blow the anarchists to hell.' They were allowed to savor the terror of this promise for some minutes before the attempt was made to set off the explosive. The detonators failed, however. The prisoners were then forced to run a gauntlet of bayonets and thrown into a lorry where they were beaten again. Hales was hit in the temple with a rifle butt.

"They were transported to Bandon Barracks and stood up against a wall in front of a firing squad. The officer in charge demanded that they salute the British flag. This they also refused. They were not shot—that was just another way of torturing them—but they were beaten unconscious. When Tom Hales recovered his senses he saw another British officer taking snapshots of the incident for his personal collection.

"Harte and Hales continued to be beaten and brutalized by men working in shifts. Pliers were used to tear flesh from their bodies. At one point Tom Hales was dragged to the top of a staircase by the hair of his head, then thrown down the stairs and attacked with fists and feet at the bottom.

"Both men are now in the Cork Military Hospital. If they survive, they will be deported to Pentonville Prison. One may only speculate about the treatment awaiting them there."

When Henry called in to Bushy Park to deliver his articles, Erskine Childers remarked, "You're still limping a bit, I see. Anna said it was too soon for you to be going off like that. Frank and I've talked it over, and we'd prefer if you stayed here for a while. There are plenty of things to write about in Dublin until you're fit again."

Henry decided to stay in Dublin, at least until his hip was thoroughly healed. He knew he stood an excellent chance of being arrested, but that was a secondary consideration.

He was needed.

Precious summed it up best: "Nothing's the same when you're not here, Uncle Henry. It's like there's a big hole where you're supposed to be."

Louise Kearney reincorporated Henry so smoothly into life at number 16 it was almost as if he had never been away.

As a bonus he received a cordial note from Ella Rutledge. "On the twentieth of September we shall be having a small party to formally announce Madge's betrothal, just a gathering for family and close friends. I do so hope you will be able to attend."

Chapter Twenty-six

Ned flung aside his pencil with a grunt of exasperation. Síle looked up from her mending. Precious was hard on clothes. "What's wrong?"

"I'm not making much headway with my novel, Síle. Maybe I should have taken Henry's advice and written about the Rising. But those memories still hurt too much."

"What you're doing seems to be causing you some pain," she commented.

"It's just . . . I wish I hadn't learned the rules of writing. It would be so much easier if I didn't know them—or had the courage to disregard them."

"You've never had trouble disregarding rules."

"This is different. You don't understand."

Staring at the sheet of paper before him, he did not see Síle wince. "I'm sure I don't," she said stiffly. "I didn't have your education."

"*Alanna,** I didn't mean it like that. I just—"

"I know. We're getting on each other's nerves, that's all. It happens sometimes."

"What you need is a holiday," said Ned.

She laughed. "How could I?"

"Even Louise takes a holiday sometimes. You know she's

*Irish term of endearment

off to visit her friend Maggie Walshe in Balbriggan tomorrow."

"She always goes on the twentieth of September, because it's her friend's birthday and they have a party in the evening," Síle replied, adding wistfully, "It sounds lovely."

"Then why don't you and Precious go with her? Get out into the country, enjoy the fresh air, and come back the next day. It will do the child a power of good and you too."

"Louise and I can't both be away overnight, Ned. Who would mind this place?"

"I shall, of course. I'm not helpless, you know. And the lodgers won't care who's here as long as the lamps are lit and there's a fire on the hearth when they come in. You just go and enjoy yourself." He gave her a gentle spank on the buttocks, then let his hand linger, cupping her warmth until she turned to him with eyes humid with desire.

T H A T night as they sat down at the table Precious exulted, "I'm going to the country tomorrow, Uncle Henry—I'm going to ride horses!" Her face was flushed, her eyes very bright.

"Don't lose the run of yourself entirely," Louise warned. "Balbriggan's not a farm, it's a village, and we'll only be there overnight. I doubt if there'll be any horse riding."

Henry winked at the girl. "Don't look so disappointed, Little Business. Tell you what: I've been making some inquiries, and I've found a man who can teach you to ride. He runs a livery stable beside the Smithfield Market."

"Where they have the horse fair?"

"Know all about that, do you? Well, you can start lessons next weekend if you like. I'll walk you over there myself and buy you lunch someplace in the city afterward."

"Clever strategy," Ned said, "presenting us with a fait accompli."

"I'm learning from master strategists," Henry told him.

Precious was too excited to eat. She only fiddled with her food and was packed off to bed early.

By the time unexpected last-minute details were attended to next morning, Louise was almost frantic. "We're all behind like the cow's tail!" she complained as she hurried out the door. "Do come along, or we'll miss our train."

Síle lingered in the hall to give Ned a final embrace, then ran after her.

HENRY had long since left the house. He had a round of calls to make to the various businesses who employed his services as a freelancer; plus, his work load for the *Bulletin* was drastically increased. Attacks on Catholics in Belfast had multiplied.[1] Hundreds had been driven out of the city by Orangemen and their houses burned. Between August twenty-second and September third, thirty-one Catholic men and women were murdered by loyalist mobs and members of the UVF.

A member of the British cabinet suggested shooting "a hundred Sinn Féiners a day" to cow the rebels.

The IRA undertook nearly a thousand raids for arms.

The condition of the hunger strikers in Cork Jail deteriorated. Crowds daily gathered outside the walls to pray. But world attention was focused on the man in London's Brixton Prison. An appeal for Terence MacSwiney's release was refused by Lloyd George. Winston Churchill came out strongly against any concessions for Ireland.

Every week the *Irish Bulletin* published a summary entitled *Acts of Aggression Committed by British Crown Forces*. "On Thursday the following residents of Dublin City were arrested in their beds without warrant or charge." Thirty-eight names followed: dentists, county surveyors, music teachers, milliners, mineral water salesmen . . . all deemed enemies of the Crown and arrested without a scrap of corroborating evidence.

Week after week. Month after month.

"Someday our little *Bulletin* will be a priceless historical document," Kathleen McKenna predicted.

Dublin Castle was distributing its own propaganda to counter the *Bulletin*. A four-page news sheet entitled the *Weekly Summary of Outrages* was being circulated that depicted the Republicans as a gang of degenerate criminals holding the nation in thrall, while the Black and Tans were portrayed as valiant rescuers arriving in the nick of time. The *Weekly Summary* contained no mention of the hundreds of arson attacks, beatings, and murders being perpetrated by the British side.

"With the *Bulletin*," Desmond FitzGerald told his staff, "we're fighting for the possession of history."

Notices were posted on walls throughout Dublin offering cash rewards for information on IRA members. Citizens were warned to disguise their handwriting. "This is a marvelous opportunity," Henry commented, "for any vindictive person to have someone he dislikes arrested and get paid for it."

Meanwhile in Brixton Prison Terence MacSwiney was slowly sinking. Mindful of what had happened with Thomas Ashe, the authorities were reluctant to force-feed him. But neither would they let him go.

Cruel jokes were being made about him from the stages of English music halls. The least vicious was, "Save money—let the vulgar Irishman swallow his pride if he's hungry. He's only getting what he deserves for trying to bully his betters."

When this was reported in the British papers, Henry responded in the *Bulletin* with a rare show of petulance. "Vulgarity, like bullying, is an acquired characteristic. If we Irish are guilty of either, we learned it from our neighbors."

SHORTLY before noon, on the morning of September twentieth, a new story was breaking. Henry and Frank Gallagher were walking together along Arran Quay when a member of the Dublin Metropolitan Police came running toward them. Both men tensed until they recognized him as a faithful subscriber to the *Bulletin*. Frank caught him by the arm. "What's wrong, Declan?"

"I'm after being in Upper Church Street," the policeman panted. "Some British soldiers with a lorry had called in to the bakery for provisions when half a dozen men in civilian clothes came walking down the street and pulled guns on them. There was a shootout; a couple of the ambush team were hit and several soldiers fell. I just stood there with me mouth open, gaping like a trout, I was that stunned. Then I saw one young chap's gun jam. He knelt down beside the lorry to free it, then stood and fired again, but he didn't hit anything. The bloody gun jammed a second time; meanwhile his pals scarpered. When he looked around and saw he was alone, he dived under the lorry—Hoping to get away in the confusion, I expect. But the soldiers grabbed him and pulled him out. I'm on my way to the station now to report."[2]

He ran off while Frank and Henry hurried to the scene. By this time the street was crowded with curious spectators: working-class men and boys in caps, a few businessmen in hats, a scattering of women. Soldiers were demanding that no one leave the scene until they had been questioned.

Henry began methodically working his way through the crowd, interviewing anyone who would talk to him.

Several knew the young man who had been captured. They identified him as Kevin Barry. He was only eighteen, a Belvedere College boy who was studying medicine as well being as a member of the Republican Army. Witnesses agreed that Barry had not shot anyone himself. Unfortunately, he was the only member of the ambush team whom the soldiers caught. It would go hard with him.

SÍLE was enjoying her little holiday inordinately. Balbriggan was on the seacoast some twenty miles north of Dublin, unremarkable except for a thriving English-owned hosiery business. The little town had its full complement of churches and pubs. Rows of tiny cottages occupied by factory workers were interspersed with shops on the main Dublin–Belfast road and lined the narrow laneways.

Louise's friend Maggie was a popular woman married to the owner of a butcher's shop. The couple lived over the shop with two daughters and a grown son. Maggie's birthday every year was something of a local tradition. By late afternoon her female friends had taken over both the living quarters and the shop, while their menfolk retired to their locals.

Laughter and banter and gossip, mothers and daughters enjoying themselves together, complaints about husbands and brothers and praise for sweethearts and sons. Someone had brought a fiddle; several of the women danced together on the sawdust-covered floor of the shop. Endless platters of food were served, and endless pots of tea.

Síle Halloran was welcomed into the group as if she had grown up in Balbriggan. No one aside from Louise Kearney knew her background. She might have been any respectable married woman in any ordinary village.

She had never been happier.

This, she thought to herself, was what she had been missing and never knew it. Normal life. She resolved that when they went back to Dublin the next day she would start getting around her own neighborhood more. Meet other women, make new friends. She had been hiding out in number 16 from possible confrontation with her past. But that was years behind her now, thanks to Ned. Time to live, she thought resolutely. Time to live.

The evening was crisp and cool, a perfect autumn night. The men were still at the pub when Maggie made up pallets for her daughters and gave her guests from Dublin their bed. Síle thought she was too excited to sleep, but as soon as her head touched the pillow the world faded away. She drifted smiling into a dream.

HENRY Mooney was attending Madge Mansell's engagement party, which included dancing and a late supper. Ava had taken charge of planning the wedding. It would take place as soon as the bride was twenty-one. In the meantime Madge was being praised, petted, and bullied by a growing contingent of women. Every detail of the event was discussed as if a matter of vital national significance.

"It will be the social event of the season," Ava assured Henry.

"Is your own family coming?"

"My family." Ava gave a contemptuous sniff and changed the subject.

The prospective bride, Henry thought, looked stunned. Her young man, a barrister friend of Edwin's, looked positively terrified.

But Ella Rutledge was beautiful.

In the back of Henry's mind lurked the incident in Upper Church Street earlier that day, and the young Republican called Kevin Barry who had been marched off to an uncertain fate. He was determined not to let it spoil his evening, however—not with Ella Rutledge smiling at him as if there had never been any tension between them. It might have been the occasion, it might have been the champagne, but as they were eating supper she leaned against his shoulder and whispered, "I do hope you will call more often. You don't need an invitation, you know. Just come. We've . . . I've missed you."

THE sound of gunfire came through the open window like a crack of lightning.

Síle sat bolt upright in bed.

"Merciful hour!" Louise cried, clutching at her. "Did you hear that?"

Síle said tightly, "I think we had best get dressed."

A few minutes later Maggie Walshe's husband came running up the stairs. "There's been a brawl in the pub. One man's shot dead and another's wounded."

"Will there be trouble?" His wife was still in her night-dress with her hair hanging in a long braid down her back. As she spoke she caught the sides of her nightdress in her hands and clutched the material as if for support.

"What do you think, woman? I didn't see what happened myself, but I heard the dead man's one of the Black and Tans from the depot at Gormanstown. Maybe the IRA shot him." Walshe turned to Síle. "Gormanstown's not three miles from here. Somebody's sure to ring them from the hotel; they'll be on us before you know it."

Maggie Walshe began to cry. Slow, helpless tears; the tears of ten generations of being a victim. Her husband cursed in a methodical monotone and began searching for some sort of defensive weapon. When all he could find was his wife's broom, he ran down to the shop and brought back his knives and a meat cleaver.

Síle willed herself to stay calm. "We'd best shutter the windows," she told Maggie Walshe.

Black and Tans in the armored cars called Crossley tenders roared into Balbriggan. Pulling up in front of the first public house they came to, they broke down the door, grabbed bottles of liquor, and set the place ablaze. Then they ran out into the road and began firing their weapons at random.

Someone screamed.

The Tans surged through the village, breaking windows and singing "We're the Boys of the Bulldog Brigade" at the top of their lungs. Then they began lighting torches.

The frightened little company above the butcher shop heard the street door being battered down. Immediately thereafter came the first whiff of smoke. "You murderin' gobshites!" Walshe cried. Waving the meat cleaver, he pelted down the stairs with his wife behind him, tugging at his coat and tearfully begging him to come back.

He flung open the door leading from the stairway into the shop. A blow from a rifle butt knocked him to the floor.

Smoke billowed through the open doorway and up the stairs, driving the women back into the living quarters.

Síle took charge. Stripping the covers from the nearest bed, she ordered, "Knot all the sheets together to make ropes and fasten them to the heaviest pieces of furniture, then climb out the back windows to the yard. Hurry!"

Leaving them to it, she felt her way down the smoky stairwell to see what could be done for Maggie's husband. The far side of the shop was in flames, but there was no sign of Walshe. When she took a step inside to make certain he was gone, Síle stumbled over the meat cleaver. Just then a line of fire ran past her, feeding on the sawdust on the floor, and roared up the stairs.

Escape that way was cut off.

Síle snatched up the cleaver and ran for the door.

A different kind of chaos met her in the road. The night air was cool after the heat of the burning building, but here too was roaring: the roaring of the Black and Tans. Looting was well underway. Men and women were being dragged from their premises into the road, where the men were beaten with fists and rifle butts while their womenfolk were pawed by drunken soldiers.

One of the Tans caught sight of Síle standing in the road, uncertain which way to run. "C'mere, ya Irish bitch!" he shouted. "Lemme show ya wot a real man is like!" He held his rifle to one side and began gyrating his pelvis obscenely.

In his leering face Síle suddenly saw all the men who had abused and degraded her. The men who had tried to kill Ned. The men who kept Ireland on its knees.

Her scream of rage soared above the drunken singing and the roar of the fire, the smashing of glass, and the crashing of timbers. She felt no fear, no hesitation, only the fury of a hunted animal driven too hard for too long.

Síle flung herself at her tormentor.

He took an instinctive step back and tried to fend off the crazy red-haired woman.

But no power on earth could stop her taking revenge. Not this time.

With a wild cry of his own, the Tan drove his bayonet through her body.

At first all Síle felt was the force of the blow, like being kicked in the belly. She looked down in disbelief to see steel plunging into her midsection. Then everything inside her stopped at once. Frozen. Skewered on icy hot steel, on burning cold steel. She could not breathe. The meat cleaver fell from fingers gone numb.

After that came the pain. Pain beyond imagining, tearing her in half.

Síle writhed on the bayonet, trying to turn and look back. "*Precious . . .*"

Her mouth filled with blood.

The man shouted at her, "Gor blimey, ya stupid bint, wotcha do that fer? Wotcha hafta go and do that fer? I ain't never kilt no woman before."

Her slumping body was a dead weight on his blade. He tried to shake it off. When that failed he lowered her to the ground and braced his foot against her belly so he could pull the bayonet free. "She made me do it—she come at me with a cleaver!" he protested to anyone who would listen.

No one did.

• • •

HENRY returned very late to number 16. He was in a buoyant mood, a rainbowed soap-bubble of a mood. He did not want to talk to anyone for fear a pinprick might explode his joy, so he went straight to bed. He hardly slept. He could not remember when he had felt so flooded with energy. By morning he was up and dressed and out of the house without seeing anyone.

Recalling Tom Barry's description of the torture of Hales and Harte, he was worried about young Kevin Barry. The best source for information would be one of Michael Collins' agents. It was still early enough to catch Ned Broy before he went to work in Dublin Castle, so Henry walked to a coffee shop he knew Broy frequented on his way to work. Accidental meetings in informal surroundings were always safest. Besides, it gave Henry the opportunity for a hot breakfast.

He was just beginning his meal when Broy appeared. Like all men recruited for the Dublin Metropolitan Police force, Broy was broad-shouldered and muscular, standing well over six feet tall. Added to this he had trained himself to show no expression, no matter what happened. Some said this unnerving impassivity was his most effective weapon. When he recognized Henry, Broy greeted the journalist with the faintest of nods, then took a seat at an adjacent table so the two could talk across the backs of their chairs.

"You know anything about the arrest of a lad called Kevin Barry?" Henry asked out of the side of his mouth as he pretended to devote himself to buttering a scone.

"Heard something yesterday," Broy muttered. "Involved in an IRA attack on a party from the Duke of Wellington's Regiment. Two soldiers dead, one probably dying."

"Where are they holding Barry?"

"Dunno, but I'll find out when I go to the Castle. Won't be until this afternoon, though. First there's this Balbriggan business."

Henry put down his scone. "What Balbriggan business?"

"Last night a hundred and fifty Black and Tans from the military depot at Gormanstown sacked Balbriggan. They destroyed forty-nine houses, four pubs, and the stocking factory. At least two civilians were killed. I'm supposed to—"

Henry was running for the door.

He reached number 16 as a member of the DMP was leaving. The policeman had taken off his helmet and was carrying it under his arm.

Henry brushed past him. Ned Halloran was standing in the hall, his face as empty as a sheet of blank paper. "What's happened?" Henry grabbed his friend by the shoulders. "I just heard about Balbriggan—tell me what's happened!"

Ned's mouth worked, but no sound came out.

"Were they hurt? Look at me, Ned!" Henry's clutching fingers bit so deep they reached the far place to which his friend had retreated.

Ned's green eyes slowly focused. In their depths Henry saw the signposts of his own heart obliterated.

No. God no.

In a voice of ashes Ned whispered, "Dead."

Unsay it. Unsay that word. "I don't believe you." Shock rolled over Henry. "There must be some mistake. Not Síle! Not Precious!"

"Precious," Ned echoed hollowly.

Don't tell me, don't make it real, I can't stand this.

"She . . . woke up with a cold yesterday. We made her stay here. She was so . . . angry . . ." Ned swallowed hard. When he spoke again, it was one long ascending moan. "It's Síle, Henry. Sweet Christ, they've killed my Síle!"

This time the undertakers were real.

LOUISE draped all the mirrors with black crepe and stopped all the clocks. Time itself had stopped at number 16.

Ned asked Father O'Flanagan to conduct the funeral service. "My wife was a dedicated Republican," he told the priest who was also vice-president of Sinn Féin. "She fought with Countess Markievicz in Stephen's Green and she nursed the wounded in the GPO." These were the credits that mattered. Nothing else needed to be said.

• • •

Requiem Mass in the gloom and glamour of the Pro-Cathedral, a stone's throw from the General Post Office. Familiar faces and strangers. Louise sniffling into her handkerchief. Father O'Flanagan attributing more glory to the deceased than she had ever known in her lifetime.

In a driving rainstorm they buried Síle Duffy Halloran in Glasnevin Cemetery. A Republican honor guard. The coffin draped in an Irish tricolor. Michael Collins among the mourners at graveside, with his bared head bowed.

Ned would not let anyone stand close to him. Would not let anyone comfort him. His grief was as scorching as his passion had been and could not be shared. He clung to a strip of sanity as thin as the rind pared from a cheese. On either side of that strip was a howling void. The easy thing would be to turn loose and tumble down, in madness forgetting. Forgetting the death of those days that were never to be. The aborted future.

Laid in the grave with Síle.

If only I still had the comfort of faith, Henry was thinking. *When I was a little boy I was sure I'd meet my father again in heaven.*

But he had gone from devoted to diverted, and did not know how to find his way back.

The gravediggers were throwing down hay to deaden the sound of falling earth when it was shoveled back into the grave.

Precious stood beside Henry, clinging tightly to his hand as the first clods went down. "I'm not going to cry, Uncle Henry," she said in a hoarse whisper. "My mama was very brave and I'm going to be brave too."

It was Henry who wept.

• • • •

LATER he wrote to his sister Alice in the convent and asked her to pray, to a God Henry was no longer sure he even believed in, for the soul of a woman she had never known. "Síle was a good person, a much better person than she ever knew," he explained. "Ask God not to judge her harshly. Her faults were those of desperation and we are all desperate, one way or another."

Chapter Twenty-seven

THE sacking of Balbriggan made international news. Photographs taken of the destruction—the roofless houses, the smoldering ruins—horrified people far from the shores of Ireland. The village was described as "looking like a Belgian town that had been wrecked by the Germans in the war" by no less a personage than Herbert Asquith, former prime minister of Great Britain.[1]

A number of Republican prisoners were quietly transferred—or released—from Cork Jail. Henry captioned his article: "The Government's Guilty Conscience."

But eleven hunger strikers remained within the grim prison walls—and one in Brixton Prison.

On the twenty-first of September an IRA flying column ambushed five Black and Tans in West Clare and left them lying dead in the road. In reprisal the Tans attacked nearby Ennistymon and Milltown Malbay. The first person they shot to death was an old man driving a haycart. Next they shot a young schoolteacher, then a twelve-year-old boy who was carrying water to put out the fire destroying his house. The rampage finally ended hours later at Lahinch, where the terrified citizenry took to the fields as their town hall and homes were burnt to the ground.

In an interview given to members of the American press, General Macready remarked that it was "only natural" that men under his command should act on their own initiative.[2]

On the twenty-second an unarmed civilian registered as John A. Lynch of Killmallock on the registry of the Royal Exchange Hotel, Dublin, was shot dead by members of the RIC as he lay in his bed. There was speculation that he had been mistaken for Liam Lynch, who was now commander of the Southern Division of the IRA.

A few days later Republicans stormed the police barracks at Trim, in County Meath, and seized its store of weapons. Two hundred Tans and Auxiliaries retaliated by sacking the town.

On the twenty-eighth Liam Lynch and Ernie O'Malley led an IRA raid on the military barracks at Mallow, which they captured. In reprisal Crown forces sacked the town.

People in Ireland began bitterly referring to the conflict as the Tan War.

Even the English press was horrified. The London *Times* spoke for many: "The accounts of arson and destruction must fill English readers with a sense of shame. The name of England is being sullied throughout the empire and throughout the world by this savagery."[3]

I could show them real savagery," Henry said to Louise. "Ned Halloran. God help anyone who crosses him now."

Ned went to Michael Collins and demanded to join the squad. Collins refused. Ned returned to number 16 in a towering rage. "Mick's not discriminating against you," Henry tried to tell him. "It's just that you're out for revenge and he won't allow it."

"Will he not, the bloody hypocrite!" Ned slammed his fist against the wall so hard the sound reverberated through the house. He did not feel the pain. "He avenged Tom Clarke and Seán MacDermott!"

"That's different," Henry said. Knowing it was not.

Ned hit the wall again, harder.

Henry laid a restraining hand on his arm. "Please, Ned, we're all grieving."

Ned whirled away. For a moment Henry thought he would hit him, so livid and furious was the face he turned on his friend. "You don't know anything about it!" he cried.

Don't I?

For Ned Halloran there was only one loss: his. He clutched his grief to his heart like a trophy and refused to acknowledge anyone else's pain. He began avoiding number 16, leaving without explanation and returning at all hours, sometimes filthy, sometimes with a split lip or a bloody nose.

One night in the Oval Bar Henry confided to Matt Nugent, "I'm afraid Ned's going to get himself killed."

"Nobody can stop him if that's what he really wants to do. Give him time, though, and he'll come to terms with it." Nugent gave Henry a searching look. "You will too."

"What d'ye mean by that?"

"You were fond of her yourself, weren't you?"

"I was," said Henry, his mind retreating to a middle distance. "Fond of her."

A member of the British parliament wrote a letter to the London *Times* in which he suggested a truce with Ireland, unhampered by any preliminary conditions, to be followed immediately by a conference between representatives of the British government and Dáil Éireann.

General Macready expressed himself as unalterably opposed. Martial law, he insisted, was the only way to solve the Irish problem. "The civil authorities must be prepared to shoot down rebels like the mad dogs they are."

"There is no Irish problem," Henry angrily wrote in the *Bulletin*. "Only an English problem."

THE Dublin Metropolitan Police force was composed of Irishmen. Many of them were dismayed at being ordered to shoot other Irishmen. An emissary was sent to Sinn Féin asking for a guarantee that policemen would not be shot if they stopped carrying guns. Michael Collins agreed, with the added proviso that the police must no longer support military raids. From October the DMP ceased to be active against Republicans.[4]

• • •

CIRCULATION of the *Irish Bulletin* had increased to six hundred, forcing the purchase of the long-desired new rotary duplicating machine. Desmond FitzGerald and Kathleen MacKenna went to purchase the contraption at Gestetner's, and Joe Hyland delivered it to the *Bulletin* office in his taxi.

More staff was needed, too. Kathleen MacGilligan was employed for dispatch work, and a young woman called Sheila Murphy to help with the statistics. Someone said she was one of the Big Fellow's girlfriends; someone else said that could apply to half the women in Dublin.

Collins, however, was seeing more of Kitty Kiernan than of anyone else, as Henry very well knew. When he spoke of her there was a tone in his voice that Henry recognized.

ON the night of October eleventh Dan Breen and Seán Treacy were just falling asleep in a Republican safe house. Suddenly there was a crash of glass. British soldiers burst into the room. "The damned Castle spies had found us at last," Breen told Henry later. "But we fought our way out, though we had to kill some soldiers to do it. Next thing I knew I was running barefoot through Dublin, half-blinded by blood pouring from a wound in my head. I thought Seán had been killed for sure, but he got away without so much as a scratch on him.

"I knocked on a strange door and they did what they could for me, then took me to the Mater Hospital. There the nuns, bless 'em, hid me in the maternity ward. While I was lying in a bed half-conscious the place was surrounded by troops. The soldiers happened upon another badly wounded Republican they mistook for me. The poor fellow died while they were dragging him out of the hospital. They thought they were rid of Dan Breen.

"Meanwhile Seán Treacy was trying to organize a rescue for me before the British realized their mistake. He was so worried about me that he forgot to look after himself. A gang of Auxiliaries and G-men caught him and shot him dead in the street." Dan Breen's tough bulldog features softened, melted with grief. "He was the best friend any man ever had, Henry. The best friend."

The seventeenth of October saw the death of the Cork hunger striker Michael FitzGerald.

Members of Sinn Féin in Bandon awoke to find red crosses painted on the doors of their houses. That same night the Essex Regiment was turned loose in the town. Later a military lorry laden with the dead and dying went careening into Cork City, followed by soldiers who set about wrecking everything they could. The Harrington brothers sent Henry a long, detailed list of casualties and damages, to be published together with similar lists from Tuam and Mallow and a score of other towns.

O n October twenty-fifth hunger striker Joseph Murphy died in Cork Jail. A more famous Republican preceded him by hours. Terence MacSwiney had died at 5:40 A.M. in Brixton Prison after seventy-four days without nourishment.

Henry was in the *Bulletin* office when the word came through. The peripatetic newsletter had moved yet again. Thanks to the late-night efforts of the office boy and two of Collins' men, the paper was now being printed and prepared for mailing on the second floor of number 11 Molesworth Street.

· Frank Gallagher appeared in the doorway. "Terry's gone," was all he said. He was white-faced and looked very fragile. Gallagher had a special horror of hunger strikes.

"I never really thought they'd let it go that far," said Anna Fitzsimons. Her voice was shaking.

"I never really thought it would go any other way," Henry replied. He folded his arms on his desk and put his head down on them.

H e n r y was thankful for his work. Addressing the grief of others gave him a legitimate outlet for his own grief; the intensely personal loss he could not express. He wrote: "Terence MacSwiney has now joined the heroes of Easter Week, standing shoulder to shoulder with them in sacrifice. To Mrs.

MacSwiney and little Máire we offer the consolation of knowing that the Irish nation shares their loss. The name they enshrine in their hearts shall be forever enshrined in ours."

Terence MacSwiney had fought to stay alive as long as possible to draw attention to his cause, and in this he had succeeded. Foreign correspondents had flocked to cover the story. It was carried as a major news item in Rome and Paris and New York. The world had watched his protracted martyrdom with increasing dismay, and when at last he died, international condemnation of British policy was scathing.

In an attempt to shift the blame, Winston Churchill said, "It was during the silly season the lord mayor of Cork announced his determination to starve himself to death. He did not want to die, and the government did not want him to die; but MacSwiney had many friends in Ireland who wished him to die."[5]

Although she was opposed to her husband's hunger strike, Muriel MacSwiney had traveled to Brixton and remained there for most of his ordeal. But neither she nor his brothers and sisters were allowed to be with him at the end. Nor was his body immediately released. The authorities were alarmed by the ever-increasing crowds outside the prison.

Cables of protest were pouring into London.

Richard Mulcahy sent a military honor guard to escort the body back to Ireland. Upon arrival in England they were arrested. As the coffin was transported through London on its way to the port at Holyhead, thousands of ordinary English men and women lined the streets in respectful silence.

MacSwiney's family had arranged to take the body to Dublin for a large funeral procession, but they were prevented by force. When the coffin reached Holyhead it was shipped straight to Cork, where it was dumped on the quays like abandoned cargo, covered by an old tarpaulin.

Terence MacSwiney was buried in Cork City on the thirty-first of October. A day of national mourning was proclaimed by the Dáil.

At the request of Arthur Griffith and Michael Collins, the remaining nine hunger strikers in Cork gave up their protest.

On the first day of November eighteen-year-old Kevin

Barry was hanged in Mountjoy Prison. An immense crowd gathered outside the prison before dawn, praying and pleading for mercy for the young man. To no avail.

In the House of Commons J. H. Thomas read aloud an affidavit from Kevin Barry, giving full details of the extensive torture he had undergone in an effort to get him to identify those who had carried out the shootings in Church Street. Barry went to the gallows without ever revealing their names.[6]

That same day a young Galway woman called Ellen Quinn was sitting on a wall beside the road, nursing her baby. As a party of Black and Tans drove past in a lorry, one of them casually shot her in the stomach. It took her seven hours to bleed to death. The military later claimed her shooting was a precautionary measure.

"And wisely so," Henry commented in the *Bulletin*. "Taking the precaution of killing an Irish mother will prevent her giving birth to more rebels. It is certain, however, that this sort of action will create other rebels sprung from the wombs of other Irish women."

Six unarmed Republicans were captured by Black and Tans near Cork City. When their mutilated bodies were finally returned to their relatives by the RIC—without explanation or apology—they could be identified only by their clothing. One's heart had been cut out; another had lost his tongue; a third's nose had been cut off.

IN the days following Síle's death Henry hardly thought of Ella Rutledge. She was at the far periphery of his thoughts, which formed concentric circles. Precious was on the innermost ring; his work beyond that. Ned was somewhere farther out, unreachable. He was only at home intermittently, but he had begun writing again. He showed some of his novel to Henry. It was no longer a lighthearted adventure tale; jagged angry words slashed the page like shards of broken glass.

Henry understood all too well. There was a darkening of the world. The streets were grayer, the skies were lower. Hope walked arm in arm with her ugly twin, despair.

At night he slept with one arm on the side table by his bed, where his revolver lay in easy reach. During the day, if he did not have it on him, it was under his mattress. Louise found it there but never commented; she merely put it back.

As for Precious, she confounded them all by drawing into herself and healing from the inside out. Immediately after the funeral she had unable to sleep, unable to eat, hardly able to talk. When Father O'Flanagan called at the house, she listened politely as he offered spiritual consolation, but her eyes were distant. Nothing he said touched her. Yet with each day that passed she battled her way back. They watched her forcing herself to eat without being pressured, heard her first valiant efforts to make normal conversation. Saw the child they loved returning, unbroken.

Michael Collins inquired about Ned's family one morning when he called in to the *Bulletin*. "I don't know where Precious gets her inner resources," Henry told him.

"Was she not born poor?"

"She was," Henry replied, surprised as ever by how much Collins knew.

"Well, the poor learn early that they must rely on themselves. Didn't your mammy ever tell you, 'Like the river, we sparkle more in sunshine, but our strength comes from the rain'?"

"Were you born poor, Mick?"

"Not really; I was born lucky. My ancestors were once lords of Ui Chonaill, though all that's many times gone. But my family still has ninety acres near Clonakilty, a place called Woodfield. It's a good farm. With so many of us in the family it's quite self-sufficient."

"I didn't know about Woodfield."

"I imagine there's a lot about me you don't know. For instance, my father was the seventh son of a seventh son. He was sixty years old before he finally married a local girl called Marianne O'Brien, and seventy-five when I was born—the youngest of his eight children," Collins added.

"An exceptionally vigorous man," Henry commented admiringly.

"You don't know the half of it. He lived through the Famine and was educated in an outlawed hedge school before he joined the Fenians. Then he went right on educating himself. He had a great love of learning, my father did. He was fluent in Irish and French and had a working knowledge of Latin and Greek. I was seven when he died, but I remember him well."

"My father's dead too. I was older than you, though, when it happened. Not that it makes it any easier."

"Is your mother still alive?"

"She is. But we're not close."

Collins gave Henry a look of focused concentration, diamond-hard. "Both our friends and our enemies think we'll never die, but we will. In the meantime you should cherish your mother. Mothers are sacred."

"If you knew my mother," Henry said, "you wouldn't be so reverential about her."

Collins was sitting on the edge of Henry's desk, swinging one foot. He had brought a top-secret government document to be published in the *Bulletin* to embarrass the British, but it was temporarily forgotten as he reminisced. "You wouldn't know it to hear me swear now, but I was a reverential kid. Reverence was not only instilled into me by my father; it seemed a natural trait. Great age held something for me that was awesome. I was much fonder of old people in the darkness than I was of young people in the daytime. It's at night that you're able to get the value of old people. And it was from listening to the old people that I got my ideas of nationality."[7] He paused, rummaged in his pockets. "Say, Henry, do you have any fags on you?"

"I gave them up."

"Just like that?"

"Just like that." *No point in admitting how hard it was to Mick Collins, for whom nothing is hard.*

"Maybe I should give them up too. I'm becoming a slave to cigarettes, and I'll be a slave to nothing."

"There speaks the Fenian's son," said Henry.

" 'Sure and what would the cat's son do but kill the rat?' "

Collins quoted in his broadest West Cork accent. Producing a folded document from an inside pocket, he dropped it on Henry's desk. "Here, print this in the next edition. Show the feckin' bastards we know their secrets. Make 'em squirm."

Chapter Twenty-eight

November 16, 1920

RUSSIAN CIVIL WAR ENDS—BOLSHEVIKS
TRIUMPH

OUTSIDE lay the cold sunshine of a winter afternoon. Inside the dark, malt-scented sanctuary of the Oval Bar, Henry Mooney sat alone at a table, playing with his empty pint glass on the tabletop, making interlocked wet rings, blurring them, making new ones. He had come in for his customary Tuesday pub lunch and lingered, unwilling to face the world again. So many terrible stories to tell. His mind wandered. *Síle.* Exquisite pain in the remembering. An affirmation of the futility of striving. Why bother? It all came to the same thing in the end.

At the other side of the room a man stood up against the bar and began singing in a clear tenor voice. Such impromptu performances were a part of pub life, rewarded with appreciative audiences who might or might not sing along as the spirit moved them.

Oh think not my spirits are always as light
And as free from a pang as they seem to you now;
Nor expect that the heart-beaming smile of tonight

Will return with tomorrow to brighten my brow.
No, life is a waste of wearisome hours
Which seldom the rose of enjoyment adorns;
And the heart that is soonest awake to the flowers
Is always the first to be touched by the thorns.

Henry joined in the last lugubrious lines, then raised two fingers to signal the publican for a refill.

The singer launched into the second verse.

The thread of our life would be dark, Heaven knows!
If it were not with friendship and love intertwined;
And I care not how soon I may sink to repose,
When these blessings shall cease to be dear to my mind!
But send round the bowl, while a relic of truth
Is in man or in woman, this prayer shall be mine—
That the sunshine of love may illumine our youth,
*And the moonlight of friendship console our decline.**

A fresh pint arrived, brimming, at Henry's table. *"The moonlight of friendship . . ."* God help Ned. He raised the drink to his lips. *"The sunshine of love . . ."* He set the drink down untasted. *Sunshine. Precious, battling back.*

Henry, who had always decried the Irish habit of making an icon of tragedy, suddenly realized he was doing the same thing.

Ella Rutledge. He said the name in his head like a talisman. *Ella Rutledge.*

HENRY stood on the footpath, gazing at the front door. Once or twice he turned to look at the gleaming black Delage motorcar parked at the curb. At last he went up the steps and knocked. The housemaid seemed surprised to see to him. "Why, good afternoon, Mr. Mooney. Are you expected?"

*"Oh Think Not My Spirits Are Always As Light," by Thomas Moore

The *Irish Times* lay on the table in the hall atop several other newspapers. While he waited for Ella, Henry scanned the headline story about the end of Russia's bloodbath between the Whites and the Reds. *Civil war: the most uncivil of all wars. Brother against brother, father against son. How could they? Thank God it's over, anyway.*

His eye fell on a brown envelope that had slid off the table when he picked up the *Times*. The address was in Anna Fitzsimons's familiar handwriting. He bent to retrieve it just as Ella appeared. "Henry! What a pleasant surprise."

"I'm surprised myself," he said, handing her the envelope. "I didn't know Edwin subscribed to the *Irish Bulletin*."

"Why? Because it's nationalist? And what makes you think it's for Edwin?" As she put the envelope in her pocket there was an edge to her voice: unexpected steel beneath the plummy accents. "Perhaps you should have asked me before you jumped to conclusions, Henry."

Before he could respond Edwin appeared in the door of the drawing room. "I thought I heard your voice, Henry. Wonderful bit of timing. Come inside with us; we're looking at sketches for a proposed conservatory and I should value your opinion. Oh, I don't believe you've met Major Wallace Congreve? He's an old friend of ours—he served with Father in the army."

The major was a heavyset man in his early fifties, with brilliantined hair and a pencil mustache. His features might have been handsome once, but were blurring under the influence of too much food and drink. When he moved he creaked slightly, as if he were wearing a corset. His conversation was liberally peppered with the names of mutual friends and references to shared history. Henry had no opportunity for a private conversation with Ella until she walked him to the door after less than an hour. He did not really want to go, but Congreve made him feel like an intruder.

The maid brought his coat and held it while he shrugged into it, then vanished at a wave of Ella's hand. Henry could not ask the question on his mind about Major Congreve; not with the doors still open and the man just inside. Gesturing toward the papers on the hall table, he asked instead, "Is that your *Bulletin*, Ella?"

"Of course it is. I read every article you write."

"Surely there's very little in them that you agree with."

"How would you know? You and I discuss everything under the sun except politics. And religion."

Henry found himself defending his good manners. "I was taught that those two are forbidden subjects in polite conversation, Ella."

"Yet in Ireland they are central to who we are," she retorted. "How could you possibly propose marriage to a woman without knowing her opinions on both?" Suddenly her cheeks dimpled; her eyes danced. "Or perhaps you weren't proposing marriage at all, but something else?"

Caught off guard, Henry floundered. "Of course I was proposing marriage. I would never dream of . . . I mean . . . But it was just a wild notion, I thought you understood . . ."

"So on mature reflection you take it back?" She was definitely laughing at him. Henry made a grasp for emotional equilibrium and missed. His face betrayed his confusion.

Ella was instantly contrite. "I'm sorry, I shouldn't be teasing you at a time like this. We read Mrs. Halloran's obituary in the *Times* and I know she was a friend. You have my sympathy."

The mention of Síle was like cold water poured over Henry. He drew a deep, steadying breath and buttoned his coat. "Thank you."

"She must have been an extraordinary woman."

He paused in the doorway, forced, as always when confronted with such a statement, to be objective. "I don't suppose you could call Síle Halloran extraordinary. Come to think of it, there are hundreds like her in Dublin. You couldn't tell the story of the city or the times without them."

It was too late in the day to go back to work, and he was not in the mood anyway, so he set out on one of his rambles through the city. Picturing Ella's face as he walked, listening again to her words: "I read every article you write."

Major Congreve's features swam into memory and shattered the mood. *Is that man courting Ella? He certainly seemed attentive. But what could she possibly see in a man old enough to be her father? Him and that ridiculous mustache. Surely she wouldn't* . . . Henry reached in his pocket for cigarettes, remembered he had quit. Swore under his breath.

Who knows what's going on in the mind of a woman? And why did she mention my proposal?

On the morning of November twentieth Michael Collins paid another visit to the *Bulletin*. He handed Henry a decoded memorandum on Dublin Castle stationery. "For some time we've known there's a deliberate shoot-to-kill policy to eliminate what the government calls "Sinn Féin extremists." In this document is proof that Field Marshal Sir Henry Wilson, chief of the imperial general staff, has assembled a company of specially trained British intelligence officers and sent them to Dublin with orders to destroy my organization."[1]

"Rather like your squad eliminating G-men and spies," Henry commented dryly.

Collins ignored the remark. "They're lodging in private houses around Dublin and posing as ordinary citizens. They're old Mideast hands, most of them, and they tend to meet at the Cairo Café, so they've been nicknamed the Cairo Gang. I have no doubt that if they can get me out of the way, Wilson will have them target the members of the Dáil next.

"We're meeting in Vaughan's Hotel tonight to finalize a plan of our own. That's where you come in, Henry. Today's Saturday; I want the *Bulletin* to publish this document verbatim on Monday. Stencil in the Castle letterhead if you can."

"Why on Monday in particular?"

"Do you recall our conversation about political assassinations?"

"I do of course."

"Well, let's just say no one's going to wipe out the government of the Irish Republic again."

•   •   •

NED Halloran left number 16 without explanation that evening. He had not returned by the time Precious went to bed, so Louise took the child a cup of hot cocoa and Henry read to her from the evening papers until she fell asleep. In the kitchen later he told his cousin, "I made Little Business a promise before Síle died and tomorrow would be a good time to keep it. Whatever about Ned, life goes on for that child."

Sunday morning dawned clear and crisp. There was no sign of Ned, who either had not come home at all or had left the house before anyone else was awake. Henry and Louise took Precious to the earliest Mass. Henry did not stand in the back of the church with his arms folded, but occupied a pew with his womenfolk. Afterwards they went back to number 16, where Louise helped Precious dress for her first horse-riding lesson.

When they competed in sidesaddle classes at the Dublin Horse Show, Ascendancy ladies wore beautifully fitted broadcloth riding habits custom-tailored by Wm. Scott & Co. Ursula Halloran would learn to ride wearing an old woolen jumper and a pair of boy's knickerbockers from a secondhand clothes stall in Moore Street—and the gloves Henry had given her.

For his sake she was pretending more enthusiasm than she felt. Síle's death was still too recent. Yet as they neared Smithfield, Precious began to walk faster. Henry trailed along in her wake, amused that the girl could be excited by something as commonplace as horses.

Animals of every description were part of Dublin street life. The cobbles were always smeared with fresh dung. Livestock markets proliferated. Drovers brought herds of cattle up the North Circular Road, with unruly bulls occasionally breaking free to demolish a shopfront or trample an onlooker. Flocks of sheep clogged side streets while dogs barked and frustrated pedestrians prodded the creatures out of their way. Homegrown pigs and poultry were pursued down laneways by barefoot urchins. Thousands of screeching caged birds were transported through the city to the bird market in the Liberties, sold to hang in residential windows and sing their sad lives away.

The horse was special, however. In the years following the Great War Dublin was still heavily dependent upon horsepower. Sometimes as many as five hundred horses would be lined up along O'Connell Street in the morning, harnessed to the service of coal merchants, bakeries, dairies, breweries, delivery wagons of every description, and, in spite of the growing influence of the motorcar, a predominance of horse-drawn cabs.

Central to this equine power grid was the Smithfield Horse Fair, where almost every horse, pony, or donkey in the city was sold at some stage in its life. Although the fair was held only on the first Sunday of every month, in her imagination Precious could see thousands of animals on display. They drew her like a magnet. She could not have said why; she knew only that the attraction had always been there. By the time they reached the livery stable her heart was racing. A row of equine faces gazed at her from the loose boxes. "Hello," she called softly. Ears pricked; a blaze-faced chestnut nickered.

While Precious went from one horse to another, crooning in a wordless language, Henry took the liveryman aside. "You understand I want her to have proper lessons?"

"Same as I'd teach me own children. By spring she'll be riding like one of them centenaries."

"Centaurs," Henry corrected absently. "Listen here to me. She's not to get hurt."

"Well now, horses ain't house pets, they—"

"She's not to get hurt!" Henry paused, dropped his voice to a conspiratorial level. "You know Michael Collins?"

A respectful light came into the man's eyes. "Don't know him, know of him. The Big Fellow."

"That's the one. He's a close friend of mine, and neither one of us would like it if this child got hurt. Do I make myself clear?"

The liveryman nodded vigorously. "None o' the lads'll so much as spit in her path. When she rides out, I'll run alongside, and if she falls I'll catch her. I swear it on me sainted mother!"

Henry smiled to himself. *So that's what having power feels like.*

A piebald cob was brought out for Precious: white with large irregular blotches of black across its body, and sturdy legs. "The tinkers call these broken-colored horses," the liveryman explained, "but this was no tinker's horse. This is a right fine animal, this is, and we have a proper lady's side-saddle too."

A flicker of contempt crossed the girl's face. "I shan't require a sidesaddle, thank you. I'm not a proper lady."

The liveryman glanced toward Henry, who bit his lip to keep from laughing. "Better do it her way," he said. "She knows what she wants."

A regular saddle was produced and the stirrup leathers shortened to accommodate the little girl's legs. The liveryman led the cob to a mounting block. "Step up on this," he instructed, "then put your right leg over the horse . . . There you are now. Like a reg'lar centenary."

Precious sat quietly for a few moments, absorbing the wonder of the living, breathing animal beneath her. Looking down at the people around her. Looking out across Dublin from a height.

Until that moment she had been little. On a horse, she was little no longer.

THAT same morning Michael Collins' squad, augmented by members of the Dublin Brigade, approached seven different private houses and the Gresham Hotel. Each group was provided with a list of names and physical descriptions. They waited until the clocks chimed nine, then struck simultaneously across the city. Housemaids responding to a knock on the door were ordered at gunpoint to identify the bedrooms of the British agents, most of whom were still asleep. At the Gresham the head porter was forced to give the room numbers of two more.

When one member of the squad found his intended victim not at home, he vented his frustration on the man's mistress by spanking her with her lover's sword scabbard.[2]

According to the official government statement, fourteen British secret agents were shot dead that morning. The actual number killed may have been as high as nineteen or twenty.

A witness described one of the murder scenes as looking like an abattoir.

As news seeped out, there was panic in the city. Hundreds of military and civil-service personnel besieged Dublin Castle, convinced they would be the next targets. One British secret agent broke under the strain and shot himself.

By the time Henry and Precious left Smithfield, newsboys were already shouting in the streets. BLOODY SUNDAY! screamed the banner headline in a special edition of the *Times*. Henry immediately bought the paper and read it aghast. Now he understood why Collins wanted him to print the decoded document on the following day.

Precious stood watching his face while he read, then silently extended her hand for the paper.

"You don't want to read this, Little Business."

"I'll worry more if I don't know."

What sort of childhood is this for anybody? He handed her the newspaper. Precious ran her eyes swiftly over the story. Her expression did not change, but Henry saw her brace her shoulders. Then she folded the paper and put it under her arm. "We had best go straight home, Uncle Henry. The streets won't be safe, will they?"

"I'm afraid not, Little Business."

Looking up at him, she forced her special, radiant smile. "But it was a wonderful morning."

In Dublin's Croke Park, the Mecca of Gaelic football, there was a match that Sunday afternoon between Dublin and Tipperary. Eight thousand men, women, and children gathered to watch the traditional rivals battle it out. Many of them stood on Hill Sixteen at the far end of the playing field, so named because its terraces had been constructed from rubble left after the 1916 Rising. Somewhere underneath was even the wreck of the De Dion Bouton motorcar that had belonged to The O'Rahilly, and been used as a barricade.

The match had hardly begun when a number of military lorries drove up and surrounded the grounds. Tans and Auxiliaries leaped from the trucks. While an officer was telling the gatekeepers they had come to search for known Sinn Féiners, his men set up machine guns on the canal bridge and indiscriminately opened fire on the crowd. A Tipperary player, Michael Hogan, and eleven spectators were killed outright. Fifty-seven suffered serious bullet wounds, and hundreds more were injured in the stampede that followed.

Dublin was convulsed with horror.

THAT night was an anxious one at number 16. No one knew where Ned was. Henry and Louise tried half a dozen times to get Precious to go to bed, but finally they gave up. She fell asleep on the black horsehair couch in the parlor—with her riding gloves on. Only then was Henry able to carry her upstairs and tuck her into bed.

Ned arrived shortly after midnight. His face was haggard and he seemed dazed. Henry was waiting for him in the parlor. "What in God's name have you been up to?" he burst out angrily.

"You heard, I suppose? About the Cairo Gang?" Ned slumped into the nearest chair. "I went to Mass," he said dreamily, rubbing his thumb along the arm of the chair, back and forth, back and forth. "Sure a lot of us did. We prayed for their souls."

"Were you one of the men who shot them?"

Back and forth. Eyes lowered, watching his thumb. "I told you, Mick wouldn't let me join the squad."

"It wasn't just the squad and you know it. According to the newspapers there were members of the Dublin Brigade as well. Most of them got away, but there were a couple of running gun battles, and at least one man was captured."

"Mick will get him out. He's good at that." Ned leaned his head against the back of the chair. "I'm so tired," he sighed. His eyelids drifted down until the long lashes brushed his cheeks. He reminded Henry of a weary boy. Of Precious falling asleep on the couch.

"What about Croke Park, Ned?" Henry persisted. "This morning's work brought all hell down on a lot of innocent people."

"That wasn't meant to happen. Mick tried to get the game cancelled, but the GAA said the crowd had been gathering since morning and there was nothing that could be done."[3]

"He knew there would be reprisals when he gave the order to exterminate the Cairo Gang. Damn it, Ned, were you one of the killers?"

"The British are the killers." Ned opened his eyes; they met Henry's for the first time. Green eyes, cold as the sea, pitiless as fate. "They killed my Síle." He stood up abruptly. "I'm going to bed."

ON Monday the *Bulletin* printed the stolen Castle document as justification for the murders of the Cairo Gang.

Even Dublin Castle dared not try to publicly justify what had happened in Croke Park. However, the British cabinet was informed that "there is no doubt that some of the most desperate criminals in Ireland were among the spectators."[4]

Three prisoners who had been held in Dublin Castle since Saturday night—two Republicans and a civilian arrested by mistake—were beaten by their captors, then bayoneted and finally shot. It was claimed that they had tried to escape by threatening their guards with hand grenades, the presumption being that they had smuggled these grenades into the Castle and kept them on their persons for twenty hours without being discovered. A highly suspicious series of photographs was released to the press, showing three men sitting with their heads bowed so their faces could not be recognized, then leaping toward the window while their guards crouched behind overturned furniture. When the bodies were released for burial, their faces were found to have been badly battered post-mortem.

Michael Collins insisted the two Republicans be buried in full uniform, and attended their funeral Mass himself, risking identification and arrest. Afterward he helped carry the coffins. A photographer for the *Evening Herald* managed to snap a picture of him that appeared in the first edition. The squad called on the newspaper immediately afterward and the picture was deleted from later editions.

On November the twentieth Professor Eoin MacNeill was arrested without warrant or charge.

On the twenty-seventh the IRA took the war to the enemy.

In Liverpool a Republican squad set fire to fifteen cotton warehouses and timber yards. Warnings were given in advance and no one was injured, but the damage to property was extensive. The alarmed British government responded by erecting barriers across the approaches to Downing Street, and the public galleries were closed in both the House of Commons and the House of Lords. Scotland Yard was called in to protect politicians.

In Dublin, Arthur Griffith was arrested. He joined Eoin MacNeill in Kilmainham Jail—which had been called the Dismal House of Little Ease when first used as a prison in the twelfth century.[5]

For months Griffith had been working behind the scenes to encourage a truce between the British government and the Irish. Following Bloody Sunday he had remarked in *Young Ireland* that violence was at best only one aspect of national policy. A politician walking a very careful line, he was trying not to upset either side before a truce could be negotiated. But his comments were enough to draw the wrath of Dublin Castle. As far as the Castle was concerned, Griffith was Sinn Féin and Sinn Féin was the enemy.

Henry wrote in an article for the London *Daily News*, "By arresting that great pacifist, Arthur Griffith, Dublin Castle has gone a long way toward silencing the moderate voices in republicanism that urge constitutional political solutions. Is this the British intention? In a plan worthy of Machiavelli himself, does Lloyd George mean to reduce us to such extremes that any method of suppression is justified?"

To his surprise, they printed it.

Two days after Griffith's arrest Eoin MacNeill was unconditionally released.

From prison, Arthur Griffith appointed Michael Collins to serve as acting president of the Dáil in the continuing absence of de Valera.

• • •

IN West Cork the Tans had been conducting a terror campaign since summer. They would come roaring into a village, order everyone—men, women, and children—into the street, search and abuse them for hours, sometimes stripping the men naked, sometimes pistol-whipping them. When a very elderly priest objected to their shooting some of his parishioners for sport as they worked in their fields, the Tans shot him too.

ON the twenty-eighth of November Tom Barry's flying column ambushed an Auxiliary patrol at Kilmichael, on the Macroom road. Eighteen Auxiliaries were killed. Three Republicans also died, an unusually high number for a guerrilla operation.

On November the thirtieth Eoin MacNeill was rearrested—still without warrant or charge.

Dublin Castle was seizing and releasing individuals in a dizzying round meant to frighten and intimidate. They did not seem to care who they took, or why. Some men would never leave prison alive.

A young tenement girl the same age as Precious was shot dead by British soldiers in the streets of Dublin as she scavenged for food.

GENERAL headquarters of the Irish Republican Army was a movable feast. Henry found the chief of staff working in the carriage house behind his home in the suburban village of Rathmines. On the two and a half acres that comprised the property, Mulcahy's wife had begun creating a small farm. Her butter-and-egg money would be a welcome addition to her husband's income. In the young state, even the head of the army had to count his shillings and pence.

Inside the carriage house maps were tacked on every wall. Richard Mulcahy sat behind a table, poring over papers. In an article for *Collier's Weekly* in America, Henry had written, "General Richard Mulcahy is a quiet, gracious, unassuming man, simple in his tastes. He does not drink and attends Mass at seven every morning. It is unusual to describe a military man as unassertive, but that is the case with him. He is the opposite in temperament from Michael Collins, who served as director of intelligence on his staff."

Mulcahy glanced up with the abstracted air of a man who must call his concentration back from far places: one swift blink, a sudden and sharp refocus. Taking off his reading spectacles, he said, *"Dia dhuit,** Henry," in impeccable Irish. "Welcome to GHQ. Did Mick send you?"

"I'm here on my own. I have a personal matter to discuss with you."

"Go on into the house and have Min give you a cup of tea." Mulcahy issued the invitation as a courteous command; he was a cool, practical man who dealt with each situation as it arose in precisely the same manner. "I'll be with you in a few minutes," he added.

"Min" Mulcahy—the former Mary Josephine Ryan—was as ardent a Republican as her husband. She and her sister Phyllis had been the last two to see Sean MacDermott alive, aside from the firing squad. While he waited for Mulcahy, Henry persuaded her to retell a story she must have told many times before.

"We waited for hours and hours at Kilmainham, and were finally shown to Sean's cell at three o'clock in the morning.[6] It was gritty dark hole with a bucket in the corner and a plank bed. Do you take sugar, Mr. Mooney? . . . Really— that much? Anyway, there were two soldiers there all the time, watching us. They had a lantern, because there were no lights in that part of Kilmainham. You can't imagine how dark and grim it was."

Henry said soberly, "I think I can."

"Seán could tell how miserable we were. He wanted to make things easier for us, so he chatted about people we knew and made little jokes as if we were sitting around a table at Bewley's, having our coffee. Then he tried to give us some keepsakes for various other girlfriends of his. We all loved him, you know. He borrowed a penknife from one of the soldiers and scratched his name on the few coins he had left

*Hello; literally, God with you.

and some buttons he cut off his clothes. I can see him to this day, Henry—that beautiful head like some old-time Celtic prince, bent over his work." Her eyes filled with tears. "The last thing we heard him say as they took us out was 'God Save Ireland.' Half an hour later they shot him."

Dick Mulcahy entered the room. Thirty-four years old, a slender man of average height, he carried himself with the bearing of a professional soldier. His was a long, narrow face, with sharply cut features and deep-set eyes. An air of imperturbable calm: the sort of man who could hold an army together under fire.

"You shouldn't keep talking about that, Min," he said to his wife. "It just upsets you." He turned to Henry. "We're expecting our first, you see, and she needs to take care of herself."

"That's what I want to talk to you about. Taking care of someone."

"Sorry?"

"My friend Ned Halloran. Dublin Brigade."

Mulcahy nodded. "One of the best. What about him?"

"Let me tell you some things about him you may not know. Both of Ned's parents went down with the *Titanic*; he himself narrowly escaped. He's still suffering from a severe head wound he received Easter Week. And now his wife's been murdered. I don't think he can cope anymore; he's on the verge of a complete breakdown."

"Soldiers have come back from the trenches with something they're calling shell shock," said Mulcahy. "Dreadful. There's simply a limit to how much any man can take. It differs with individuals, though."

"I can assure you Ned has reached his limit. He's behaving like a man who doesn't care what happens to him, and in that state he's bound to be caught by the British. You know what they did to poor young Kevin Barry. Prolonged, systematic torture. It would go much worse with Ned Halloran, who really does know secrets they'd give anything to get. The point is, Ned has a motherless young daughter who needs him sane and alive. So I'm asking for your help while there's still time."

Min Mulcahy stretched out an imploring hand to her husband. "Oh, do help them. You heard—he has a baby, Dick!"

Henry did not contradict her.

Mulcahy smiled tenderly at his young wife, a smile that revealed another and very different man. "All right, Min, all right. Don't fret now." He put one arm around her and hugged her to him. They had been married only a year. "Tell me what you have in mind, Henry."

Two days later Ned was summoned to GHQ. The next morning over breakfast he asked Precious, "How would you like to live down the country?"

Louise Kearney put down her fork. "What's this about?"

"I'm being transferred out of Dublin effective immediately. Orders from the top. The IRA in Clare are running their own show a bit too much for General Mulcahy's liking, and he wants someone from headquarters down there to keep him informed. He selected me personally because I know the area. It means a promotion; I'm to be a communications officer."

Precious looked stricken. "What about Uncle Henry and Auntie Louise?"

"We'll be living with your uncle Frank and my aunt Norah instead, and my two little sisters, Lucy and Eileen. They're only a few years older than you, so it will be like having sisters yourself. If all goes well, we'll be with them in time for Christmas."

For the first time since Síle died, Henry noticed a touch of color in Ned's cheeks. *I did the right thing*, he thought with relief. He smiled encouragingly at Precious. "You'll be having a country Christmas, Little Business. Just imagine."

"But I don't want to leave you."

"Oh, you'll see quite a lot of me. This hip of mine's healed and I'm ready to report the action from the front lines again."

"There are plenty of front lines right here in Dublin," Ned commented. "All the action a man could . . ." His eyes narrowed with suspicion. "Say, Henry, did you have anything to do with sending me out of the city?"

"Me? I don't have any influence at GHQ—I'm not even in the army. I'm not a fighter, remember?"

As Henry helped Louise clear the table she whispered to him, "He'll never forgive you if he finds out. He'll accuse you of trying to run his life instead of trying to save it again. That's getting to be a habit with you, isn't it?"

"Ned would do the same for me," Henry assured her.

Chapter Twenty-nine

DESPITE the approach of Christmas, Kingsbridge Train Station was almost empty. In the current tense situation people were not traveling unless they must. After Henry saw Ned and Precious onto their train, he slouched through the echoing station, feeling achingly alone.

Good things do come out of bad, he tried to comfort himself. *Ned could never go home while Síle lived. Everyone in that part of Clare would have remembered her as the girl who ran away with the cattle dealer. She'd be marked for life, even if they never found out she'd become a whore in Dublin afterward. Not that that's so unusual. This city is full of whores. And priests. And soldiers. To tell Dublin's story you would have to tell about all of them. But no woman could survive what the big mouths and the little minds would have done to Síle if she went back to the country.*

Now she was a heroine, buried in the designated Republican plot in Glasnevin. Except for himself and Ned, no one knew all of her story.

Perhaps every person is a mystery. No matter how straightforward the exterior, inside is all myths and mazes.

His thoughts expanded to a spiral, inevitably led to Ella Rutledge. *Someone else who has a lot more to her than appears on the surface. Fascinating to explore. If she'd let me.*

If she'd let me . . . A kaleidoscope of erotic images shim-

mered behind Henry's eyes: Ella in a froth of silk lingerie
. . . Ella unpinning a mass of fragrant hair . . . Ella—

His neck burned red. He glanced around as if afraid passersby could read his mind. *Stop that*, he told himself
sternly. Stop that. But he walked on dreaming.

Henry intended to stay in the city for the holidays. He
would miss Ned, and most particularly Precious, but they
needed time to settle into their new surroundings. Besides,
he had promised to attend not one but two parties on Christmas Eve: one given by the irrepressible Michael Collins and
the other in Herbert Place.

A murmur of hope ran through the capital. As a result of
intensive pressure at home and abroad, Lloyd George was
said to be considering the possibility of a truce. In the House
of Commons he stated on the tenth of December that he
believed the majority in Ireland were anxious for peace.

Almost immediately, however, he announced that any
meetings to discuss a truce would have certain precondi-
tions. It must be understood that the six counties of northeastern Ulster would be accorded separate treatment, and
also that under no circumstances would the government
agree to any proposal for the secession of any part of Ireland
from the United Kingdom.[1]

Dublin Castle added its own precondition. No truce talks
could take place without a surrender of IRA weapons.

"No army in history ever surrendered its arms *before* a
truce was established," Henry pointed out in the *Bulletin*.

The murmur of hope dwindled, died.

On the tenth of December the *Irish Independent* reported,
"Today Woodrow Wilson, former president of the United
States, was awarded the Nobel Peace Prize. Paralyzed since
his stroke last year, Wilson was not able to accept in person.
President Warren G. Harding sent an emissary in his name."

•   •   •   •

ON the tenth of December Lord-Lieutenant French placed counties Cork, Kerry, Limerick, and Tipperary under martial law. The following night Auxiliaries and Tans rampaged through the streets of Cork City, setting fires. Soon a baleful orange glow stained the sky. Shops were looted; Patrick Street was gutted. City Hall was demolished, as was the Free Library. While members of the fire brigade tried to fight the rapidly spreading conflagration, two were shot by the military. Dawn revealed the main thoroughfare clogged with wreckage and smoldering debris.

Within hours the great country houses of Protestants in County Cork began to go up in flames.

"Do you want to go down there?" Frank Gallagher asked Henry.

"I've seen it before, remember? Dublin, 1916. I don't have to visit Cork to describe what they've done to it. I'm sick to my back teeth of seeing beauty destroyed."

"That's all right—we have someone in Cork who can bring us an eyewitness account. Young fellow named Ellis who used your name as a recommendation, in fact. He's working on the *Cork Examiner*."

Three days later the military authorities issued a proclamation to the effect that any person convicted of specified offenses would be liable for execution. These offenses did not include arson, looting, or murdering Irish civilians. They did include the "unofficial" possession of firearms or explosives, the wearing of a Republican uniform or "clothing likely to deceive," and harboring, aiding, or abetting rebels.

One of the first to be arrested was a reporter named Ellis, who was taken off a train from Cork when he was found to be carrying documents meant for the *Irish Bulletin*.

ON December twenty-third the Government of Ireland Act became law. It was to be officially implemented in May.

ALSO on December twenty-third, Eamon de Valera at last returned to Ireland. For months he had been developing connections in the United States that would be useful to the infant Republic. Clan na Gael, the Ancient Order of Hibernians, the Friendly Sons of Saint Patrick, and other prominent Irish-American organizations had hosted him as he criss-crossed the country. He had met with state governors, addressed state legislatures, been given the freedom of cities, and received honorary degrees. Every major newspaper carried photographs. If Arthur Griffith represented the face of Sinn Féin to Dublin Castle, then Eamon de Valera had become the face of Ireland in America.

He had also learned a great deal about the fierce infighting between the various Irish-American factions, each with its own vision for "the Ould Sod."

Henry was on hand at the docks to cover de Valera's arrival in the predawn hours. To avoid calling unnecessary attention, the welcoming party was small, just a few members of the Dáil and an IRA bodyguard. They waited with ill-concealed impatience. Henry's willpower finally deserted him. He borrowed a cigarette from one of the TDs and went stamping up and down the dock, trying to keep his feet warm.

The relatively short voyage from Liverpool to Dublin across the Irish Sea was often rougher than the Atlantic crossing. It proved so again. De Valera disembarked suffering from seasickness. *I'll describe him as looking stern and statesmanlike*, Henry decided.

"How's it going?" de Valera asked one of the men who was hefting his luggage.

"Great! The Big Fellow is leading us and everything is going marvelous."

Henry saw de Valera's lips tighten. Striking the guard rail with his hand, he exclaimed, "Big Fellow! We'll see who's the Big Fellow . . ."[2]

I don't think I'll print that.

They accompanied de Valera to a safe house arranged by Michael Collins: the home of a prominent Dublin gynecologist who was popular among the wives of British officers. As Henry was leaving the house, he met Cathal Brugha arriving. "Dev's home and dry," Henry remarked to him on the steps.

Brugha gave a brusque nod. "Now we'll get things

straightened out, and not before time. With the Chief back as president of the Dáil, Collins won't have it all his own way anymore."

So the rumors I've been hearing are true, Henry thought. *There is antipathy between Brugha and Collins.*

The men who had brought Ireland this far along the road to freedom were all strong-minded individualists; nothing less could have succeeded. Among such men there would inevitably be deep philosophical differences. De Valera had succeeded in holding them together before he went to America. Would he be able to do so now? Henry wondered. Or would the British, scenting cracks in the structure, find ways to drive wedges between them?

Never underestimate Machiavelli. I'd wager Lloyd George has read him too.

On Christmas Eve pedestrians shopping in Grafton Street were held up by Auxiliaries and searched at gunpoint. Dashing angry tears from her eyes, Kathleen McKenna stormed into the nearest teashop and borrowed a pencil from the proprietor so she could write down every detail to report in the *Bulletin*.

Meanwhile, Henry was running his own last-minute holiday errands. He encountered one of Collins' men on a bicycle, frantically pedaling from neighborhood to neighborhood as he delivered a myriad of presents to the Big Fellow's friends and acquaintances. He pulled up at the curb, panting. "Been looking for you, Mooney. Mick wants you to know the party tonight will be at the Gresham Hotel."

"Are you serious? That's one of the most public places in Dublin."

The other man shrugged. "Some of the boys won't go; they claim it's suicide. But the Big Fellow's assured us we'll have a private room. Not to worry."

Not to worry. My God, how long does he expect his remarkable luck to hold?

Knowing the Collins party would run very late, Henry decided to go to the Mansell party first—while he was still sober. He bathed and dressed in his best suit, ruefully noting

that the cuffs of his suitcoat were beginning to show signs
of wear. Financially he was stretched thin. Added to the
Limerick tithe was the expense of the horse trainer for
Saoirse. But that was one expense he could not begrudge.
Besides, it was over now.

His surprise Christmas present to Precious had already
been delivered.

Henry was smiling to himself as he knocked on the door
in Herbert Place.

The house was lavishly decorated with massive swags of
greenery, crimson velvet bows, candles on every available
surface. Tides of people ebbed and flowed through the reception rooms. Laughter and conversation. Body heat rising
through perfumed air. Silk and velvet frocks; army officers
in dress uniform. Linen-draped tables with bowls of creamy
eggnog and sparkling punch, and a selection of whiskies for
the men. Chamber music emanating from a quartet discreetly
concealed behind a jungle of potted palms. Ella Rutledge
looking superb in pale blue chiffon with a handkerchief hem.

She greeted Henry with exactly the same degree of
warmth she bestowed on every guest—among whom, he noticed to his chagrin, was Major Congreve.

A huge Christmas tree in the style beloved of the late
Queen Victoria stood in the exact center of the room. Henry
had given a great deal of thought to Ella's present. He was
anxious to see her expression when she opened it.

When he handed her the carefully wrapped package, she
said, "How lovely, Henry! Thank you so much."

She put it, unopened, with the array of others beneath the
tree.

After the first toast to the season, Major Congreve took
center stage as if it were his right. He had an inexhaustible
repertoire of war stories featuring himself as hero and had
soon gathered a coterie of admiring women.

The man's all gab and guts, thought Henry sourly. *How
much of that is he making up? I could tell some war stories
if I wanted to. I know things that damned Congreve doesn't
dream of.*

A blur of faces. Making small talk with strangers. Aware
of political lines, the need to be careful. Trying to catch a

glimpse of Ella. Always with someone else. Being charming. Very much in demand. The rest of the room invisible, its occupants boring, an interference.

He stole a surreptitious glance at his watch. "I have another party to go to," Henry apologized to Ava. "I'm really sorry, but—"

As if she had picked up his message by invisible telegraph, Ella was beside him. "Surely you're not leaving so soon."

Her obvious regret was the best thing that had happened so far. "I'm afraid I must. I promised."

"Well, then, wait just a moment." She ran across the room and swooped down beside the tree, then came back holding a gift-wrapped box. "Take this with you and open it when you open your other presents." So swiftly he almost thought he imagined it, she rose on tiptoe and kissed his lips. "Caught you under the mistletoe," she added, pointing to a sprig hanging above him.

Then she vanished into the crowd.

The next thing Henry knew he was standing outside the house, holding her present. Tasting her kiss. Feeling a charge of electricity run through him from his mouth to his groin to his knees.

Under the nearest street lamp he opened the box. It contained a tril-by hat.

THE Gresham was overflowing. Another sort of Christmas crowd here: louder, impersonal. Henry took off his precious new trilby and shouldered his way through the thronged lobby until he found the night manager. "The Big Fellow," he whispered under his breath, extending a coin. "Private room."

"I'm afraid all the private rooms were booked already, Mr. Mooney. You'll find your party inside." The man nodded to indicate the public dining room.

Henry felt a prickle of alarm. "Could you not put him someplace less obvious? Or better still, talk him out of this altogether?"

"Two chances of that: slim and none. You didn't really expect me to argue with *him*, did you?"

"I s'pose not. Well, at least keep your eyes peeled and let us know if . . ." Henry offered another coin.

"Keep your money. I won't let anything happen to the Big Fellow if I can help it."

The party was in full swing by the time Henry arrived. Collins' bravado was not shared by everyone. Fewer than a dozen men were present. Five were members of the squad; the rest were trusted agents. Henry remarked as he sat down, "You lot would make a great Christmas present for the Castle." The words were hardly out of his mouth when he saw the night manager in the doorway, signaling frantically. A moment later six uniformed Auxiliaries stalked into the dining room.

People froze with their forks in midair. Food and conversation dried on their lips.

The Auxiliaries split up and began working their way around the large room, searching guests at random. Michael Collins said under his breath, "False names, everybody. And let me do the talking." When two men came to his table, he greeted them cheerfully. "What are you chaps looking for, an invitation? Pull up a couple of chairs if you like—we don't stand on ceremony around here." Collins seemed as relaxed as if they were old friends.

Henry could feel the sweat rolling down his back.

When Collins was searched, a bottle of whiskey was discovered in his hip pocket. "It's a gift for my landlady—how else is a fellow supposed to get clean sheets?" The Auxiliaries laughed and set the bottle down on the table.

For once Henry did not have his notebook on him. A notebook was found in Collins' possession, however, and one of the Auxiliaries began flipping through the pages. "I can't read your writing," he said suspiciously. "What's this? Rifles?"

Collins stood up and peered over his shoulder. "Refills," he corrected. "Say, can a fellow go to the toilet?"

The other man took a blurred photograph from his pocket. Studied it, looked searchingly at Collins. "We'll go with you. There's a few more questions to be asked." Both then escorted Collins to the toilets while his party remained at the table, trying not to look as guilty as they felt.

Long minutes passed.

"I better go see what's happened," Liam Tobin said. He sauntered out of the room with his usual loose-jointed, lazy gait. An onlooker would have thought him unconcerned unless they noticed the muscle twitching in his jaw.

Tobin was barely out of sight when the remaining Auxiliaries approached the table.

Henry braced himself in his chair and smiled up at them. "All through?" he asked brightly. "Did you find any of those Republican bastards? No? Sorry about that—it's tough to have to waste your Christmas Eve chasing the likes of them. Say, would you like to have a drink before you go? To make up for your trouble?" He held up Collins' bottle. The men grinned. Tension diminished a notch. Henry looked toward the doorway, where the waiters were hovering nervously, and signaled for a second bottle.

Chairs were pulled out, glasses filled. Henry turned the full force of his most amiable persona on the Auxiliaries, bombarding them with pleasantries. Collins, Tobin, and the two guards returned to find him leading the party in drinking a toast to the king.

"For a while there, I thought I was going to have to grab one of their guns and make a break for it," Collins managed to whisper to Henry. "But they couldn't identify me."

"You're too cocksure by half," Henry retorted. "You've taken ten years off my life tonight."

When the public dining room was finally closed for the night, the Auxiliaries staggered out with their arms around the shoulders of Collins' men, singing "Good King Wenceslas."

Two days after Christmas Henry received an ecstatic letter from Precious.

"Dearest Uncle Henry,

"How can I thank you! He is here, Saoirse is here and he is mine! The man who brought him from Limerick rode him all the way and led another horse to ride back. He said I should get on Saoirse immediately, while he was tired. That way he was calm for our first ride together. Horses remember things like that.

"His coat is very shaggy but Uncle Frank says that is just winter hair and he will shed it out. Papa taught me an Irish saying. *Is minic a rinne bromach gioblach capall cumasach.* Which means, A raggy colt often made a powerful horse.

"Saoirse is still gentle with me but he is not dull. He is full of spirit. Sitting on him is like riding the wind but I am not afraid. I have fallen off twice already but it did not hurt. Lucy and Eileen have a fat pony called Tad but they do not ride him much anymore. I shall ride Saoirse every day no matter what the weather. I wish Mama was here to see him. But I think she is, don't you?"

She signed the letter "Little Business."

I think she is, don't you?

Chapter Thirty

FROM her bedroom window on the second story Ella Rutledge looked down at the street. Assessing the weather. Deciding what to wear. New Year's Day, 1921, had begun with a rare, light fall of snow, but already it was melting. The cobbles would be slippery with brown slush. Buttoned boots, then, even if they were out of fashion. And a fur.

The family occasionally spent Christmas in Belfast, where snow was more common and seemed to last longer. Strange, what a difference a few miles could make.

With a sigh, she seated herself at her dressing table and peered at her face in the looking glass. The light from the window revealed dark smudges under her eyes. A woman's beauty melts away like snow, she thought. Men are more fortunate; other qualities matter more than appearance.

Her gaze turned to the silver-framed photograph on her dressing table. Her favorite Christmas present. It was a cabinet portrait taken by Kcogh Bros. Ltd., Dorset Street, and the subject obviously was unused to having his picture taken. His pose was stiff and his smile self-conscious, but there was no mistaking his gentle good humor.

Ella smiled back at Henry Mooney.

She knew he had been to Belfast during that long spell last year when he was traveling around the country and she never saw him. One of his articles in the *Bulletin* had described the Marching Season as observed firsthand; even hinted that he had been shot during a riot. Yet all he ever told her was that he was "indisposed." There were many things Henry never talked about.

Such a gulf between them. Background, religion, class.

A frown etched Ella's forehead.

Class. The arbitrary division labeling this person one thing and that person another. Who made such decisions? Who had the right?

Wallace Congreve was of her class; a man who would ensure that her life continued in familiar patterns. He was older, but she was no longer a young girl herself. She could hardly expect a romantic prince to sweep her off her feet. Their mutual friends expected they would marry when she was ready to take off the ring another man had given her.

Wallace took it for granted.

Ella studied the face in the photograph. Henry Mooney took nothing for granted. He had not even noticed the mistletoe.

Wallace Congreve had. Kissing her wetly, sliding his hand down from her waist to her buttocks. Trusting the impeccable manners that had been drummed into her since childhood to prevent her making a scene in front of their friends. The next time it happened he would open his mouth wider and attack her tongue with his. He would grope her more intimately, perhaps even give her a pinch to demonstrate his dominance. She knew the steps as well as she knew the steps she had learned in dancing class.

On the third of January an IRA officer died of influenza in Galway. A prisoner at Earl's Island, he had been visited by a reporter who described his condition as so critical that prison authorities finally agreed to send him to hospital. He expired before he could be given a bed.

General Macready responded by issuing a new order: "No pressman is to visit Irish prison camps."

Henry reported, "The magnificent eighteenth-century mansion of Mountshannon, in County Limerick, which was the home of the former lord chancellor of Ireland, John Fitzgibbon, the earl of Clare, has been burned by members of the Irish Republican Army. It is a loss to the architectural heritage of the nation."

The counties of Wexford, Waterford, Kilkenny, and Clare were put under martial law. The whole of southern Ireland was now at the mercy of military governance. On the first of February a man of known Republican sympathies was arrested and charged with being in possession of a revolver. His brother also was arrested for failing to inform against him. When the owner of the revolver was executed without trial, Dublin Castle reported in its *Weekly Summary*, POTENTIAL MURDERER SHOT.

ON the cold, damp evening of January twentieth Henry Mooney was passing Devlin's Pub on Rutland Square—commonly called Parnell Square by the city's Irish population—when he recognized a familiar black bicycle leaning against the wall of the building. Michael Collins laughingly referred to Devlin's as "my unofficial office" and often slept in a room at the back.

Suddenly Henry felt the need of a hot whiskey.

He found Collins in his room, with a face like thunder. "Look at this letter I just received, Henry. From de Valera."

Not Dev. Not the Chief. De Valera; spoken through tight lips.

The long letter was typewritten, no doubt by de Valera's secretary, Kathleen O'Connell. It suggested that Collins go to America so the Republic "would not have all our eggs in one basket" in case of a coup on the part of the British.[2]

As Henry read, Collins gave a bitter synopsis. "De Valera wants me to make a report to the minister for defense on the possibilities of sending munitions from the U.S. And also execute any commissions the minister requests. In other words he wants me out of his hair, and to add to the insult, I'm to be taking orders from Cathal Brugha. That way de Valera can take over the military as well as the Dáil. Well, I'll tell you something, Henry. I won't do it. The Long Whoor won't get rid of me as easily as that!"

·   ·   ·

THE twenty-first was a Friday. Ella had agreed to a late lunch with Wallace Congreve after visiting a friend in the Rotunda Maternity Hospital. Bad weather had kept her housebound for days, and she was eager for an outing. Besides, in the very proper dining room of the Kildare Street Club Wallace would have to behave himself.

Steps of the dance.

She telephoned for a motorcab to carry her across the river to the Rotunda, then back to the club on Stephen's Green. The vehicle arrived late. "There's trouble in the streets, Missus," the driver explained to Ella. "I'm not sure you'd want to be going out."

"I'm not sure I want to be staying in," she retorted, burrowing her hands into her fox muff for warmth.

A chill wind sliced across the city. As they neared O'Connell Bridge they met a contingent of soldiers setting up traffic barricades. A British officer in full battle dress thrust his head into the cab, gave Ella a polite salute when he saw she was a lady, then told the driver, "You can't go this way—we're not letting anyone through for a while."

"What's the problem, Captain?" Ella inquired.

"Tanks, Miss."

"What sort of tanks? Water tanks, you mean?"

"No, Miss, army tanks. They're taking up positions now in the docks and the market areas. We're holding back the traffic until they're in place."

"This is outrageous. I have a friend in the Rotunda Hospital with a new baby; how am I supposed to visit her?"

"You can drive down as far as Islandbridge; they'll let you through there. You might not be able to get back, though. There are some reports of snipers, and we may have to close off a number of streets until we've flushed them out."

"What sort of snipers?"

"Rebel scum, Miss. But we'll get rid of them for you."

Ella clenched her fists in her muff. "Turn around and take me home," she ordered the cab driver. "Then I would appreciate your carrying a message to Major Wallace Congreve at the Kildare Street Club." She handed the driver one of her calling cards. "Tell him I'm not in the mood for luncheon today."

ON the fourth of February Sir James Craig succeeded Sir Edward Carson as leader of the Ulster Unionist Party. Carson was now MP for the Belfast constituency of Duncairn, joining the Tories at Westminster.

Fifteen members of the Cork Brigade were betrayed by an informer as they gathered in a cottage at Clonmult. A mixed force of soldiers and Auxiliaries surrounded the cottage and set the thatch roof ablaze. The officer in charge ordered the Republicans to come out with their hands up. When they obeyed, the Auxiliaries opened fire without warning and shot nine dead. Five more were wounded before the army officers could stop the slaughter.

The six IRA men who survived Clonmult were executed on a winter's morning when sea mist mingled with the smoke of coal and turf fires in the skies over Cork City. Outside the barracks wall, Tomás MacCurtáin's widow led the wives and mothers of the condemned men in prayer. They were close enough to hear the rifle fire, volley after volley, with fifteen-minute intervals in between to make the anxiety of waiting more agonizing.

That afternoon six British soldiers were shot dead in Cork City in reprisal. Some of them were barely old enough to shave.

Twenty thousand householders in Cork City were ordered by the British military to post a list of the occupants of their houses on the door, giving the age, sex, and occupation of each person.

DESMOND FitzGerald was arrested at his home on the eleventh of February. He was taken to Dublin Castle, whose reputation for the treatment of prisoners was appalling. His wife immediately appealed to personal friends who worked for the United Press and the *Manchester Guardian*. They contacted the publicity man at Dublin Castle and made clear to him what sort of publicity would result from any damage to FitzGerald.[3]

Within a few days Desmond FitzGerald was transferred to Kilmainham and given a cell in the new section.

The *Bulletin* announced, "Mr. Erskine Childers, although not a member of Dáil Éireann, has been appointed to take the place of Mr. Desmond FitzGerald as director of publicity."

HENRY Mooney was invited to dine in Herbert Place. Finding himself the only guest for once, he took the opportunity to introduce the subject of politics. He began by applauding the work of the Sinn Féin courts.

Edwin disagreed. "They have no business usurping the powers of the official government."

"That government was failing in its responsibility to govern fairly," said Henry. "Besides, the Dáil is the democratically elected government of Ireland now."

"We don't live in a democracy, we live in a monarchy," Ava chimed in.

"With a representative parliament and an electoral system," Henry reminded her. "Being subject to Britain is not the will of the majority of the Irish people. We voted for an independent republic in—"

"Overturning the rule of law is a crime," Edwin insisted.

"Yet that is exactly what mankind has done since civilization began, brother mine," Ella remarked. "There would have been no social progress otherwise. Didn't the Magna Carta overturn an unjust rule of law?"

"Throw out all laws and lawyers too, then!" Madge cried, waving her hands dramatically. "Leave everything up to the people in the street!"

"Then you would have mob rule," warned Henry.

Edwin said, "But isn't that what you're advocating? Henry, why are you not content to live beneath the Union Jack? Is flying an Irish tricolor worth the loss of a single life?"

"That's easy for you to say when you've always enjoyed the privileges of the ruling class. You don't know what it is to be beaten and oppressed, to have your land taken from you and your religion discriminated against, to see your children forced to emigrate or starve."

"But things have changed. We live in enlightened times."

"Maybe you do, Edwin, but the majority of the people of Ireland are still as oppressed as ever, socially and economically if not physically."

"I simply cannot accept that. Our government has given them every opportunity to better themselves."

"To make better unskilled laborers and cannon fodder for the empire," Henry retorted.

Voices were raised and positions defended with passion. After allowing it to go on for some time, Ella cleared her throat and spread her smile around the table like butter on a hot scone. "That was lovely. You've spiced up our evening, Henry; we do so enjoy a spirited debate." On cue, the subject was changed.

"Any disagreement in my family always turned into a full-blown row," Henry said to Ella later. "Nothing was ever forgiven, much less forgotten."

He regretted this personal admission—until she took his hand and gave it a gentle squeeze. "We're civilized people. You can fight with us and we'll still love you in the morning."

On the fourteenth of March six Republicans were hanged at Mountjoy Prison, the largest number ever executed there in a single day. The other prisoners heard them calling a cheery goodbye as they were led out.

The lord mayor of Limerick, Michael O'Callaghan, plus the former lord mayor and another of the town's leading citizens were shot dead in their homes in a single night. The lord mayor's wife was severely wounded. Though she identified the gunmen as Black and Tans, only a military inquiry was held. No charges were filed.

Dublin itself was not yet under martial law, but a state of war existed between Michael Collins and Dublin Castle. He was being hunted as no man had been hunted in the history of Ireland. Sinn Féin was described by the Castle as crime incarnate and the returned Eamon de Valera as belonging to a race of treacherous murderers.

The redoubled efforts on the part of the Castle's propaganda machine meant more work for the Irish Bulletin. Henry's war-correspondent trips were brief. Invariably his presence was required back in the capital the next day, either for the *Bulletin* or to complete some of the other freelance writing by which he was supporting himself. He managed to find time to spend with Ella Rutledge, but had yet to visit County Clare.

Ned wrote to say that Sarsfield Maguire was hoping for some articles from Henry. As for himself, Ned commented, "All I do is arrange phone calls and send telegrams. I might as well go back to work on my novel."

Henry told Louise, "At least he isn't surrounded by reminders of Síle. Being back home with his own people is bound to help distract him from his grief."

"Do you never want to go back home, Henry?"

He shrugged. "I'm not sure where home is."

In hopes of capturing wounded Republicans, Dublin Castle issued orders for any Irish person suffering from "suspect injuries" to be turned over to the authorities at once. When hospital staff refused to comply, the raids began. Patients were seized without explanation or apology. A fourteen-year-old boy who had been injured while blowing up stumps on his father's farm was forcefully dragged away from his mother and the doctor and died in the military hospital.

The Tans and the Auxiliaries made the hunting of Republicans a sport.

The IRA continued to strike back. Infected by the upward spiral of violence, they became more violent themselves. Their officers tried hard to maintain the high standards of decency that had hallmarked the Irish Republican Army since 1916, but it was not always possible.

Brutal deeds were reported on both sides.

Responding to a formal protest of his Irish policy on the part of English ecclesiastics, Lloyd George said, "So long as Sinn Féin demands a republic, the present evils must go on. So long as the leaders of Sinn Féin stand in this position, and receive the support of their countrymen, settlement is in my judgment impossible."[4]

IN response to a whispered summons delivered by a man in a dark overcoat, on the eighteenth of April Henry strolled the short distance from number 16 to Moran's Hotel at number 71, Lower Gardiner Street. The hotel was a favorite Republican gathering place. He found Collins sitting by himself in a private room, drinking whiskey. It was obvious he had drunk quite a lot already. He did not even glance up when Henry entered.

"I have a story for you. Write it down just as I dictate it, will you? See if one of the more sympathetic British papers will buy it from you. Tell them it's typical of what's happening in Ireland today."

Henry pulled up a chair and got out his notebook. "Go ahead."

Collins stared into his glass as he dictated. Slowly. Careful not to slur his words. "Two days ago His Majesty's security forces attacked a farmhouse in County Cork. The house was occupied by eight young children, their maiden aunt, and a housekeeper. The children's father was away, attending a meeting of Cork County Council. The family had recently been left motherless. The mother had been seriously ill for months, and the stress of repeated raids in the neighborhood had contributed in a large measure to her death. You getting all this, Henry?"

"I am. Go ahead."

"Ignoring the pleas of the women, the soldiers threw everyone out in the cold. They piled up hay and straw against the house and farm buildings and set them afire. They even stripped the harness from a team plowing a nearby field and threw that into the flames. The Collins family home and everything in it was burned to the ground. Furniture, clothes, toys even. Things lovingly accumulated over generations, all gone." Collins raised his eyes. "They knew where they could hurt me most."

"Mick, I'm so sorry."

"Don't be sorry for me." The lips that women loved to kiss curled into cruelty. "Be sorry for those shitty bastards if I ever get my hands on them."

REPORTERS were flocking to Ireland. A tiny fledgling republic struggling against the might of an immense empire made for dramatic headlines. Foreign journalists were eager to interview Irish men and women who were fighting for freedom. Dublin Castle made every effort to prevent their stories being told, including having press passes revoked.

"Right now we're an eight-day wonder," Henry said to Matt Nugent in the Oval Bar, "but once the shouting's over and everyone goes home, the British propaganda machine will go grinding on, presenting us to the world as consummate villains."

"We aren't the only ones to suffer their tender mercies," Nugent replied. "Did you know there was serious rioting when the Indian parliament opened in January? Some fellow called Mohandas Gandhi is the head of the Indian National Congress, and has sworn not to co-operate with the British authorities. He describes them as 'this satanic government.' "

Henry chuckled. "A man of taste and perspicacity. What else do you know about him?"

"It's your shout," Nugent reminded his friend. When fresh drinks arrived he went on. "Like Arthur Griffith, Gandhi advocates nonviolence, but the British Empire reacted to his call for independence just as they did to ours—repression, beatings, imprisonment. The Amritsar Massacre. Now frustrated mobs are attacking road convoys and burning English property, and the British press is calling the 'ungrateful' Indians names unfit to print."

"It must be difficult for the imperialists," mused Henry, "to watch their colonial holdings trying to shake themselves free. They're baffled that we even want to. It's easy to underrate independence if you've always had it, I suppose. Only another colony that's had to fight for its freedom can understand how we feel."

That night when Henry went to Herbert Place to take Ella

out to dinner, he arrived early—an almost unheard-of occurrence in Ireland. She was not ready. He had to cool his
heels in the drawing room and make small talk with Edwin
while his mind was upstairs with her. *Ella in her chemise.*
Ella brushing her hair.

He hoped her brother could not read his mind.

ELLA was indeed in her chemise, frowning at a selection
of frocks laid out on the bed. "Which one should I wear,
Madge?" she asked her sister, who was lounging in a slipper
chair.

"Do you want to look elegant or do you want to look
gorgeous?"

"What do you mean by that?"

"I mean, are you dressing to impress other people or to
make Henry want you?"

"Madge, I'm astonished!"

The younger woman just laughed. "Well, you do want
him to desire you, don't you? You can't tell me it hasn't
crossed your mind."

Blushing but smiling too, Ella admitted, "Madge, whenever he speaks to me in that deep voice of his I can feel my
toes crossing and uncrossing."

ON the third of May the Government of Ireland Act officially came into force. The *Irish Bulletin* printed the news
in a stark black box, like a funeral announcement. That night
Henry wanted to get drunk—grimly, furiously drunk. Instead he went to see Ella Rutledge.

His face told her everything. He was not looking for romance. This was a man in pain. "Come in and sit down,"
she said gently, "and I'll ring for a drink."

"Best not. I already thought about that, but tomorrow
won't be any easier with a sore head."

They sat close together in the drawing room. "Do you
really think having two parliaments is such a bad idea?" Ella
asked. "Perhaps it will ease the tension. I'd love to see things
go back to being the way they were. The Belfast of my

childhood was a kindly, tolerant place before Edward Carson curdled it with obstinacy and hate."

"The Government of Ireland Act won't make things any better," he told her, "because it isn't meant to. Lloyd George's intention in partitioning us is to create a society too divided to function. Then he and those like him can cry, 'Ah, we told you you weren't fit to govern yourselves!' That way they're justified in refusing to grant us independence. And if they succeed here, what's to prevent them from doing the same thing in . . . in India, say? Imperialism breeds a curious mentality, Ella. There is a type of individual who is determined to be right, no matter what the cost to others."

Ella said, "That's not limited to imperialists. I call it 'last wordism.' Long ago, my father made a rule that no one in this house was ever to try to have the last word."

"Your father was a wise man."

"He was. I wish you had known him; he would have approved of you."

What did Tom Barry say? You need caution and courage in equal measure, and in that order. I think I've been cautious long enough. "I wish I had known your father, Ella. Then I could ask him for your hand in marriage. Now I'm not sure who to ask."

Her lovely face was grave.

Oh, God. I've ruined everything.

Ella lifted her left hand and removed the circlet of diamonds from her finger. Then she extended the ringless hand. "Why not ask me," she said.

Two Irish-Americans who had met de Valera in New York successfully smuggled a few dozen Thompson machine guns into Ireland. They held informal training sessions to familiarize the IRA with the new weapon. Henry received a note from Tom Barry. "You should see the dandy toy the Big Fellow just sent me. It goes rat-a-tat-tat. Come down and I'll let you play with it some time."

A larger consignment of Thompsons was arranged through Clan na Gael. British intelligence agents in America did not have Michael Collins to thwart them; U.S. Customs learned of the shipment and seized it before it ever left New York.

The potential threat they represented did not go unrecognized. In Britain the voices calling for a truce grew louder. Lloyd George's coalition government, shaky at the best of times, was forced to rethink its position, particularly in light of the fact that the number of nonmilitary persons being killed by Crown forces in Ireland was averaging almost one a day. Should that statistic be made public, the results could be dire for international relations—and commerce.

Two of the most influential British newspapers, the *London Times* and the *Daily Mail*, began clamoring for a peaceful settlement in Ireland.

HENRY wrote to Ned, "We've not yet told anyone, but Ella Rutledge has consented to become my wife!" He overcame his journalistic scruples to insert an exclamation mark, but even that was not sufficient. The next sentence was in block capitals. "I AM GOING TO MARRY ELLA RUTLEDGE!"

Ned replied, "We were absolutely gobsmacked by the news. Congratulations from us all. Precious in particular is over the moon. She likes Mrs. Rutledge very much and insists on being part of the wedding party. She wants to carry the bride's train or throw rose petals or something, so you had best keep her in mind when you start making plans."

Louise Kearney was not as wholehearted in her approval. Over meals she would gaze fixedly at Henry and clear her throat as if about to speak, then remain silent. Finally he could stand it no longer. "What's the matter, Louise? If something's on your mind, it's not like you to keep quiet about it."

She turned crimson and twisted her hands together in her lap. "Henry, Mrs. Rutledge is a sonsy* woman, I grant you that. But she's also one of them."

Henry was amused. "One of them what?"

*Lively and comely

"English." The word came out in a hiss.

"Louise, that's sheer bigotry. Besides, the Mansells aren't English, they're Anglo-Irish."

"Sure and that's worse. Don't I have friends who clean houses for that sort and have to whistle for their wages?" She gave a contemptuous sniff. "Jumped-up gentry with empty pockets, giving themselves airs. Silk stockings and no breakfast."

"You've met Ella's family. They aren't like that."

"If you say so. But they seemed toffee-nosed to me, especially that Ava. Do you really suppose they will they let her marry a Catholic?"

ON the twenty-second of May King George visited Belfast for the formal opening of the new northern parliament. To the surprise of many, he personally revised the speech written for him and concluded by saying, "The future lies in the hands of my Irish people themselves. May this historic gathering be the prelude of the day in which the Irish people, north and south, under one parliament or two, as those parliaments may themselves decide, shall work together in common love for Ireland upon the sure foundation of mutual justice and respect."[5]

AT Westminster Sir Edward Carson was proving to be something of a problem. His outspoken prejudices were deemed unhelpful in the changing political situation. So he was granted a life peerage as Baron Carson of Duncairn and appointed to serve as a lord of appeal. Thus effectively sidelined, Carson remarked with great clarity of hindsight, "I was only a puppet, and so was Ulster, and so was Ireland, in the political game that was to get the Conservative Party into power."[6]

"Why did he not realize that sooner," Henry asked bitterly, "when it could have done the people of this island some good?"

THE *Bulletin*—from its twelfth hideaway, a stately home in Longford Terrace, Rathgar—published the latest compilation of statistics. Justifying their actions on the grounds that Ireland was in a state of war—while simultaneously refusing to acknowledge members of the Irish Republican Army as prisoners of war—the British military was hanging or shooting prisoners without any pretense of a trial. Furthermore, all coroners' inquests had been cancelled.

THE afternoon of May twenty-fifth was warm and sunny, with a light inshore breeze. Emmet Dalton, a former major in the British army who was now the IRA's director of training, had selected a fine day for the Dublin Brigade's maneuvers.

Splitting into two groups, the brigade sent one detail to prevent the central fire brigade from answering calls. The second and larger group surrounded the magnificent domed Customs House on Eden Quay. James Gandon's architectural masterpiece housed nine administrative departments, including income tax and local government records.

The Republicans ordered the large building evacuated. The frightened staff obeyed, but the head caretaker vehemently refused. After a brief argument, they shot him. Then they ran from room to room with paraffin and matches.

The time spent evacuating the building was sufficient to allow an alarm to be raised. As the Republicans left the building, the first lorry load of Black and Tans arrived. Gunfire once more rattled along the quays. Five members of the Dublin Brigade were killed and almost eighty arrested, but nothing could arrest the fire. The flames had tons of paper to feed upon.

For the rest of the day the skies above Dublin sagged with smoke. Crowds gathered to gape at the fire, which continued to blaze throughout the night until the great copper dome collapsed with a roar that was heard for miles. By morning only the blackened walls were standing.

Henry was sickened, and not just by the wanton destruction of a beautiful building. When Frank Gallagher asked him to write a triumphant article about the burning of the

Customs House, he refused. "I can't condone what was done there," he said bluntly. "In destroying the records of the administration of Ireland we're destroying our own records. We are Ireland."

This was the kind of thing he had feared when he arranged for Ned to go to Clare. Otherwise Henry had no doubt Ned would have been inside the Customs House with matches in his hand.

Ned affirmed his belief by writing jubilantly, "Thank God for that fire! All those birth certificates burned—now no one can prove Precious is not my daughter."

No one doubted that de Valera had ordered the attack on the Customs House, though he was not acknowledging it publicly. "He's waiting to see whether the action proves to be an asset or a liability to him," Matt Nugent said to Henry in the Oval Bar. "You have to admire Dev. He knows when to keep his head below the parapet."

"He knows how to turn a situation to his advantage, too," Henry replied. "To make up for those who were killed and captured he's amalgamated Collins' men into the Dublin Brigade. That puts them under Cathal Brugha as minister for defense, and thus directly under Dev's control."

"What does the Big Fellow think about that?"

Henry shook his head. "I wouldn't like to be the one who asks him."

At the end of May Anglo-Egyptian relations hit a new low as Egyptian nationalists rioted in Cairo and Alexandria, demanding independence. British soldiers quelled the potential uprising with rifle and bayonet.

In June the British military arrested Eamon de Valera and imprisoned him in Portobello Barracks. The arrest took place without bureaucratic sanction.

• • •

THE destruction of the Irish income tax records forced the British government to confront the reality of the losses they were suffering. Michael Collins and the IRA were running circles around Crown forces.

Field Marshal Sir Henry Wilson and Lloyd George had a serious disagreement over Irish policy which led to the prime minister refusing to reappoint Wilson chief of the imperial general staff. As a parting shot, Wilson flatly informed the cabinet that the British troops in Ireland were so demoralized they would all have to be replaced by October. To attempt to reconquer the country, he said, would require an additional one hundred thousand specially recruited men at the minimum, total martial law, and prohibition of all civil traffic except by special license. The cost to the British exchequer would be staggering.

Wilson went, but his words echoed in number 10 Downing Street.

EAMON de Valera was released from prison without explanation.

Within days Arthur Griffith, Eoin MacNeill, and Desmond FitzGerald were released as well.

ON the twenty-fourth of June Lloyd George sent a formal invitation to de Valera. He was asked to attend a conference together with Sir James Craig, who now bore the title of Premier of Northern Ireland.

Anticipating a truce, an editorial in the *Westmeath Independent* proclaimed triumphantly, "English rule is broken in Ireland. No English policies, good or bad, will stand. The Irish people will govern themselves."[7]

Henry Mooney cut out that column to save with his treasured copy of the Proclamation of the Republic. In the peace and quiet of his room at number 16 he began work on an article of his own. The first paragraph read, "1776—America. 1789—France. 1921—Ireland. This will go into the history books as the year Ireland won her own War of Independence."

He put down his pencil and sat for a long time staring at the words. "Nineteen twenty-one," he whispered. Then he went out alone to stand under the night sky. The hem of heaven was embroidered with stars.

DE Valera declined Lloyd George's invitation. His response stated, "We most earnestly desire to help in bringing about a lasting peace between the peoples of these two islands, but see no avenue by which it can be reached if you deny Ireland's essential unity and set aside the principle of national self-determination."[8]

In the *Clare Champion* Henry explained, "Had Eamon de Valera accepted Lloyd George's invitation to attend jointly with Sir James Craig, it would have amounted to an acceptance of Craig's right to govern part of Ireland against the will of the national majority. We must obtain freedom from foreign domination for all our people, not just some. But we are almost there. The war is won. It only remains to win the peace."

IT's down to politics now," Henry told Ella when he called at Herbert Place that evening. "The two sides will negotiate until they find a position their supporters can live with. If Dev keeps his nerve and doesn't give way, Britain will have no choice but to accept the Republic. After that there can be real peace between our two countries. After all, many in Britain are our friends—or our relatives."

"Like my cousins in London," said Ella. "You'll meet them one of these days."

"Mmm. What will they think of you marrying a Catholic? For that matter, what does your family here think?"

"So far I haven't told anyone but Madge. She was worried that when she married I would be left as—how did she put it?—the last leaf on the tree. So I—Oh, hullo, Madge. Were you eavesdropping?"

"Of course not, since I already know your secret," Madge replied, hurrying across the room to plant a kiss on Henry's cheek. "I'm delighted for you both. I think Edwin will approve too—he likes you tremendously."

"And Ava?"

Madge made a face. "Don't worry about Ava, Henry. Let me tell you one of our secrets. When Sir Rhys Mansell came to Ireland to beat the recalcitrant natives into submission, he made one of those natives his mistress. After the rebellion was put down, he went back to England; but she was an Irish Catholic peasant, so he could hardly take her with him. He left her here with a bun in the oven, and that's our famous Mansell connection. Descended from an illegitimate son. If dear Ava tries to pretend this family's too good for the Mooneys, you just laugh at her."

Laugh at Ava. And the cousins in London. And the relatives in Belfast. And the priests who will want her to convert and demand our children be raised as Catholics. And her Protestant friends who will be horrified. Laugh at those who will very rightly be concerned about what Ella's getting into.

She hasn't told people yet because she's afraid to. I don't blame her.

Henry did not take a cab back to number 16. He walked, with his coat collar turned up against an insistent drizzle.

In marrying Ella Rutledge he would be taking a leap of faith: faith that their feelings for one another would be enough to overcome all obstacles.

Chapter Thirty-one

ALTHOUGH he had declined Lloyd George's invitation
to a conference, de Valera organized a conference himself.
He wanted members of the Dáil to consult with what he
called "representatives of the political minority," the loyalists living in the six counties in contention, and gain their
consent to a truce proposal on Republican terms.

De Valera set the date for the Fourth of July—American
Independ-ence Day.

The conference was held at the Mansion House. On de
Valera's orders the American flag was flown from the front
of the building to honor the day. Four representatives from
the loyalist side attended, but Sir James Craig refused to
come.

None of the press was invited. The negotiations were held
behind closed doors while an anxious crowd waited in the
street, seething with speculation.

On the fifth of July a British emissary, General Smuts,
arrived from London to hold private talks with de Valera.

When the conference concluded three days later, Desmond FitzGerald gave the *Irish Bulletin* its lead story: "Eamon de Valera, the president of Dáil Éireann, will be
traveling to London on the fourteenth of this month to meet
with the British prime minister at Downing Street. In the
meantime General Macready has been invited to the Mansion House to discuss principles governing a possible truce."

Ireland held its breath.

When General Sir Neville Macready, wearing full military uniform and with a revolver in his pocket, arrived at the Mansion House, he found the footpath lined with Irish men and women on their knees, saying the rosary. To his amazement, they greeted him warmly. "It's peace you've come to bring us, then?" said one white-haired woman with a careworn face. "May God bless you."

ON July eleventh a special edition of the *Bulletin* proclaimed, ANGLO-IRISH TRUCE SIGNED:

"The British army has agreed to bring in no more troops, conduct no provocative displays, and engage in no pursuit of Irish officers or men. For its part the Irish Republican Army has agreed to abandon its attacks on Crown forces, conduct no provocative displays, and cease interfering with government property and otherwise disturbing the peace. Republicans are given leave to go home, but asked to hold themselves ready for mobilization at short notice for the duration of the truce."

Henry could not resist adding, "After more than seven hundred years of subjugation the Irish Republican Army has made foreign occupation of Ireland untenable."

THE *Bulletin* staff held a little party. Emotions were mixed. "I'm so thankful for the truce," Kathleen McKenna said to Henry. "My brother Tadhg's in prison; now he'll be released. But all the same . . ." Her eyes swept around the room.

Henry understood. "It could mean the end of the *Bulletin*. When it's no longer needed we'll discontinue publishing."

She was biting back tears. "I can't imagine what life would be like without the *Bulletin*."

Frank Gallagher interjected, "I can tell you what it will be like. We'll have peace in Ireland. We won't need to tell the stories no one else dare tell. You girls have been champion, you know. You've carried the bur-den while we were in and out of jail or risking our necks down the country."

Embarrassed, Kathleen lowered her eyes. "It was our privilege, Gally."

"Well, it was appreciated, and we want you each to have a little memento. Bring them over here, Henry, will you?"

The "little memento" was a special edition of the *Bulletin* that Gallagher had inscribed on a stencil. The headline read MAKERS OF THE REPUBLIC. Beneath was a recognizable likeness of Kathleen McKenna, sketched by Ella Rutledge from a photograph. In cartoon style, it depicted her wielding a cudgel in one hand and a revolver in the other. The figure was labeled "The Dáil Girl." A much smaller figure carrying an attaché case was identified as "The Mere President."[1]

EAMON De Valera issued a proclamation that read, "During the period of the truce each individual soldier and citizen must regard himself as a custodian of the nation's honor. Your discipline must prove in the most convincing manner that this is the struggle of an organized nation."[2]

WHAT does that mean, 'the period of the truce'?" Louise Kearney asked Henry. "Isn't this peace?"

"It's just a temporary respite," he told her. "A quiet time in which to see if we can come to a settlement."

"And we're supposed to trust the British to abide by their agreement?"

"We have to trust them, Louise, and they have to trust us. If we can't take at least that small step, how can we go any further?"

She folded her arms atop the shelf of her bosom. "When they arrested you they came bursting into my house without my permission and pawed through my cupboards and went off with my valuables in their pockets. How am I supposed to trust people who're after doing that?"

The IRA felt the same way. Republicans stayed close to home with their weapons at the ready, expecting to be called up again any time.

Civilians were overjoyed. The capital went *en fête* as it had with the announcement of the Armistice of the Great

War. Curfew was rescinded. Nationalists flew the tricolor and sang "A Soldier's Song" and shouted "Up the Republic!" without fear of arrest.

Michael Collins made a trip home to Cork.

Henry Mooney also took advantage of the general euphoria to give himself a brief holiday. Laden with small presents for everyone, he caught the early morning train for Clare.

Frank Halloran met him at the station with the pony and trap. There was another horse alongside: a glossy dark gray, almost black—a spirited young animal who danced and tossed his head and flirted with the bit as if it were wrapped in thorns. He was ridden by a girl almost as leggy as her mount. She rode bareback, at one with the horse.

Henry hardly recognized Precious. It occurred to him that Ned and Síle might have underestimated her age. They had guessed she was born in 1910, but her small stature could have been the result of malnutrition.

"Uncle Henry!" she cried as she slid off and ran to embrace him.

Seven months had wrought a remarkable change in Ursula Halloran. She was both taller and heavier. Her hair had become a healthy, lustrous nut-brown, hanging over one shoulder in a heavy plait; but the most noticeable change was in her face. A scattering of golden freckles dusted her skin like speckles on a blackbird's egg. The underlying bone structure was being sculpted by the onset of puberty. Cheekbones were emerging. Eye sockets had acquired a definite arch. "Papa's off with the lads," she told Henry as she squeezed the breath out of him with a mighty hug, "but he'll be at the farm in time for dinner. Aunt Norah and the girls are waiting; I insisted on welcoming you first."

Over her head, Frank caught Henry's eye. "When this one insists . . ."

Henry chuckled. "You don't have to tell me."

Precious vaulted back onto the horse and rode beside the trap as they drove to the farm. "Don't you have a saddle for that animal?" Henry called to her.

"Don't need one."

"I suspect your Aunt Norah's scandalized to see you riding like that."

Precious laughed. "She is of course. But I just give her a hug and go on."

Frank laughed too, the rusty rumble of a man who did not laugh very often.

"How are Lucy and Eileen taking to her?" Henry asked him in a low voice.

"They seem to think she's a force of nature and let her be."

"I'm amazed at how she's grown."

The girl interjected, "Aunt Norah says cities are no good for Irish people, they stunt us."

"Are you still earwigging, Little Business?"

She grinned. "I am of course. And I'm ever so much stronger. Here, we'll show you." Holding the reins in one hand, she twisted the fingers of her other hand into the horse's mane and drummed his sides with her heels. Saoirse leaped into a gallop.

Girl and horse thundered toward the nearest stone field wall. Henry thought his heart would stop. "Mind yourself!" he cried, but Precious paid no attention. When she leaned forward and made a clicking noise, Saoirse lifted into the air like Pegasus.

Henry was badly shaken. "Don't ever do that to me again, Little Business," he called as she came trotting back through an open gate.

Her laughter pealed. "Oh, Uncle Henry, Saoirse can go much higher than that!"

I'D think about marrying myself, Henry," said Frank Halloran as they sat down to dinner, "if I could find a young woman to help with the farm. A strong woman with sturdy legs, beef to the heels like a Mullingar heifer."

"You don't want a wife, you want a milk cow. I'm afraid my Ella wouldn't suit you." *My Ella.*

Ned said, "Ella Rutledge would suit any man who admires grace and beauty. You have a treasure there, Henry. You're not going to have an easy time of it, though."

Norah Daly glanced up from serving the mashed parsnips and carrots. "Why is that?"

"Mrs. Rutledge is not of our faith."

Norah gasped. "You don't tell me! Henry Mooney, you've proposed marriage to a *Protestant*? What were you thinking of at all?"

"The rest of my life," said Henry.

Later he and Ned went for a walk together. Feeling every inch a country man, Henry broke off a stalk of grass and chewed it contemplatively as they strolled around the farm. Grain was ripening in the sun. The three young girls were singing together as they weeded the vegetable patch. Outside the barn, Frank was sharpening a scythe on the scythe stone, *whiss-whiss, whiss-whiss*, never missing a beat. Country rhythms, pastoral and eternal.

"This is what one misses in Dublin," remarked Henry. "Here everything is about living and growing."

"You've been in the city too long. You forget how much slaughtering we do."

Henry gave him a sideways glance. "Does that include Michael Brennan's flying column?"

"We've won more skirmishes than we've lost. That's what war's about."

"Seen much skirmishing yourself, have you?"

Ned spun around to face him. "You know I have not," he said in an angry voice, biting down on the words. "You know exactly what my orders are."

"I told you before that—"

"The Volunteers are one big family," Ned interrupted. "I think you forget that, Henry. Dick Mulcahy's secretary was with me in the GPO, and when I asked him why I was given the only noncombat assignment in Clare, he told me. You arranged it. I'm no fool; it was easy enough to figure out why. You wanted me out of Dublin and away from Síle's grave."

"Ah, Ned, that wasn't the—"

"Away from Síle's grave," Ned said again. He turned away and strode off. His rigid shoulders were a harsh punctuation mark in the gentle poetry of landscape.

Henry watched for a few moments, then hurried to catch up. Ned did not acknowledge his presence.

Just walk. Give him time to calm down. At last Henry

asked brightly, "How are people here reacting to the truce?"

He had to repeat the question before Ned replied in a sullen, uninflected voice. "I took the news to Brigadier Brennan in Kilmaley and then went with him and the flying column to Ennis. In front of the Clare Hotel we were surrounded by a crowd of people cheering and hugging each other—even a British sergeant with the Victoria Cross on his tunic. When we went on to Limerick the next day, the same scene was repeated. Our men were carrying rifles, and so were the Auxiliaries and Tans. The two sides circled around each other like dogs in the road. There were a lot of itching trigger fingers, but no one fired a shot."[3]

Henry looked out across the rolling hills of Clare. The real Ireland, uninterested in the petty convulsions of men. "Ned, if we do reach a settlement with Britain . . . do you think we'll all be able to live together again?"

"I don't know, Henry. That would be asking a lot of human nature." He hesitated, then added, "Friends come and friends go, but an enemy is forever."

On the train back to Dublin Henry was deeply troubled. Ned's attitude perplexed him. He tried to tell himself it was just resentment at his interfering. Ned would get over it—would even be grateful to him, someday. Yet at the back of his mind, a warning bell chimed a discordant note.

The next day, although Henry hated visiting cemeteries, he went to Glasnevin and stood for a long time beside Síle's grave with his head down and his hands folded.

I'm doing my best for him, Síle. For him and Precious.

Afterward he walked aimlessly, going for a little journey around the inside of his head. Eventually he found himself beside the Royal Canal. The dark water mirrored a solitary swan drifting as aimlessly as himself.

Swans should be in pairs. They mate for life, don't they? Henry cupped his mouth with his hands and called, "Why don't you go and find her, wherever she is?"

Slowly the regal head turned on the imperial neck. The bird looked at him across the water. He could swear their eyes met. Man and animal were briefly locked in an intense moment that transcended species. Then with a great flapping of wings the swan ran along the surface of the canal and leaped for the sky.

Whether drifting on the water or soaring in the sky it was at home, a creature in its element. Yet in the moment of takeoff the swan was vulnerably awkward.

So are we poor lonely humans, Henry mused, *caught between earth and heaven*.

THE cease-fire was in place but the hard work still lay ahead. When they met in the Oval Bar, Matt Nugent told Henry, "The British press is using this as a propaganda opportunity. They claim their government made an exceptionally generous offer it didn't have to make, and if we Irish are so ungrateful as to refuse the terms, there is every moral justification for crushing us by force. They say telegrams of congratulation are pouring in to Lloyd George."

"I'll just bet they are," said Henry.

Michael Collins was also back in Dublin. He was furious when the British announced that the remaining imprisoned Dáil Deputies would all be released save one. The exception was a close friend of Collins, Seán MacEoin. In a highly charged meeting with other members of the cabinet, Collins said he was willing to call a resumption of the war if all the TDs were not freed at once.

Equally furious that Collins would jeopardize the truce for the sake of one man, de Valera had no choice but to agree. The demand was passed on to Downing Street. MacEoin was released with the others.

When Eamon de Valera departed for London to discuss the next phase of the peace negotiations he took with him Erskine Childers, who was now serving in the Dáil as TD for Wicklow, as well as Arthur Griffith and Count Plunkett. Michael Collins was not invited.

Once they arrived in London, de Valera left his party at the hotel and went alone to 10 Downing Street. The prime minister welcomed him with all the pomp and circumstance of empire: red carpets unrolled, flunkeys in livery opening doors, much bowing and scraping, photographs for the newspapers. Attired in a beautifully cut morning coat, Lloyd

George radiated self-assurance: a leonine mane of white hair; a strong-featured face; dark eyebrows flared like butterflies' wings above wide-set, hypnotically brilliant eyes. The prime minister employed his features as an actor might, appearing ingenuous or shrewd, a sympathetic friend or a dangerous enemy as the situation required. A flair for drama was his stock in trade.

Beside him de Valera appeared gawky and foreign-looking. A man not in his element.

Once the ceremony was over and the two were seated in a private chamber, Lloyd George began the conversation by asking de Valera if there was a word in Irish for "republic." De Valera told him of two, the more literal being *poblacht*. But there was also *saorstat*, or "free state." Lloyd George smiled and said "Free State" was a fine name and need not be changed. He repeated it frequently during their meeting. From this de Valera inferred an acceptance of the Republic, as he told the others when he returned to the hotel. He had three more meetings with Lloyd George, and wrote to Michael Collins, "The meetings have been between us two alone as principals . . . You will be glad to know that I am not dissatisfied with the general situation."[4]

De Valera had yet to learn just how slippery the Welsh Wizard could be.

On the nineteenth of July an interview with Sir James Craig was published in which the northern leader made it obvious that Lloyd George had assured him the six Ulster counties would be held apart from the "Free State."

A heated exchange followed between de Valera and Lloyd George. The prime minister then handed de Valera a proposal by which Ireland would be granted partial dominion status within the British Commonwealth—described as "the great association of free nations over which His Majesty reigns." The proposal ignored the principle of self-determination for Ireland as a whole according to majority vote, and offered a far more restricted autonomy than that enjoyed by other dominion members such as Canada. It also copper-fastened Northern Ireland as a separate polity. The Free State was further expected to assume responsibility for a share of Britain's debts.

De Valera felt certain that his people would not accept less than the Republic. Nor would he. He told Lloyd George he would not even take the document home with him for consideration, and he and his party returned to Dublin.

The British sent the document after them.

ON the twenty-ninth of July an Austrian who had been wounded and gassed during the Great War became the new president of the National Socialist German Workers Party. Adolf Hitler, who was scathing in his condemnation of democracy, had begun his climb to power.

Chapter Thirty-two

August 26, 1921

EAMON DE VALERA CONFIRMED BY DÁIL
ÉIREANN AS PRESIDENT OF THE IRISH REPUBLIC

THE damned Delage was parked in front of Herbert Place
again. Polished and gleaming. Cushioned leather upholstery
and patented shock absorbers. Henry stared at it with incre-
dulity.

How dare he pay a call on my fiancée!

The voice of common sense cut in. Major Congreve was
an old friend of the family. There was no reason why he
should not call.

*Ella still hasn't told anyone about our engagement. In-
cluding that damned major, I'm sure. Why not? I want to
shout it from the rooftops.*

Too many years of observing politics and politicians had
made Henry cynical. He had learned to expect hidden mo-
tives. *What if she's keeping her options open for a better
offer? Maybe she's decided she doesn't want to live on a
journalist's income and doesn't know how to tell me.*

He gave himself a mental shaking. *Ella's not like that.*

But that other voice in his head, like the droning of a
poisonous insect, went on. *How do I know what she's like?*

I've never pretended to understand women. The closest I came was Síle . . .

He put his foot of the bottom step and looked up at the door. The polished brass knocker. The gleaming nameplate.

Turned. Looked back at the motorcar.

Patented shock absorbers.

Damn.

As he raised his hand to the knocker, the door opened and Congreve himself emerged, chatting back over his shoulder. He nearly knocked Henry down before he saw him. "I beg your pardon, old man."

"I'm not your old man," Henry said. "And *I'm* not old," he added. He could not help it.

Congreve paused; took a good look at him. Read his eyes. "Is something amiss?" he asked politely. Then he turned and called into the house, "Ella, your friend the newsman is here, looking like thunder."

"Your friend the newsman"—as if I deliver the papers!

Henry was growing angrier by the moment. Brushing past Congreve, he stalked into the house. Ella gave him a startled look but lingered at the door long enough to tell the major goodbye, then followed Henry into the drawing room. "What on earth is wrong?"

"Nothing's wrong."

"Don't bite my head off, Henry. Wallace is right, you do look like thunder."

"Wallace?"

"Major Congreve. Surely you remember him."

"Surely I do. How could I forget him? More to the point, how can you forget him?" The words were tumbling out without his permission.

To his relief, she laughed. "Why Henry Mooney, you're jealous."

"I am not jealous."

Ella smiled. "A man hates for a woman to suggest he's jealous, while a woman hates if a man is not." Her dimples mocked him.

"Are you ever jealous?"

"My goodness, Henry, what a direct question! If I answered I should lose all my womanly mystery."

She was playing, but he was serious. "You'll never lose your mystery," he assured her, "not for me. Sometimes when you put your hand to your chin just so"——he demonstrated—— "and gaze off into space with that faraway look of yours, I imagine that's exactly how the moon must regard the earth."

For once Ella was caught off-guard. "What a poetic thing to say."

"I mean it. I always mean what I say to you."

They stood looking at one another. Around them the atmosphere thickened, throbbed.

Ella's social graces came to the rescue. Gesturing to Henry to take a chair, she plied him with the distractions of tea, biscuits, and light conversation. He sat in the chair, drank the tea, and responded automatically to the conversation while he tried to bring his rebelling emotions under control.

Since she agreed to marry him Ella had permitted Henry certain liberties—a tender kiss on the mouth, a lingering hug that left the shape of her body imprinted on his. He had not attempted to go farther. Either they were out together in public or there were other people in the house who might enter the room at any time. He had never been invited upstairs, nor did he expect to be. A respectable courtship had certain rules.

Suddenly he was tired of rules. Tired of flirtatious games. *I'm too old for this.*

She went on talking vivaciously, but he who made his living through words had no interest in words, could not even hear them, was receptive only to the fall of light on her skin, the halo of light trapped in her hair. His eyes fastened on the delicate blue vein visible on the inside of her wrist when she made some graceful gesture. Within that vein pulsed life. Hot. Insistent.

"I want you," he said.

The flow of chatter stopped abruptly. "I beg your pardon?"

"I want you. Desire you. Want to make love to you. Do you understand what I'm saying?"

"Of course I do, Henry, and that's very flattering, but——"

"But nothing, damn it."

She raised her eyebrows.

"Damn it," he repeated, emphatically, so there was no mistake. "I'm a grown man and yes, sometimes I swear. That's me. I won't apologize for being what I am. Or for desiring you. Wanting to make love to you. *Making love.* Surely you've made love before," he added with a cruelty he did not intend and immediately regretted.

"Of course I have. With my husband." Her cool tone carried no inflection whatever. He had no way of telling if she was angry.

But he had gone too far to turn back. "What do you think that phrase means, Ella? I'll tell you: making love means building something. Do you want to make love with me? If not, tell me now."

"What's this about? Wallace Congreve?" Still cool. Still self-possessed.

"Not at all; it's about you and me. I hate games playing; I see it all around me every day, and I don't want it in my personal life as well. Perhaps the men in your set conform to—"

"The steps of a dance," she interrupted.

"What?"

"Nothing. Go on."

"I'm just telling you I want simple honesty. You haven't set a date for the wedding; you haven't even announced our engagement. There must be a reason. I'm not a wealthy man and never will be. Sometimes, with enough provocation, I am a profane man. And I'm Catholic, we mustn't forget that. If you have the slightest reservations about marrying me, say so now. I won't hold it against you. I only want your happi—"

"Hush." She rose from her chair and crossed the space between them in one graceful step to take his hand. "Come with me, Henry."

"Where?"

"Come with me. Now."

He followed her upstairs.

Up three flights of stairs, to the rooms on the top floor.

Deep inside him was a harpstring tuned too tight, right to the breaking point. He could hardly bear to watch as she turned the key in the door. "Welcome to my studio," she said.

They entered a long room that ran halfway across the front of the house. A row of windows let in a flood of clear light. "Edwin had this fitted up for me, and no one ever disturbs me up here," Ella said. "They have strict orders." But she locked the door anyway.

Henry absorbed the room through his pores. *Her private place.*

Faded floral wallpaper, bare floorboards, a worktable spread with newspapers, an old daybed with a chintz cover. In her studio the elegant and fastidious Ella Rutledge became a different person. Carelessly scattered around the room were canvases, stretchers, unfinished oil paintings, and dozens of sketches and watercolors. A charcoal drawing in progress waiting on an easel; a wire armature for figure study slouching on a candle stand. Jam jars crammed with brushes, pens, pencils. Smeared palettes, wadded cloths, tubes of paint, a half-empty bottle of turps, pots of watercolors, art books opened to illustrations for study and weighted down with a variety of unlikely objects.

"What's the daybed for?"

"It's warm up here, so sometimes I get sleepy in the afternoons. I like to lie down for a little while and then go back to work."

"Are you sleepy now?"

"No."

"Ella, are you sure you—"

"Hush," she said again. She opened her arms and gathered him in.

Watching his face as if his thoughts were printed there, she let him undress her. It certainly was not the first time Henry had undressed a woman, yet never before had he handled garments of such daintiness. The delicate ribbons and frothing laces and tiny pearl buttons of Ella's underclothing were meant to be handled only by a lady's maid. Being allowed to touch them was a greater triumph than any he had experienced with women whose clothing was blatantly intended to entice the male. Henry was elated—and awed.

"You are very beautiful," he whispered.

"Not as beautiful as Ava."

This time he said "Hush."

The skin over her collarbones was as thin and fine as silk. He brushed it with his lips almost reverently, then moved farther down. Seeking. Finding. Losing himself in her.

She inhaled sharply.

"Am I hurting you?"

"No."

He knew a great deal about giving pleasure to a woman, but surely the skills learned from Monto whores were not appropriate here. He fought to control himself, to be a gentleman. Be gentle. So . . .

Flooding incandescence, and the enormous release of energy that follows giving in to a long-suppressed desire.

A great moan was wrung from him.

Much later, deeply moved, he murmured, "You leave me speechless."

He could feel her laughter. "That's a first."

"Do I talk too much?"

"Sometimes you don't talk enough. I never realized there was so much passion in you, damn it."

Henry raised himself on one elbow and looked down at her in surprise.

"I swear too," Ella Rutledge told him.

He was halfway back to number 16 before he realized she still had not set a date for their wedding.

EAMON de Valera leaned back in his chair and surveyed Henry across his desk. He remained an austere figure, but an element had been added. His spectacles did not quite conceal a new wariness in his eyes. "Is this interview for the *Bulletin*?" de Valera inquired politely.

"I freelance as well," Henry reminded him. "In the *Bulletin* you'd be preaching to the converted, so you might prefer me to offer this to some of my connections abroad."

"When I appointed Desmond as minister for propaganda, perhaps I should have made you his deputy."

Henry shook his head. "I don't want to be part of government. I think I have more to contribute this way."

"And fewer limitations," the other said surprisingly. "Go ahead, then. Ask your questions."

Taking out his notebook, Henry read, " 'Dáil Éireann has supported President de Valera by unanimously rejecting the peace terms offered by the British government. As a result threats of renewing the war are being made in the House of Lords. Meanwhile Lloyd George has been quoted as saying that dealing with de Valera is like trying to handle mercury with a fork.' " Henry looked up. "May I have a quote from you, sir, on the prime minister?"

De Valera put two steepled index fingers to his lips and withdrew into a brief, contemplative silence. When he flung his hands apart the decision was made. "As the president of the Republic I think it best not to engage in personal remarks. I am no longer to be regarded as a party leader— and you can quote me on this—but as one who represents the entire nation.

"I have one allegiance only: to the people of Ireland. The whole and united Republic of Ireland, that we genuinely believe to be the only means by which this island will have peace. We have fought honorably to achieve this end. We cannot change our position because it is fundamentally sound and just, as the rest of the world recognizes."

I wonder if he can speak without making a speech? "May I have a few words on your vision of the Republic, *Taoiseach?*"

At the word Taoiseach de Valera allowed himself a very faint smile. Then he reached out and peremptorily helped himself to Henry's notebook and pencil. Turning to a fresh page, he began sketching a series of geometric figures. To each he ascribed an identity: the government, the economy, the educational system, the agricultural community—the Church. Interconnecting lines showed the relationships of these entities to one another, presenting a balanced structure.

Just what one would expect from a mathematics teacher, Henry thought.

Underneath his drawing de Valera printed in block letters, BY CONSENT OF THE GOVERNED.

At the conclusion of the interview Henry thanked de Valera and rose to go. One final question hovered on his lips, however, and de Valera saw it there. "Is there something else?"

"In reappointing the ministries, Michael Collins was returned to finance. Considering the fact that it was he who forced the British to the truce table, do you not think he should be offered—"

"No," said Eamon de Valera.

DEAREST Girl," Henry wrote, "I am running between appointments all day and may not see you until after tea time, but I want you to know you are in my thoughts. If you remember where I left my last kiss, imagine that I just put another one there." He folded the note, tucked it into an envelope, and sent it via the first small boy. He had begun keeping an assortment of small change for the express purpose of paying for such messengers to Ella.

Their relationship had entered a new realm. He was allowed caresses of the most intimate nature when no one was looking. The glances Ella gave him in public were those of a woman in love. With difficulty, Henry refrained from insisting that she set a wedding date. From his own experience he knew that grief was heavy, leaden, but happiness was ephemeral and must not be examined too closely. His possession of Ella Rutledge seemed a miracle of such ephemeral magic that pressure would destroy it, just as a touch would destroy a cobweb pearled with dew on a May morning.

He would trust, and wait. In the fullness of time all would be arranged.

Henry very much wanted to believe that.

In the meantime he held long, one-sided conversations with her in his head when he first woke up in the morning, conversations in which he expressed anxiety about the difference in their backgrounds, concern over the uncertainty of his financial future, and most of all his need for reassurance on a level other than the sexual. When they were together he never repeated these conversations. Instead he was relaxed and confident, the very picture of an accepted suitor.

•   •   •   •

ONE night after a cabinet meeting Henry saw Michael Collins in Devlin's. Collins greeted him by asking, "D'you happen to know the Irish synonym for 'deceit'?"

Henry chuckled. " 'The smile of an Englishman.' "

The other man nodded, unsmiling. "Precisely. Henry, I worked as a civil servant in England; I know the bureaucratic mind over there. I've tried to warn Dev, but he won't listen to me. Lloyd George and his crowd have dazzled him with all that fancy show. All that smiling. He's still exchanging letters and telegrams with them, trying to arrange a peace agreement, but he doesn't appreciate the nature of the people he's dealing with."

"Oh, I think he does," Henry replied, recalling the wariness he had seen in the president's eyes.

The duel between de Valera and Lloyd George became a war of words as each sought a phraseology that would seduce the other into a compromise. Desmond FitzGerald kept Henry apprised of developments. Understanding the language of persuasion, the weight and nuance of the most insignificant word, the journalist felt a mounting sense of frustration.

Michael Collins was equally frustrated. "I'll tell you exactly what's happening," he told Henry. "We won the war, but now Lloyd George is trying to claw back everything we won."

Lloyd George was arranging another conference, but when de Valera asserted that Ireland would enter negotiations as an independent and sovereign state, the prime minister cancelled it.

De Valera wrote to Lloyd George, "We request you to state . . . whether this is a demand for surrender on our part, or an invitation to a conference free on both sides and without prejudice should agreement not be reached."[1]

The prime minister replied, "The position taken up by His Majesty's government is fundamental to the existence of the British Empire and they cannot alter it. My colleagues and I remain, however, keenly anxious to make in cooperation with your delegates another determined effort to explore every possibility of settlement by personal discussion. We therefore send you a fresh invitation to a conference in Lon-

don on 11 October, where we can meet your delegates as
spokesmen of the people whom you represent with a view
to ascertaining how the association of Ireland with the community of nations known as the British Empire may best be
reconciled with Irish national aspirations."

FitzGerald showed Henry a copy of the prime minister's
letter. "This isn't for publication, of course; matters are far
too delicate. But I want you to see what we're dealing with."

Henry read the letter twice. "Christ in a convent! Lloyd
George makes it sound as if he's offering everything, but
he's offering nothing. Surely Dev won't fall for that."

"He can't afford to be seen as refusing to enter into discussions, either. We've fought bloody hard to be recognized
as a constitutional government, Henry, and now it's time to
behave as constitutional governments behave. We must be
willing to talk rather than shoot."

"You're right so. We've won everything we can with the
gun. We'll just have to trust that Dev's too clever to let them
take it away from us."

Arthur Griffith drafted de Valera's reply to the latest British offer. "We agree that conference, not correspondence, is
the most practical and hopeful way to an understanding. We
accept the invitation and our delegates will meet with you
in London on the date mentioned."

So far, de Valera had not given anything away.

A new wave of excitement was building in Ireland. People
were aware that treaty negotiations were in the offing, and
many considered the acceptance of the Republic a foregone
conclusion. "Sure," they said to one another on the street,
"between the Big Fellow and the Long Fellow the British
stand no chance."

In advance of the actual negotiations the conservatives in
the British parliament began placating Sir James Craig. He
received surreptitious disbursements of arms and money on
a grand scale, enabling him to fund a new militia called the
B-Specials, composed almost entirely of members of the Orange Order. The purpose of the B-Specials was to carry out
a campaign against Irish nationalists in the north similar to
that undertaken by the Black and Tans in the rest of Ireland.
The conservatives wanted to be certain Craig had enough

firepower to resist any effort to unite Ireland. In return the Unionists would continue to support them in Parliament.

When the IRA learned about the B-Specials, anger boiled over. The most militant of the Republicans was Cathal Brugha—who in his body carried twenty-five metallic reminders of 1916. In the almost daily cabinet meetings now being held, he repeatedly urged that all attempts at negotiation with the British be broken off.

"The only thing keeping him in check is his personal loyalty to Dev," Collins told Henry.

"De Valera's in much the same position as Lloyd George," the journalist commented. Collins gave him a quizzical look. "By that I mean Dev's trying to hold disparate factions together and carry them along with him, just as the prime minister's trying to control a coalition. I don't envy either man."

Collins said, "People think I'm a firebrand, but I'm nothing compared to Cathal. A few months ago he proposed sending a squad to London to assassinate the entire British cabinet."

"My God! That really would have put the cat among the pigeons. The British would not have stopped until they'd exterminated our whole race; it would be Cromwell all over again, only worse."

Collins nodded. "I told him he'd get none of my men for that. And do you know what he said? 'I don't need any of *your* men.' "

In the months to come, those words would take on a sinister meaning.

Now that de Valera had agreed to the October conference there was intense speculation as to who would constitute his party. On the night when the cabinet met to take that decision, Henry waited for Desmond FitzGerald in the Wicklow Grill until long after closing time. The proprietor cleaned tables and mopped the floor around him, and out of sympathy kept his cup filled with strong tea. He twice refilled the small sugar bowl on the table.

At last Desmond FitzGerald peered through the glass door panel and Henry beckoned him in. He was ashen with fatigue.

"What happened?" Henry asked eagerly.

"Is that tea hot? Never mind, just give me some." Fitz-Gerald took Henry's cup and drained it in one long gulp. He shuddered. "Christ, man, what do you have in there?"

"Just sugar. The milk in that jug's sour."

"Do you always put a little tea in your sugar?"

"Never mind about that, tell me who's going to London." Henry opened his notebook.

FitzGerald dropped wearily into a chair and began counting off on his fingers. "The delegates are Arthur Griffith, George Gavan Duffy, Robert Barton, Eamonn Duggan, and Michael Collins. Erskine Childers will be chief secretary to the delegation, and—"

"Michael Collins! Are you sure?"

"Of course I'm sure. When I left, Mick was still arguing with the Chief about it. Neither he nor Arthur Griffith want to go, and Cathal Brugha and Austin Stack have refused outright. Dev let them off, but he's determined about the other two."

"Mick wanted to go badly enough last time."

"I know, but now he's dead against it. The British think of him as an elusive demon they can't defeat, which gives him a certain mysterious glamour—and great value as a gun held to their heads. He says if they see him in the flesh and realize he's an ordinary man they won't be afraid of him anymore."

"Mmm," said Henry, "he has a point there. But the same thing was just as true last time. There must be another reason why he doesn't want to go."

"If there is, he didn't tell us. Mick can argue all he likes, but in the finish-up he'll obey orders."

"So he'll be at Dev's side."

Desmond FitzGerald slumped deeper in his chair. "That's just it. He won't be at Dev's side. Arthur Griffith's heading the delegation with our own Kathleen McKenna as his private secretary. The Chief's not going at all."

THE next day Henry went looking for Michael Collins. For once Collins was impossible even for his friends to find.

Henry left messages for him in all the familiar haunts, then went back to number 16 to work on an article he was preparing about the upcoming peace talks. As so often, he lost himself in the work. Louise had to knock twice on his door before he heard her.

She hissed in a stage whisper, "He's here."

"Who's here?"

"The Big Fellow. Down in the parlor."

"Well, show him up, woman. I'm sure he doesn't want to talk in a room as public as your parlor."

Louise Kearney was thirty years older than Michael Collins, but there was no mistaking the nature of her excitement. By the time she reappeared with Collins she had smoothed her hair, licked her lips, and pinched her cheeks to make them even redder. Her eyes were very bright and she was breathing hard.

A certain mysterious glamour, Henry thought, amused.

Collins flung himself down on Henry's bed as if it belonged to him. "You were looking for me?"

"I'm writing about the delegation that's going to London and I would like to include a statement from you."

"I'm being sent against my will. That's not a statement for publication, but it's God's truth. I'm a warrior, not a politician."

"Mick, you've worked in London and, as you reminded me yourself, you know the scene over there. Dev may genuinely believe you're the best person for the job. Remember the adage 'It's the old dog for the hard road.' "

Collins rolled onto his side and propped himself up on one elbow. "Hell with that, Henry. Let me remind you of another saying. How about 'lamb to the slaughter'? This is Dev's way of getting rid of me. The man's as subtle as a Jesuit, trying to make being sacrificed look like an honor."

"What do you mean, 'sacrificed'?"

"Dev can't refuse what appears to the world as an honest offer of negotiation, so he's sending us to make a final attempt. If we succeed you can be sure he'll take the credit. If we fail, however, we'll get the blame. And Arthur Griffith already told Dev straight out that we won't get the Republic. He's convinced Lloyd George will never accept it."

"You can't put the entire onus on Lloyd George," Henry replied. "He has Tories and Whigs to deal with—not to mention James Craig and his Unionists."

"I understand that. Damned politics." Collins sounded disgusted. "Christ, I just made another plea to the Unionists myself. I published an article in every northern newspaper that would carry it, urging them to join us and help govern their own country instead of leaving it up to Westminster. They're ignoring me." Dropping his voice, he said, "I have another reason for not wanting to be away from Ireland right now. Not important in the grand scheme of things, but . . . I've been seeing one particular young lady who means a lot to me."

Henry chuckled. "A certain Miss Kiernan from Longford?"

Collins nodded. "Unfortunately my pal Harry Boland likes her too. Now he's off to America on IRB business, and I think he's going to ask her to join him there and marry him."

"I had no idea things had gone that far."

"They shouldn't have," Collins replied. "I should have forced the issue sooner; I plan to marry her myself."

"Does Harry know?"

"These days we talk about everything but Kitty. It's—"

"It's a very awkward situation," interjected Henry. "Surely you'll have some time off during the conference, though."

"In a manner of speaking," the other replied. "Arthur and I are supposed to come back from time to time to report to Dev personally."

"Well, you can plead your cause with Miss Kiernan then. Just don't let your personal life distract you from the larger picture."

"No bleedin' chance of that," said the Big Fellow.

Chapter Thirty-three

I intend to go to London to cover the Anglo-Irish Conference," Henry told Ella Rutledge.

"How wonderful!"

"There's a lot of us going. Every major newspaper is sending reporters, and the freelancers are fighting for accommodations. London hotels are said to be ruinously expensive, so I was hoping . . ."

"Hoping what?"

"There might be someone in the city whom I could stay with." He drew a deep breath. *I should have forced the issue sooner.* "Future family."

He halfway expected her to balk, like a horse refusing to jump a fence. Then she gave the sort of mysterious little woman-smile he had never understood. "Of course. I shall write to them tonight and tell them of our engagement, and ask them to look after you while you're in London."

My God. As simple as that. Emboldened, he took one step further. "What about our wedding date? In case anyone asks."

"Oh, whenever you think. Shall we say . . . this time next year? Perhaps the first Sunday in October? That will hardly give me enough time to prepare, but I can get busy right away."

Henry would have given anything he possessed to be able

to sit down that night with Ned Halloran and talk about the strange and incomprehensible ways of women.

ON the seventh of October the delegates were conferred with credentials by the Dáil. On the eighth Ella gave Henry a letter of introduction to the London cousins. "Good luck," she said.

"I'm not sure luck matters so much. Audacity seems to work better," he told her. But he took care to supply himself with an assortment of presents: marzipan and handkerchiefs embroidered with Limerick lace for the women, and Irish whiskey for the men.

THAT evening Michael Collins went to confession. Afterward he asked the priest, "Will you say a prayer for Ireland, Father?"

Then he went to ask Ned Broy to accompany him to London as his personal secretary.

HENRY Mooney also paid a last-minute call to a priest. He found Father O'Flanagan in the Sinn Féin office in Harcourt Street. Michael O'Flanagan, whose dynamic organizing skills had been partly responsible for Sinn Féin's electoral victories, was sitting behind a desk trying to shore up a toppling tower of file folders. He glanced up hopefully as Henry entered the room. "I don't suppose you know where—"

The journalist held up his hands. "I do not know, there's no point in asking me. Talk to the office girls."

"You seconded the best of them to the *Bulletin*. That's why there's a problem now. But not to worry, I'll get it sorted. In the meantime, did you want something?"

Henry shifted from one foot to the other. He should have had this conversation sooner, but there was so much going on, and he had not really been sure of Ella . . . "I need some information about getting married."

"That's grand! Congratulations. Who's the lucky girl?"

"Her name is Ella Rutledge. Mrs. Rutledge—she's a widow. And a Protestant, Father. Anglican. Church of Ireland." He spun it all out as if it would somehow make a difference.

"I see." The priest's expression did not change by a whisker, yet Henry had the distinct impression that blinds had been drawn down. "Have you actually proposed?"

"I have, and she's accepted. We plan to marry early next October."

"You should have come to me sooner, Henry. Surely you're aware we do not approve of anyone marrying outside the Church."

"It happens, though; I know of several instances myself."

"It happens," the priest agreed gravely.

"What I need to know, Father, is what restrictions the Church will place on the marriage."

"First you will have to apply for a special dispensation, and both you and Mrs. Rutledge will need to talk with your parish priest."

"I don't really have a parish priest," Henry said, refusing to sound apologetic. "I'm not much of a churchgoer."

"I see." A long pause. Then, "Very well. I'll give you the benefit of my counsel."

"And support?" Henry urged.

The priest gave him a long look. "And friendship," he said.

"Then as a friend, tell me what we need to know."

"Under the canon law governing mixed marriages, there can be no Mass celebrated."

That's not so bad. I won't mind and I'm sure Ella won't.

"Secondly, since 1908 both partners are required to give a promise in writing that any children will be raised in the Catholic Church. You must make that very clear to the lady in question, and the promise must be filed with the Church before a priest will consent to marry you. Should you undertake to be married by anyone other than a Catholic priest, your marriage will not be considered valid in Ireland and your children will not be legitimate."

"I can't tell Ella that!"

"I'm sorry, Henry. There are no exceptions."

• • •

Iᴛ was one of those radiant autumn mornings that occasionally enrich Dublin by standing guard in russet and gold against the approaching winter. The air was liquid spice. Even the aroma from the Liffey was tolerable.

Ella Rutledge was among the throng of well-wishers who came to the docks to see the delegation depart. She was wearing a fawn Norfolk jacket and walking skirt and a lemon-colored silk blouse, and just before Henry boarded the boat she kissed him in front of everyone.

He had not yet told her of his conversation with Father O'Flanagan. In the last-minute rush of events there was no convenient time.

The jubilant crowd on the Dublin docks radiated optimism like heat from a stove. People were convinced the treaty delegation was going to achieve Irish independence. In the gilding sunlight, with Ella Rutledge smiling up at him as he leaned his elbows on the top rail of the boat, Henry believed it himself. *There's no advantage for Britain in holding on to Ireland against her will. Far better for the Crown to acknowledge Ireland's nationhood and have her as a friend and ally. Which we will be if they treat us fairly. Surely our lads can convince them.*

When the boat docked at Holyhead, its passengers traveled on to London by train, arriving at Euston Station. They were welcomed by an immense crowd that seemed to include every Irish man and woman in London and not a few sympathetic English people. Cheers and applause; tricolors waving exuberantly. Adults pointing out well-known personalities to their children: "Remember him, now. Remember that you saw Mr. Arthur Griffith. And there's Mr. Childers, who wrote that famous book. Wave to him!"

After an exhaustive round of handshaking and back pounding, the delegates and their staff finally managed to reach the fleet of official motorcars waiting for them, like a swarm of huge black beetles, and were whisked away.

"Two residences are being put at the disposal of the delegates," Henry jotted down. "One in Hans Place and the other in Cadogan Gardens. The latter will house the secretaries and the Republicans who have been brought along as general dogsbodies." He crossed out the last two words and substituted "attendants."

Henry's personal welcoming party arrived at the station in two private motorcars. As they introduced themselves, he assigned names he knew to faces: Ernest and Winifred Mansell, Donald Baines, Ruth Mansell Moore, Ninian Speer. With the exception of Winifred, all were related through ties of blood. They shared a Mansell ancestor who had begun as a ship's chandler in Dublin in the eighteenth century, then moved to England and expanded into importing linen, cotton, and ramie. Now the family was heavily invested in stocks and shares. "Everyone's doing it," Donald Baines assured Henry as they drove through London. "Postwar boom, you know, businesses growing like weeds. Opportunities everywhere for a shrewd man, what? Can't help making money. Give you a few tips myself if you like. Though I'm sure you have your own broker, of course."

Ernest and Winifred Mansell were a silver-haired couple in their late middle age who had grown so alike they might be mistaken for brother and sister. If one started a sentence, the other finished it seamlessly. They rarely spoke directly to each other; it was as if their thoughts flowed together into a river. *Ella and I will be like that someday*, Henry promised himself.

For the duration of the treaty talks he would stay in the Mansells' home, with the other cousins taking turns driving him around the city or wherever else he wanted to go. "That's not necessary," he assured them. "I don't want to be any trouble. You're good enough to put me up and—"

"Nonsense," Ruth Moore interrupted. "We've been eager to meet you, and this is a perfect opportunity to get to know one another. I do so hope we shall see a lot of you while you're here."

She was one of those women whose age was unguessable as a result of having enough money to take excellent care of herself. She was also wearing a very short skirt, only a few inches below her knees. The delighted Henry hardly knew where to look.

"Be careful," warned Ninian Speer. "Ruth's already survived two husbands and is holding auditions for a third."

"But he would have to have money," Ruth said. "Do you have money, Mr. Mooney?"

He was startled. No Irish person would ask such a question. Becoming aware that the others were watching him covertly, he launched into a circumlocution that lasted for several minutes and avoided giving a straight answer.

Later, in the Mansells' elegantly appointed guest room, he sat down to jot a quick note to Ella. "Your relatives seem most amiable," he commented. But he soon discovered that their English manners were a wall to hide behind. He could not tell what they really thought about anything. He could not even tell if they liked him.

At dinner there were snatches of conversation that by themselves meant nothing, yet were cumulatively disturbing. "Henry, did you know her first husband by any chance? No? What a pity. Fine man, John Rutledge. Artistic, like Ella. They had so much in common."

"I think education is so important, Henry, don't you? Of course Ella will want her children to attend school here in England. They should have every opportunity."

"When we visited Florence before the war . . . were you ever in Florence, Henry? No? Everyone should see Florence—a man can hardly call himself cultured otherwise."

"You want directions to what? Oh, the Catholic church. I forgot . . . yes, of course we shall take you. Do you want to go to confession, communion, that sort of thing? Or just call in out of courtesy?"

AT eleven in the morning on the eleventh of October, 1921, Michael Collins, whose father was the seventh son of a seventh son, sat down with his fellow delegates to negotiate the future of Ireland. They had been given plenipotentiary status by the Dáil, officially investing them with the power of independent action. However, they were to keep the Dáil fully apprised of developments, and Collins and Griffith were expected to report back personally during the negotiations.

Across a dividing sea of highly polished mahogany in the cabinet room in Downing Street the Irish delegates and secretaries faced the prime minister; Baron Birkenhead, the lord chancellor; Austin Chamberlain, the leader of the House of Commons; and Winston Churchill, who was now secretary of state for the colonies. These four were flanked by the attorney general, the secretary for war, and the chief secretary for Ireland. Seven formidable men.

Outside, journalists thronged Downing Street, interviewing recognizable dignitaries, people who merely looked important, casual passersby, and when all else failed, one another. Henry chose instead to walk the few blocks to Hans Place and interview the delegation's housekeeper.

During a conversational skirmish at the door they discovered that both had County Clare antecedents. The housekeeper promptly invited him in. She showed him to a small anteroom where she fed him endless potted meat sandwiches and gossip. Among the tidbits Henry learned was that Michael Collins held himself apart from the others. He came and went alone, or accompanied only by Ned Broy, and never told anyone where he was going or when he would return.

Mick needs privacy to keep in contact with the IRB, Henry thought to himself. *He has more people to report to than just Eamon de Valera.*

Henry was still there when Robert Barton returned to Hans Place late in the afternoon to change his shirt and collect some more documents. "It's obvious," Barton confided to Henry, "that the British are more interested in Michael Collins than in any of the rest of us. He fascinates them. Even the prime minister hangs on his words. But this is going to be an uphill gallop, Henry, and no mistake. Our side's ill at ease because it's our first introduction to diplomacy. The other side's in familiar surroundings where they've met and defeated a hundred opponents. You should see the place. We sit there in a solemn row with the portraits of past prime ministers glowering down at us from the walls. And maps; great pull-down maps showing the extent of the empire. Lloyd George keeps referring to them as if talking about his own private game preserve."

Henry said, "They're just trying to impress you, Bob—to intimidate you into losing your nerve."

"Oh we realize that." Barton gave a faint smile. "George is a barrister and Eamon's a solicitor, remember. They know about courtroom tricks."

As the days went by, it became clear that the British had other weapons at their disposal. Lloyd George set about dividing the Irish delegation with surgical skill. By dismissing Barton, Duffy, and Duggan as opponents and patronizing them verbally, he cast doubt on their abilities. Meanwhile he concentrated on Griffith and Collins, flattering them as equals with whom he could do business.

When Barton and Duffy responded with hostility to British suggestions on trade, Griffith rebuked them at the conference table.

The thin edge of the wedge was in; would be driven deeper.

Kathleen McKenna told Henry when he waylaid her on her way back to Cadogan Gardens one evening, "Because Erskine and his cousin Bob Barton are both English—what de Valera calls 'intellectual Republicans' "—Lloyd George's flunkeys are treating them with a deference that's beginning to grate on Arthur's nerves. He's distancing himself from them emotionally; he can't help it.

"And it's not just him. Every time Erskine asks that something be repeated so he can be certain of the exact wording, the prime minister deliberately calls attention to the delay. Makes it seem frivolous, unnecessary. You can see Mick holding his temper and trying not to be impatient, but now he's unhappy with Erskine too."

Henry frowned. "I don't like the way this sounds."

"Neither do I. But if I try to say anything about it, my 'female intuition' is simply dismissed. Yet I can see numerous undercurrents developing that the British know how to exploit and we don't."

"Damn it, Kathleen, we don't have centuries to learn to be their equals at political maneuvering. It's all happening right now."

"I know," she said sadly.

• • •

GRIFFITH and Collins were invited to meet Lloyd George at Winston Churchill's house for protracted talks. They dutifully reported the conversation in full to their colleagues. However, Lloyd George made veiled references to the meeting in front of the others, implying that some secret agreement had been reached to which the remainder of the Irish delegation was not privy.

Michael Collins was not fooled by Lloyd George's games; by his theatrical performances, his aggressively beetling brows, or his seductive voice which he played like a musical instrument. But there was no doubt the prime minister's tactics were effective. Even the most intelligent man could not help being worn down day by day by a consummate gamesmaster.

ERNEST and Winifred Mansell owned a large, half-timbered mock-Tudor house in Kensington, replete with every modern convenience. Their cook was a brawny-armed Scotswoman whose frequent booming guffaw rang through the house, giving the lie to the dour Scot stereotype. The housemaids were competent, dark-eyed Welsh girls, with accents like water running over pebbles.

As the autumn days darkened, Michael Collins felt increasingly lonely. He wrote impassioned letters to Kitty Kiernan. But though lonely, he was not alone. Ned Broy hovered close like a guardian angel while Collins maintained his usual frenetic pace between appointments and attended an astonishing number of social engagements as well. Now that his cover was blown, he was seen everywhere. For a gunman he moved in the best circles. His friends in London society included the painter Sir John Lavery, whose wife, Hazel, was a famous beauty and devoted to the cause of the Republic. She persuaded Collins to sit for his portrait, and also arranged glittering dinner parties at which he was the star attraction. In other circumstances Michael Collins would have enjoyed himself immensely.

But these were not other circumstances. This was life and death for a nation.

When Kitty arrived in London for a visit, her presence did not provide the respite Collins needed. He was under too much strain to be the playful Michael she knew, and her Catholic conscience would not allow her to relax. She could not bear knowing that people were gossiping about them; worse still, she heard gossip concerning Collins and other women. The heightened tension resulted in unpleasant scenes, and Kitty returned to Ireland. From there she tried to mend the damage with loving letters to a man who scarcely had time to read them, but faithfully responded almost every day.

HENRY Mooney, who rarely went to Mass, began attending regularly in London. Fully aware of the hypocrisy of his defiance, he flew his Catholicism like a flag. When he met Erskine Childers for a quick drink, he remarked on this to his friend. Childers, born and bred a Protestant, smiled. "Under the skin of every Irish Catholic lurks a pagan anarchy, Henry. Sometimes it bursts through in unexpected ways. In your case it's a reverse form of religious rebellion. Don't worry, old chap. When you get back to Dublin, you can ignore the Church again."

LLOYD George arranged to have separate meetings with Collins and with Griffith. With one he discussed matters relating to the military and the manning of coastal defense, while with the other he went into detail about commercial trade arrangements and the appointing of commissions. For each meeting his associates produced a huge portfolio of papers—thousands of details to be discussed and agreed upon, every word and phrase carefully chosen by experts at political language.

· · ·

DURING a break in the talks one afternoon Collins emerged from Downing Street at the trot. Henry had to sprint to catch up with him before he ducked into a waiting motorcar.

"Have you a moment to speak to me, Mick?"

Collins blinked, then held open the car door himself. "Sure. Sit in." The Big Fellow was dressed in a black suit and a stylish homburg and had grown a little smudge of dark mustache in an effort to look like a plenipotentiary. As the two men settled back on the seat, he said, "It's good to see your friendly mug, Henry. I know I promised you an interview this week, but between the jigs and the reels they're keeping us pretty busy."

"That's all right, I understand."

"You want to do it now?" When Collins ran a hand through his thick hair, Henry noticed with surprise that its dark brown was lightly flecked with silver. Michael Collins was only thirty.

"Not right now," Henry told him. "Mainly I just want to know how you are."

"Damned nice of you to care. I'm frustrated, that's how I am. I came to this conference to call a spade a spade. It's the only name I know it by. But to be a politician one needs to have the ability to say one thing and mean another; one needs to be abnormally successful at the art of twisting the truth. Can you wonder that I think and think and yet never manage to achieve peace of mind?"[2] Collins gave a great sigh, like a man struggling beneath the weight of the world.

"As for the prime minister," he went on, "I find his attitude particularly obnoxious. He's all comradely, all craft and wiles, all arm-around-the-shoulder—this man who wanted me dead just a few weeks ago. In my time I have told men and women what I thought of them. I've cursed them—and they understand me all the more for it. But what can one say to a politician?"

"Maybe you don't belong here, Mick."

"Damned right I don't belong here. I'm beginning to think none of us do. Arthur Griffith is the only one with any claim to being a politician, but he's probably the least well equipped."

Henry was surprised. "Why do you say that?"

"Because he always tries to see the best in people. Arthur just doesn't know human nature the way I do." Staring morosely out the window, Collins went on: "Know what I just discovered? Erskine's been sending back secret reports to de Valera that the rest of us knew nothing about. The British consider Erskine a renegade Englishman and don't trust him, and now I can't trust him either. Damn it, Henry! Dev demands that we act in consultation with him—never mind about this power of independent action we're supposed to have—but he does just as he pleases without bothering to consult with us. He acts as if what matters most is not the conference, but maintaining his personal authority. It's impossible to pin him down and find out what he does want us to do," Collins concluded sourly.

Kathleen spoke of undercurrents. Sounds like it's the power struggle going on between Mick and Dev that's the real danger.

IN Ireland, Cathal Brugha wanted Austin Stack appointed deputy chief of staff of the IRA. Richard Mulcahy opposed the appointment, seeing it as a move to undermine Michael Collins in his absence. In London, Lloyd George established a principal conference attended by Griffith and Collins, and subconferences attended by the lesser players.

On the twenty-fifth of November Michael Collins and Arthur Griffith traveled to Dublin for an urgent meeting of the cabinet.

Behind the scenes in Ireland, Cathal Brugha was fighting with savage tenacity to retain the Republic and settle for nothing less. Behind the scenes in London, Erskine Childers was drawing up endless fact sheets and memoranda for the delegates to the same purpose.

Meanwhile Lloyd George continued to bring a hundred subtle, clever, relentless pressures to bear on the Irish, designed to convince them they could not hope to prevail against the will and might of the empire.

· · ·

HENRY snatched every scrap of information about what was going on behind the door at 10 Downing Street. He wrote to Ned Halloran, "There are so many bargaining points and they each gain significance in turn. From day to day it's hard to know which rock the agreement might break upon. All I know for certain is, it may well break."

By return post he received a terse note from his friend. "We're ready in the west."

What had become of that bright autumn morning, Henry wondered, when he stood at the rail of the boat and looked down at Ella, smiling and waving in the sunshine?

GRIFFITH and Collins returned to London in somber mood. When they arrived, Henry tried unsuccessfully to get an interview with either.

He began to avoid Ella's relatives as much as possible without being obvious. They were too polite to discuss the conference in front of him, but its unspoken presence was a specter at their table. Without anything being said he knew which way their sympathies lay—with their conservative Tory pocketbooks. The Union was good for business. Any rejection of the Union was therefore bad. As long as he maintained the persona of objective journalist, his Irishness could be politely ignored, like a speech impediment; but if he once let his mask drop and his nationalism show through, he would become, quite literally, beyond the Pale.

AT last Henry managed to have a quick word with Michael Collins as the Big Fellow was rushing from one appointment to another. He was shocked at the way Collins looked. "Great God's ghost, Mick! Are things that bad?"

"Oh, the negotiations are still trundling on. Arthur's convinced that moderation will win more for us than taking a hard line, and I've come round to his way of thinking. De Valera won't agree, but I can see that the advantages of dominion status to us, as a stepping-stone to complete independence, are immeasurable."[3]

"So you're willing to entertain a compromise?"

"I'm considering it."

"You don't sound very happy about it. If you don't genuinely believe it's the right thing to do, Mick, hold out."

"Hold out?" Michael Collins regarded him with haunted
eyes. "While I was in Dublin last time I had a long meeting
with my own lads."

The IRB, Henry interpreted. "And?"

"I asked them for a report on our level of military pre-
paredness in case the negotiations fall through."

"And?"

For the first time in Henry's memory, he saw Michael
Collins' broad shoulders sag. "According to their best estimate, the IRA has four feckin' bullets left per man."

Henry felt cold in the pit of his stomach. "Does Dev
know?"

"Oh yes," said Collins wearily. Closing his eyes, he
leaned his head back against the leather upholstery. "I'm
sure Dev knows."

Collins could be highly dramatic when the mood took
him, but this was no performance. In the flatness of his voice
Henry heard the sound of unvarnished truth.

HE wrote tender letters to Ella, who wrote tender letters
back to him: bits of family news, gossip about mutual acquaintances, trivia. By common consent neither wrote anything very serious. These were love letters.

Henry had never received a love letter before. He went
into a shop in Bond Street and bought a japanned box to
keep them in.

IN late November Eamon de Valera began driving across
Ireland, accompanied by Cathal Brugha, meeting with IRA
officers and giving inspirational speeches to their men. In
ringing tones he exhorted them to fight for Ireland to the
last drop of blood. "No offer will be accepted by the nation
if that offer deprives us of the essentials of freedom. Freedom is a thing that you cannot cut in two—you are either
all free or you are not free. It is, therefore, for complete

freedom that we are struggling, and we tell everybody that this nation will continue to struggle for its freedom until it has got the whole of it."[4]

On the first of December a "Proposed Articles of Agreement" was delivered to the Irish delegation. Britain was offering dominion status and the title of Irish Free State, with six counties of Northern Ireland to be excluded from the Free State if the majority so wished. A British governor-general would be appointed and an oath of allegiance to the British sovereign demanded. Defense of Irish coastal waters would remain under the control of the British, who were to be given unlimited access to Irish ports and allied facilities. The Free State would also assume liability for a portion of Great Britain's debts and military pensions.

Arthur Griffith left London early the next morning to take the document to Dublin. De Valera drove up from Clare to meet him. After heated discussions, the president and the majority of the cabinet rejected the British proposal on the third of December. Griffith was instructed to return to London and tell Lloyd George the Irish would not accept either the oath or partition.

Eamon de Valera was working on an alternative of his own. Referred to as Document 2, this proposed an external association with Britain which would not require the swearing of an oath of allegiance to the Crown. Meanwhile, in London, Duffy, Barton, and Childers set about drafting a new and less objectionable oath, one that did not promise to "be faithful to H.M. King George V, his heirs and successors by law."

But Lloyd George was not interested in alternatives. To compromise at this stage would be to lose control, and he had no intention of losing control.

At a full meeting of both delegations in Downing Street he produced a document to which Arthur Griffith had earlier agreed. The document proposed setting up a boundary commission to reconsider the divisions created by the 1920 Government of Ireland Act. It had been presented to Griffith as a harmless quid pro quo, a bargaining chip to encourage the Irish to be more flexible on the questions of sovereignty and alliance. At the time, Griffith had considered it so minor he not even mentioned it to the others, even Collins.[5]

But, Lloyd George now stated, in accepting a boundary commission the leader of the Irish delegation had also accepted the existence of boundaries. Boundaries defined partition: partition de facto as well as de jure.

The Irish delegation sat stunned.

The Welsh Wizard's eyes blazed with cold fire. "Are you now going back on your word?" he challenged Griffith.

Arthur Griffith, ashen-faced, squared his shoulders. "I have never gone back on my word, whether given to friend or enemy," he said with dignity.

Leaning toward him, Lloyd George purred, "Then since your delegation has accepted partition, you can no longer refuse to sign the Proposed Articles of Agreement on those grounds. This treaty constitutes Britain's final offer, and your time has run out. Sign now or . . ." The prime minister straightened up and raised his voice to its full power. "If the Sinn Féin representatives refuse the oath of allegiance and refuse to come within the empire," he cried dramatically, sweeping his piercing gaze around the room, "it means war in three days!"[6]

For a moment there was absolute silence. Then Griffith protested, "I cannot sign that document without referring it back to Dublin!"[7]

"Dublin, may I remind you, has already seen the Articles of Agreement," Lloyd George asserted. "As plenipotentiaries you are fully empowered to act on behalf of those you represent." He produced two envelopes and held them aloft, drawing all eyes. "Here I have two letters. Both are addressed to Sir James Craig in Belfast, and one will be sent tonight at ten o'clock. Either I tell him you accept our final proposal, or I tell him we are going to war. Winston says we can put two hundred thousand armed men into Ireland in a matter of days if need be.

"Peace or war! Which is it to be?"

Chapter Thirty-four

Precious heard the postman's bicycle coming up the road before anyone else did, and ran out to meet him. She returned to the house carrying a letter. "It's from Uncle Henry in London. May I have the stamp?"

Ned said indifferently, "You can have the whole letter."

"But it's addressed to you."

Ned shrugged.

Precious ran her thumbnail under the flap and opened the envelope without tearing it, so Aunt Norah could use it for storing seeds. As she read the letter she began to smile. "The Irish delegation is leaving London now, he says, and he plans to come to Clare for a visit while the cabinet is holding closed meetings in Dublin. Oh, Papa, how wonderful!"

"Wonderful that he never bothered to ask first," Ned growled. "Just took for granted that he'd be welcome."

"But of course he's welcome. This is Uncle Henry we're talking about."

"Your Uncle Henry," Ned retorted. "Not mine."

When Henry arrived on a bleak December day, Frank and Precious met him at the train station. "You're always very welcome here," said Frank, "but I should think you'd rather be with Mrs. Rutledge."

"She met me at the boat yesterday and we spent the afternoon together," Henry replied. *Together in her studio amid the smell of oil paints and turpentine. The daybed. Ella's flesh golden and glowing . . .*

He gave himself a tiny shake. "I . . . mmm . . . need to have a little quiet time to myself just now, though. She understood."

He was not sure she understood. The disappointment on her face had been all too plain. But after a few glorious hours together when they talked about nothing and their bodies said everything, he had left before the conversation could come around to the wedding. He felt shredded. He could not summon the strength to deal with the religious problem yet.

"London was desperately hectic," he said aloud. "We agreed that a few days' rest in the country would do me good."

"Would you not go to your family in Limerick?"

"Sure and I'd have no peace in Limerick. Any time I walk through my mother's doorway I'm likely to be greeted with *ri-rá* and *ruaille buaille.** Besides—" Henry winked at Precious—"my family's here."

She winked back. "That's how we feel too. But you'll have a wife and family of your own one of these days. And I'm to be an attendant at the wedding, remember? You are still getting married next October, aren't you?"

"If she'll still have me by then." *What a politician I'm becoming—never a straight answer.* His most ardent desire was to put his head down on a pillow that smelled of Atlantic wind and sleep until the cares of the world went away.

You lot are dreadful gosterers, have ye nothing to do but talk?" Norah Daly asked as she removed the half-full plate from Henry's place. "Look at that, you barely touched your food."

"I ate all I could, honestly."

She pursed her lips. "They ruined you in London, so they did. Took your nice healthy appetite away from you."

---

*Irish for uproar; commotion and tumult. Pronounced "ree-raw" and "roolya boolya."

While the others barraged Henry with questions, Ned Halloran sat silently at table with his eyes on his plate.

"Go on," Frank urged, leaning forward over his own neglected meal. "Finish telling us about the treaty negotiations."

"Please, Uncle Henry," Precious implored, "we want to hear every detail. You were right there, it must have been dreadfully exciting."

He shook his head. "Heartbreaking, more like. I don't know that we ever had a chance, Little Business. It was impossible to know what de Valera intended; he stayed at a distance so he couldn't be pinned down. Meanwhile there were so many letters, telegrams, documents, discussions, conversations, subconferences—at various times the Irish representatives separately, in London or Dublin, agreed, or partially agreed, to a number of aspects of the British proposal without ever accepting it in its entirety. The British kept copies of everything, including transcripts of every conversation. Our lads tried to do the same, but there was so much going on at so many levels their secretaries couldn't cover it thoroughly.

"At last Lloyd George plucked a combination of words from all that avalanche of language and used it against us. He pinioned poor Arthur Griffith and proved to him that he had already accepted too much to turn back. Griffith was compelled by his own honor to sign. The prime minister convinced him it would mean war otherwise."

Precious had been following his narrative intently. "Was Lloyd George bluffing?"

"That goes right to the heart of the issue," Henry replied. He had long since ceased to be surprised by the girl's perspicacity. "But it's a question no one dared ask at the time. I have a hunch he was bluffing, but I can't prove it. It doesn't matter anyway now; the treaty's been signed."

At last Ned looked up. "What about Mick Collins?"

"Lloyd George had made Mick all sorts of grandiose but vague offers of important posts within the empire 'afterward.' But he never won him over. And when it came to the sticking point, Mick stood by Griffith, though he must have been mighty angry at having the boundary commission agreement sneaked past him. But that was Lloyd George's doing; he didn't hold it against Arthur.

"Mick told the other delegates exactly how depleted our army was in terms of men and materiel, and asked if they wanted to send our lads out to be slaughtered. In the end, he persuaded them. At two-thirty in the morning, so worn out they could hardly see to write their names, they all signed. Signed their names in Irish, every one—that beautiful flowing old Irish script that owes nothing to the Anglo-Saxon.

"Next day the London papers quoted Winston Churchill as saying . . . wait a minute, I have it here . . ." Henry rummaged in the pocket of his waistcoat and withdrew a press clipping. He read, "Michael Collins rose looking as though he were going to shoot someone, preferably himself. In all my life I have never seen so much pain and suffering in restraint.'[1]

"When I managed to have a few words with Erskine Childers later," Henry added, "he told me that Mick had said, 'I've signed my own death warrant.' "

Ned pushed his chair away from the table and stood up. "From his mouth to God's ear. He deserves to die for what he did." He stalked from the room.

Hastily excusing himself, Henry followed him outside. He caught up with him just as Ned was heading for the barn. "What's the matter with you, Ned?" he wanted to know, putting a hand on his friend's shoulder. "Mick had no choice. If he'd rejected the Treaty he would have condemned Ireland to a much worse war than anything we've endured so far."

Ned whirled to face him. His green eyes held a deadly glitter. "Take your hand off me."

Henry drew back in astonishment. "I don't understand."

"I'll spell it out for you if you're that thick. My Síle died for the Republic, and now Mick's pissed it all away."

"She didn't die for the Republic, Ned," Henry said, realizing that his friend's loss was still paramount in his thoughts, coloring everything. "Síle's death was no more than a terrible accident—she was in the wrong place at the wrong time. You mustn't try to make a martyr out of her."

Ned's eyes narrowed to slits through which a tormented soul peered. "You never liked her."

"That's not true."

"You never approved of her because of her past."

"That's not true either. I have nothing against the girls who work in Monto. I could hardly condemn them when I used to spend so much time with them myself. Besides, Síle was extraordinary. Once I got to know her, I loved her just as much as—" Henry stopped abruptly. Once again his treacherous tongue had gone too far.

The festering abscess of Ned's anger swelled; burst. "The devil take your soul, Henry Mooney! Aunt Norah told me you'd been in love with my wife all along, but I didn't want to believe her. Now you've admitted it yourself. How could you do that to me? I thought we were friends."

"We are friends, the best of friends; you've got the wrong end of the stick entirely. When I said I loved Síle, I meant I admired her for—"

"Don't try to play word games with me—you're a master of words like your British pals!"

Henry fought back a rising tide of anger. "That's not fair, Ned. I love Ireland as much as you do." *Change the subject, get him talking about something else.* "So does Mick Collins. He simply believes, and I have to agree with him, that we can't force acceptance of the Republic right now. It will take a lot of hard work. For one thing, we have to get the twenty-six counties on their feet economically, then win the Unionists over and convince them their best interests in the long term lie with the rest of us. You must understand that . . ."

"I understand that you were making love to my wife behind my back, you bastard!" Ned exploded. "Just look at you. It's written all over your face. While I was in prison, was she in your bed? Did the two of you have a good laugh at my expense, poor dumb sod gone off to fight for Ireland?" He whirled away and ran into the barn.

Henry was aghast. He must tell Ned, make him believe *. . . Believe what? That I didn't love her? I can't leave it like this; he's hurting too much. I have to make him understand that nothing ever happened between us. Couldn't*

*have. Síle's fidelity was above reproach. That's one of the
reasons I loved her.*

Ned returned from the barn. He was carrying a rifle.

"I want you off this farm," he said furiously. "Get your
things and leave now. Tell them inside anything you like.
But go back to Dublin on the next train. If you ever set foot
on this land again, you're a dead man."

"Ned, you don't mean this. You're not thinking clearly.
Just listen to me . . ."

Ned raised the rifle.

"You're bluffing."

"Like your friend Lloyd George? You're about to find
out." Ned's cold green eyes sighted along the barrel. Taking
aim on Henry's heart, he drew a deep breath and held it so
as not to spoil the shot.

Henry quickly raised his hands palm outward. "You win,
I'm going." He turned and headed back toward the house.
By the thread of icy sweat trickling down his spine he knew
that the rifle was leveled on him all the way.

Chapter Thirty-five

H ENRY had longed for the peace and quiet of Clare. Instead he found himself on the train headed back to Dublin, into the eye of the storm.

He believed Griffith and Collins had done the best they could under the circumstances and gained all the concessions they thought possible. Indeed, they had achieved a greater degree of autonomy for Ireland than she had possessed since the English conquest of the island began. But would it be enough to satisfy the Republicans?

Is it enough to satisfy me? I too had tears in my eyes at the sight of the flag of the Republic flying above the GPO. How can we accept the indefinite postponement of a dream we've held, if only for a few moments, in the palm of our hand?

The Dublin to which Henry returned had changed considerably since the ebullient October of 1921. Now people were edgy, uncertain. Details of the Treaty were being published in the papers, but the language was tortuous and every element was subject to more than one interpretation.

"Plain folk can't make any sense of them," Louise complained to Henry at number 16.

"That's not surprising. The negotiations weren't really about agreement, they were about coercion."

"What does that mean—'coercion'?"

"Powerful pressures that can work and work on a mind until the strongest resolve crumbles."

When he called next day at Herbert Place, Ella welcomed him warmly. "I hope you're going to stay in Dublin longer this time."

"I am going to stay longer. The country wasn't . . . well, it didn't do for me what I'd hoped."

"You don't look very rested," she admitted. "You poor old dear." She stroked his cheek with her fingers, but although there was no one else in the house but the servants, she did not invite him upstairs.

"Have you had any letters from your cousins in London in the last few days?" he asked casually.

"Why?"

"I just wondered. I had the impression they didn't think very much of me."

"Of course they liked you."

"As a prospective husband for you?"

"Who I choose to marry is my own business," she said in a crisp tone.

But she had not denied receiving letters from London.

Pressures, Henry thought. *Coercion. How does anyone know what's going on behind his back?*

When he returned to number 16 Henry sat down with the separate notebook in which he kept the names and addresses of all the newspapers and periodicals in Ireland, Britain, and America who now bought material from him. Was there enough work there to support a wife properly?

Properly. By whose standards? How can I compete with what some Englishman could give her?

On the fourteenth of December Dáil Éireann convened in the Convocation Hall of the National University to debate acceptance of the Treaty. Henry Mooney was among more than a hundred journalists crowded together at one end of the room. He wrote in his notebook: "Eamon de Valera immediately took over the proceedings to deliver a long speech, partially in Irish, exonerating himself in advance. It was obvious that sides already were being taken. Deputies changed their seats in order to be close to those with whom they agreed."

On the sixteenth the British parliament voted to accept the Articles of Agreement for a Treaty Between Great Britain and Ireland.

Dáil Éireann was still debating ratification. De Valera called on the delegates to reject the Treaty in favor of his own Document 2, but it was not seriously considered. They knew it stood no chance with the British.

THE Ulster Unionists were volubly unhappy about the Treaty. Lloyd George had promised Craig nothing would be agreed without referring back to him first. But when Griffith agreed to sign the document, the prime minister had pushed ahead and committed His Majesty's government without any further consultation with Belfast.

Sir Henry Wilson, newly elected Unionist MP for North Down, was scathing in his personal condemnation of the Treaty. He saw any agreement with the Irish as surrender to an enemy he had been unable to crush.

In the matter of the boundary commission—that rock over which Arthur Griffith had stumbled—Lloyd George had in-dicated that the wishes of the inhabitants of the six northern counties would be consulted. If this was allowed, the Un-ionists knew that Tyrone and Fermanagh would choose to stand with the south, reducing Ulster's economic viability. "Our northern areas will be so cut up and mutilated that we shall no longer be masters in our own house," protested the Unionist MP for South Antrim.[1] Lloyd George was forced to artful negotiation—and once again the skilful manipula-tion of words—to reassure the Unionists that the boundary commission would be entirely under their control.

Yet it was the oath of allegiance to the king that most upset the Dáil delegates.

During thirteen days of debate the atmosphere in the Dáil became increasingly acrimonious. Some of the delegates kept their tempers under control, but Michael Collins turned the air sulphurous with profanity. From the reporters' gallery

Henry could see expressions of distaste on the faces of Cathal Brugha and Eamon de Valera.

De Valera, who had gone to great lengths to avoid taking active part in the negotiations, now blamed Griffith and Collins for not referring everything back to him before signing.

For its part, the Treaty delegation blamed de Valera for his vacillation about decision making and the ambiguity of his instructions, which were more confusing than helpful. Michael Collins—who had shaved off his mustache since returning to Ireland—remarked that the president was a captain who sent his crew to sea, then tried to direct operations from dry land.

Meanwhile the language of the Treaty confounded the Dáil delegates almost as much as the man in the street. Without clarity it was impossible to argue the terms on their merits. Ancestral passions, long historical memories, personal allegiances, fear of war, and fear of cowardice took over.

Tom Clarke's widow wrote to a friend, "Great God, did I ever think I'd live to see it, to see men who were the bravest, now fooled and blinded by a juggle of words into the belief that this Treaty means a realization of our highest ideals."[2]

By contrast Richard Mulcahy said, "I see no solid spot of ground upon which the Irish people can put its political feet but upon that Treaty."[3]

Constance Markievicz mockingly suggested that Michael Collins should marry Princess Mary and unite the two countries that way.

Those, like Richard Mulcahy, who supported Arthur Griffith deplored the lack of a constructive alternative to the Treaty from its opponents.

On one side were the pragmatists; on the other side, the idealists. In the middle was No-Man's-Land.

Businessmen, the press, and the Church supported the Treaty. So did majority of the plain people of Ireland. Conditioned by centuries of servitude, they were unwilling to risk losing what had been achieved on a gamble to win it all.

However, some units of the IRA, particularly the Southern

Division, were bitterly opposed. Commanders such as Liam Lynch and Ernie O'Malley thought it a grave mistake not to carry on the fight. Young men who had grown up vowing to die for the Republic agreed with them.

It was to this side that Eamon de Valera threw his enormous personal prestige. With him he carried the women whose support and devotion had been critical in bringing Ireland this far. Of the six female deputies in the Dáil, four were related to martyred Irish patriots. As Margaret Pearse said, "We will hold what they upheld."

LATE one night—far too late for convention—Henry went to Herbert Place. After a long wait, Tilly Burgess answered his knock at the door. The maid had thrown a wrapper over her nightclothes and her eyes were puffy with sleep. "You can't call on ladies at this hour!" But he insisted.

When Ella came down to him she was fully dressed, but her night-braided hair was twisted into a knot atop her head and hastily pinned. "Is something wrong?" she asked anxiously.

"I couldn't sleep, that's all. I kept thinking about you, and the future. This business about the Treaty . . . I don't know where it's headed, Ella. I've been pacing the floor for hours, worrying."

Her worried expression melted into compassion. "Oh, my dear, you take things too personally. It's only politics."

"Of course I take things personally—I'm only human!" he snapped. "And politics is no small matter. It's behind everything that's gone wrong in Ireland."

"Perhaps it's all for the best, Henry. Things usually are, you know."

His nerve endings were too raw to be placated. "You're saying that because you're quite content to be part of the empire. That filthy old pirate Britannia's made your family wealthy, hasn't she?"

"That's unfair, Henry."

"I'm sorry. I lost the run of myself, I didn't mean to imply . . ."

"Of course not." She patted his hand. "I understand, dearest. Truly I do. You're just tired and strained; let's forget we ever had this conversation. I'll ring for Tilly and . . . no, I'll go to the kitchen myself and make us some cocoa. Would you like that?" She smiled tentatively. "A chance to see if your bride-to-be knows her way around a kitchen in case we can't afford a cook?"

He tried to match her smile, her deliberate lightheartedness. But he imagined he saw a new wariness in her eyes.

Maybe she's realized I'm not good enough for her. Maybe Mam was right about me all along and I've only been fooling myself.

IN an effort to encourage acceptance of the treaty the British government announced a general amnesty for all Irish political prisoners. If he had been facing Ned Halloran across a chessboard, Henry would have taken the opportunity to remark on a clever use of pawns. But he did not have Ned to talk to anymore.

Precious wrote: "I'm sorry if you and Papa have had a row. He won't speak about it, so I don't know what happened. But I love you just the same and wish you a very happy Christmas." She included a handmade card depicting a girl and a black horse kneeling together beside the Christ Child's manger. The figures in the pen-and-ink drawing had been reworked several times, with the nib of the pen digging into the paper as the youthful artist became more impatient.

The Dáil recessed for Christmas on the twenty-third with no end to the debate in sight. During the public sessions the galleries had been packed with people eager to see the duel between Collins and de Valera—and not disappointed. Both men were at the top of their form. Passion crackled through the air like the electricity sparking through the electroliers that lit the hall. Henry dutifully reported their exchanges to periodicals at home and abroad, but with a sinking heart.

Because he could no longer share his thoughts with Ned, he wrote to Precious. "They're all good people," he told her. "Courageous, principled people who genuinely believe they know what's right for Ireland. If either side were acting out of self-interest or malice it would be different, but when it comes to decency there's nothing to choose between them. That's where the tragedy lies.

"After the Dáil adjourned I noticed Mrs. Pearse talking with Count Plunkett and Kathleen Clarke. Mrs. Pearse's two sons, Count Plunkett's first-born son, and Mrs. Clarke's husband lie buried in quicklime in the grounds of Arbour Hill Prison, victims of a British firing squad. How could people who have sacrificed so much for the Republic be asked to relinquish it now?

"Just across the room from them was Arthur Griffith, that sincere and brilliant man, who has dedicated his life to trying to improve the lot of the Irish people. And Mick Collins, a gunman in the process of evolving into a statesman, or I'm no judge of human nature. Were they wrong to try to save the Irish people from a devastating all-out war?

"It's an impossible question to answer, Precious. Had the vote been taken before the Dáil adjourned for Christmas, I think the Republicans would have carried the day. But during the recess press and pulpit, both of which are for the Treaty, will have time to exercise their influence." He could not help adding, "If you wonder why the Catholic Church supports the Treaty, the answer will tell you a lot about the establishment itself. Many individual priests are staunchly republican, but the hierarchy see the handwriting on the wall. They know which side will win. The Church, with so much property to protect, will always side with Power."

HENRY took little pleasure in the Christmas of 1921. He gave and received presents, went to Mass, attended parties, smiled, talked, ate and drank . . . yet he felt hollow inside, like someone sitting at the bedside of a critically ill patient through a dark and lonely night.

Precious wrote, "I have been thinking about your letter, Uncle Henry. I have been trying to be a TD in my mind and decide how I would vote. It is so hard to know. If only we could step into the future and then look back. But we shall step into the future. It is waiting for us, and it will be shaped by what they decide in the Dáil. I pray they will make the right decision."

She signed the letter not Precious, nor even Little Business, but Ursula.

All over Ireland people were praying that the Dáil would make the right decision.

What would that be?

ON the second of January, 1922, a number of Dublin's bridges were formally rechristened. Wellington Bridge—known locally as the Ha'penny or the Iron Bridge—became Liffey Bridge. Richmond Bridge was changed to O'Donovan Rossa. Queen Street Bridge was thenceforth to be known as Queen Maeve Bridge and Kings Bridge as Sarsfield.

The Irish were taking over.

Dáil Éireann reconvened on the third. Henry Mooney listened intently to the last impassioned arguments about the Treaty, transcribing as many as he could. At her request he sent copies to Clare addressed to "Miss Ursula Halloran."

On the seventh of January a vote on the Treaty finally was taken in the Dáil. Among those who voted "Is toil"—quite literally, "I desire"—were Arthur Griffith, Michael Collins, Seán Milroy, Eoin MacNeill. W. T. Cosgrave, and Richard Mulcahy. Those voting "Ní toil," "I do not desire," included Eamon de Valera, Mrs. Margaret Pearse, Constance Markievicz, Cathal Brugha, Harry Boland, and Erskine Childers. Childers—thin and deadly pale—was physically shattered by what he saw as the betrayal of the Republic. He made no secret that he blamed Collins entirely.

The Treaty was accepted by Dáil Éireann with a vote of 64 to 57. The nation would have a chance to make its own decision in the upcoming general election, which would be seen as a referendum on the Articles of Agreement with pro- and anti-Treaty nominees fighting for office.

When the huge crowd in the street outside heard that the Treaty had passed the Dáil, they broke into a spontaneous cheer.

Inside the hall was a very different scene.

As if a line had been drawn across the floor with the tip of a sword, the vote separated friend from friend. Former comrades-in-arms gazed at one another across that line.

To the background accompaniment of the cheering in the streets, Eamon de Valera announced, "It will of course be my duty to resign my office as chief executive."

"No!" cried Michael Collins.

De Valera ignored him. He went on, "The Irish people established a Republic. The Republic can only be disestablished by the Irish people. Therefore, until such time as the Irish people in regular manner disestablish it, this Republic goes on."[4]

In an attempt to defuse the situation, Collins appealed to de Valera to help form a committee to maintain public order during the transitional time ahead. Many of the spectators thought he would accept—until Mary MacSwiney, sister of the dead lord mayor of Cork, leaped to her feet. "This is a betrayal, a gross betrayal!" she cried. "It is only a small majority, and that majority is not united. Half of them are looking for a gun and the other half are looking for the fleshpots of the empire. I tell you there can be no union between the representatives of the Irish Republic and the so-called Free State."

Addressing the room, de Valera said in a strangled voice, "I would like my last word here to be this: We have had a glorious record for four years; it has been four years of magnificent discipline in our nation. The world is looking at us now . . ." His voice broke. The man they called the Chief folded his arms on the table in front of him and put his head down on them while his long body shook with sobs.

Many of the women in the hall and not a few of the men began weep-ing too.

Henry Mooney saw a long look pass between Michael Collins and Harry Boland, on opposite sides of the hall. Both had tears in their eyes.

Paindrops.

On the ninth of January, Eamon de Valera formally announced the resignation of himself and his entire cabinet and led his supporters from the Dáil.

Chapter Thirty-six

Henry tilted back his chair and surveyed the calendar on the wall. "It's the first of February. The Feast of Saint Brigid. First day of spring."

"It is," Louise Kearney agreed absentmindedly. She bit off a thread, knotted it, and went on mending sheets. Lodgers were very hard on sheets. A few minutes later she glanced up. "Henry, why are you pulling faces?"

He paused in the ruminative examination of his mouth with his tongue. "Took a blast of cold wind in the street yesterday. Must have had my mouth open."

"D'you have a bad tooth?"

"Mmm."

She put her sewing aside. "There's a pliers in the scullery. I could—"

"Don't even think it. I'd rather be shot again."

"Then promise me you'll go to a dentist."

"Mmm." He resumed his contemplation of the calendar. "Little Business will be confirmed in a few months."

"I thought you told me she likes to be called Ursula now."

"She does."

"Will you be going down to Clare for her confirmation?"

"Ned won't want me there."

"You'll have to face him sooner or later, Henry, and try to patch up your differences, whatever they are."

He had not explained them to Louise; had not explained

them to anyone. The assumption was that he and Ned had quarreled over the Treaty as many in Ireland were doing, and he let it go at that.

Some pains you just have to swallow and keep to yourself. I wonder: When you fill up to a certain point with your secret pains, do you begin to die? Is that what old age really is?

He stood up. "I'd better get on my bike, Louise. I've an interview this morning with the president of the Dáil."

"Well, why are you spoonybrassing around here, mortal man! Get your hat while I brush your coat. Do you have a clean handkerchief? Do you want some meat sandwiches to put in your pocket? Hurry up, Henry, don't keep Mr. Griffith waiting."

AFTER de Valera's departure from the Dáil Michael Collins had nominated Arthur Griffith to replace him as its president. On the fourteenth of January the Dáil had elected a provisional government that was to operate while a constitution for the Free State was being drafted and accepted. Under the terms of the Treaty, if this did not happen within one year the administration of Ireland would revert to Britain.

The chairman of the Provisional Government of Ireland was Michael Collins, and its offices were in the former Royal College of Science.

Collins did not intend to wait for the national election, but had set about organizing matters as swiftly as possible to keep Ireland in Irish hands. Within days, a contingent of the newly designated Free State National Army took over Beggars' Bush Barracks in Dublin while the British were still moving out. The former RIC Depot in the Phoenix Park was to be used for the new Civic Guards. In the aftermath of the Rising the British had allowed the Irish economy to disintegrate drastically, while the return of demobilized soldiers from the Great War had added to the already staggering unemployment. Recruitment offices for the Free State Army and the Civic Guards were unable to keep up with the flood of applicants. They included unemployed Volunteers, demobilized members of the British army, raw farmboys, and tough, illiterate gutties from the slums of Dublin.

The Provisional Government was up and running.

HENRY met Arthur Griffith in his office. Griffith began by apologizing. "There are books and papers and cartons everywhere, I'm afraid, both coming and going—Dáil material, Provisional Government business. . . . If you can find anything to sit on, please do, Henry. Just mind that one of my staff doesn't whisk it out from under you and leave you sitting on the floor."

"At least when you're on the floor you can't fall any farther."

"I must remember that. Now if you have questions for me, I can give you half an hour if you don't mind interruptions."

"I'm grateful for whatever time you can spare," Henry assured him. He thought Griffith looked ill, but did not say so. None of the Treaty delegation had looked hale and hearty when they returned to Ireland. "I would appreciate your thoughts on the new cabinet and the way ahead for the Irish nation, Mr. Griffith. My articles are now being published in America and on the Continent, so I can assure you a wide audience."

"At least some good has come out of this frightful business. People everywhere want to know more about Ireland."

Henry raised his pencil. "May I quote that phrase: 'frightful business'?"

"I would prefer if you did not. We must look buoyant and optimistic."

"Are you optimistic, sir?"

Griffith took off his spectacles and wearily rubbed the bridge of his nose. "You've always played square with us, Henry, so I'll answer your question . . . but off the record. I'm quite worried about the situation. The majority of the people support the Treaty; you know that and I know that. But there are very strong emotions on the other side and Dev knows how to play on them. He insists that his heart tells him how the Irish people really feel . . . and he wasn't even born in Ireland. It is very arrogant of him," said Arthur Griffith, the least arrogant of men.

Henry smiled. "Do you not recall what the Duke of Wellington said when someone accused him of being Irish because he was born in Ireland? He said, 'Being born in a stable does not make one an ass.' Or something to that effect."

Just then two men came in with a hand truck and began piling up boxes. "Those are for the City Hall, mind you," Griffith said. One of the men nodded. "And that lot over there go to the Castle."

"How strange it is," remarked Henry, "for the Dáil to be sending documents to Dublin Castle."

"I can't quite get used to it myself. Unfortunately I couldn't be at the Castle on January sixteenth for the official handover of the place. I was struggling with a mountain of urgent government business elsewhere."

"Mick told me he went to the Castle in a taxi," Henry said. "The British had everything organized in advance. When he came swaggering in, some officious little bureaucrat complained that he was seven minutes late. Threw their whole timetable off. So Mick told him, 'Blast you, sure and you people are over here for seven centuries. What bloody difference does seven minutes make now that you're leaving?'"

Griffith managed a tired smile. "You have to admire his nerve. I was at the Mansion House later when he announced that he 'had received the surrender of Dublin Castle which was now in the hands of the Irish nation.' I know perfectly well the British had not meant the handover as a 'surrender,' but Mick made it into one."

Henry smiled too. "I only wish the men who died in 1916 could have been here to see it."

"They should never have died, Henry," Griffith insisted. "No one should ever have died."

"Name me one nation that was born bloodlessly."

"We have to complete the winning of this one bloodlessly, but it won't be easy. Imagine the scene: Michael Collins and his ministers in City Hall, surrounded by the ruins of one administration and trying to put another together while the Republicans are cursing them through the keyhole."

Henry chuckled. "Metaphorically speaking."

"Not necessarily. It could really happen. Remember that two years ago the Irish Republican Army voluntarily placed itself under the control of the Dáil. Now the Dáil has voted for the disestablishment of the Republic, replacing it with a Free State. That's thrown the relationship between the government and the army into disarray.

"To make matters more difficult, the Provisional Government's just appointed Richard Mulcahy as minister for defense to replace Cathal Brugha. It will be an unpopular decision with many Republicans. Brugha is one of their greatest heroes. Last night de Valera met with the senior officers and asked them to give Mulcahy the same cooperation they gave Brugha, and asked Mulcahy himself to take no action that would split the army."

Henry said, "That's a hopeful sign, is it not? Dev always was good at holding opposing sides together."

"That was then and this is now," replied Griffith. "I'm not convinced he wants to hold them together. If the army does split one branch will be composed of veterans of 1916 or men who devoutly wish they had fought in 1916. It won't be over for them until we have the thirty-two-county Irish Republic their comrades died for. If Dev tells them to continue the fight, they will."

When the interview was over, Griffith put one hand on Henry's sleeve. "Now may I ask you a question? Off the record?"

"You may of course."

"Which way do you go in this?"

"As a journalist I'm strictly neutral, but . . . I tell a lie. That's pretentious and it's not even true. My head accepts the Free State as a political expedient. But my heart is with the Republic."

"Ah," said Arthur Griffith sadly. "That's the problem, isn't it?"

THAT night Henry took Ella to dinner at the former Metropole Hotel. The Dublin landmark, which had been destroyed by British artillery during the Rising, was now rebuilt. The occasion marked its official reopening as the Metropole Cinema, Ballroom, and Restaurant. He hoped the ambience would put her in a good mood.

"Everything smells new," Ella remarked as they waited to be shown to their table. "How appropriate for a new Ireland."

"A fragment of a new Ireland," Henry said under his breath.

"Sorry?"

"I asked if you would like an aperitif before dinner."

"Wherever did you learn that habit?"

"In London."

"How cosmopolitan you've become," she teased him. "But now we really must discuss the wedding. I know men aren't terribly interested in such things, but Ava says we must have your guest list as soon as possible, and—"

The headwaiter interrupted to lead them to their table. Blessed distractions: being seated, unfolding napkins, consulting the menu. Henry ran an exploratory tongue around his sore mouth. *Something soft, I think. Soup.* "Ah yes, the wedding. I've been meaning to talk to you about that." At that moment their drinks arrived. While Ella toyed with a dry sherry, Henry took a large swallow of whiskey. Then another. It burned all the way down. "It's time we . . . mmm . . . faced up to certain difficulties, Ella." He cast a wild glance around the room, wondering what would happen if he threw down his napkin and ran for the door.

"Are you jilting me?" Ella's eyes sparkled with mischief.

"Under no circumstances! It's just that . . ." Choosing his words carefully, he circled closer to the real problem without tackling it head-on. "Well, we do come from different backgrounds."

"Henry, why are you trying to put silly little obstacles in the way now?"

Silly little obstacles. Henry stared down into the amber liquid at the bottom of his glass. *Be brave, Mooney. You can't put this off forever.* He drained the last drops of whiskey.

"Then there's the matter of religion," he said. Keeping his eyes fixed on her face, he repeated what Father O'Flanagan had told him.

To his amazement, Ella smiled. "I knew that already, dearest. I made it my business to inquire a long time ago."

His jaw dropped. "How long ago?"

"Around the same time I began subscribing to the *Irish Bulletin*."

"You were a mile ahead of me! I must confess, I don't understand women at all."

Her dimples winked at him. "You're the only man I know who's brave enough to admit that. It makes me love you all the more."

"So although you knew what was involved, you agreed to marry me anyway?"

"Did you think me so shallow I would only love a Protestant? Henry Mooney, I never suspected you were such a bigot." But she laughed. Ella Rutledge reached across the table and caught both his hands in hers, and laughed.

LOUISE too was laughing as she told Henry, "I just had to wait up to give you this letter. It arrived this afternoon, and the stamp is one of the first issued by the new government. It has 'Saorstat Eireann' on it, see?"

"What's so funny about that?" Henry wondered.

"The posts-and-telegraphs lad who delivered it obviously has no Irish. He said it meant 'Sore-arse Erin.'"

A committee was appointed to draft the new constitution, for which purpose they took over a room in the Shelbourne Hotel, overlooking Stephen's Green.

"Nice work if you can get it," Henry Mooney commented.

As the military handover continued and more and more British barracks were turned over to the new Free State Army, the divisions within the army became more apparent. The brigades began to split into pro-and anti-Treaty, with the anti-Treaty men racing to occupy buildings ahead of orders. Digging in, entrenching.

But the British soldiers were leaving. That alone was a

wonder. People flocked to their churches to offer prayers of thanksgiving.

Henry wrote, "After more than seven hundred years of foreign occupation the liberation of Ireland comes like a sunrise. Like every sunrise it ushers in an unpredictable new day. What now? This is a nation in a state of becoming. This is a people terrified of change, yet embracing change in an act of awesome courage.

"Over the centuries the English destroyed our confidence as a race. That is how they held us in thrall so long. As long as we try to compete with them at being Englishmen we will always be second best.

"But we can be the best Irishmen ever."

WHEN he contemplated the upcoming changes in his own life, he had to admit to himself that he was terrified. And exhilarated.

ON the twelfth of February Eamon de Valera opened his campaign against the Treaty. He argued instead for his own Document 2 and an external association with Britain that would give Ireland complete sovereignty. One of the many items in the Treaty that he rejected was the retention of an armed British presence in Ireland's ports and territorial waters. Britain had insisted this was necessary for its own national security.

De Valera's concern was only with Irish national security.

As the British military relinquished its hold, the Free State Army continued to expand. Henry reported to his readers that General Eoin O'Duffy had been named chief of staff, succeeding Richard Mulcahy. New uniforms were hastily designed and ordered. The departing British turned over a number of their weapons. The first armored vehicle the Provisional Government received was a Rolls-Royce Whippet with a rotating turret containing a Vickers machine gun. The Whippet was delivered to Portobello Barracks in Dublin, but within a matter of days was sent to Limerick on a training and reconnaissance mission.

"There's trouble down here," a colleague at the *Limerick Leader* informed Henry by telephone. "When the British troops pulled out of Limerick Barracks they handed them over to the Free State Army, but Commandant O'Malley of the Mid-Limerick Brigade has sent for anti-Treaty men from Tipperary to try to seize both the barracks and King John's Castle. The pro-Treaty men are holding them off and some sort of compromise seems likely, but I don't like this, Henry. I don't like this one bit."

"Neither do I," Henry admitted.

At that moment the telephone operator cut in. "Nor me. If anyone tries to seize the telephone exchange I'm going home."

Henry wrote to his brothers, asking them to keep a closer eye on their mother's cottage. "We may be in for a turbulent time," he wrote without giving details.

On its return trip to Dublin the Whippet stopped at Templemore Barracks for refueling. The crew was met by men in uniform who politely informed them they were now prisoners of the Irish Republican Army. They were soon released and put on a train for Dublin, but the armored car was sent back to Limerick and turned over to Commandant Ernie O'Malley of the Irish Republican Army.

The first parade of the Free State Army in their new dark green uniforms was lustily cheered in Dublin.

THE Sinn Féin Árd Fheis was held on the twenty-second of February. The two army factions, represented by Seán MacKeon for the Free Staters and Dan Breen for the Republicans, met at the Mansion House to try to resolve their differences. Both sides argued earnestly but without rancor. Neither would move. Although the negotiators remained personal friends, they left the conference more philosophically opposed than ever.

After heated discussions between Eamon de Valera and Michael Collins, the Provisional Government agreed to postpone the general election for three months. In the meantime the new Free State constitution would be published to help clarify the issue for voters.

Chapter Thirty-seven

February 28, 1922

EGYPTIAN INDEPENDENCE PROCLAIMED BY
LORD ALLENBY

EGYPTIAN NATIONALISTS CLAIM FRAUD AS
BRITAIN WILL RETAIN SUEZ CANAL AND LARGE
MILITARY PRESENCE

ON the fifteenth of March, 1922, Eamon de Valera assembled the Dáil delegates who had voted against the Treaty and formed a new political organization under the name Cumann na Poblachta, the Republican Party. It was opposed by the entire British establishment and many elements of the Irish press as well. Most nationalist newspapers agreed that the Treaty was a stopgap measure on the way to full independence.

Many of the plain people of Ireland still saw the Chief as their leader, however. Membership in his new party grew rapidly.

Erskine Childers invited Henry to join the staff of the party's weekly journal, which was to be called *An Poblacht*—The Republic. Henry politely declined. "I don't think it would be in my best interests, Erskine. I'm getting married in the autumn, you know, and I can't do anything that might adversely affect my income. For a freelance journalist to be so closely associated with one political group would . . . well . . . you understand."

"I thought you had more guts than that, Henry."

"This isn't about courage. Did I not work for the *Bulletin* when the entire British government was after our scalps?"

His argument was lost on Childers, who had never needed to worry about money.

MONEY was the last of the obstacles, the one Henry could never discuss with Ella, who so freely dismissed all the others, making molehills of his mountains. He wanted more for Ella than she seemed to want for herself. He found it hard to accept the unselfishness of women. *Maybe*, he thought, *I just don't trust happiness*.

ON the twentieth of March Eamon de Valera spoke to a large crowd in O'Connell Street. Henry Mooney was among those who heard him outline the major points of his proposed Document 2. De Valera then warned his audience, "if we continue on that movement which was begun when the Volunteers were started, and we suppose this Treaty is ratified by your votes, then these men will have to march over the dead bodies of their own brothers. They will have to wade through Irish blood."[1]

His words struck a responsive chord with many. "Bugger an oath of allegiance to the Crown!" a man near Henry stated emphatically. "Bugger dominion status too. And bugger Mick Collins while you're at it. I ain't no Free Stater, I'm a Republican, and I have the bullet in me leg to prove it. Give us the Republic, Dev!" he shouted.

An echo of his emotion ran through the crowd, an angry muttering that seemed to gather in strength like an ocean wave.

Then someone else called out, "I can shout 'Up the Republic,' but how the hell am I supposed to shout 'Up the External Association' and keep a straight face?"

The crowd roared with laughter and the tension eased. For a while.

WHEN Henry called at Herbert Place that night to take Ella to dinner, he found the atmosphere uncharacteristically somber. Ella met him with reddened eyes. "We've just heard from my aunt in Belfast with details of the dreadful rioting up there, Henry. We're so worried about Mother's family."

The British government, confident that the Treaty would be accepted in southern Ireland, was tightening its control over the north. Unionists and Orangemen were freely given licenses for guns. Murder gangs composed of members of the Royal Ulster Constabulary were joining with the B-Specials to conduct a pogrom against Catholics. Belfast had erupted in violence.

"Surely there's no trouble in the area where your relatives live," Henry said to Ella.

"Not yet, but Uncle Will's business downtown has been burnt out because he employs Catholics. Aunt May is terrified their house will be next. She says they can hear gunfire and people shouting in the streets at night."

"If you'll promise to stop worrying," Henry said, "I'll tell you something that not many people know yet. Michael Collins is meeting with Sir James Craig to sign a pact of co-operation to restore peaceful conditions in the north. Craig will agree to recruit Catholics into the Northern Ireland constabulary and to protect the citizenry from sectarian violence. Collins will agree to take action against the IRA units operating in the north from bases in the south."

"Are you sure they'll both keep their word?"

Henry answered cautiously. "Mick always keeps his—in his own way." He did not repeat to her a remark one of Collins' aides had made: "Mick's like a tinker swapping donkeys at the fair. He's suspicious of what he's getting, but happy enough that he's not giving an honest beast either."

IN the Craig–Collins Agreement Michael Collins tried to build into the partitioned counties a parity of esteem under the law. But as the days went by, it became obvious that Craig was not living up to his side of the arrangement.

Nothing was done to prevent sectarian assaults on Catholics. If anything, they were more frequent and more brutal than ever.

"This is what comes of trusting the British," Eamon de Valera told his followers. "By accepting the Treaty we abandon our countrymen in the north to a cruel fate. We must fight for them; we must fight for all of Ireland."

HENRY called upon the minister of defense for an interview about the situation. Richard Mulcahy looked more grave than Henry had ever seen him. "I can't give you anything you can print, not right now," he said. "The situation is . . . delicate, to say the least. I've sent a memorandum to Arthur Griffith voicing my concern about the increasing loyalist violence and the part the British are playing in financing and arming those responsible. It's up to Arthur to make representations directly to the British government."

"Is that all you can do?"

"No." Mulcahy dropped his voice. "This is strictly off the record. I want your word that you won't breathe it to a living soul. Ever."

"You have it," vowed Henry.

"I've arranged with Liam Lynch and the IRA executive committee to send some of the Republican guns north for the defense of the Ulster Catholics. Whatever about borders and treaties, we mustn't abandon our people stranded up there."[2]

"Does Mick Collins know you did that?"

"Who do you think suggested it? Mick's furious about the pogrom; in fact, he's come close to walking away from the whole process.

"We couldn't send arms direct because the weapons we have were given to us by the British and they could identify them. But with Mick's knowledge and support I'm replacing what Liam sends north with guns from the Free State arsenal."

Wheels within wheels, Henry thought. Aloud he said,

"Given the tensions right now, do you trust Lynch?"

Mulcahy's eyes snapped. "Trust Liam? Of course I do. We were comrades in arms."

On the twenty-sixth of March the Irish Republican Army held a convention. Liam Lynch was elected chief of staff. A new IRA constitution was to be drawn up as soon as possible.

On the eighth of April Winston Churchill, speaking at Dundee, Scotland, said, "It is possible that Irishmen will kill and murder each other and destroy Irish property and cripple Irish prosperity for some time before they realize that they, and they alone, will have to pay the bill in life and treasure."[3] Four days later he announced that an additional four thousand rifles, twenty-two hundred revolvers, six machine guns, and large amounts of ammunition had been given by Britain to the Free State Army. He implied that further arms to use against the Republicans would be supplied as needed.

From Belfast, Sir James Craig announced the appointment of Sir Henry Wilson as his personal military advisor.

In the dead of night on April thirteenth, members of the First and Second Battalions of the Dublin Brigade of the Irish Republican Army drove through the city in motorized vehicles laden with sandbags and rolls of barbed wire. They parked behind the Four Courts and quietly made their way inside.

The Four Courts, another of James Gandon's masterpieces, extended almost five hundred yards along the north side of the Liffey. The immense structure consisted of a main block in the classical style, fronted by a Corinthian portico and linked by arched gateways to two flanking wings. The name was taken from the four courts—Chancery, King's Bench, Common Pleas, and Exchequer—that opened off the central rotunda. Rising above the rotunda was a huge masonry drum supporting a copper-clad dome much larger than that of the Customs House. Its dominating grandeur was visible for miles. Since the Act of Union the Four Courts had been the most visible symbol of British law in Ireland.

Under the direction of Rory O'Connor, Liam Mellows,

and Ernie O'Malley, the Republicans bolted the exterior doors of the Four Courts and fortified the windows with sandbags. They also began digging a tunnel into the sewers to use as an emergency exit.

As they worked they sang rebel songs.

Before dawn another company from the Dublin Brigade seized Kilmainham Jail.

HENRY Mooney awoke to a fist pounding on his door. He pulled himself out of a deliciously erotic dream of Ella Rutledge and reached for the pistol in his bedside locker. While he fumbled with the weapon, fuzzily trying to remember how to use it, the door was flung open.

"For God's sake, Henry, don't shoot me!" cried Frank Gallagher.

"Jaysus on toast! What are you doing here?"

"Why don't you have a telephone installed in this house?" Gallagher countered, panting.

In hasty sentences that tumbled over one another, he related the night's events while Henry pulled on his clothes. "As soon as this gets out, every newspaperman in Dublin will be heading for the Four Courts," Gallagher said, "but the Republicans have asked for you in particular. They want to give you their official statement."

"Are you serious?"

"I am of course. Come on . . . and you'd better bring that pistol with you. God knows what Dublin's going to be like an hour from now."

The two men ran at top speed through the early morning streets. The customary drays, floats, and delivery carts were already making their rounds and shop owners were unlocking their premises, but there was a tentative air about everything. People glanced nervously over their shoulders. A woman sweeping the pavement in front of a greengrocer's shop called out to Frank and Henry, "Where you lot goin'?"

"The Four Courts," Henry replied, checking his pace.

"Wouldn't go down there it I wuz you. Them rebels has started all over agin." She shook her head. "More shootin' and killin' and it ain't nuthin' to do with me. I'll still have to be sweepin' me footpath t'morry."

At the foot of O'Connell Street, where the mighty bronze statue of Daniel O'Connell the Liberator brooded, the two men turned right and sprinted along the cobblestone quays. Bachelor's Walk, Ormond Quay Lower, Ormond Quay Upper with the ancient bulk of Christ Church across the river— they could go no farther. A company of Civic Guards was installing barricades at Chancery Street and at the foot of the newly renamed O'Donovan Rossa Bridge. Beyond the barricade Henry glimpsed Republicans patrolling in front of the Four Courts with rifles on their shoulders.

Several reporters were already at the barricade, trying to get the attention of a short, dark man in a tweed coat, who had just emerged from the east gate. Rory O'Connor, a former member of the Irish Republican Brotherhood, had been director of engineering for the army since 1918. O'Connor ignored the clamoring reporters, but when he saw Henry he came down to the barricade to meet him.

"Hullo, Henry. I'm glad Frank was able to find you for us."

"Hullo, Rory. I—"

Another reporter rudely thrust himself between them. "Who are you?" he shouted at O'Connor.

"Just what do you think you're doing?" someone else cried.

"I am an officer of the Irish Republican Army," O'Connor said crisply, "and we have taken over these premises as our general headquarters. The ongoing battle for the Republic will be organized from here—where British law no longer pertains. Now I have some further remarks for Mr. Mooney, if you will excuse us?" He nodded to the Civic Guards, who obligingly opened the barricade and let Henry through.

"Will you see that what I am about to say gets the widest possible distribution?" O'Connor asked Henry as the two men moved away from the increasing frenzy at the barricade.

"You may be certain of it. And I appreciate the opportunity."

"It's difficult to know who to trust," said O'Connor. "I

recall that Mick Collins once gave a private interview to an American reporter called Carl Ackerman who was working for the *Philadelphia Ledger*—and as a secret informer for the British.[4] The things Mick told Ackerman went straight to Lloyd George." O'Connor gave a sardonic smile. "The Big Fellow's not always as smart as he thinks he is.

"But we know you, Henry, and we trust you. You've always given everybody a fair shake, and there's not many doing that these days."

Henry waited with pencil poised.

"Here's what we want to tell people," said O'Connor. "Write it down just as I give it to you. There is nothing in our actions in the nature of a revolution or a coup d'état. The Republican Army is not now associated with any political organization. But I am safe in saying that if the army were ever to follow a political leader, Mr. de Valera is the man.

"My comrades and I recognize Dáil Éireann as an institution, but the majority in the Dáil have done a thing they had no right to do. A people must never be encouraged to surrender their independence."[5]

He stopped speaking. Henry stopped writing. "Is that all?"

"That's all. There's nothing more to say—except thank you for coming. And wish us luck." O'Connor saluted smartly, turned on his heel, and marched back into the Four Courts.

A bemused Henry returned through the barricade. The crowd of reporters had grown substantially and were elbowing one another in their effort to interview him, but he managed to push his way through to where Frank Gallagher was waiting for him.

"Well? Did he talk to you?"

Henry showed him the notebook. Gallagher read swiftly, then grinned. "Good on you," he breathed. "Oh, good on you, lads! Go for it, give 'em hell! Up the Republic!" he shouted loudly enough for the men in the Four Courts to hear.

Henry was dismayed. "Do you realize what you're encouraging?"

"Course I do. The Free State's nothing but a ploy to keep

disobedient children in line with false promises. Griffith and Collins made a dreadful mistake, but it's not too late to undo it." Noting Henry's expression, Gallagher added, "I take it you don't agree?"

"I *can't* agree, Frank. Mick Collins intends to use the Free State as a cover while he deconstructs the Treaty bit by bit, until we have the Republic after all. It may take years, but my conscience tells me that's the only reasonable approach."

"Then you must go with your conscience," Gallagher said sadly, "and I with mine." He held out his hand. "Will you shake with me, Henry? For friendship's sake, and while we still can?"

Henry seized his hand and pumped it hard. He did not trust himself to speak around the lump in his throat.

ALERTED by the Republican action, the Free State Army hurried to strengthen its position. By the sixteenth a pro-Treaty company was occupying Sligo Town Hall, and there were troop movements throughout the island.

With the IRA men in the Four Courts now a symbol of open defiance, law and order was breaking down. Violent crimes were on the increase.

Henry wrote of the gathering storm: "Neither the Provisional Government nor the Republicans have right totally on their side. If one party occupies a fixed point and a second party occupies another fixed point, and neither of them is willing to give an inch, there is only one solution—not war, which is merely an extension of the same principle, two parties on opposing sides. The answer is for both parties to move to a third point, as in an equilateral triangle. There something can be fashioned which is neither one nor the other, but the best of both."

He hoped de Valera would read his words, particularly the part about the equilateral triangle. The image might appeal to the mathematician in him.

A forlorn hope, a shouting in the wilderness.

•   •   •

THE IRA in the countryside took over a number of barracks formerly occupied by pro-Treaty troops, some of whom stayed on to join them. The Republicans were disorganized, however, because their brigades were still accustomed to operating autonomously. They were also having trouble provisioning themselves. The Dáil was allocating money only for Free State troops. As they had done in 1916, the Republicans applied to local shopkeepers for supplies and left receipts. When that proved insufficient for their growing needs, they began to raid banks and seize Provisional Government funds.

To counter the losses of men to the Republican side, the Free State Army further increased recruitment. Inexperienced soldiers were inclined to shoot at shadows. In Dublin tensions mounted as the sound of random gunfire was once more heard in the streets.

The Republicans were still ensconced in the Four Courts, issuing appeals to the nation to keep on fighting until the battle was won. Among their number was young Seán MacBride, the son of Maud Gonne MacBride and the executed Major John MacBride.

IN Northern Ireland Catholics continued to be killed with impunity. Whole families were beaten to death. Parents were slain in front of their children. A five-year-old lad named John Devlin was shot in cold blood while innocently playing in the street with his friends, and died the next day. No one was arrested.

In reprisal a Protestant family was bombed out of their home. Two of their sons were shot. When Henry called upon the Mansells the day the story broke in the papers, he found Edwin stiff with outrage. "Damned papist savages," he said. "Murdering innocent people."

Our molehills are becoming mountains again, Henry thought.

The IRA began conducting armed raids along the border. Loyalists were convinced, not without justification, that they meant to sweep aside the boundaries and reunite the island by force. There were more shootings, woundings, killings.

Sir James Craig introduced a draconian measure called the Special Powers Act that made the possession of firearms punishable by death. But the legislation was only employed against Catholics.

ON the twentieth Michael Collins made a speech in College Green. In an article for the *Longford Leader* Henry reported, "The crowd the Big Fellow drew was larger than the one that had gathered to hear the Long Fellow. Collins urged the people of Ireland to support the pro-Treaty candidates in the upcoming election, because the Treaty would give them the freedom to get freedom. He also assured his audience that the boundary commission would transfer large areas of Northern Ireland to Free State jurisdiction."

"I hope he's right," Henry remarked privately.

That same week members of the Irish Republican Army marched down Grafton Street carrying rifles. The Civic Guards watched them without interference.

"This is agony," Henry wrote to Ursula in Clare.

On the twenty-fifth of April an officer of the Third Cork Brigade of the IRA was shot dead when he called at the house of a Protestant family near Bandon on business. Within days ten Protestants in the area had been shot dead.

An outraged de Valera announced, "The German Palatines, the French Huguenots, the English Protestants flying from the fires of Smithfield . . . in this land of ours always found safe asylum. That glorious record must not be tarnished by acts against a helpless minority."[6]

Pro- and anti-Treaty representatives met at the Mansion House to try to resolve their differences. Although a Dáil committee was appointed to explore possible solutions, Cathal Brugha flatly stated that he was sick of politics. He would never fire a shot against comrades, he said, and preferred to die by an English or Orange bullet.[7]

The conference ended in failure.

DURING the first week in May open fighting broke out in Kilkenny and there were casualties on both sides. The matter was patched up, but only temporarily, when Free State and Republican forces agreed between themselves to share the local army barracks.

AMERICA was experiencing a postwar boom. New magazines appearing almost weekly were clamoring for material. They paid amounts that seemed to an Irishman incredible— as much as a penny a word. Henry was finding them a ready market for his work. But when he referred to "raindrops glittering on a blackthorn hedge" in an article on the looming civil war in Ireland, he received an unsettling response from America. "Please send us more writing with Irish color," he was urged. "Our readers also would love reminiscent pieces about the Ould Sod and the Little People."

"Irish color." What in God's name is that—words written in green ink? The Ould Sod. The Little People. I'm trying to tell them what's really going on in Ireland, and what they want is flights of fancy. But they were willing to pay for it; oh yes, they were willing to pay. The question of being able to support a wife seemed settled.

ON May twentieth an agreement was taken to defer the formal decision on the Treaty until after the general election. "The makeup of the new Dáil will determine the outcome," Henry reported.

General Macready, who was still in Ireland, began concentrating the remaining British forces in Dublin. If the Republicans won the election, he intended to seize the capital city immediately.

MEMBERS of the IRA were sending Catholic children from Northern Ireland to safety in the south. Families were opening their homes to as many as they could take. A number from Belfast had already arrived in Dublin when the Provisional Government announced they must be sent back as soon as possible. Granting them refugee status, it declared, might prejudice the new government's own fragile position.

Henry's article about the children's plight appeared in several newspapers, including the *Clare Champion*. Within days he received a letter from Ursula Halloran.

"Dear Uncle Henry,

"Those poor children must be as frightened as I was when Papa found me. They do not understand why anyone should hate them. Neither do I, and I want to do something for them. You know everybody who matters. Can you arrange for a few of the littlest ones to come to us instead of being sent back? Uncle Frank and Aunt Norah say we can care for at least half a dozen here on the farm, for as long as needs be. I have already told Lucy and Eileen they must help." *I'll just bet you have, Little Business.* The letter continued, "I am sure Papa will agree with the plan, although he is not here now."

That last sentence chilled Henry. If Ned was not at the farm, he must be away with the Army. The Republican army. And this time he would not be content to serve as a noncombatant.

When Henry told Ella about the refugee scheme, she asked if he was taking the children to Clare himself.

"I need to stay in Dublin to cover the election campaign. I'll put them on the train, and Ursula and Frank will meet them at the other end."

"I shouldn't think the poor mites will be in any condition to make such a journey alone. Let me accompany them, Henry. I should like to meet the rest of the Hallorans. Besides, I can serve as interpreter. I understand a strong Belfast accent, and that's not something everyone can do."

"There's no need for you to involve yourself in this."

She gave him a look of mock severity. "Since the ship of our lives is in your hands, the least you can do is let me take an active part in sailing it."

"Aye aye, Cap'n," Henry said with a chuckle.

No matter what had passed between himself and Ned, he felt confident no one at the farm would be so untactful as to mention Síle to his fiancée.

• • •

ELLA stood at the window, watching Henry walk away down the street. She did not hear her brother come up behind her until Edwin said, "Are you sure you know what you're doing?"

"Helping some children who need help, Edwin."

"That's not what I mean. This marriage of yours. Perhaps it is . . . ill timed."

She turned to face him. "I thought you liked Henry."

"I do, very much. But listen to me, Ella. You know I have only your best interests at heart. Every day clients are coming into my office to update their wills because they expect another war. Perhaps a resumption of the Anglo-Irish conflict, perhaps civil war among the Irish themselves. We—"

"I am Irish by birth," she interrupted, "and so are you."

"We are British," he replied firmly.

"If I were marrying Wallace Congreve would you be objecting now?"

"If you were marrying Wallace you would continue to enjoy the sort of life you've always had, and there would be no question about which faith your children were raised in."

"It's the same God, Edwin! If that's your only objection it isn't good enough."

"In normal times I would agree with you," he admitted, "but these are hardly normal times. Think of what's happened to Uncle Will and Aunt May. I don't want you caught in a crossfire, which you might be with a Catholic husband. As your nearest male relative I'm responsible for you."

"Have you never heard of women's suffrage?" she cried in exasperation. "Since 1918 women over thirty have actually been allowed to vote! Well, I'm over thirty now, and I'm going to marry Henry Mooney with or without your approval. And I'm taking those children to Clare, too."

Edwin was astonished. "I've never known you to be headstrong, Ella."

"Perhaps I've never known myself."

• • • •

In late afternoon the Pro-Cathedral was almost deserted as Henry slipped into a rear pew. There were only two or three shawled women and an old man mumbling his rosary, rattling the beads against the back of the pew in front of him.

Kneeling, Henry bowed his head over his folded hands and closed his eyes.

I always seem to be asking you for something. Yet I don't uphold my end, do I? I hardly remember the last time I went to Mass—Christmas, I suppose. And never confession. You know my sins already; I don't feel any need to tell them to a priest as well. You will absolve me or not as you see fit. You are all-powerful, and I'm not. That's the problem. I'm doing my best, but I beseech you to help me protect the people I care about.

He silently recited the names of those he loved most, and behind his closed lids pictured each familiar face in turn: *Ella. Ned. Little Business.*

Síle. Rising unbidden from a walled-off compartment of his heart.

On the twelfth of June, Grace Gifford Plunkett, widow of Joseph Plunkett, reputedly was seen on the roof of the Four Courts, blowing a trumpet to summon all true Republicans to the aid of the men inside.

That same day Henry put Ella and six little refugees from Belfast on the train. While the porter loaded her crocodile-skin suitcase and their shabby bundles into the railway carriage, the children clustered around Ella, pressing against her with instinctive trust. Henry stood with his hands in his pockets, rocking back and forth on his heels.

"Henry Mooney, why are you smiling like that?"

"I was . . . mmm . . . imagining these were your chicks, Ella. Yours and mine."

Her cheeks turned pink. "Is that what you want? Six children?"

"I want all that God sends us, I suppose."

"Oh my. You *are* Catholic, aren't you."

"This doesn't have anything to do with religion. I simply love you."

Her blush deepened. "Please, Henry, people will hear you." But she was pleased. "I wish you were coming with us."

"I do too, but remember you promised to be back here by the sixteenth in time to vote. Meanwhile, enjoy yourself. Get to know Ursula, she's something special. You can explain the meaning of the word 'precocious' to her if she doesn't know it already."

Henry watched the train pull out of Kingsbridge Station, following it as far as he could with his eyes.

Chapter Thirty-eight

Henry spent the next several days trying to cover as many political speeches as possible. The campaign was not without its lighter moments. While Michael Collins was making an impassioned pro-Treaty speech from the back of an open motorcar in Sligo, a Republican jumped into the front seat and drove the car away at high speed. Collins had to vault over the back, to the vast amusement of the crowd.

He laughed too.

On the morning of the fifteenth Henry received a telegram from Ella, telling him she would be on the last train that night. He met her at the station with an armful of roses.

"You look tired," were her first words to him.

"And you're positively glowing. Your visit to the farm must have done you some good."

"I loved it—and Ursula. You're right, she is something special. She told me her father has been teaching her at home, but that's not enough for such an exceptionally bright girl. There are some fine schools on the Continent educating young women to a high standard; perhaps, if I make some inquiries, her father might consider one for her."

"Did you see Ned?" Henry asked warily.

"No, he's with the Republican forces somewhere. Frank

did mention that you and he had a disagreement—over the Treaty, I gather."

"Mmm."

"Well, you must mend your fences with him before the wedding, Henry. I know you'll want him for your best man. Ava already has him on one of her interminable lists."

"Mmm," Henry said again.

"And your family," Ella went on, while he collected her suitcase and they went in search of a cab. "We really must pay a formal call on your family soon, so I can get to know your mother and your brothers and sisters."

Get to know my mother. Great bouncing Barabbas!

That night Henry composed a long-overdue letter to Hannah Mooney and one for each of his siblings. He felt as if he were dropping bombs into the pillar letterbox on the corner of Talbot Street.

The first reply came from Pauline. "Mam says," wrote Henry's sister, who no longer seemed to have opinions of her own, "to tell you that widow is marrying you for your money."

Of course she is, Mam. Why else would any woman marry a worthless creature like me? With a start Henry realized he was talking out loud. *Does everyone carry on lifelong one-sided conversations with their parents, or is it just me?*

Neither Bernard nor Noel responded to his letters. Alice wrote to say she did not think she would not be allowed out of the convent to attend the wedding, so she would not bother Reverend Mother by asking.

THE long-promised constitution for the Irish Free State did not appear in the daily newspapers until the morning of polling day. As soon as he was dressed, Henry went to the nearest newsagency to get the morning papers. Between bites of egg and sausage he fumed to Louise, "What are they playing at, waiting until today to publish? Now most of the voters will go to the polls with no idea what they're voting for."

"Maybe that's for the best. A lot of them are like me,

Henry. They know they can't understand the issues, so they'll vote for the man."

Stabbing his forefinger at the *Irish Times*, Henry said, "Here's a perfect example. The bishop of Cloyne has a letter in here saying he's subscribed to the election campaigns of pro-Treaty candidates. That's the same as telling his flock to vote for them. So they will, I'm afraid. Without bothering to think for themselves, they will."

"I thought you supported the Treaty."

"I support the right of the people to make up their own minds, Louise."

"But the newspapers say the Treaty is best for us. You know we believe what we read in the papers. Why, we trust you, Henry, almost like we trust the Church."

She meant it as a compliment.

Henry gave her a long, thoughtful look. Then, leaving his breakfast to go cold, he went to his room and began work on an article that could not possibly appear in print for several days. He felt compelled to write it anyway.

"Who appointed journalists unimpeachable arbiters of the truth?" he asked his readers. "As a journalist myself I can tell you that each of us, no matter how loudly we proclaim our objectivity, has a personal opinion. These opinions influence our writing down to the choice of the most insignificant words. Through language we manipulate the reader in ways he does not suspect. Intentionally or not, we seek to make him—or her—think as we do.

"So I tell you this: do not take anything you read in the papers at face value. Question it, test it, bring your own critical faculties to bear. For too many centuries we Irish have accepted whatever 'truth' we have been told by figures of supposed authority. It is time we thought for ourselves."

Then he put on his hat and went out to vote.

FROM London, Sir Henry Wilson denounced both the Treaty and the election, and reiterated Britain's right to Ireland. He urged Sir James Craig to prepare for all-out war against the Republicans.

.   .   .

Two days after the election, while the votes were still being counted, the IRA held another convention at the Mansion House. Henry applied to cover it, but admission was strictly limited. He waited outside in a driving rain until at last he saw Tom Barry coming out, then hurried to intercept him. "What's happened in there, Tom? Is there any chance you might rethink your position and make it up with Richard Mulcahy and Michael Collins?"

Barry paused to talk under the shelter of Henry's umbrella. "None whatever. Dick Mulcahy is the finest executive officer I ever saw. He's calm, meticulous, and his integrity is beyond question. But we no longer accept his authority as minister for defense. He's a by-the-book soldier, and we can't fight this war by the book."[1]

You underestimate him, Henry thought, recalling Mulcahy's secret arrangement with Lynch to send guns to the north. But he had given his word never to tell anyone.

"As for Mick," Barry went on, "personally I'm as fond of him as I ever was, and that's considerable. But the Brits have got to the Big Fellow—he's singing off their hymn sheet now. And we won't."

"So things go on as before?"

"Not exactly. You may not know this, but Collins and de Valera have been working together on a pact to reunify the army. More discussions, negotiations, all that class of thing. When it was presented tonight, Liam Lynch and some of the IRA executive supported the pact, but many of the lads wouldn't wear it. Too much has happened; they don't trust any political scheme anymore.

"I brought forward a proposal to give the British seventy-two hours to get out of the country altogether, then terminate the truce. That would free us to launch an armed attack on the six counties and take them back. I'm convinced action is all we need to unite the army again, but Lynch and his crowd didn't agree. My motion was defeated. Narrowly," he added. "So we've done what we had to do."

"What does that mean?"

"It means the Republicans who agree with me have re-

pudiated Liam Lynch and appointed a new chief of staff.
Joe McKelvey. He's a good man, a Tyrone man; he's been
up in Belfast personally, defending our people there."

"But what about General Lynch?"

"We're going to lock him and his crowd out of the GHQ."
Tom Barry turned up his coat collar and squinted at the rain.
"I have to make a quick trip down to Cork, but I'll be back
in a couple of days. There's a lot of work to be done if
we're not going to lose the Republic altogether." Snapping
Henry a quick salute, he sprinted into the night.

*Dear Christ, another split. Is there no end to it? It's as
if some natural law is in force, with pressure causing each
splinter to splinter further.*

Next day Liam Lynch set up a GHQ of his own in the
Clarence Hotel.

Although no journalists had been allowed to attend, the
Freeman's Journal published an account of the ill-fated convention. The editor, Seán Lester, accused Tom Barry and
those he called "fire eaters" of advocating a parliament of
gunmen.

Rory O'Connor issued an order to have the presses of the
Journal smashed and the premises burned.

However, Cathal Brugha assured the editor of another
newspaper, "So far as my influence goes, no journalist shall
ever be molested."

Henry was furious at the attack on the *Journal*. He
marched up to the Four Courts to remonstrate with the Republicans inside, but was not allowed in.

*I'll have to wait till Tom Barry gets back. He'll see me.
Please God he will listen to me. We can't go this route.*

On the twenty-second of June Ireland was electrified by
news of the assassination of Sir Henry Wilson.

That night when Henry knocked on the door in Herbert
Place the parlor maid told him, "I'm sorry, Mr. Mooney, but
Mrs. Rutledge is not at home."

"But she's expecting me. We have a dinner engagement."

The maid looked embarrassed. "I've been instructed to tell
you Mrs. Rutledge is not at home," she repeated.

Instructed? "Who told you to say that, Tilly?"

"Mr. Mansell, sir."

"I see." Henry did not see at all. "What about Madge? Or Ava?"

"Oh, they really are out, sir," the girl said brightly. "They've gone to see the new play at the Abbey with Miss Mansell's young man. But Mr. Mansell is waiting for you in the library. I have orders to take you to him as soon as you arrive."

Edwin stood up when Henry entered the room. "Henry, we have a bit of a problem here," he said, gesturing toward the day's newspapers strewn across the reading table. "I hope you will understand my position."

"What's this about?"

"I assume you know Sir Henry Wilson's been shot dead in London by members of the IRA?"

"I was at the *Evening Mail* office when the news came in," Henry replied. "Wilson was shot outside his house in Belgravia; the police already have two men in custody. Their names will be in tomorrow's editions. What's that to do with me?"

"Do you approve of Wilson's murder?"

"I won't shed any tears for him. With the exception of General Macready he was the most hated man in Ireland. But I don't approve of murder, his or anyone else's."

Edwin selected a newspaper from the pile. "Here's a report of the IRA burning Mount Talbot at Athleague. We used to go to parties there, and the Talbot girls are great friends of my sisters'. If the rebels had gone only a mile or so farther up the road, they might have burned Beech Park too. What do you have to say to that, Henry?"

"Surely you know me well enough to know that I deplore such acts."

"Yet are you not a Republican sympathizer?"

"Are you cross-examining me? I thought you were a solicitor, not a barrister. But to answer your question, I'm an Irish nationalist—I've never made any secret of that."

"You're a Republican," Edwin said again. Around the eyepatch he still wore, his face suffused with blood.

"If you're asking if I support the ideal of an Irish Republic, I do," Henry said evenly. "A republic is a state in which supreme power is held by the people or their elected representatives rather than a monarch. No more just system has yet been devised."

"You call it justice to send two thugs to shoot an old soldier dead in the street?"

"An old soldier? Come now, Edwin, you know what Wilson was—a hate-filled Ulster bigot who loathed Catholic Ireland. He was doing everything he could to keep the pot boiling in the north so the British government would launch a new invasion of this island."

"So you do approve of killing him."

"I can't believe I'm hearing this. I don't know where you got the idea that I—"

Edwin picked up yet another of the papers and held it for Henry to see. It was folded open to his article about making up one's own mind. "Do you deny you wrote this?"

"Of course I don't deny it. I said some things that needed to be said. But what possible inference can you draw from—"

" 'We manipulate the reader in ways he does not suspect,' " Edwin quoted. "Indeed you do. Since Ella's known you she has changed, and not for the better. She used to accept the advice of her menfolk. That's how it should be; the ladies do not have our experience of the world. But lately she has become quite headstrong, which I attribute entirely to your influence."

"Perhaps she always could think for herself," Henry said. "Did you ever consider that possibility?"

Edwin ignored the question. "I am afraid that any further association with you might compromise my sister's safety. Since her husband's death she has been my responsibility, and I have to do what's best for her. No matter what it takes," he added.

"What's that supposed to mean?"

"I never mistook you for a fortune hunter, Henry, but you must realize that Ella has money. Or rather, she is a beneficiary of the trust our late father established for us. As head of the family I control that trust, and if necessary I will cut her off her income to prevent her marrying the wrong man."

Henry was rigid with anger. "I don't want Ella's money! We won't need it. I can support her adequately."

"But surely you would not wish to be the cause of her disinheritance?"

"Does she know we're having this conversation?"

"I asked her to stay upstairs so you and I could discuss some serious matters in private. She may have suspected it had something to do with the marriage, but I gave no details. At first I thought she would refuse—that's what I meant about her becoming headstrong—but at last she agreed. I trust you will be equally reasonable."

"Reasonable? Do you think it's reasonable to try to break off our engagement without even consulting her?"

"My sister isn't thinking clearly right now. Taking those children to Clare is a perfect example. There's military activity all across the country; anything might have happened."

"Well, it didn't. I arranged to have two members of the army in her railway carriage with orders to look out for her. They wore civilian clothes so she didn't notice them, but she was protected the whole time she was away. They came back to Dublin when she did."

"Which army, Henry?"

He hesitated. "The IRA."

"The IRA," Edwin repeated. "That says it all, doesn't it? I think you had best go now."

Henry squared his shoulders. "I have no intention of leaving this house tonight until I see Ella. I asked Republicans to look out for her because they happened to be personal friends of mine."

"And I'm Ella's brother. I cannot allow her any further involvement with—"

"All right then!" Henry burst out. "I admit it, I'm for the Republic heart and soul! But if I had to fight tomorrow, it would be on the side of the Provisional Government, because that's the legally constituted—"

"You admit your republicanism without shame?"

"You're a monarchist," Henry countered. "Are you ashamed?"

Edwin's visible eye blazed. "Of course not! Henry, I demand that you leave now."

"Not without seeing Ella."

"I could call the servants and have you thrown out."

Henry doubled his fists at his sides. From deep within himself he summoned the unyielding strength, the simmering anger, the latent male aggression he had suppressed all his adult life. "You could try," he said grimly.

Until that moment Edwin had thought of Henry Mooney as a temperate man. An amiable, easygoing man. Now he realized his mistake. Waistcoat and watch chain concealed a tiger's heart.

"I'll see Ella now," Henry Mooney growled. "And if you try to stop me, I swear I'll go through you for a shortcut."

He strode from the library. Up the stairs, three at a time. Edwin, disconcerted, hurrying behind.

"Ella!" shouted Henry. His deep voice reverberated in the stairwell. "Ella Rutledge! Where are you?"

Chapter Thirty-nine

THAT same night Commandant-General Tom Barry of the IRA was captured by Free State troops. Disguised as a nurse, he had been attempting to rejoin the garrison in the Four Courts. He was taken to Mountjoy Jail as the first Republican prisoner of the Irish Civil War.

Henry made every effort to get in to see him, but even Richard Mulcahy would not issue him a pass. "This isn't a good time to interview an IRA commandant, Henry."

"But you're an IRA commandant. Or were."

"You know what I mean."

"Sadly, I do."

On his way down Kildare Street Henry saw Liam Tobin coming toward him. His languorous pace was easily recognizable. "Liam! Are you going for a pint?"

Tobin stopped. "Might be. You buying?"

"You've been around the Big Fellow too long."

Tobin grinned. "You pump me for information, you pay."

It took several drinks before Tobin proved a good investment. Laconic as always, he replied to Henry's questions with monosyllabic answers—until Henry asked about the assassination of Wilson. Then he said with obvious relish, "Didn't we do good! Mick himself ordered that, you know. That's one less British bastard to piss all over the Irish."[1]

"D'you think the British government knows Mick was behind it?"

"Not at all—they're convinced he's their man." Tobin gave a contemptuous snort. "As if the Big Fellow could be anybody's man but his own."

The results of the election were not announced until the twenty-fourth of June. Six hundred and twenty thousand votes had been cast; over 78 percent had been for pro-Treaty candidates.

L OUIS Kearney looked up as Henry entered the parlor. "What are you doing back? I thought you'd be out until all hours; I don't even have your room swept yet."

"I'm sorry, Louise. I seem to be at sixes and sevens, so I thought if I came home for a while . . ."

"If that tooth's still bothering you, put oil of cloves on it."

"It's not the tooth."

She folded her arms across her apron and gave Henry a knowing look. "Exactly what happened between you and Mrs. Rutledge? You've been like an antiChrist since you saw her last."

Don't tell anyone your personal business. "Nothing happened."

He slumped into an armchair beside the hearth and stared at the cold ashes.

H ENRY struggled to find some humor to lighten his personal gloom. In a piece for his American markets, he related, "The *Irish Times* newspaper in Dublin still has its own horse and delivery cart, which is more useful in the narrow laneways of the capital than a motorized lorry. A young apprentice recently was asked to take the horse to be shod. Misunderstanding directions, he took the unfortunate animal to the knackers and had it shot instead. *Times* deliveries were late that day."[2]

But soon there was nothing lighthearted left to write about.

• • •

THE British government assumed the assassination of Wilson had been carried out on orders from the hard-line Republicans in the Four Courts. General Macready was told to dig them out or bomb them out. When he delayed, Michael Collins, as head of the Provisional Government of Ireland, was ordered to remove them from the Four Courts immediately.

Winston Churchill told the House of Commons that refusal to comply would bring the Treaty crashing down.

The arrests of known Republicans accelerated. Women were not spared. Eventually some four hundred would be jailed, including Maud Gonne MacBride, Grace Gifford Plunkett, Terence MacSwiney's sister Mary, James Connolly's daughter Nora, and Dorothy Macardle, who had worked for the Republican Publicity Bureau.

THE twenty-seventh of June was a dull, rainy day. Lowering clouds created an atmosphere so heavy that Henry left his windows wide open when he went to bed, so he could catch the least breath of moving air.

Sometime during the night he dreamed of Ella.

Ella in a carriage drawn by two white horses. The horses were running away and Ella was screaming, calling to him to save her. Him with his feet stuck in a bog, unable to move.

Mam behind him saying, "I knew you'd let me down."

AT four a.m. the army of the Provisional Government attacked the Four Courts with heavy artillery. The roar echoed through the city, tumbling frightened Dubliners from their beds. It was followed immediately by rifle fire and the unmistakable chatter of machine guns.

Henry met Louise on the stair landing. She had not even put on a dressing gown, but wore only a flannel nightdress with all the color washed out of it, and her nightcap askew. "Merciful hour!" she cried, crossing herself. "Is it the end of the world?"

"I'll go find out. You stay here, Louise, and keep the other lodgers here too if you can. After I've gone, bolt the door behind me."

He took his revolver with him.

In the cold gray light of early morning the scene on the quays was a cruel reminder of 1916. Once again British guns were bombarding Dublin—only this time they were manned by Irishmen. The long frontage of the Four Courts was being targeted by two borrowed eighteen-pound field guns firing from Winetavern Street across the Liffey.

Henry Mooney had not cried since Síle's funeral. Pain-drops burned his eyes now.

Chapter Forty

HENRY joined the growing crowd watching the bombardment of the Four Courts from what they believed was a safe distance. The field guns were being fired at five-minute intervals, but bullets from both sides were constantly spanging off the cobblestones. Lancia armored cars had been drawn up in front of the gates of the Four Courts to prevent the Republicans inside from using the armored Whippet they had captured from the Free State forces. On the south side of the Liffey, more Lancias were providing cover for the eighteen-pounders and their crews in Winetavern Street.

Among the gasping, pointing spectators Henry saw a photographer who worked for the *Times*. The man was trying to adjust a large box camera atop a tripod. Every boom of the guns threatened the contraption's delicate stability.

Henry went over to him. "I never thought I'd see this," he remarked, shaking his head.

"Shouldn't have come to it at all," the photographer replied irritably. "Put your hand on that bleedin' thing and hold it still, will you? The Irregulars were given an ultimatum at four this morning. They could have marched out with their hands up and their heads high and no blame on them. Instead they refused. Stubborn bog-trotters. What the shite do they think they're doing?"

"Who ordered the shelling?"

"Emmet Dalton, I heard."

As the gunfire intensified, O'Connell Street and the bridge became clogged with spectators. Traffic was stopped in every direction. The unarmed Civic Guard fell back and the Dublin Guard Brigade, armed members of the Free State Army, began trying to clear the area. Henry obediently turned his back on the Four Courts and walked east along the quays, following the river toward the sea.

Behind him the field guns roared.

People streamed past him going the opposite way. In spite of the effort to keep them back, the crowds were moving in again. The roar and rumble of destruction mingled with shouts and cheers. Henry shook his head. *The fatal attraction of . . . et cetera.*

Emmet Dalton, a militant Treatyite, might have given the actual orders for the shelling, but the instructions had to have come from Michael Collins. Henry could imagine what private agonies Collins was suffering. On behalf of the north he had been working behind the scenes with Lynch and the IRA executive. Now he was attacking those same Republicans. *To keep the British from moving back in and taking things out of his hands,* Henry thought.

Ironically, thanks to the latest split, Liam Lynch was out of the line of fire.

Henry crossed the Liffey by the bridge near the unrepaired Customs House. Barricades were being set up there by men in Republican uniform. He then worked his way back along the quays, skillfully avoiding Free State soldiers who were also erecting barricades. Dublin was his city now; he knew every sheltering doorway, every rat-infested laneway.

Reporters and rats, he thought sardonically, *we go where we like.*

The Clarence was one of many hotels whose staff knew Henry. In developing his contacts, he had bought them drinks and listened sympathetically to a catalogue of their family and financial woes. When he entered the lobby the desk clerk beckoned to him. "You'll be wanting to see Commandant Lynch I expect, Mr. Mooney. He's still upstairs."

"Will he see me?"

"No chance whatever. Them other reporters over there—" the desk clerk indicated a score of Henry's colleagues

thronging the lobby—"they want to see 'im too. But the
general gave strict orders to let no one come up."

Digging in his pocket, Henry produced a gold sovereign.
"How's that son of yours, the one with the bad chest?" he
asked as the gold magically changed hands and disappeared.

The clerk dropped his voice. "The service stairs from the
kitchen is down that passage—turn to your right then right
again. Second door on yer left. And I dint see ye go up."

Most of the IRA executive were crowded into a room on
the second floor of the hotel. One or two nodded to Henry
as he stood in the doorway. He caught sight of Liam Lynch
in the far side of the room, deep in conversation. Lynch was
a big man who, in his late twenties, looked older. A steep
brow, combined with the rimless spectacles he wore, gave
him a scholarly look. In one of his articles Henry had written: "Liam Lynch is a shrewd judge of men who at the same
time wants to believe the best of everybody, which makes
him popular with the troops in the field. His absolute faith
in his men is legendary. Although he is adaptable in military
situations as a good commander must be, when it comes to
the cause of the Irish Republic Lynch is unmovable."

Now Liam Lynch glanced up, saw Henry, smiled fleet-
ingly, but waved him away.

Henry continued to stand in the doorway.

At last Lynch came over to him. The commander's voice
was slightly husky, accented with his native Limerick as he
said, "I suppose it would do no good to ask you to leave?"

"None whatever—I'm getting pretty good at refusing that
request. Can you tell me what's going on?"

Behind his glasses Lynch's eyes glinted. "I'm off to Cork
in a couple of hours to muster the Southern Division, and
I'm leaving Oscar Traynor to direct operations here in Dublin."

"What operations?"

"We're going to defend the Republic in arms, Henry. To
the bitter end. I was in the Four Courts last night only hours
before the shelling began, and I've come back with a document the officers there signed. We've healed the split between ourselves and them. We'll be fighting shoulder to
shoulder against the Free Staters now."

Lynch gave Henry the text of a proclamation which would be handed out to the reporters in the lobby. "Fellow citizens of the Irish Republic. The fateful hour has come. At the direction of the hereditary enemy our rightful cause is being treacherously assailed by recreant Irishmen. Gallant soldiers of the Irish Republic stand rigorously firm in its defense. The sacred spirits of the Illustrious Dead are with us in this great struggle. 'Death Before Dishonor.' We especially appeal to our former comrades of the Irish Republic to return to that allegiance and thus guard the Nation's honor." The document was signed on behalf of the Irish Republican Army by its commandant generals, including Liam Mellows, Rory O'Connor, Joseph McKelvey, Ernie O'Malley . . . and Liam Lynch.[1]

Winston Churchill was bombarding Michael Collins with offers of additional help to crush the Republicans. He ordered General Macready to place howitzers at the disposal of the Free State troops, and cabled, "Aero planes manned by their own pilots will carry out any action necessary."[2]

Collins declined the offers.

Oscar Traynor had established headquarters in the Hammam Hotel on the east side of O'Connell Street. Other officers took over adjacent buildings and barricaded the area to create a defensive block. A detachment of Fíanna boys, some still in short pants, had stationed themselves in North Great George's Street, eager to defend the Republic.[3]

Free State troops had hoped to keep the fighting contained to the Four Courts, but soon there was skirmishing throughout north Dublin. Snipers took up positions. Figures in uniform, bent double, ran from doorway to doorway. Motorcars and horse-drawn vehicles of every description were commandeered to block off streets.

Henry worked his way back and forth across the neighborhood he knew so well. Ducking; crouching. Talking to anyone who would talk to him. Men on either side, many of whom he knew personally. Patting his pocket to make sure his pistol was still there. But whom would he shoot?

The gunfire continued for almost eight hours. Shopkeepers boarded up their shops. A tangle of tram wires littered O'Connell Bridge, and the laneways north of the Liffey were obscured by smoke smelling of cordite. Henry could not eat, could not relax, wandered into the few public houses still open and out again without even having a drink.

The IRA was installed in Moran's Hotel at the corner of Gardiner and Talbot streets. As Henry passed by, he observed the upstairs windows bristling with guns.

Rifle fire crackled dangerously close.

Henry ducked into the lobby of the hotel. Most of the men he saw were men he knew. They were willing to talk to him, but, as one explained, "That cute whoor Collins has cut communications outside the city. The Staters have seized the rural phone exchanges so we can't get any information about what the boys are doing down the country. All we know for sure is that the Southern Division is out there somewhere. If they can get this far, maybe we can trap the Staters in a pincers movement."

Ned Halloran's out there somewhere too, Henry thought glumly. *Angry and with scores to settle. Probably get himself killed for sure this time.*

During a lull in the gunfire he sprinted up Gardiner Street to number 16 to make certain his cousin was all right. He found her anxious and angry but safe enough. Gardiner Street was not in the immediate area of action, at least not so far.

"What about Mrs. Rutledge?" Louise asked.

"I'm on my way there next."

"Would you not telephone? You said they have one."

"The phones aren't reliable right now."

Taking his bicycle from the shed, he followed a zigzag route across the city. Once he was south of the Liffey it was quieter. By the time he got to Ballsbridge it was hard to believe a war was going on. Life in the affluent suburb continued serenely undisturbed. *So Ella's safe enough for now,* Henry thought with relief. *But if I could just see her for a moment, to be sure . . .*

He had just reached Herbert Place when a black Delage came roaring around the corner and almost knocked him over. Henry leaped off the bicycle, shouting, "What the hell do you think you're doing!"

Surprisingly, the man stopped the car. When he stepped

out of his vehicle, Congreve did not look apologetic. "I didn't recognize you," he said in a cold voice.

"Would it have made any difference? You can't go speeding around the city like that—you might kill somebody."

"Don't talk to me about irresponsible behavior," Congreve retorted. "A band of Fenians has taken over the Kildare Street Club. It's absolutely shocking. These people call themselves Republicans but they're nothing more than barbarians. I gathered up my things and left, as any gentleman would."

Henry glanced at the piled-up luggage in the back of the car. "Where will you stay now?"

"Edwin Mansell will put me up, of course. He has no more patience than I do with this sort of carry-on."

The journalist set his jaw. "I don't think that's a very good idea."

"My dear fellow, you have no say in the matter. He tells me you've been forbidden the house."

"We're not in the house now," Henry said, measuring Congreve with his eyes. The man was no taller than he and looked considerably less fit. *Drives everywhere in that damned motor.* "And you're not going to be."

"You arrogant puppy!" Congreve took a deep breath as if pumping himself up to fight. But Henry did not give him time.

One hard fist to the jaw. Congreve's eyes going blank, the man suddenly sitting down hard on the curb.

Henry stood over him, waiting. Feeling suddenly, violently, confident.

Congreve fingered his jaw. "I think you broke it," he muttered.

"I doubt it, but if I did there are plenty of doctors in town," Henry nodded his head. "Back that way. And plenty of hotels and boardinghouses, too."

Congreve glared balefully up at him. "I'll have you arrested."

"Oh, I don't think so. The police will have other things to worry about for quite a while."

The major slowly got to his feet. He did not take his eyes off Henry, watching him as he would have watched a snake that might strike at any moment. With an exaggerated air of courtesy Henry opened the car door. "Sir," he said.

Congreve did not respond to the sarcasm. He edged past Henry into the safety of his car. Before he could slam the door, Henry closed it gently. "There's plenty of room for you to turn your car," he said. "I'll direct you if you like. Or we can go another round if you'd prefer."

Congreve snarled something under his breath. With a great grinding of gears he made an awkward U-turn, then sped away.

Henry watched the car disappear from view. Only then did he realize he was grinning. *Guess I'm one of those barbarians with no sense of decency. Wait until Edwin hears about this.*

The grin faded. His fist was throbbing painfully. Feeling eyes upon him, he turned and looked up.

Ella Rutledge stood framed in her bedroom window, looking down at him.

Henry's breath caught in his throat. He tried to read her expression, but she was too far away. *Sweet Christ, I just confirmed all the terrible things her brother's undoubtedly been saying about me!*

He stood gazing up at her. She made no gesture, just watched him. *What must she think of me?* His shoulders slumped. Retrieving his bicycle, he set off for Gardiner Street.

IN mid-afternoon Eamon de Valera drove into the city from Greystones. He went direct to his office in Suffolk Street, from which he issued a statement of defiance. "At the bidding of the English, Irishmen are today shooting down, on the streets of our capital, brother Irishmen. In Rory O'Connor and his comrades lives the unbought indomitable soul of Ireland. Irish citizens! Give them support!"[4]

ADDRESSING an emergency meeting of the Dáil, the new minister for justice, Kevin O'Higgins, said, "We have very good reasons to believe that our attack on the Four Courts anticipated by a couple of hours the creation of conditions which would have brought back the British power—horse, foot, artillery, and navy—in hostile relations to this country."[5]

HENRY felt as if he were being slowly squeezed in a giant fist. Men he knew and liked were doing their best to kill other men he knew and liked. That night he wrote, "Both sides are grimly determined. The air of fraternal high spirits that the Volunteers exuded during the Rising has changed to one of the fratricidal ferocity." He stared at that last sentence, hardly able to believe he had written it.

Even several large whiskies failed to help him fall asleep.

The gunfire resumed at dawn.

Casualties were mounting. The women of Cumann na mBan were assisting the doctors and nurses who tended the wounded—on both sides.

The field guns had been moved to Bridgefoot Street near the Brazen Head Inn, which claimed to be the oldest public house in Ireland. From that vantage point the gunners continued to blow chunks out of the facade of the Four Courts.

Henry crossed the river and, avoiding military cordons, made his way to the Dáil office. He was relieved to find it open. Kathleen McKenna looked up from her typewriter as he entered. Her face was drawn, her eyes red-rimmed from lack of sleep. "Good morning, Henry."

"Nothing good about it, as far as I can see. Where is everyone?"

"The officers are all at their posts. Emmet Dalton is directing the shelling, and Paddy O'Daly—you know him, he was one of Mick's Twelve Apostles—is in charge of the attack force."

"I mean the men who're responsible for this fiasco in the first place."

"You can't blame Arthur for this," she said quickly. Protectively.

"I wasn't going to. Where is he?"

"Up on the roof, I think. Watching. He's taking it very hard; we're all worried about him."

"Collins and de Valera, where are they?"

"Mick—I mean Chairman Collins—is in conference with Minister Mulcahy. I can't speak officially for Dev; he's on the other side now. But according to our latest intelligence he's reported back to his old battalion and asked to be sworn in as an ordinary soldier. He's been posted to the Hammam Hotel."

"Jesus in a jaunting car! Don't the Republicans know better than to concentrate their leadership in one place?"

Kathleen said, "We believe they're hoping to find a way to evacuate the Four Courts garrison. Rory O'Connor dug an escape tunnel leading to the sewers that empty into the river, but they forgot the river is tidal. The sewers are flooded now."

Henry groaned. *War*, he thought to himself, *is fifty percent farce*.

THE battle went on. Windows along the quays, many of them only recently replaced after the Rising, were smashed again by artillery concussion or snipers. Dubliners who lived in the center of the city huddled, terrified, in their homes, but the churches and some pubs remained open.

The day gave way to a second night of gunfire, ambulances, chaos. Street lamps, were, for the most part, unlit. Henry heard children in a laneway chanting a mocking singsong. At first he thought it was just some of the doggerel beloved of street children; then he stopped to listen. "England gave the orders, and gave the cannon too, For England's bloody vengeance must be satisfied anew."[6] Henry dutifully copied down the words, though he doubted anyone would print them.

NEXT morning he awoke with the profound conviction that the universe was run by a cosmic comedian with a bizarre sense of humor. A civil war was raging in Dublin and he had the worst toothache of his life. His jaw was so swollen he could hardly close his mouth.

Rain was drumming on rooftops. The field guns had not

yet resumed, but machine guns were clattering in the distance as Henry left the house. Only a few civilians—the poor to whom the streets were home—could be seen. Dublin had the look of an abandoned city. Trash and sodden newspapers littered empty streets.

As Henry made his way toward the scenes of yesterday's action, the pace of the gunfire began to pick up. The artillery roared again.

He paused to chat with a tubercular newsboy sheltering in the doorway of the boarded-up Singer Sewing Machine shop on Talbot Street. The lad, who was sitting dejectedly on a stack of yesterday's unsold papers, said, "Them Free Staters got them Republicans pinned down in that block o' buildings either side o' the Hammam Hotel. They shoot at any man what tries to look out a winder."

When Henry reached the corner, a uniformed member of the Dublin Guards informed him, "Some of our men managed to get into the west wing of the Four Courts during the night. Now the field guns are concentrating on the part of the building still held by the Republicans. The government means to end this thing today. There's over two thousand men ready to storm the place, and ambulances and motorcycles and everything down there. I have orders not to let anyone go any farther in that direction."

"That's where I need to be, unfortunately," Henry replied, showing his press card.

The soldier shrugged. "Sorry."

Give a man a uniform and a little power and he goes mad.

"D'jou say something?"

"Sorry," Henry muttered. "I must have been talking to myself."

He backtracked up to Parnell Street, then zigzagged by way of Capel Street—where a nest of IRA snipers allowed him to pass unmolested—to King Street and thence to Church Street. There a sandbag barricade blocked his way. He could see a thread of unusually black smoke rising from the direction of the Four Courts. "What's happening down there?" he asked a soldier in Free State uniform.

"A fire at the rear of the building," the man said. "There

was a truce earlier to let the Irregulars evacuate their wounded, but we'll have them all out soon."

Irregulars again. Not Republicans anymore; they must be called by a more derogatory title. While Michael Collins is still hoping for a way to save the Republic.

Henry continued working his way around north Dublin, talking to anyone he could find. Occasionally glancing at the smoke still rising from the rear of the Four Courts. Listening to the gunfire.

The pain in his jaw grew progressively worse. He finally found a chemist's shop that was open and asked for oil of cloves, but there was none in stock. The shop had been depleted of everything by soldiers provisioning both sides. "You should go home and put a poultice on that jaw," the chemist advised him. "I think I'll go home myself. There's no point in keeping the doors open when you can't do business."

The smoke at the rear of the Four Courts was becoming thicker as Henry once more tried to approach the area. When he happened to glance down a crooked laneway, he saw something that stopped him in his tracks.

HECTOR HAMILTON, PAINLESS DENTIST read a neatly printed card in the second story window of a narrow brick building. Inside the room a light was burning.

There is a God after all.

Henry took the stairs two at a time.

The door on the second-storey landing was ajar. Inside was a man on his knees, fiddling with the adjustment of a dentist's chair. He jumped up when Henry knocked. "My first patient of the day!" he exclaimed brightly.

Henry nodded. It was easier than speaking.

"Sit here and let's have a look." The dentist was a stringy middle-aged man with quick nervous movements, like an excitable bird. He talked continuously, the sort of person country folk described as "all chat and chortle." When his fingers fluttered close to his patient's sore mouth, Henry shrank back in the chair.

"Open up now," Hamilton said, "This will only take a minute . . . That's a good fellow."

Henry mumbled, "You sure this is painless?"

"Absolutely."

The next quarter-hour was the most painful Henry had ever endured. At the end of it, Hamilton triumphantly flourished a bloody molar. "Never seen a longer root," he announced happily.

"Keep it. Frame it." Henry rinsed his mouth and spat blood. "I thought you said it was painless."

"It didn't hurt me," Hamilton chirped. "Ha, ha."

"Ha, ha," echoed Henry. "Maybe it didn't hurt you, but I will. I'll wring your neck with pleasure."

"An hour from now you'll be singing my praises. Sit still while I pack that hole with cotton. Tell all your friends about me, will you?"

At that moment the room reverberated to the sound of a shell exploding somewhere nearby. Hamilton flinched violently. For a moment the dentist's mask of jollity slipped and Henry saw naked fear in his eyes.

"That was too close. I'd go home if I were you," Henry advised. Then he realized that the little man's clothes were very wrinkled and there was a growth of stubble on his face. "Have you been sleeping here?" he guessed.

"I . . . uh . . . yes. I have digs in Hammond Lane, you see. Right by the Four Courts. Since the shelling started I can't get home. Not that there's anyone waiting for me. The wife died years ago, and the children are . . ." He gave an eloquent shrug that somehow encompassed all birds flown from the nest.

"Listen here to me," said Henry. "Close up shop and go to Lower Gardiner Street, number 16. Tell Louise Kearney that Henry Mooney sent you, and she's to give you a basin of hot water and a proper bed." Taking out his watch, Henry added, "It's a few minutes after twelve, but tell her I said you should have a good breakfast too."

"I thought you wanted to wring my neck."

"I still do," Henry assured him, "but it can wait. In the meantime do as I tell you."

The grateful dentist shook Henry's hand. "The extraction is free, Mr. Mooney, there's no charge to you."

"Nonsense," Henry replied, digging into his pocket, "I

always pay what I owe. Now let me tell you the safest route to Gardiner Street."

The two men left the building together. Henry turned toward the river and Hamilton went the other way.

The Free State forces were distracted by watching the fire that now engulfed the rear of the building, so Henry was able to get closer to the Four Courts than he had since the bombardment began. When no one was looking, he managed to slip between a pair of armored Lancias and enter the gate nearest the east wing.

A moment later the world exploded.

Chapter Forty-one

Henry was flung violently onto his back.

The shock of concussion numbed; the roar of collapsing masonry deafened. All the breath had been knocked out of him. A gasping inhalation made his chest muscles spasm with pain.

God in heaven, it is the end of the world.

A huge pall of dust and smoke boiled outward, enveloping the universe and Henry Mooney.

HailMaryfullofgracethe-Lordiswiththeeblessedartthouamongstwomenandblessed isthefruitofthywombJesus.

He could not breathe, could not see. Another desperate inhalation, but nothing filled his lungs.

HolyMarymotherofGodprayforussinnersnowandatthehour ofourdeathAmen.

The next thing Henry knew he was on his hands and knees. Crawling. Crawling because it seemed the only safe form of locomotion. Crawling not away from, but toward, the direction of the explosion. *Men might be dying in there.* He rubbed his arm across his face to clear his eyes and looked up—then recoiled from what he saw.

An immense column of dark smoke towered hundreds of feet over the Four Courts. Within the column leaped tongues of lurid red flame, like a vision of hell.

Henry staggered to his feet. A piece of blazing debris fell

on his shoulder. He brushed it away only to be inundated by similar material. Tiny hot sparks stung his face and hands like vicious insects while he slapped frantically at his clothing to keep from being set afire.

Around him soldiers were running in every direction. Shouting, cursing, gesticulating. Waving their rifles in the air. Getting in each other's way.

Flames leaped toward the great dome, clawing with crimson fingers as if guided by a malign will. Meanwhile a rising wind caught the smoke from the explosion and rolled it toward the east, resculpting it into thunderheads. From them fluttered a strange snow. Millions of minuscule pieces of paper began falling over Dublin.

Henry tried to reach the central block, but his way was blocked by men and vehicles. To approach further would be to risk getting shot. At that moment no one seemed quite sane, and certainly no one was in charge.

As the first fire brigade vehicles came screaming down the quays, a figure clambered over the rubble with his jacket on fire and lurched straight toward Henry. Tall, thin. A crop of black curls.

Whipping off his own jacket, Henry ran toward the man and enveloped him in fabric while he beat desperately at the flames.

Please God. Just this once more. Not Ned. Please.

A stench of scorched fabric and hair. A muffled voice gasping, "Jaysus, stop, will you? You've put out the fire but you're suffocating me."

Henry peeled away the jacket to find a smoke-blackened but unfamiliar face staring at him. "Bless you," the stranger murmured.

"Here, let's get you out of this." Henry led him away from the conflagration. "You sure you're not injured?"

The other man coughed, shook his head, gingerly felt his arms and torso. "Don't seem to be. A bit shaken, that's all."

"What the hell happened in there? Did the field guns . . . ?"

"Not the guns. Us. Our main munitions dump was in the cellar of the Public Records Office."

Henry gazed dumbfounded at the blizzard of tiny bits of

paper drifting down upon them. The entire contents of the Public Records Office, historical records and legal documents of every description, some dating back to the twelfth century. Falling like the snow of other days.

"What set off the explosion?" he asked through dry lips. "The fire I saw earlier?"

"I dunno; maybe some of our officers did it on purpose. Couldn't let the enemy have our ammunition and gelignite, could we? They're going to overrun this position soon; we already had the whole place mined to take out as many as we could. Say, that was a bloody brave thing you did, coming to help me. Didn't you realize the bloody traitors might shoot you too?"

"Traitors?" Henry repeated blankly.

"The bloody Free Staters, of course. But they won't win. To get back the Republic we'll kill every one of them if we have to—unless they kill every one of us first."

Henry did not return to number 16 until very late that night. Louise was waiting for him. "What's happened how are you I thought you were dead!"

"Take it handy, Louise. I'm not even hurt."

"But just look at you! There's blood and soot all over you."

"I was helping get some of the wounded out of the Four Courts. At the time of the big explosion almost forty Free State soldiers had reached the central hall, and many of them were badly hurt. Miraculously, though, no one was killed. Even me," he added with a weary chuckle. "Blocks of masonry were flying through the air like kites. It's a sight I'll never forget, and I hope never to see another like it."

"I was terribly worried because I didn't know where you were or what was happening. None of the lodgers went to work today, so I tried to get one or two to go looking for you, but nobody would. Cowards. I'm going to raise their rent."

"Did a man called Hamilton show up here?"

"He did, the poor soul, and him exhausted. I gave him a meal and the room across from yours and haven't seen him since."

Henry longed for his own bed, but Louise had planted

herself between him and the staircase. "Is the fighting over?"

"Only at the Four Courts," he replied. "Around three-thirty the Republicans raised a white flag on a pole and asked for terms, but Paddy O'Daly insisted on unconditional surrender. At last Liam Mellows and Rory O'Connor led their men out. A lot of them were just lads, leaning against each other, they were so weary.

"A surrender document had already been drawn up. Leave it to Mick Collins to think of that in advance. Ernie O'Malley signed the surrender for the Four Courts garrison and myself and some of the other press men served as witnesses. Then O'Daly demanded the Republicans turn over their weapons, which they did—except for O'Malley. He threw his revolver into the river. I heard him say, "Here's an offering for Mother Liffey.""[1]

"What about the rest of the city, Henry? What's happening there?"

"The Republicans are holding the east side of O'Connell Street and they have posts in the Rotunda, Lower Abbey Street, Moran's Hotel, and what's left of the Customs House. They mean to fight to the last man—or woman. There's a contingent of Cumann na mBan nurses in the Hammam Hotel."

Louise crossed herself. "God-a-mercy."

ONCE more there was hand-to-hand combat in the streets of Dublin. Snipers, grenades, armored cars, landmines . . . the entire ugly paraphernalia of war. Free State forces, working street by street and house by house, took over four hundred Republican prisoners. During the first days of July most of the east side of Upper O'Connell Street was destroyed when the Crown, the Granville and Hammam hotels were bombarded by Free State troops. Artillery demolished the temporary GPO and the Hibernian Bible Society as well.

Curious crowds gathered behind sandbags to watch the final hours of the drama. Oscar Traynor and most of his staff had taken up headquarters in Barrys Hotel in Great Denmark Street, from which base they ordered the evacuation of the O'Connell Street positions. Cathal Brugha, together with seventeen men and three women, refused to leave the Hammam. They held out until evening, when Brugha finally ordered everyone out before the building collapsed. They surrendered to a company of Free State soldiers in a laneway at the rear of the hotel. But Cathal Brugha was not with them.

Henry sadly recorded: "Suddenly Cathal Brugha appeared in the doorway of the blazing hotel. He had a revolver in each hand. Friends and enemies alike called to him to surrender. He shouted, 'Never!' and ran forward firing both guns in the air. A volley of rifle fire cut him down.

"Ironically, the bravest man in Ireland died at the hands of his former comrades-in-arms."

Next morning Henry managed to speak briefly to Michael Collins. The chairman of the Provisional Government was, as usual, on his way between offices, loaded down with three briefcases. While he paused to talk to Henry, a member of his former squad stood less than two yards away with one hand in his pocket. The man never moved, but his eyes were never still.

Collins was visibly grieved at Brugha's death. "Cathal was so sincere I would have forgiven him anything. At his worst he was a fanatic, but he fought in what has been a noble cause. At best I numbered him among the very few who would have given their all so this country should have its freedom."[2]

"That sounds like a speech. Can I quote you, Mick?"

"You can of course. I'm not ashamed of my admiration for a brave Republican. You'll not hear *me* calling any of *them* traitors," he added with ill-concealed bitterness. "Speaking of brave Republicans, did you hear about Ernie O'Malley?"

"What about him?"

"He's escaped. Simply strolled away while O'Daly was gathering the prisoners in the old distillery before transporting them to Mountjoy." Abruptly, Collins flashed the old grin. "Ernie saw his chance and took it; I couldn't have done better myself."

"Good on him," Henry could not resist saying. "Listen here to me, Mick. Can you give me a pass to the Four

Courts? I'd like to write an eyewitness account of the damage."

"Just don't get yourself killed too," Collins warned. "The feckin' place isn't safe."

The area was still barricaded and heavily patrolled to keep back the hordes of sightseers. Continued explosions of the munitions stored in the cellars had made the situation too dangerous for the fire brigade, so the fire had been allowed to burn itself out. What remained was a blackened shell.

An eerie echoing place as sinister as a murder scene and giving off the same chill.

The pillared drum that had supported the dome was gutted. The great copper dome had collapsed, a ruin of melted metal, into the rotunda below. Daylight streamed through gaps in the walls torn by artillery fire. In the chambers off the central hall the marble floors were buried beneath a welter of charred debris, torn blankets, stale food, burnt paper, and broken weapons. It was possible to trace the painful evacuation, chamber by chamber, as the Republicans were driven back from their positions and eventually crowded together into the farthest reaches of the building.

It's the GPO all over again, Henry thought. *The future the same as the past. Round and round we go and nothing changes.*

He returned to number 16 in a grim mood. As he put his trilby on the hat rack he told his cousin, "This war isn't over; it's only beginning, Louise. And it will be worse than the Tan War ever was. I've seen their faces. I've heard their voices. O'Connor and Mellows and Barry are in prison, but the rest will carry the fight out of the city and all over Ireland. I need to pack my suitcase."

She was startled. "Leave Dublin, you mean? Now? Why?"

"Today Michael Collins told me the Provisional Government's decided to reinstitute censorship to withhold vital information from the IRA—another unpleasant policy we've inherited from the British. It means that all sorts of things can happen without anyone knowing—unless someone makes a mighty effort to record what's really going on. I've elected me. Most Dublin journalists are unfamiliar with the countryside, but I know it like the roof of my mouth, so I'm going back in the war-correspondent business. Besides, it will give me a chance to look for Ned."

"I thought he was in Clare."

"According to Little Business he hasn't been at the farm for weeks."

"But what about Mrs. Rutledge? Should you not be staying here for her sake? For that matter, Henry, should you not . . ."

Her voice went on but he was no longer listening. Instead Henry was standing once more on the staircase in Herbert Place. Edwin below him and Ella above, emerging from her studio with her hair disheveled and a smear of yellow paint on her cheek.

". . . bring her back here with you?" Louise was saying.

His eyes stared past her into memory. "Funnily enough, that's what I meant to do."

"Then why didn't you? Was she not willing?"

"She was. I wasn't."

Edwin shouting at his sister, "If you leave this house with this man you can never come back!"

Ella, stricken, tears filling her eyes. "Brother mine, say you don't mean that."

"Oh, but I do. If you go off with a Republican, I never want to hear your name spoken again."

You weren't willing?" Louise was struggling to understand. "But I thought you loved her, Henry."

"With all my heart."

"Then why?"

"That's why."

His cousin clucked her tongue. "You're as daft as a brush, Henry Mooney."

I suppose I am, he thought as he climbed the stairs to his room.

When he had closed the door behind him, he sat down and looked once more at an article he was working on. "From the day of their founding, the Irish Volunteers possessed an extraordinary esprit de corps," he had written. "Youthful fellowship, ardent patriotism, and the chivalrous ideals of those who inspired them worked a special alchemy. They lived life to the full yet were ready to die without hesitation for one another. In a few short years the tight-knit family of the Volunteers accomplished more for Ireland than generations had done before them. Yet those same men are now divided by a civil war. There is nothing more cruel."

Henry put the article aside and stood up. Moving briskly in a futile attempt to keep ahead of the pain, he began to pack his suitcase.

Before leaving Dublin he telephoned the office of the *Clare Champion*. He was not sure the phone call would be put through, but the Dublin operator proved to be a Clare woman. Henry had once reported glowingly on her sister's wedding, and after a few moments of chat she made the connection for him. "I have to listen, though," she warned. "But I won't cut you off unless you're talking sedition."

"How do you define 'sedition'?"

"I have no idea," she replied with a laugh.

Over a crackling connection Sarsfield Maguire told Henry, "The Republicans are solidly in control in Ennis. Liam Lynch is reported to be attacking the government garrison in Limerick."

"If the IRA's holding Ennis, is Ned Halloran with them?"

"Don't think so; I certainly haven't seen him. But Michael Brennan's commanding the Free Staters in Limerick now. Could Halloran be with them?"

"I seriously doubt it," said Henry.

"What's happening your side of the country?"

"De Valera was among the Republicans who escaped Dublin; he's with the IRA in Clonmel. Ernie O'Malley's seized Enniscorthy."

"Can you get us an exclusive interview with either of them? We could print it once the government comes to its senses and lifts the censorship."

"Afraid I can't help you right now, Sarsfield. I'm coming west myself."

Leaning his forehead against the train window, Henry stared through smeared glass at the landscape rolling past. Jammed against his feet was his suitcase, which contained twelve new notebooks, his clothes, and his pistol.

• • •

WHEN Henry reached Limerick his first stop was the *Limerick Leader*, where he was told, "Liam Lynch has set up headquarters just outside of town. He's engaged in truce talks with Michael Brennan at the moment. Brennan says he might agree to a truce with the Southern Command to keep them from marching on Dublin. But even if there is a truce, it might not last. General O'Duffy wants to defeat the IRA outright, on the battlefield."

"What have you heard from the rest of the country?" Henry wanted to know.

"Ernie O'Malley's in Wexford. He's captured Wexford town and allowed the Free Staters garrisoned there to leave unmolested. Bloody shame we can't print that; it's a good story."

Henry's next call was to his mother's house. Before he had taken off his hat, his mother was berating him for leaving her alone to be murdered in her bed.

"Since you warned us, Bernard's taken to sleeping here most nights and Noel looks in when he can," Pauline assured Henry. "You needn't worry; we haven't seen any soldiers. They're on the Cork road or the Dublin road but they don't come this way."

In Hannah Mooney's imagination, however, the house was surrounded and under fire. "Ye'll stay here where you belong and that's all I'm going to say about that!" she shouted at her oldest son.

Out of the side of his mouth Henry said to Pauline, "Someone once suggested I cherish my mother, and I thought this would be a good time to give it a try. I must have been mad."

When he left the house he could hear Hannah shrieking after him, but he did not look back.

Henry checked into the Glentworth Hotel, which was bravely attempting to conduct business as normal. As he stood at the front desk the bark of a rifle sounded in the street outside. The desk clerk flinched violently. "Doesn't that bother you?" he asked the new guest.

"I've heard plenty of gunfire lately," Henry told him. "I duck, but I don't flinch."

He began searching out old contacts and learning as much as he could about the situation. No one could tell him anything about Ned Halloran. In the confusion of the moment it was impossible to locate anyone below officer rank by name.

"Liam Lynch appears to be fighting a largely defensive war," Henry commented in his notebook. "The IRA is winning some victories but their overall situation is not good. This war blew up without their being prepared. Now they are sending for the Republican forces in the north to come to their aid, leaving the Ulster Catholics unprotected against Protestant abuses. This will mean a cessation of hostilities in the Six Counties, but at a dreadful price.

"Lynch's opposite number, Eoin O'Duffy, is making sure the Free Staters are constantly resupplied by the government, but the Republicans have to commandeer supplies from the citizenry, or get them through outright looting. This is undermining the popularity they enjoyed when they were fighting the Tans." He chewed on his pencil for a moment, then added. "Note: the Free Staters want to be called 'the National Army,' just as they want the Republicans called 'Irregulars.' "

Put a label on something. Create an image and convince people that the label is the reality, he thought sourly. *Like the "Sinn Féin Rebellion."*

No sooner was a truce effected between Lynch and Brennan than word reached the city that massive Free State reinforcements from Dublin were on their way toward Limerick. Lynch was expected to fall back.

"Not many of our boys have any great mind for killing former comrades," a Republican confided to Henry. He recorded the conversation in his notebook for inclusion in his next report to the American newspapers, adding, "From my own observation I believe this to be true."[3]

On sudden impulse, Henry set off for Ennis. He had little hope that Ned would have returned to the farm, and did not know what he would say to him if he had. Ursula would be there—Ursula, who was so straightforward and saw things so clearly. She had become like the Pole Star to Henry, a fixed point in a dizzily wheeling firmament.

Only Norah Daly was in the house when Henry arrived unannounced. He had hitched a ride from the train station on a haywagon, arriving at the farm with prickles down the back of his neck and wisps of hay on his suit. Norah helped him brush off his clothes, then took him into the garden, where six rosy-faced children were playing under the supervision of Lucy Halloran. He hardly recognized them as the pale, frightened little refugees from Belfast. "They'll have to go home when it's safe, of course," said Norah, "but there's no hurry at all. We love having them here."

A few minutes later there was a thunder of hooves and a wiry girl on a dark horse came galloping up to the house. When she saw Henry outside, she let out a whoop of delight and slid from her mount. She had the same strangling hug for Henry as always—stronger than ever because she was very fit.

"Take it easy, Little Business!" he protested.

"I'm Ursula," she reminded him. "Little Business is a nickname for a little girl."

"You'll always be a little girl to me."

She relinquished her hold and stepped back. "No," she said, fixing him with her direct gaze. The blue eyes of her childhood had become grayer, smoky. "No, I won't."

The adults went inside for tea and conversation, leaving the children to play. Henry learned that Ned had not been home in many weeks. An occasional note was passed to his family, giving no more information than that he was well and thinking of them. But he could be anywhere—anywhere with the Republican forces.

"Of course we're all Republicans here," Ursula said proudly. "Both Norah and I have joined Cumann na mBan. Each branch has its own intelligence officer; did you know that, Uncle Henry?"

"I'm going to be sorry I asked this, but are you an intelligence officer, Little . . . Ursula?"

Her eyes gleamed. "Not yet, but maybe when I'm sixteen. In the meantime there's lots to do, though. We carry messages and act as couriers—I'm to learn to drive a motorcar as soon as I'm old enough!—and arrange for safe houses, and even paint news on walls so our lads will know what's happening elsewhere."

Henry gave a wry chuckle. "Going to put me out of business, are you?"

"Oh, Uncle Henry, we have to counter the effects of censorship somehow. Is that not what you're doing?"

"I can't publish anything that would be useful to the Republicans. Only the Free State gets good press. Meanwhile I'm trying to collect information that will give a true picture of what happened when this is over."

"I hope you're going to tell everyone just how terrible the Free Staters and the British—"

"Whoa there!" Henry held up his hand. "I said a true picture. Do you have any idea how monstrous a civil war is, Ursula? There are good people on both sides. On all sides, for that matter. When it's over, and it will be over, hatred must be forgotten. If I write anything that perpetuates it, I become part of the evil."

She gave him a measuring look. "Are you on Collins' side, then? Papa said you were."

Henry had never lost his temper with the girl, but now he came close. "God's garters! I'm trying very hard not to be on anyone's 'side.' I'm for Ireland and what's best for Ireland."

"So is Papa."

Henry's shoulders sagged. "I know."

Norah changed the subject. "How is Mrs. Rutledge? We like her so much. Will you tell her that you saw the children and they're well?"

He smiled and nodded, not trusting himself to speak.

"And your wedding in October—will you still have it then? In spite of, well, in spite of everything?" Something in his eyes alerted her and she dropped her voice. "Everything is all right between the two of you, is it not?"

"It is," he said. "Everything is just grand."

Before leaving Ennis, Henry called in to the *Clare Champion* for the latest news. "The IRA in Cork City has taken over the *Examiner* and made Frank Gallagher editor!"[4] Ma-

guire told him excitedly. "Gallagher's a friend of yours, is
he not?"

"I hope so," Henry said.

Maguire went on: "They're holding a line whose northern
borders extend from Enniscorthy to Kilkenny and south of
Limerick. In addition to Ennis there are strong pockets of
resistance from Galway to Donegal. None of this can be
published, of course. Makes the IRA look too good. But
we're quite free to publish stories that show the Free State
Army winning. For example, we just learned that Seán
MacEoin has captured the bridge at Killaloe. Now the way's
open for him to march straight into Limerick with a large
force. I'd say the truce between Lynch and Brennan will be
broken by sundown tomorrow."

Henry borrowed a bicycle and hurried to Killaloe in hopes
of an interview.

MacEoin had set up temporary headquarters in the Lake
Hotel on the Ballina side of the bridge. Leading up to it was
a narrow road choked with military vehicles of every description. Across the river, easily visible from the hotel
grounds, was the ancient ring fort where Brian Bóru had
been born a thousand years earlier.

On the front steps of the hotel stood Commandant
MacEoin, supervising the loading of his personal gear into
a lorry. His green Free State uniform was crisp and new.
His brown boots were highly polished. "You can tell your
readers that Limerick will be secure in government hands
very soon," he assured Henry. "The Irregulars are only
trained for guerrilla warfare, and they're underequipped for
that. With our armored cars and field guns we have an in-
surmountable advantage."

"You sound very confident."

"I am, Mooney. I learned my optimism from Liam Lynch,
in fact. Many's the evening we've talked philosophy together. Liam never entertains the possibility of losing."

"But one of you must," Henry pointed out.

"Indeed," MacEoin gravely replied, "one of us must."

Henry returned the bicycle to the *Champion* with his interview. Then he set off to cover the war.

The Provisional Government broke the Limerick truce.

After two days of fierce fighting and considerable destruction of property, Free State forces held undisputed control of the city. Lynch fell back to Kilmallock and another hard-fought battle.

Following the shifting tides of war was not easy. The Republicans were blowing up bridges and mining trains to destroy government supply lines, making rail travel unreliable. Occasionally Henry was able to hitch a ride, but it was almost impossible to borrow a bicycle; most of them had been commandeered by the IRA. At last Henry found a lanky farm boy who produced a rusty machine from beneath a haystack and sold it to him for an exorbitant price.

One of these days I'm going to learn to drive and buy a motorcar, he promised himself. *Something bigger than a damned Delage.*

Chapter Forty-two

On the twelfth of July a War Council was appointed by the Provisional Government. Michael Collins was made commander in chief of the Free State Army. Eight days later the Dáil was informed that both Limerick and Waterford were under the total control of the government.

Henry Mooney was in Carrick-on-Suir at the time, observing Republican preparations to defend against advancing government forces. Anxious citizens watched from doorways. One little golden-haired child ran out into the road chasing a hen, and her mother dashed after her to carry her back into the safety of the house. At the doorway the woman paused with her hand cradling the back of her child's head, and glanced fearfully up and down the street. Both directions.

"It is neither Free Stater nor Republican the people fear," Henry wrote. "It is simply War."

For the sake of the townspeople the IRA ultimately decided not to try to hold the town, and fell back.

As he was riding his bicycle down a lonely country road a sudden spate of machine-gun fire burst from a hedgerow. Bullets slammed into the plowed field beside him, sending up sprays of dirt from the furrows like hailstones striking a pond.

Rifle fire responded from another hedgerow.

Wouldn't do any good to show 'em my press card, he thought, pedaling furiously until he was out of range.

THE pace of war increased. Henry saw dead men piled in ditches and streams of blood running between the cobbles of village streets: the nightmare landscape from his childhood come back to haunt him.

At three in the morning, when he surveyed the landscape of his own life and saw it littered with loss, he thought he would welcome the oblivion a bullet could bring.

A few nights he spent in hotels; most he passed in army encampments. Talking a little, listening more.

"I really thought the Big Fellow would break the Treaty, unite the IRA, and march on the north," a Republican told him. "We'd have followed him to hell itself if he'd done that. Why didn't he?"

When his travels took Henry behind Free State lines, he frequently observed photographers making a pictorial record of well-equipped, confident troops. Often the shots were artificially composed to show Free State soldiers vanquishing an unseen enemy. "On whose orders?" Henry asked a cameraman.

"Desmond FitzGerald," was the reply. "He's a blinkin' genius at propaganda."

Once, in a sunlit field, Henry saw a photographer recording a company of captured Free State soldiers playing a game of hurley while their Republican guard stood watch, cheering the good plays.[1]

For some the sunlight was blotted out forever. On the last day of July, government soldiers came upon two Republicans in the Grand Hotel in Skerries, in North County Dublin. One was the quartermaster for the Eastern Command of the IRA—Harry Boland.

A scuffle ensued during which Boland was shot in the stomach. He was taken to Saint Vincent's Hospital in Dublin, where a letter was found in his pocket from Michael Collins. The letter expressed profound disappointment at Boland's loyalty to de Valera. "Harry—it has come to this! Of all the things it has come to this. It is in my power to arrest you and destroy you. This I cannot do."[2]

Boland's sister visited him in hospital. When she asked who shot him, Boland replied, "The only thing I'll say is that it was a friend of my own who was in Lewes Prison with me. I'll never tell the name and don't try to find out. I forgive him and want no reprisals. I want to be buried in the grave in Glasnevin with Cathal Brugha."[3]

Two days later he was dead.

Michael Collins remarked, "I'd send a wreath, but I suppose they'd return it torn up."[4]

HENRY Mooney wrote, "Depending on one's viewpoint there are several names for the war which ended with the truce of 1921: the Tan War, the Anglo-Irish War, the War of Independence. But there is only one name for what is happening now: the War of Brothers."

THE fighting grew increasingly desperate in the south. Almost every town and village was the subject of an intense struggle. The commander in chief of the Free State forces was driving himself and all those about him at a fever pitch. Only a proportion of the government troops were former Volunteers; the majority were raw recruits who had to be transformed overnight into an efficient fighting force. With his energies concentrated on the war, Collins was forced to leave more and more of the business of running the country in the hands of others. He resigned as chairman of the Provisional Government and W. T. Cosgrave was appointed acting chairman.

In his early forties, Cosgrave was a refined-looking man with a sharply cut nose. He had once possessed a flowing mane of golden hair and a matching mustache, but these had been shaved off by British prison guards after Easter Week, 1916. They grew back but were never as luxuriant again. W. T. was considered a good choice as chairman; the sort of man who would value principle over power. With him in charge, Collins could devote himself to strategy.

The war must be won so that the peace could be built along with the new state.

Ships from Dublin, heavily laden with munitions, traveled around the coast to land government troops in Cork and Kerry. They included members of the Dublin Guard, which in turn included former members of Michael Collins' assassination squad. Hardened men trained to unquestioning violence at the command of their leader.

The government's plan was to encircle the IRA in its stronghold and force a final victory. It was more likely that the conflict would become a grim war of attrition in the rural wilderness.

Henry reached Cork City on the tenth of August, only hours ahead of the Free State forces. The IRA was tearing up roads and railways and blowing up bridges to slow their progress. However, the Free State Army was launching a three-pronged attack supported by reinforcements landed on the coast, and the outcome was inevitable. Michael Collins, Cork man to the soul, was determined to claim the southern capital for the government.

Before the fighting for the city began, Henry called in to the *Cork Examiner*. To his relief, Frank Gallagher gave him a friendly welcome and a typist to transcribe his most recent notes. "Don't suppose I could use your telephone?" Henry ventured. "I would like to get a call through to Dublin."

"So would we all," Gallagher replied. "Give it a try." But after a frustrating half hour listening to crackling wires, dead lines, and operators who pretended not to hear him, Henry gave up.

"I'll wager the Free Staters can make a phone call if they want to," said Gallagher resentfully. "Say, would you like to go for a jar while it's still quiet?"

As the two men were getting their hats, they heard the roar of engines in the street.

They ran outside.

A large convoy of lorries and motorcars, bristling with guns, had set out from IRA headquarters at Union Quay. Republicans rode on top as well as inside. Henry was astonished to observe none other than Erskine Childers crouched on a running board. He looked very small and slight in his mackintosh; his face was shrunk nearly to the bone. Before Henry could call to his old friend the car roared past and was gone.

Henry ran into the street and finally succeeded in flagging down a lorry. "Where the hell are you going?"

The front-seat passenger, a rugged mountain man with forty years of living ground into the seams of his face, was crying. "We been ordered to evacuate. They tell us we don't stand a chance here."

His words confirmed what Henry already knew. Yet hearing them, and seeing the defeat and bafflement, the rage and grief contorting the faces of the departing men, was like a blow to the belly. For one irrational moment he wanted to shout at them, "Stand and fight! You mustn't give up!"

The driver of the lorry leaned across his passenger to say, "I'd step back if I were you. We've our ordnance crammed into these things, piled in any old way just to get it out of the city. This lorry's loaded with bombs, and I can't vouch for their stability."

Henry took a hasty step backward.

The vehicle pulled away.

An hour later, Collins' men strode in to the city unchallenged. "Local boy makes good," Frank Gallagher observed to Henry Mooney. "I suspect you'll be able to get that telephone call through in another hour or so."

"What are you going to do?"

"Stay here with the paper, I suppose, like the captain of a sinking ship."

Collins himself did not enter Cork City with the Free State Army. The commander in chief was conducting a tour of inspection through the southwest and was currently believed to be in Tralee, but was expected within a day or two.

He did not arrive. When Henry finally got his telephone call through to Dublin, he was told by a distraught Kathleen MacKenna, "Oh, Henry, Arthur's dead!"

"What are you saying? Arthur who?"

"Arthur Griffith. He died of a cerebral hemorrhage this morning. We've sent word to Mick Collins to come back for the funeral."

• • •

EAMON de Valera, who was being hunted by government
forces, did not dare appear in public at Arthur Griffith's
funeral.

Tributes were pouring in. The one Henry chose for the
articles he would send abroad came from Seán MacEoin,
who said, "Griffith sacrificed his life—a life of great ability—for the Irish people. He was the poorest man in Ireland
when he died."[5] Henry added, "Though no one would know
it to look at him these past months, when he was worn down
by overwork and constant strain, Arthur Griffith was only
fifty."

Michael Collins, holding his face in rocklike impassivity,
marched at the head of the funeral procession. He was not
yet thirty-two.

"He looks ten years older than he did the last time I saw
him," Henry told Louise afterward. "Black hearses, black
horses, and black hats—this isn't the Dublin I fell in love
with years ago."

"What about the woman you fell in love with? Would you
not stop here a few days before you go back down the country, and see her?"

"I am going to remain here for several days," he replied.
"I need some time to polish my articles for abroad before I
send them."

"That doesn't answer my question."

Henry pretended not to hear.

THE war had not touched Herbert Place. As he stood across
the street from Ella's house, Henry wistfully observed the
serene residential neighborhood. Leafy trees, blooming gardens. A nanny pushing an elaborate Victorian pram with a
long fringe to protect its small occupant from the sun.

It might almost have been last year: the year of hope,
1921.

He thrust his hands deep into his pockets and turned away.
Walking, solitary, through Dublin. Back towards the north
side.

• • •

H ENRY hoped for a personal interview with Michael Collins about Arthur Griffith. As usual, Collins was making room in his crowded schedule to meet journalists and to see prominent visitors from abroad. The Provisional Government must be seen to be functioning. In addition he was trying to balance the competing agendas of military and civic government, and the stresses between north and south. The date of his wedding to Kitty Kiernan had been set as August twenty-second. That was now postponed.

Before Henry had a chance to talk with him, on the twentieth of August Michael Collins left the city. "The commander in chief has gone south to resume his tour of inspection," Henry was told when he called at Collins' office. "He's taken Emmet Dalton with him. They'll be in Cork City all day tomorrow."

Unsatisfied with the answer, Henry next paid a call on Liam Tobin. "Was it not reckless of Mick to go to Cork right now? The county's still anti-Treaty almost to a man. Liam Lynch has some two thousand men in the area."

Tobin replied, "The Big Fellow's not worried. You know what he said to me? 'Och, no one would shoot me in me own county.' "

"Not on purpose, perhaps, but . . . Why is he really down there? Surely he has plenty of staff officers for inspection tours."

"Well . . . you can't print this, Henry, until he gives the word . . . but he's hoping to meet with de Valera and arrange a truce. He told me he's going to try to bring the boys around.[6] He's persuaded a number of prominent Cork men to support the initiative. Mick's not as reckless as he seems."

Henry briefly closed his eyes. "Thank God."

He returned to number 16 to work on other articles, but found himself writing a letter to Ursula instead.

"It's only a matter of time until the war is over," he told her. "Collins' people believe it will be a few weeks at the most. If you have any way to get in touch with your father, please ask him to contact me. I shall be at Louise Kearney's for another week or so, possibly longer." He stared at the paper for a while, then added, "If you don't hear from Ned, write to me anyway. Just to write me."

Three days later, as Henry was coming downstairs for his tea, the first of Louise's lodgers returned from his day's work. The man had a special edition of the *Irish Times* in his hand and a stunned expression on his face.

Henry took the paper from his nerveless fingers. With a sense of disbelief he read: "General Michael Collins, commander in chief of the National Army, was the victim of an ambush by Irregulars at Béal na mBláth, between Macroom and Bandon, on last night (Tuesday). At the end of the engagement, which lasted close upon an hour, the commander in chief was fatally wounded by a single shot to the head. The killer or killers have not yet been captured."

Both our friends and our enemies think we'll never die, but we will.

OVER seven hundred Republican prisoners were being held in Kilmainham Jail. When they learned of Collins' death they went down on their knees to say the rosary for the repose of his soul.

Richard Mulcahy issued an order to the Free State Army. "Stand by your posts. Bend bravely and undaunted to your work. Let no cruel act of reprisal blemish your bright honor. Every dark hour that Michael Collins met since 1916 seemed but to steel that bright strength of his and temper his gay bravery. You are left each inheritors of that strength."[7]

Messages of tribute poured in from far beyond the shores of Ireland. Not only his friends, but his enemies, saluted him. Lord Birkenhead, who had taken part in the Treaty negotiations, said, "He was a complex and a very remarkable personality; daring, resourceful, volatile and merry. I have never doubted that both he and Mr. Griffith, having once given their word, would sacrifice life itself in order to carry out their promise."[8]

In a letter to Collins' sister, the cynical and witty Dublin-born playwright George Bernard Shaw wrote, "Tear up your mourning and hang up your brightest colors in his honor, and let us all praise God that he had not to die in a snuffy

bed of a trumpery cough, weakened by age, and saddened
by the disappointments that would have attended his work
had he lived."

HENRY tried to write an obituary, but the memory of
Mick's living face kept getting in the way. *What in God's
name can I say about him? Who could sum him up in a
paragraph, or even a volume? Mick was a law unto himself:
brilliant, boisterous, exuberant, maudlin . . . occasionally
immature. It's easy to forget how young he was.*

*He cold-bloodedly sent men out to kill, but what else does
a commander do in a war? He was also a warm, loving
man, totally devoted to his family and his people. A hero to
suit the need of the time. If he had lived, he might have
matured into a great statesman. But how does one come to
terms with the contradictions in his character?*

*Don't we all have them? What did Little Business say?
"I'm lots of different people. So are you."*

So are all of us, Little Business, Henry thought, putting
aside his pencil. *So was Michael Collins.*

COLLINS' funeral was the largest in living memory. In
Queenstown Harbor a crowd watched in a numbed silence
as his body was loaded on board ship to be transported from
Cork to Dublin, it not being deemed safe to send it by land.
Candles were burning in every window. When the ship
pulled out of the harbor, the mournful sound of a solo trumpet floated out across the water.

In Dublin mourners converged on the capital from the
four corners of Ireland. A Requiem Mass was celebrated in
the Pro-Cathedral; then the coffin was placed on a gun carriage for a procession which wound through the city before
making its sorrowful way to Glasnevin Cemetery.

The crowds were so dense at times it was impossible to
move at all. Men wept as openly as women.

Henry waited for the cortège in Merrion Street, outside
Government Buildings. As the procession was approaching,

a man standing beside him muttered under his breath, "It's a trick, you know."

"Sorry?"

"A trick to confuse the British. The Big Fellow's pulled some good ones in his time, but this takes the biscuit. Wait till the minister for finance gets the bill for this funeral! But it'll be worth every farthing. Just when the Brits think he's dead and take their eye off 'im, Collins'll sneak up on their flank and . . . and . . ." The man could not sustain the dream. Taking a handkerchief from his pocket, he blew his nose with a great honk.

A woman in the crowd turned to glare. Beneath the brim of her fashionable black hat, Henry recognized Ava Mansell. They exchanged nods; then she came over to him. "What a sad day this is, Henry."

"Indeed it is." He restrained himself from looking past her, searching for another face. "I trust you're not here alone?"

"Oh no, Edwin and Madge are with me." She gave a vague wave. "They're over there, engaging a motorcab for the drive to Glasnevin."

"Ella didn't come? Is she ill?" he asked anxiously.

"Nothing physical. She's just not going out much these days. You broke her heart, you know."

"I *what?*"

"It's a wonder I'm speaking to you at all, Henry Mooney, after you hurt her so terribly."

"What are you talking about, woman?"

"Don't play the innocent with me—I'm sure you know quite well. We returned from the theatre one night to find her in tears and Edwin in a perfect fury. Neither of them would say what had happened, but we got the impression you'd abandoned her."

Henry was deeply shocked. "Abandoned! My God. Nothing could be further from the truth."

People in the crowd around them were openly eavesdropping. The Irish loved gossip even more than funerals.

Taking Ava by the elbow, Henry steered her back from the street to a sheltering doorway. There he described his encounter with Edwin, concluding, "I love Ella deeply. I've never wanted anything but her happiness, Ava. You must believe that."

"What I believe isn't important. The fact remains, she's miserable. It's making me miserable too, because she's dearer to me than my own wretched relatives."

Her choice of adjectives surprised Henry. "Wretched?"

Ava's lips curled with contempt. "To my family I was never more than a commodity on the marriage market. But the Mansells love the person I am, warts and all, bless them."

Glimpsing the vulnerable woman behind the beautiful mask, Henry felt a sudden, unexpected kinship. "My mother despises me," he admitted. Ava lifted her eyebrows. He went on, "I've been a disappointment to Mam since the day I put on long trousers. And if my brothers and sisters speak to me at all, it's to complain. Ella is so lucky to have the family she does! That's what it comes down to—not politics or money or religion. I love her too much to destroy her relationship with her family. Rather than forcing her to choose between us, I simply left. Maybe a person has to be without something to know how much it's worth," he added.

Ava studied his face intently. "Does Ella know about your family?"

He shook his head. "I'm a very private person."

"So you left without explaining any of this to her?"

"I did what I thought was right, Ava."

"What you thought was right. Men!" She rolled her eyes heavenward. "You took it on yourself to act on her behalf. If that's not typical of the arrogant, pig-headed attitude that has subjugated women for so long!" Ava sounded disgusted. "Explain something else, Henry. Ella said she saw you in the street one day, fighting with Wallace Congreve. She thought you would come for her then. But you turned and went the other way."

"I hoped she would at least wave to me, give me some sign. When she didn't . . ."

"Ella can be pig-headed too, Henry. She felt it was up to you to make the first move. Instead you seemed to be abandoning her all over again—at least that's how she saw it."

"She's wrong! I'd fight for her to my dying breath. I'd

fight Congreve or anyone else . . . except her own brother."

"Well, I can fight him." Ava lifted her chin. "You wait right here, Henry Mooney. Don't dare step out of this door-way until I come back."

Before he could stop her, she melted into the crowd.

Henry tardily realized that the funeral cortège had passed. It was already moving away up the street. He had intended to follow, marching with the thousands who would accom-pany it on foot all the way to Glasnevin. Then he saw Ava coming back toward him with her arm firmly linked through Edwin Mansell's.

She pulled her husband into the doorway beside Henry. "Now then. I know people think I'm a frivolous fool with nothing in my head but clothes and parties, but that's be-cause I can afford to be. I have Edwin. You," she added to her husband, as if there were some danger he might not know whom she meant. "I've given thanks for you every day since we married and I want the same thing for Ella. Henry Mooney's a fine man and you know it, yet you've driven him away with your bloody-minded nonsense. You so rarely lose your temper that when you do, you make a fool of yourself. But this time I won't have it."

Her well-modulated voice filled with steel. "I won't have it, Edwin Mansell. You tell Henry that he is welcome in our house anytime and that you will be proud to marry your sister to him, or I will not sleep under your roof tonight. I'll take a suite at the Shelbourne and stay there until you come to your senses."

Fascinated eavesdroppers were gathering around the door-way.

Edwin muttered, "Ava, this is no place for—"

"This is the perfect place for! Did you hear what I said? If you didn't, all these people are witnesses and I'm sure they will be glad to repeat my words for you."

Edwin gave Henry an embarrassed look from his good eye. "I don't know what to say."

"Say yes, *avic*!" urged one of the onlookers. "We can fight each other but sure there's no fighting the women."

"I mean it," Ava warned her husband. "I expect you to be big enough to admit you were wrong. We shall be 'at home' as usual this coming Thursday, Henry, and I expect you to call. Tell him, Edwin."

"You see what I'm confronted with?" Edwin said to Henry instead.

"I'm beginning to."

Edwin summoned a rueful smile. "A good officer knows when he can no longer hold a position. I suppose there's nothing to be done but apologies. God knows I could use a friend at court," he added, holding out his hand.

Henry gave it a hearty shake.

"That's better," Ava said with an air of satisfaction that reminded Henry of Little Business dusting the parlor at number 16. "Now we must be on our way to the cemetery. Henry, would you care to share our cab?"

"I . . . mmm . . . I think not, thank you. I want to walk with the procession. He was my friend."

"Very well then. We'll expect you on Thursday afternoon at two." She steered her husband away as efficiently as she had steered him to Henry.

The journalist gazed in awe at her departing back.

"Yer wan," said an onlooker, a man whose rough clothes and rougher speech identified him as a Dublin guttie. "She a gorjus mot like that 'un?"

Henry blinked. "She's not a classical beauty like her sister-in-law, but to me she's . . ."

"S'all right," the other replied consolingly. "Me oul wan's no oil painting neither. But oo looks at the mantelpiece when 'e's pokin' the fire?"

In spite of himself Henry smiled.

The smile grew, spread across his face like sunlight thawing ice. It was inappropriate given the day, but he could not help it.

He began running to catch up with the funeral cortège.

WILD rumors were racing through the city: Collins had been shot by one of his own men; he had been the hapless victim of a ricochet bullet; he had been assassinated by the British because they were afraid he would abandon the treaty and go back to the Republicans.

When it was learned that Eamon de Valera had been seen in the village of Béal na mBláth only minutes after Collins' military convoy passed through, some believed the story of the attempted truce negotiations. Others insisted upon a more sinister interpretation.

A wave of anger unlike anything that had gone before swept Ireland. The fighting had stopped on both sides as a mark of respect during Collins' funeral, but now it resumed with unprecedented savagery.

HENRY was anxious to go down the country and try to learn the truth. After Thursday.

For Michael Collins the world had stopped permanently. For Henry Mooney it had stopped until Thursday.

Chapter Forty-three

Henry arrived at Herbert Place scrubbed, brushed, and polished, nattily attired in his best suit, his trilby, and an expensive new Arrow shirt with a collar so stiff it already was chafing his neck. His pocket watch informed him the hour was half past one. Ava had been explicit: *we'll expect you at two.*

Do everything right this time, you eejit. Don't go banging on the door early like an overanxious schoolboy.

But I am overanxious. What if Ella won't see me? What if . . . what if . . .

He bit his lip and turned away. Half an hour. Thankfully, he had something to keep him occupied. As he was leaving number 16 he had met a boy from Posts and Telegraphs coming up the steps with a letter. Addressed to Henry Mooney, in Ursula's handwriting.

Henry strolled off down the street until he was out of sight of the Mansell house, then took the letter from his pocket.

"We have news of Papa," Ursula had written. "He had not contacted us for some time, but in my new position with Cumann na mBan I have learned how to find out things through the IRA network. You will be proud of me."

I'm always proud of you, Little Business.

The letter continued, "When Michael Brennan chose the Free State side, Papa did not want to have to shoot men who had been his comrades in arms. So he joined the Eastern

Command under Ernie O'Malley. He was with the Republicans occupying Wexford Town. I suppose he did not let us know because he did not want to worry us, but he has been very ill in hospital there since the second week of August. Influenza."

Henry read the sentence again. *In hospital since the second week of August.*

A sense of profound relief washed over him. Until that moment, he had not admitted to himself just how afraid he had been that Ned Halloran's finger had pulled the fatal trigger at Béal na mBláth.

"Papa is slowly recovering," Ursula's letter went on, "but he will not be released for another few days. I am hopeful we can arrange for him to be sent home to convalesce. I looked up 'convalesce' in the dictionary you gave me so I could spell it."

At exactly two o'clock Henry knocked on the door in Herbert Place.

Ava herself opened the door. Drawing him inside, she whispered conspiratorially, "Ella doesn't know you're coming, but everything's arranged. At breakfast this morning Edwin announced that he had acted rashly when you were here last, and made a mistake he now regrets. He said he had no objections to you as a brother-in-law and hoped it wasn't too late."

"How did Ella respond to that?"

"She gave him a withering look, threw down her napkin, and left the table. She's been in her studio ever since. Go up to her."

Henry hesitated. "Will she let me in?"

"I doubt it. But this is your opportunity to demonstrate how you really feel." Ava's eyes twinkled. "The door to the studio isn't very heavy and the hinges are old—they'll pull right out of the wall under a strong enough blow. Like a man's shoulder. A determined man."

"The army needs a strategist like you," Henry remarked.

"Once you're inside," Ava continued, "tell her exactly what you told me the other day. About your mother, your family, everything. If you really love her, you must give her a chance to understand."

"Even if she does, do you think she'll forgive me?"

"I can't say if she'll ever forgive you or Edwin, but you won't know unless you try. Scoot, now." She gave him a little shove.

Lingering in the hall, Ava listened to the sounds from upstairs. A knock. A louder knock. Then a sudden ferocious crash.

Smiling, she went to the telephone and rang her husband's office. "Edwin dear," she said, "I'm afraid we shall have to replace the studio door."

D EAR Ursula,

"You cannot know how thankful I am to have news of Ned. You and Norah will take the best possible care of him and soon have him on his feet again. He has not been truly well for a long time, so perhaps this is enforced rest is just what he needs.

"On a happier note, we are counting on having you here on the twenty-first of October. If Ned does not want to come I shall understand, but Ella wants you for her bridesmaid. It is to be a very small ceremony. You will require a white dress with a blue sash, the women tell me."

A FTER so much tragedy it seemed as if the tide had begun to turn for Henry, if not for Ireland. Michael Collins' death had made international headlines. Newspapers and periodicals in America were clamoring for hard news from Ireland. "No more 'Irish color,' " Henry remarked with satisfaction to Louise as he waved a sheaf of cablegrams. "Dev laid the foundations, but Mick's tugged at the world's heartstrings. Suddenly we're important, and I'm the boyo who knows everybody that matters. The *Boston Herald*, the *New York World*, the *Dallas News*, even the *Toronto Star Weekly*— they all want me as their Irish correspondent."

"Och, you're on the hog's back now," said his cousin, beaming. "You'll be buying a house for your bride soon."

"We're going to rent one first. Take our time, find something we both really like. I'm not about to make a decision like that without consulting the Cap'n."

Louise was amused. "Cap'n—is that what you call her? And what does she call you?"

"Mr. Mooney sir," Henry replied, straightfaced.

"She does of course. While you're at it, would you ever pull the other one? It has bells on."

EAMON de Valera was being reviled in press and public. "Maybe he didn't fire the shot himself," an angry Matt Nugent said to Henry when they met in the Oval, "but his men have murdered the best chance Ireland had. And on his orders, I'd wager."

"I doubt that," Henry replied. "Dev's a complex man, but he's not an assassin. He has a very rigid relationship with God. He couldn't live with his conscience if he'd ordered Mick shot in cold blood. Until I talk to people who really know, my best guess is that a company of Republicans happened to be in the area because Dev was there, and Mick's convoy accidentally drove right into their laps, so to speak. Mick always was reckless. They may not even have known who they were shooting at when they brought him down."

"Perhaps," Nugent conceded. "If you ever learn the truth of it, will you tell me?"

Henry started to agree. Then the words of a Cork telegraph operator echoed in his memory. "Sometimes," he told Matt Nugent, "you have to forget you know the truth."

ELLA was upset. "I don't understand, Henry. We've just sorted things out between us and now you're going away again. And with only weeks until our wedding."

"Journalism is how I make my living, remember?"

"But do you have to go back to where there's fighting?"

"I've gained a reputation as a freelance war correspondent, Ella—an eyewitness. Anyone can issue statements, but what people *do* reveals the truth about them, makes them heroes—or villains." He put his arms around her and rested his cheek against her soft hair. "Don't fret, Cap'n, I know

how to take care of myself. I promise I'll be here for you
on October twenty-first."

De Valera sneaked back to Dublin with an eight-man escort
of bodyguards who later described him as being in a highly
distressed state. Even before Collins' death he had realized
a military victory was not possible. Now he hoped to regain
control of the Republican movement with himself as its head
and negotiate through politics what could not be won on the
battlefield.

To this end he discussed various options at length with
Richard Mulcahy, but nothing was achieved. Mulcahy understood the situation better than de Valera himself. De Valera had nothing to offer; he could not guarantee to bring
the Republicans back into the fold. The IRA was Liam
Lynch's now. The men who were fighting so desperately
against the idea of a partitioned Free State were the philosophical heirs of Cathal Brugha.

The Provisional Government was drawing up an Emergency Powers Bill enabling military courts to impose the
death penalty without civil trial or the right of appeal.

Tom Barry was moved to Kilmainham, then escaped during an effort to transfer him to Gormanstown. He made his
way back to Cork without being captured.

Henry Mooney was on the road again, covering a war
that had been almost over, then exploded into uncontrollable
fury.

Although he faithfully wrote to Ella every day—reassuring letters that did not convey the horrors he was witness-
ing—Henry did not always mail them. Usually he waited
until he was with National troops and asked them to post
his mail back to Dublin. The power was with the government now.

September was a brutal month. In County Mayo, the government garrison in Ballina surrendered to the IRA without
a fight and were allowed to leave unmolested. In County
Sligo, six Republicans were murdered by National soldiers

after surrendering. One of the slain men was the son of Eoin
MacNeill.

The Free State Army had landed troops all along the
southern coast. Most of the larger towns were now occupied
by Free Staters. But war raged unchecked in rural areas.
Henry saw men fight one another with guns and pitchforks,
with bombs and grenades and fists and feet and teeth. Whatever ancient code of military chivalry had once dictated their
behavior was forgotten. "Some say decency died with
Pearse," Henry wrote. "Certainly it has died with Collins.
To the very end he kept the lines of communication open
between himself and his former friends on the opposite side,
always hoping to win them back. Now that is impossible.
They fight with a boiling bitterness that summons an equal
response. No matter how this ends, the scars will last for
generations."

W.T. Cosgrave succeeded Michael Collins as chairman
of the Provisional Government. Richard Mulcahy was appointed commander in chief of the Free State Army, as well
as minister of defense. On the ninth of September, the Third
Dáil Éireann convened to elect Cosgrave president of Saorstát Éireann.

The Provisional Government had few friends. Unionists
condemned it as the creation of Catholic zealots intent on
turning Ireland over to Rome rule. Republicans reviled the
same government as a British puppet regime.

Against this backdrop Eamon de Valera was working to
recover his personal prestige. He formed a "Republican government in opposition" that included Liam Mellows as minister for defense. Since Mellows was in jail, de Valera
arranged with Liam Lynch to cosign all necessary documents.

"De Valera hopes by this means to bring Lynch back on
side," Henry wrote.

Meanwhile, in the hills of West Cork, Erskine Childers
valiantly continued to publish *An Poblacht* with the help of
a small handpress and Kathleen O'Connell, de Valera's secretary.

• • •

Dᴇᴀʀ Ursula,

"I have arranged through Richard Mulcahy for a small band of National soldiers to be on the train with you when you go up to Dublin for our wedding. They will be in civilian clothes so as not to risk drawing enemy fire. This is being done as a special favor to me, so if you ever have the opportunity, I should appreciate your thanking the minister of defense personally."

September became October, crisp and golden, the sky hazed with the smoke of turf fires, the harvested fields standing empty in the sun.

Men fought and died in those fields. Machine-gun fire stripped the leaves from hedgerows. Wide-ranging hens pecked at blood puddled in the dirt.

I love you, Ella," Henry wrote. There seemed nothing else to say, nothing else that was really important.

A thinner, hollow-eyed Henry Mooney returned to Dublin on the fifteenth of October with a slight limp and suffering from nightmares. He was willing to let Louise fuss over him, "But I can't lie in bed till all hours," he warned his cousin. "We have to find a house to rent, and quickly."

Two days later Henry and Ella agreed on a semi-detached Georgian villa on Sandymount Avenue and began shopping for furnishings together. Henry enjoyed their shopping expeditions and surprised her with his knowledgeability. "I keep making new discoveries about you," she told him. "I never took you for someone who would be interested in decorating a house."

Henry chuckled. "I'm lots of different people. I have that on good authority."

On the twentieth of October the headline in the *Irish Times* carried a shock announcement:

DAVID LLOYD GEORGE RESIGNS AS PRIME MINISTER

Both the Tory Party and the Liberals were in disarray, though it was expected the Tories would form a majority government. However, the *Times* predicted with some alarm, the British Labour Party's strength was growing.

"I'm in favor of Labour having more seats in Parliament," Henry told his fiancée that afternoon as they were pricing curtain fabric in Clery's department store. "Workingmen will be more sympathetic to Ireland; they know what it means to be the underdogs."

"No one in my family's ever been for Labour."

"Or married a Catholic," he said cheerfully. "First time for everything, Cap'n."

The war seemed far away.

THE wedding party was small, discreetly limited to Ella's family and a few close friends: some Protestant, some Catholic. Louise Kearney attended on the arm of Hector Hamilton, Painless Dentist.

The bride was a vision in pale blue lace. Her brother gave her away; Matt Nugent was Henry's best man; Ava was matron of honor. A very grown-up Ursula Halloran was bridesmaid.

"I'm sorry, Uncle Henry," she said, "that Papa wouldn't come and be your best man. But he's not even at the farm now. As soon as he was well enough he went back to the war."

"To Ernie O'Malley's battalion?"

The girl dropped her eyes. "He made me promise not to tell you what company he'd be with."

"Is he still so angry with me, then?"

"He's angry with the world. I don't know him anymore."

Henry and Ella spent a week—a whole, wonderful week— in the Shelbourne Hotel. Fresh sheets every day; fresh flowers in crystal vases. The ambient hush of deep carpeting and heavy curtains. Tall windows from which to view the sunset, and the generous stars.

And a banquet whenever they wanted. A banquet of warm flesh, of delighted laughter, of passion so fierce it seemed angry. The death of inhibition. The discovery of freedom.

To Ursula's delight, they invited her to join them for dinner before she returned to Clare. She entered the Shelbourne with the nonchalance she had shown the first time. The Free State government in Merrion Street was subservient to the Anglo-Irish Treaty, but Ursula Halloran was a child of the Republic. Her posture proclaimed that she was as good as anyone.

Young men in the lobby swiveled their necks as she walked past.

"She won't want to go back to Clare," Ella warned her husband.

Henry chuckled. "Oh, she won't stay away from her horse for too long. But somehow I can't see Little Business spending the rest of her life on a farm."

Ella agreed. She spoke again of Ursula's education, of perhaps sending the girl to a finishing school abroad.

"She has no documents," said Henry, foreseeing difficulties. "They were ... mmm ... destroyed in the Four Courts."

"You know enough people in the government to find a way around that," Ella replied confidently. "And my brother and I can help with the financial arrangements."

"I can handle them myself," Henry said, setting his jaw.

ON the first morning of November he kissed his new wife goodbye, went halfway down the street, turned, and sprinted back home for another hour. He took the afternoon train to Cork instead. Strapped to a luggage rail in the vestibule was his bicycle.

Few civilians were on the train. In Henry's carriage were two priests sharing a packet of cheese sandwiches, and a pug-nosed businessman in a suit too good for the filthy train. The other passengers were all Free State soldiers. Henry greeted those he knew with a nod and eavesdropped on their conversations. He was actually looking forward to returning to work. *This is what I do. This is what I am. For the rest of my life. Journalist.*

Husband.

Perhaps a father someday.

The train jolted over its patched and repatched rails. Henry contemplated the irony of his lifelong avoidance of violence. Now he was actively seeking the nightmare landscape that repelled and fascinated him. As a child he had believed his nightmares predicted his future. And in a strange way, they had.

His eyes drifted shut; his head fell back against the high seat. Henry had not had much sleep recently.

ON the fourth of November a house in Dublin's exclusive Ailesbury Road was raided by government troops in the pre-dawn darkness. Ernie O'Malley, who was now assistant chief of staff of the IRA, was badly wounded in the shoot-out. Sixteen bullets were taken from his body in hospital.

THE ninth of November found Henry Mooney in County Cork, looking for Erskine Childers. Like the *Irish Bulletin, An Poblacht* had been moving from place to place, often published on no more than the little handpress Childers carried with him. In spite of this the newsletter was finding its way not only to the IRA troops in the field but to the Republicans in prison, the foreign press, the European embassies in Dublin, and friends in England and America. Childers, worn to a thin white ghost of his former self, was standing by his post. It would make a moving story.

But when Henry finally found the newsletter's most recent office, two Republican soldiers were boarding up the windows. "Too bad you missed him," they told the journalist. "He's on way up to Dublin."

"Do you know why?"

"He told us before he left, and proud he was too. The Chief sent for him to become secretary of his new government."

"Dublin's not safe for men like him right now," said Henry.

"Especially if they're carrying guns," one of the men agreed.

"Does Erskine have a gun on him?"

The soldier scratched his jaw reflectively. "Well, I wouldn't say he has a gun on him." He turned to his companion. "What would you say?"

"I wouldn't say he hasn't. Are you down from Dublin?" he asked Henry.

"I am. I'm a journalist."

"Izzat a fact?" the man responded. His attitude expressed total disinterest.

But the other said, "Tell us, journalist—what news of Ernie O'Malley?"

"He's survived, which is something of a miracle. He must be made of the same stuff as Cathal Brugha. They have him under heavy guard in hospital."

"They'll never keep him," predicted the soldier.

On November eleventh Erskine Childers was arrested at Robert Barton's house in Wicklow. He was carrying a revolver which had been given to him by Michael Collins, but he did not use it to defend himself, because there were women in the house.

In London the first wireless news broadcast was made from a room in Marconi House in the Strand. No mention was made of Childers' arrest. But word spread like wildfire through Ireland.

Henry debated with himself about going back to Dublin, then decided against it. Childers would be tried before a military court for possession of an illegal firearm and the wheels of justice ground slowly. Meanwhile he would cover the war. He went looking for Tom Barry.

On the seventeenth of November the Emergency Powers Bill was invoked for the first time. Four young Republicans were executed by firing squad in Kilmainham.

Under the same act, Erskine Childers was swiftly convicted and sentenced to death. He appealed the decision. Cosgrave, under tremendous pressure to commute the death sentence, offered Childers a reprieve if he would cease all further opposition to the Free State government.

Childers refused.

He was being held in Beggar's Bush Barracks, where on

the evening of November thirteenth he was allowed a visit with his wife and son. He told young Erskine, "Never do or say anything that would cause bitterness."[1]

Next morning at first light—and while his case was still under appeal—Erskine Childers was marched before a firing party of fifteen men. He thanked his executioners, forgave his enemies, and refused a blindfold. Members of the firing squad were so distressed their hands were shaking. Childers' last words were to them. "Come closer, boys," he said gently. "It will be easier for you."[2]

HENRY was appalled. "I am sick to my soul at what amounts to the judicial murder of an elected member of the Dáil," he wrote to Ella. "Only someone who believed profoundly in his principles could have met his death as bravely as Erskine Childers did. Why are we killing the best ones? When will it stop?"

Liam Lynch sent a letter of protest to the Provisional Government. "We on our side have at all times adhered to the recognized rules of warfare. In the early days of this war we took hundreds of your forces prisoner but accorded to them all the rights of prisoners of war and, over and above, treated them as fellow countrymen and former comrades. Many of your soldiers have been released by us three times although captured with arms on each occasion. But the prisoners you have taken have been treated barbarously, and when helpless you have tortured, wounded, and murdered them. We therefore give you and each member of your body due notice that unless your army recognizes the rules of warfare in future we shall adopt very drastic measures to protect our forces."[3]

WHEREVER Henry went, he sought Ned Halloran. He heard rumors that Ned had been in Dublin with O'Malley, but left the city before O'Malley's capture. Then someone said he was with Liam Lynch. He was seen in Waterford and Youghal and Skibbereen. He could be anywhere. He was as ephemeral as Michael Collins.

Chapter Forty-four

December 6, 1922

SAORSTÁT ÉIREANN OFFICIALLY RECOGNIZED
ONE YEAR TO THE DAY AFTER SIGNING OF
ANGLO-IRISH TREATY

ULSTER GIVEN ONE MONTH TO OPT OUT

ON the seventh of December two unarmed Dáil deputies
were shot by Republicans at the Ormond Hotel on Upper
Ormond Quay. The victims were Pádraig O'Máille, the deputy speaker of the Dáil, and Seán Hales. Hales was killed.

Henry Mooney learned of the shootings through the IRA
network before the news was published in the papers.
"That's cold-blooded murder!" he told his informer.

"Execution," the other man snapped. "Hales and O'Máille
voted for the Emergency Powers Bill. They were willing to
execute our boys without trial or appeal, so now they know
what it feels like."

On the eighth of December four Republican prisoners, one
from each province, were taken out of Mountjoy and executed in reprisal: Richard Barrett, Joe McKelvey, Liam Mellows, and Rory O'Connor.

Saorstát Éireann was baptized with the blood of brothers.

NORTHERN Ireland opted out of the Free State.

HENRY went home. Home to Ella.

Tilly met him at the door of the house in Sandymount. Her services for a year had been Edwin Mansell's wedding gift. "Is Mrs. Mooney at home, Tilly?" he asked as he handed her his hat.

"She's in the linen closet, sir; we were just doing the—"

Henry ran past her. He found his wife sitting on a stool while she rearranged sheets and tablecloths. She looked up in surprise at the sound of his feet in the hall. Before she could say anything he flung himself down beside her and put his weary head in her lap.

She stroked his hair. Saying nothing. Loving.

Late that night as he lay in her arms, he remarked, "I might as well stay in Dublin, Cap'n. The war's here too; I heard rifle fire as I was coming from the train."

"I know. I have mixed feelings about it. If it keeps you close to me I'm glad, but on the other hand . . ."

"Indeed. On the other hand." Henry sighed and rolled over onto his back. "Ella, I was born before the turn of the century in a time when things still seemed clear, somehow. If a man was honest and paid his bills and lived a decent life, he knew what to expect of the world. Black and white. But now . . . but now. It's all shades of gray, Ella. Right and wrong, good and evil . . . it's all shades of gray."

THE first sitting of An Seanad, the Senate, was scheduled for the eleventh of December. Henry planned to be among the journalists covering the historic event. With An Seanad and An Dáil in place, the new Irish Oireachtas, or Parliament, would be complete.

On the morning of the tenth Dubliners opened their newspapers to read in horror that the homes of four members of the Dáil had been raided during the night and set afire.

Seán MacGarry's three children, one an invalid, had been

trapped in their rooms, and only rescued when their gallant mother fought her way through the flames to save them. Mother and children were severely burned; MacGarry's young son died in hospital.

On the twelfth the Duke of Abercorn was sworn in as the first governor-general of Northern Ireland.

On the nineteenth of December seven more Republicans were executed by the Irish Free State.

ALTHOUGH he was not in the mood for Christmas, Henry went shopping. At McBirney's Gift Exhibition on Aston Quay he bought Ella a champagne-colored crêpe-de-chine jumper with an inset lace yoke and three-quarter-length sleeves. It cost twenty-five shillings and sixpence, which seemed expensive to him until he fell in love with a silver-backed hairbrush at thirty-seven shillings and bought her that too.

Feeling suddenly impoverished, he decided on books and chocolates for the rest of his gift list. In Switzers' he found *Herbert Strang's Annual*, which promised excellent stories by popular authors for children. He bought the book for Ursula—though he personally was tempted by some of the tales he saw in *The Boys' Own Annual*

When he returned home with his packages, he found a brief letter awaiting him.

"Dear Uncle Henry,

"I am buying all the papers now, because I want to know as much as I can about what is happening. In the *Irish Independent* this morning I saw an advertisement under Public Notices: Examination for Boy Clerkships, Age 15 to 18 Years, a Competitive Examination in the service of Dublin Corporation.[2] Why could I not apply for something like this as soon as I am old enough? Why does it have to be limited to boys?

"Love,

"Ursula"

Next morning Henry exchanged *Strang's* for *Boys' Own*. At home that evening he said to Ella, "Let's start making inquiries about schools for Ursula. Abroad, somewhere. Out of Ireland for a while."

On the seventeenth of December, 1922, the last of the British troops left the twenty-six counties of southern Ireland. A day later the Free State Parliament passed its first act.

The Shelbourne dinner menu at Christmas was decorated with shamrocks only, and the dishes were described in Celtic lettering.

William Butler Yeats issued a bitter statement as his legacy to the new year. "The Government of the Free State has been proved legitimate by the only effective test: it has been permitted to take life."[3]

Confidentially, many in the government would like to execute Ernie O'Malley," a member of Mulcahy's staff told Henry, "but the minister refuses to shoot a man on a stretcher. Painful memories of James Connolly, you know. O'Malley'll be sent to Mountjoy instead, as soon as he can be moved."

Henry was hugely relieved. Every life that was spared, Republican or Free Stater, seemed like a victory.

On the second of January the minister of defense appointed Paddy O'Daly as GOC of the Kerry Command. O'Daly had a reputation as a hard man and was considered a great asset to the Free State Army.

On the thirteenth the home of W. T. Cosgrave was burned down.

On the twentieth eleven more Republicans were executed. "Callous murderers must pay the price for their bloody crimes!" gloated pro-Treaty newspapers.

Winston Churchill agreed. He referred to the late Erskine Childers as a murderous renegade Englishman, saying, "No man has done more harm or shown more genuine malice, or endeavored to bring a greater curse upon the common people of Ireland than this strange being, actuated by a deadly and malignant hatred for the land of his birth."[4]

The speech was quoted without censure in many Irish newspapers.

Hɪɢʜʟʏ incensed, Henry Mooney wrote, "We are observing the deliberate demonization of the Republicans. Influenced by a self-serving desire to be on the winning side, some people are beginning to depict them in the same terms the British government once applied to the Irish race as a whole. Thus victors justify their treatment of the vanquished.

"No one escapes the poison of civil war, however. Many Republicans now view their opponents—their erstwhile comrades-in-arms—as devils incarnate.

"In another generation, or two at the most, the men and women who are experiencing these events and personally know the other people involved will be gone. Words printed on paper will be all that remains. We owe it to the future to tell the truth, not the politically expedient truth."

His work became more important to him than ever. Lights burned very late in the house in Sandymount. Ella came downstairs at three in the morning to find her husband hunched over his desk with a map of the southwest spread before him.

"You're going back, aren't you," she said. It was not a question.

"I have to. It's where the war is. It's where I'll find the truth about what happened to Michael Collins."

"The war is here in Dublin too, Henry, and so are men who must know what happened to Collins. You're going back to look for Ned Halloran, aren't you?"

He nodded.

"But you said yourself he could be anywhere. Why there?"

"The Free State Army has driven the Republicans out of almost every place but Cork and Kerry. They'll fight to the end there, so that's where Ned will be. I know him."

"There is something very wrong between the two of you, isn't there?"

"Mmm."

"And you want to mend it before . . . before anything happens to him."

"Mmm."

"If I ask you what it is, will you tell me?"

He swiveled around in his chair to meet her eyes. Here was the real test of their marriage; now, when he least expected it. *If you really love her, you must give her a chance to understand.*

"Yes," he said truthfully. "Yes, I will tell you."

"Then I shan't ask."

He almost crushed her with his embrace. "Dear God, I love you!"

ON the eighteenth of January, 1923, Liam Deasy, member of the IRA executive and acting commandant of the Southern Division, was captured by the Free State Army. He was tried by court-martial and sentenced to death. Deasy had long been seeking a way to end the war without surrendering the ideal of a republic. The Free State government persuaded him to write a document urging unconditional surrender in return for his life. He finally agreed as the only chance for survival open to him. Copies were sent to de Valera and to Lynch.

The terms were refused. Deasy's comrades did not hold his action against him. There had been so much killing already; any effort to save one's life was acceptable.

February was a bleak month, in keeping with the nation's mood. Henry attended a meeting in Dublin to honor James Connolly, and heard James Larkin, who like Connolly was a hero of the trade union movement, make a speech urging an end to the Irish Civil War. "I ask all Republicans to give up the armed struggle and take up the political, constitutional struggle. Give up your arms. There is no disgrace in peace. There can never be dishonor in peace."[5]

The voice of sanity in the mouth of a former firebrand. But who will listen?

* * *

LIAM Lynch was on his way to the south for a crisis meeting of the IRA executive. Henry was traveling too, back to Cork and Kerry. In his railway carriage was a stern-faced matron defiantly reading a copy of James Joyce's new book. When she thought anyone was looking at her, she pretended to be shocked. The book must have been smuggled in from Paris, Henry mused, as no copies of *Ulysses* were available in Britain or Ireland.

He wondered if she would lend it to him, but lacked the courage to ask her. He turned instead to the newspapers he had bought in the railway station. "Dr. T. A. MacLaughlin has just returned from Berlin," Henry read. "Dr. Mac-Laughlin, who has been working as an engineer for Siemens-Schuckert, tells this reporter he has developed a plan for harnessing the Shannon River to provide electricity. Only a third of Dublin, a quarter of Cork City, and a fraction of Limerick City have electric power; most of the nation has none. Dr. MacLaughlin hopes to improve on that situation. He claims his scheme can raise the nation's power output from 40 million units of electricity per year to 110 million units."

Think of that! I wonder if Little Business has seen this. If she does, I'll have a letter from her next time I'm home.

Reading on, Henry learned that on the nineteenth of February, by civic order, Great Brunswick Street was officially renamed Pearse Street in honor of both brothers. By the same order Brunswick Place became Pearse Place, Queen's Square became Pearse Square, and Queen's Terrace became Pearse Terrace.

Henry folded the paper and stared out the window. *In honor of both brothers. And now we have the War of Brothers. Do you know, Pádraic? Do you know?*

THE civil war in the southwest had become bitter beyond imagining, worst of all in Kerry. From their barracks in Tralee, Castleisland, Killarney, Kenmare, and Cahirciveen, Free State troops were enforcing martial law on a largely hostile civilian population. The Free State Army held the towns . . . but the Republican Army controlled the countryside.

March found Henry in a cold, dismal room in a cold,
dismal inn on the road to Castleisland. Kerry was breaking
his heart. No part of Ireland was more beautiful to the eye
or less generous to the belly than the Kingdom of Kerry.
Starved, stony soil; stark mountains and lonely bogs. Rugged headlands defying the sea; crystal lakes reflecting the
sky. Cloudshadow and seamist and a folk memory of fairies.
Wine-red heather and glowing golden gorse and great ar-
madas of cloud sailing serenely overhead, while mountainy
men struggled with all their might to wring bare subsistence
from unyielding earth.

Deserted farmsteads bore silent witness to those who had
run off to America—there to grieve for Kerry until they
died. In the houses still inhabited, terrible stories were told
of young men slaughtered: ambushed, shot in the back,
dragged from their beds in front of their horrified children,
executed without trial. Dead Republicans were left outside
of church gates with their faces battered in by rifle butts
until their own mothers did not know them.

Suspected informers, Henry learned, were summarily
dealt with by the IRA. They were questioned, beaten, and
their property and livestock confiscated. Some were innocent. The son of one such man, furious at what had been
done to his father, had joined the Free State Army. A lieutenant now stationed at Castleisland, he was reputed to be
in charge of torturing IRA captives.

Henry copied down everything he heard, every name and
detail, as diligently as he had once done for the *Irish Bul
letin*. Soon men's memories would be blurred by experience
and time. If the truth was not captured immediately, it would
escape forever.

And the truth was appalling.

Henry observed and recorded. He crouched behind hedgerows talking to soldiers from both sides; he stood in muddy
fields talking to hill farmers who were being politicized for
the first time in their lives, and a terrible image grew in his
mind.

A terrible word.

One the bishops would never allow to be published, not
in holy Catholic Ireland.

Abortion.
Something viable and full of potential was being cruelly aborted, cut to pieces before its life could begin.

FREE State Army General Headquarters for Kerry Command was in Tralee with Paddy O'Daly, but Hartnett's Hotel in Castleisland was headquarters for government troops in the immediate area. It was the tallest building in town and the sturdiest. The fourth of March found Henry Mooney there, interviewing members of the Dublin Guard as they relaxed on a Sunday afternoon. Their relaxation was only superficial, however. Posture and language were those of men under siege. The IRA was watching them from the hills, waiting for any sign of weakness. Waiting to fall on them like wolves on lambs, like assassins on Collins.

Henry had perfected the art of encouraging confidences. Soon the soldiers were talking freely.

The casual indifference with which they spoke of torturing Republican prisoners at Hartnett Post appalled Henry. The soldiers seemed to think it an acceptable procedure. They even described the techniques employed in other barracks. "At Ballymullen they use hammers for interrogations," an officer told Henry. "If that doesn't work, they tell them they're going to be shot, march them out blindfolded, shoot all around their heads, then march them back again and say they'll be executed the next day instead. Not many men can hold their nerve under that."

"And you do things like that here?" Henry asked, trying to keep any emotion out of his voice.

"We have other methods just as effective." A contemptuous snort. "Bastards asked for it. Killed the Big Fellow, didn't they?"

Another officer remarked, "I never see anything. I look out the window and smoke a cigarette." He winked at Henry.

They all went to Mass this morning, yet this afternoon they make no apologies for torturing fellow human beings. The rules of common decency which once governed these men have been swept away. And they don't even seem to notice.

When Henry returned to the inn that evening, he could not eat. By the light of a paraffin lamp he wrote: "The greatest tragedy of the Rising was that men like Pearse and Connolly were executed. With them Ireland lost their vision of nationhood linked to human decency.

"No matter how much the British government subsequently sought to blacken their characters, both Connolly and Pearse were highly principled men. Pearse the dedicated teacher lived his life according to the tenets of his faith. Connolly the union organizer was profane and earthy but equally honorable. Between the poles of idealism and pragmatism the two envisioned a nonsectarian republic that would treat all men and women equally, with *dignity*. They were willing to fight and die to make that republic a reality for the rest of us. It was perhaps an impossible ideal, but it was the best vision of Irish nationhood anyone has ever presented.

"The future those men dreamed was shot dead in Kilmainham yard. What are we putting in its place?"

Next day he rode his bicycle deep into the rugged hills, to a mud-walled cabin with a swaybacked roof. One end of the building was sinking back into the earth from which it came. Henry whispered "Long Live the Republic" at the door and it opened at once.

While he was drinking tea with the woman of the house her husband, a graying strongly built man with a ruddy complexion, arrived. He went straight to the only window and peered out.

"Were ye followed?" his wife asked in a nervous whisper.

"Don't fret so, woman. Amn't I carrying a safe-conduct pass signed by Michael Brennan himself?" His was the classic Kerry accent: convoluted vowels that battered the neighboring consonants into submission.

"How did you get a government pass?" Henry wanted to know.

"I was in the RIC, stationed in Limerick—they didn't want us within thirty miles of our own homes—and the day before I quit to join the IRA, I went to Brennan bold as brass and asked him for one. Thought it might come in handy. He gave me two in case I lost one, and later I gave the other pass to one of our lads. Fellow called Ned Halloran who did me a good turn."

Henry leaned forward eagerly. "Ned Halloran? From Clare?"

"The same. Mount Callan accent on him most of the time, but he can talk as posh as an Englishman when he likes."

"Is he in Kerry?"

"He was last time I saw him. Someone told me the Staters caught him afterward and sent him to Ballymullen. Safe-conduct or no," the man added in a voice too low for his wife to hear.

Henry went cold. "Ballymullen Barracks in Tralee? Are you sure?"

"Can't say for certain. You know yourself, you hear so many stories. If I see him, though, I'll tell him you was asking for him."

WHEN Henry finally got back to the inn, he felt weary to his marrow. It was too late to go to Tralee that night. If Ned was in custody, perhaps he could pull some strings, get him out before something horrible happened. Henry tossed and turned in his bed, holding imaginary telephone conversations with Mulcahy and Cosgrave. At last he fell into a troubled sleep. Early next morning he set off to Hartnett Post to ask permission to use their telephone, since his inn had none.

He arrived to find the place in turmoil.

A letter in the handwriting of a known local informer had been delivered the evening before. Addressed to the lieutenant whose father had been wrongly accused of informing against the IRA, the letter gave the location of a major IRA weapons dump in Barranarig Wood, Knocknagoshel. It was sufficient to entice the Dublin Guards out of their fortress. Nine men had set off from Hartnett Post that same night.

The letter was a forgery. A mine casing packed with shrapnel and an explosive charge was waiting, buried in a lonely field at the supposed dump site. At two a.m. on March sixth, five members of the Free State Army—three officers of the Dublin Guard and two enlisted men—were blown apart by the trap mine.

The man who had been in charge of torturing IRA prisoners was decapitated by the force of the blast.

A shocked survivor had returned to Hartnett Post with the news. A party was on its way with stretchers to retrieve the injured and the bodies.

"We'll get the scum who did this," an officer assured Henry through gritted teeth. "We'll get every last one of them, never you fear. We'll give as good as we get, so we will."

Henry saw the stretcher party return. He wrote, with fingers gone cold, of the looks on their faces; of the limp arm of a corpse dangling from beneath a bloodstained blanket, swinging like the clapper on a bell.

One of the survivors was not expected to live, his legs were so hideously mangled.

Henry took the details of each man's rank and family and obtained a brief summation of his service record. "Two of the dead officers were Paddy O'Daly's friends," the duty officer said. "One of them was his best friend. He's going to take this hard, very hard. We're phoning Tralee now to tell him."

"Tralee!" With a sudden jolt, Henry remembered Ned. "Listen here to me, I desperately need to make a phone call myself; can you arrange it?"

"Not today, I'm afraid; the lines are going to be humming all day."

Within the hour Henry was on his bicycle, pedaling furiously to Tralee.

He was refused admittance to Ballymullen Barracks. "I'm sorry, sir," the sentry on duty said, "but we're not admitting any civilians at the moment."

"But I'm the press, damnit!"

"I'm sorry, sir."

"Well, can I see General O'Daly, then? He knows me."

"I'm sorry, sir. Perhaps if you come back tomorrow?"

Henry had no choice but to find a room for the night—another damp and dismal hotel, he noted sourly—and wait until dawn. Sleep was impossible. He tried to write a letter to Ella but could not do that either. For a long time he stood at the window, gazing into the moonlit night. The landscape was almost as bright as day. Not a leaf stirred on the trees.

As soon as the sun was up, he returned to Ballymullen Barracks. There was considerable activity, with increased guards at the gate and squads of armed men marching to and fro outside the walls. Lights were still burning in many upstairs windows. Obviously something had happened, but Henry was again refused admittance. "Is this about the bomb at Knocknagoshel?" he wanted to know.

"I cannot tell you, sir," was all the reply he got.

He waited with increasing anxiety. From time to time he consulted his watch. The hands seemed to have been glued in place.

At last a military lorry with its back covered by canvas drove up. At the sound of its horn a gate was opened and the lorry drove through. Trying to look as if he had permission to be there, Henry ambled over to the gate and peered in.

He counted nine coffins being unloaded from the lorry. *Nine?*

Someone noticed Henry watching and slammed the gate.

He walked up the high street to chat with the shopkeepers of Tralee, see what they knew. A few had heard vague rumors of "some trouble at Knocknagoshel" the preceding day, but nothing since. When they learned Henry was a journalist, they tried to get news from him.

He went back to the GHQ to await . . . what?

At almost three in the afternoon an officer emerged from the main door and beckoned to him. "Are you the reporter?"

"Journalist. Henry Mooney."

"Well, you'd best come inside then. General O'Daly has a statement to release, and you'll do."

Chapter Forty-five

P ADDY O'Daly looked up from behind a desk littered with papers, boxes, bits of military paraphernalia, and the dried-out remains of an uneaten sandwich. Henry remembered O'Daly from his days as one of the murderous Twelve Apostles. Then he had been a deceptively gentle-looking "civilian" with a disarming smile and a thick crop of curly hair. Now he was attired in full Free State uniform and an officer's cap crushed his curls. There was no smile.

"Oh, it's you, Mooney. Heard you were in Castleisland."

"Yesterday," Henry replied.

"Yes. So you know."

"I know what happened there. What's happened here?"

O'Daly shifted in his chair. When he spoke his voice was a rapid staccato, as if repeating words memorized by rote. "Immediately following my notification of the atrocity at Knocknagoshel, I issued an order that in future government forces are not to remove any barricades, clear any dumps, or touch any suspected mines. Irregular prisoners are to be fetched from the nearest detention barracks to remove them. This is a necessary precaution to save the lives of our own soldiers, and within hours has proved its value." O'Daly lifted a sheet of paper from his desk. "Here is a statement for publication."

Henry read: "While a party of government troops was proceeding from Tralee to Killorglin on the evening of

March sixth, they encountered a barricade of stones at Ballyseedy Bridge. The party returned to Tralee and brought out nine Irregulars who were instructed to remove the barricade. While they were engaged in doing so at about two a.m. on March seventh, a trigger mine exploded and the prisoners were killed. Three members of the Free State Army suffered shrapnel wounds."[1]

Henry felt sick to his stomach. "Prisoners from Ballymullen."

O'Daly gave a terse nod.

"May I have their names?"

"They won't be released until all the next of kin have been notified."

"Was one of them Ned Halloran?"

"Can't tell you that. It may take some time to identify them. A bomb hidden among stones does a lot of damage."

Henry stared at O'Daly. "Nine IRA men at two in the morning. The exact time and the same number of men as at Knocknagoshel."

O'Daly stared back at him. "Coincidence," he said.

BALLYSEEDY Cross was easy to find. Henry had passed by the place many times on his bicycle. But never had he seen the sight that greeted his eyes that evening. A great hole had been gouged in the road. Huge splashes of blood; gobbets of unrecognizable flesh, naked and vulnerable as meat in a butcher's window. Everywhere. On the crushed grass, in the dripping trees. The air stank of it. And of explosives. And hatred. And death.

Dear Jesus, Ned, was this how it ended for you?

Birds were picking at the shredded flesh.

A few local people appeared, tentatively, at the edge of the woods, or farther down the road, and stared. Eyes wide. Crossing themselves repeatedly. Crying, some of them. One man had a pony and trap. The pony shied violently at the smell of the blood and would come nowhere near, but stood at a distance, trembling.

A cap trampled in the mud. A broken rosary. Part of a sleeve, the buttons still bright, the hand . . .

"No!" Henry cried, the word torn out of him, wrenched from his guts by grief and horror. "No! They are us! They are *us*!!!"

He got off his bicycle and vomited into a ditch. Then he made his way to the stream spanned by the nearby bridge and washed his face. There was blood there too, a sticky puddle in the mud on the bank, but he was careful not to touch it. Could not bear to touch it. Its silent voice cried out to him.

He knelt to pray.

I don't even know what to say to you. Are you blind? Deaf? Dead? What sort of deity are you, to allow this?

"Why bother?" he asked himself aloud. He stood up and brushed off his knees. "That's me done. I'm through with God." *You hear me? Through with you!*

Remounting his bicycle, Henry returned to Tralee. He wobbled as he rode. He was trying to hold the pain at arm's length, but if his concentration lapsed to the smallest degree it rushed in on him.

By dawn next morning he was back at Ballymullen, trying to get a list of the dead. There was still none available. The guard remembered him from the day before and let him in anyway, thinking O'Daly had sent for him.

Henry pretended to take a wrong turn and wandered through the building. The barracks was depressingly grim: cell-like rooms, narrow passageways, flaking paint, insufficient light. As he passed an open doorway Henry noticed a sandy-haired Republican he had known before civil war broke out, a man who was now in the Free State Army. He was standing behind a table, sorting out personal effects taken from the pockets of dead men.

Henry entered the room and struck up a conversation, being careful not to look directly at the objects on the table. Slowly he brought the topic around to them. "The bombs at Ballyseedy did so much damage it's hard to identify the men," the soldier told Henry. "All the remains of one of them could be fitted into his tunic with the sleeves knotted. But there is something . . . wait a minute, I'll show you."

Bombs? Bombs plural?

The soldier produced a slip of paper with a badly charred

edge. The printing on the paper was almost illegible with blood, but when Henry held it up to the light and squinted, he could make out part of a safe-conduct pass signed by Michael Brennan.

That night he drank until the publican refused to sell him any more, but he was still stone sober.

Blood dripping from the trees. Birds picking at ruined flesh.

He could not go to bed because he did not dare close his eyes. The nightmare would get him if he did. His brain sat thick and heavy in his skull and he could not make it work. No moving parts. Just a dense, soggy organ; inert. He knew he should think; but he did not remember how to think.

Exhausted, he wandered the narrow lanes of Tralee and cried out in his heart for Ella, for Ursula. For somebody.

OTHER Republican prisoners were taken from their cells and transported to a barricade at Countess Bridge. Bombs in a barricade there killed four of them. Five more died in similar circumstances near Cahirciveen.

Horror upon horror. Hatred expanding outward in a great wave.

On the ninth of March Paddy O'Daly sent a message to Dublin. "It has now transpired that an Irregular prisoner, Stephen Fuller, escaped during the mine explosion at Ballyseedy. It is stated that he has become insane." A reward was issued for Fuller's immediate capture.

The mutilated bodies of eight men had been distributed among nine coffins.

Henry recognized the comment about Fuller's "insanity" as an attempt to discredit any version of the event the man might tell. But terrible stories already were circulating through Tralee and the surrounding countryside.

To Henry's frustration, the names of the dead were still not being made public.

Recalling that someone else had carried a safe-conduct pass from Michael Brennan, Henry went back into the hills, to the little cabin with the swaybacked roof.

He arrived to find a family in mourning. They had just

been notified by a government messenger of the death of their patriarch. At Ballyseedy.

As if they had heard a banshee wail on the wind, the neighbors were already gathering.

Knowing Ned might still be alive did not spare Henry from grief. No one in that cabin was spared; grief came to meet each person who entered, wrapped its cold arms around them, opened its gaping maw and swallowed them whole.

"Sorry for your trouble," Henry whispered to the widow, repeating the time-honored phrase. Then he went to stand with the other men beside the hearth. Passing around the whiskey. Smoking clay pipes. Talking in low voices.

After a time the door opened and three figures entered, two men and someone who was wrapped in a shawl like a woman, but did not move like a woman. He edged crabwise, like a man in great pain.

Curious, Henry drifted closer to hear this person say to the widow, "Sorry for your trouble, missus. My name's Stephen Fuller. I knew your husband well; I was with him when it happened. I come to tell you he was brave to the end. God took him without letting him suffer none."

The woman lifted trembling hands and put them on either side of his face, pushing back the shawl to reveal a gaunt young man with boulders for cheekbones, and haunted eyes. His face was badly bruised.

"You were with my man at Ballyseedy?"

"I was."

Suddenly her legs gave way. She collapsed as if her bones had turned to chalk dust.

While the other women rushed to help her, Henry moved closer to Fuller. "Would you be willing to talk to me?" he asked. "I used to write for the *Irish Bulletin*."

Fuller's eyes scanned his face. "No word of a lie? I used to read the *Bulletin*."

"Then you know my name: Henry Mooney. Can you tell me what really happened at Ballyseedy?"

"You can't write about it, not now," Fuller said.

"I realize that. But a friend of mine may have been there; I have to know. Ned Halloran?"

"There was no Halloran with us. It's one of my own

friends we're mourning today. Them who brought me here didn't want to, but I owed it to my friend. I'll be leaving soon, though. The IRA has a safe house for me back in the hills, and in a few days there'll be a dugout ready for me to hide in until they can get me out of Kerry. You didn't see me at all, remember."

"You have my word on it."

Fuller whispered urgently, "Don't write this down. It could mean your life as well as mine. Just listen.

"I was in a cell in Ballymullen the evening the government soldiers came for us. They told us, 'We're going to blow you up with a mine.' We were removed out into the yard and loaded into lorries, and made to lie flat in the bottom and taken out to Ballyseedy crossroads. We couldn't see nothing and they told us nothing, but we knew it was bad.

"We arrived out anyway and they marched us up to this pile of stones and logs in the road—a barricade, like, but you could see it wasn't no real barricade. The language the Staters used to us was fierce. One fellow called us 'Irish bastards,' and he an Irishman himself. One of our lads asked to say his prayers and they told him, 'No prayers. Our fellows didn't get any time to say prayers. Maybe some of you will go to heaven and meet some of our fellows there.'

"They tied us then with our hands behind us, and made us stand in a circle with our backs to the stones. And they tied our legs and tied our shoelaces together too so we couldn't run. The lad next to me closed his eyes and started praying, but I kept watching-like. The lad on the other side said goodbye and I said goodbye, 'Goodbye, lads.' And I saw them pull the trip-wire. And up it went. And I went up with it."[2]

Henry realized he had been holding his breath. "Government soldiers set off the mine themselves?"

"They did surely. More than one, I think. There was a boom and another boom, and maybe another again."

"How in God's name did you get away?"

"When I saw them pull the trip-wire I threw myself sideways-like. Next thing I knew, I was lying in a ditch with the ropes blown off me. Me back and hands and legs was burnt something terrible. Our lads was writhing in the dirt with stones raining down on them and guns was blazing, the Staters was shooting them on the ground like dogs, and everything was burning and screaming and . . ." Fuller's words ground to an agonized halt. Tears streamed down his ravaged cheeks.

Henry gave him a cup of whiskey. After draining it in one long swallow, Fuller continued. "In all that confusion no one noticed me. I crawled into the stream, right down under the surface in the muck, and escaped that way. I don't know how long I was dragging meself through the night and across the fields before I found help. It's all of a mist now. A red mist."

"Were any of the government soldiers hurt?"

"The bombs didn't take a feather out of them. They took care to stand well away while they blew us to pieces." Fuller drew a ragged breath and fixed his eyes once more on Henry's face. "What happened?" he asked in baffled tones. "All us lads who fought side by side to make Ireland free . . . What happened to us?"

"I can tell you," said Henry, "because I've chronicled it day by day. But I don't think you or I will ever understand it."

Chapter Forty-six

THE following morning the names of those killed at Ballyseedy were published and their bodies released to their relatives. As they were carried out the gates of Ballymullen, the townspeople fell upon them in outrage. "Trash coffins! Condemned coffins!" they cried, smashing open the splintery, badly fashioned boxes and lifting out the pitiful remains. Other coffins were brought and the dead men placed within them, but not before hundreds of people saw the condition of the mangled corpses.

There were riots in the streets of Tralee.

HENRY returned to Dublin. Ballyseedy had broken him. He sat on the floor with his head in Ella's lap and wept like a child.

"I've seen hell with the lid off," he told her.

Next morning he insisted on seeing Richard Mulcahy. Someone had to give an explanation.

"I realize things may have got out of hand in Kerry, Henry," Mulcahy said, "but you must not be taken in by Republican propaganda. I have great faith in the honor of our army."

"What I saw with my own eyes was a lot more than propaganda!"

"I truly am sorry for those who lost their lives."

"I believe you, Dick. I know that you personally would never have sanctioned atrocities. Any more than Liam Lynch would have," Henry added deliberately.

Richard Mulcahy winced. A tiny movement, so small one would not notice it unless he was watching for it. But that sign of pain satisfied Henry.

Mulcahy said, "You must understand that I can't talk to you about this, either on or off the record. There will be an official hearing."

"Will the press be allowed to attend?"

"I'm afraid not."

"Call me as a witness, then. For God's sake, Dick, I saw—"

"We must avoid any suspicion of using biased witnesses, Henry. Your republicanism is too well known."

"Who's going to be on the hearing panel?"

"Major General O'Daly and—"

"You're saying he's not biased? He issued the damned orders!"

Mulcahy stood up behind his desk. "It is impossible for me to believe my army could do such things," he said. "I know those men, Henry. They're the best in the world. The military inquiry will determine just what did happen, and I have every confidence they'll be exonerated. Now, you know your way out, I believe?"

Henry turned away. *It's all to be covered up, then; swept under the table. For the sake of the new state. That will be their justification.*

But how do you erase a man's memories? How do you forget the unforgettable?

HE did not write to Ursula about Ballyseedy. He could not inflict those horrors on her. He told her only that as far as he knew, Ned was not a prisoner in Kerry.

She replied that her father had sent her a brief note explaining he was with Liam Lynch but hoped to be home soon.

"You could go to Clare and meet him," Ella suggested.

"It's enough to know he's alive. I don't think this is a good time for us to confront one another."

"Would it be a confrontation, then?"

"Oh yes," said Henry. "Oh yes."

His life seemed fractured. Ireland itself was fractured. "I'm thinking of giving up journalism," he told Ella. "I can't write about what's going on in this country; I don't even want to think about it. I feel like I'm sane among madmen, and that's worse than the other way around."

She dropped her eyes so that her lashes swept her cheeks; cheeks blushing pink. "Perhaps you need some good news."

"Is there any, Cap'n? Anywhere?"

"In this house there is," Ella replied. "You're going to be a father."

The terrible world contracted; dwindled to a cold black cinder; exploded in a rose-and-gold sunrise.

HERE *I am in church again, God. At Ballyseedy I swore I'd never speak to you again. So you have spoken to me. Does that prove you exist? Or do I just want it to prove you exist?*

Henry knelt in the pew with his head bent over his folded hands. *A child. That's always been your gift to us, hasn't it?*

I beseech your mercy and protection for this tiny new person. A son. Or a daughter. If I promise not to doubt your existence anymore, if I promise not to give up on my fellow human beings . . . would it be too much to ask for this first one to be a daughter?

HE was writing again. From the haven of an upstairs room in Sandymount, looking east to the sea, to the sunrise.

"We need to reimagine the past in a more instructive mold, not as myth but as guidepost," Henry suggested, concluding his latest essay on Ireland's troubled history. "Over the centuries we have made tragedy an icon. Yet surely if we believe in God at all, we believe our Creator gave man the gift of free will. We can make the future different."

Ella read everything he wrote before he submitted it for publication. She was not an uncritical audience; if a sentence was awkward or a meaning unclear, she told him. Her knowledge of correct grammar was more extensive than his. "I've never put my education to use until now," she admitted. "I like pretending to be your editor."

He gave her a hug. "You *are* my editor, Cap'n. You're putting a polish on me."

"I enjoy working with you. Being part of a team. Henry, do you suppose someday we might buy a newspaper in a small town and publish it ourselves? I could do political cartoons. Sign them 'E. Mansell.' "

Henry held his wife at arm's length and studied her face. She was quite serious. "You amaze me," he said.

"You would like that, then?"

"Like it? Cap'n, I can't think of anything better! But we won't use your money, not a penny of it." *Not a penny of it, Edwin!*

THE war dragged on. Each side accused the other of barbarous behavior. Fact and fiction merged. Doggedly, Richard Mulcahy struggled to find a way to end it all without more lives being lost.

By late March even Liam Lynch was forced to conclude the Republicans were losing. Tom Barry in Cork still had faith in the ability of his columns as long as they were used offensively, but saw no point in wasting men on purely defensive actions, which was what the war had become. The strong support given the Republicans earlier had been eroded; people longed for a more settled economic and social environment.

Lynch called a secret executive meeting of the IRA and invited de Valera to attend. At very real risk to himself, de Valera joined Lynch and nine of the sixteen Republican commandants in a remote glen south of Clonmel. Over the next four days the military position and the possibilities for an honorable truce were discussed from every angle. At the end of that time a vote was taken to end the war.

Peace lost—by six votes to five.

The meeting was adjourned with an agreement to meet again in the second week of April, when all the commanding officers might be present.

Government forces learned of the plan. With a sense of relief at being able, perhaps, to end the war in one stroke, Richard Mulcahy issued orders to encircle and capture the entire leadership of the Irish Republican Army.

On the eleventh of April a news item flashed over the telegraph to Dublin. A few stark words with no explanation. "Liam Lynch shot dead in Kerry. Details to follow."

Henry joined the pack of reporters besieging the office of the minister of defense. Matt Nugent was among them. "There have been rumors for weeks that the IRA was ready to give up," he told Henry.

"I know; I've heard them too. So why kill Lynch now? What a waste, Matt! What a goddamned waste!"

Richard Mulcahy was not available to reporters; there were rumors that he was devastated by the news. A typewritten statement was handed out: "Liam Lynch, chief of staff of the so-called Irish Republican Army, and several of his colleagues, were surrounded yesterday by Free State troops on the slopes of the Knockmealdown Mountains in County Tipperary. General Lynch was shot long-range by an unidentified sniper, the bullet passing right through his body just above the hip. The wound appeared to be fatal. He insisted that his companions go on without him to save their own lives. When government troops reached General Lynch, he identified himself and asked for a priest. A field dressing was applied to his wound and he was brought down out of the mountains in great pain on an improvised stretcher. From Newcastle he was transported to Clonmel in an army ambulance and given every care, but to no avail. It is reported he gave his fountain pen to one of the officers who had captured him, and said, 'God bless you and the boys who carried me down the hill.' Death came to General Lynch at 8:45 yesterday evening. He has asked to be buried beside his friend Michael Lynch who died on hunger strike in Cork Jail."

Henry, tight-lipped, read the statement twice. Then he took out a pencil and drew a heavy black line through "so-called."

So Liam Lynch was gone. As for Ned Halloran . . . where was he? No one seemed to know. His name was not on any casualty list.

More than one bog in Ireland contained a Republican whose name was not on any casualty list.

On the fourteenth of April Dan Breen was captured in a dugout in the Glen of Aherlow. Starved and exhausted, he had kept himself alive by drinking melted snow. He was said to be one of the last surviving leaders of the IRA.

"I never thought they'd take Dan alive," Henry wrote to Pauline in one of the very rare letters he sent to Limerick.

The civil war was winding down; it was over in all but name. The past lay in ragged tatters, and men and women spoke anxiously of the future, with little idea what form it would take. Ireland would have to be built from scratch.

Once Henry had found the idea exciting. He was not so sure now. The task was for the young, and he did not feel young.

Forty. This year I'll be forty. How in hell did that happen?

He consoled himself that the baby would bring an infusion of youth, a return of the energy and optimism that seemed to have slipped away from him. That's what babies did. Gave a man a reason for going on.

You have to live up to a baby.

Henry began leaving his pistol at home, hidden away at the bottom of a drawer. One less weight to carry.

Frank Aiken, who had replaced Liam Lynch as IRA chief of staff, issued an order suspending offensive action from noon on April thirtieth. This did not stop the government from continuing to arrest Republicans, however.

Eamon de Valera drafted a proposal for peace containing terms that he felt would be fair to both sides. The detailed document covered a number of areas, and attempted to circumvent the oath of allegiance to the king that had been written into the Treaty.

The proposal was flatly rejected by the government.

• • •

In the pages of the *Freeman's Journal* Henry Mooney reported, "Christopher Quinn and William Shaughnessy, of the Irish Republican Army, were executed in Ennis on the second of May. They were charged with the possession of firearms and the murder of government soldiers. Rounding-up operations proceed throughout the country. Upwards of sixty Irregulars have been captured by government troops this week."

Ennis was dangerous for the IRA now. Henry sent an urgent letter to Ursula, asking for news of Ned.

She replied, "We have heard nothing from Papa since he left to join Liam Lynch. I live in fear of seeing his name listed as captured—or dead. Uncle Henry, if you learn anything please let us know!"

On the nineteenth of May Eamon de Valera, from his latest hiding place, gave an interview to a representative from the Associated Press in America. He accused the Free State government of keeping the war going deliberately. "They need to secure their mandate by another election, and they want to hold that election under war conditions," he claimed, "so the Republicans may be denied that freedom of speech and public meeting which the Free State pretends to uphold."

It was a bitter interview that many saw as the angry outburst of a beaten man.

"Don't you believe it," Henry advised Ella over the breakfast table. "Observe that Dev's thinking about elections again. He always has a fallback position."

Five days later Eamon de Valera issued a proclamation: "Soldiers of the Republic, Legion of the Rearguard: The Republic can no longer be defended successfully by your arms. Further sacrifice of life would now be vain, and continuance of the struggle in arms unwise in the national interest and prejudicial to the future of our cause. Military victory must be allowed to rest for the moment with those who have destroyed the Republic. Other means must be sought to safeguard the nation's right."[1]

Simultaneously, Frank Aiken as chief of staff issued an order to the IRA. An official cease-fire was to take place immediately. They were not to surrender their arms to the enemy, however, but to dump them—a move intended to keep the government from dealing too harshly with the Republicans in its custody, for fear of causing a renewal of hostilities.

HENRY wrote, "The Civil War is over. William Shaughnessy of Ennis was the last man to be executed in the struggle for an Irish republic. One might say the first was Pádraic Pearse. And who won the war? Not the Irish people. They had voted for the Republic. Michael Collins and the leaders of today's government accepted the Treaty only as a stepping-stone to that goal. But now the Treaty is the law, and the Republic is, once more, a distant dream."

THE government began counting the cost of the war. During his time as minister for justice, Kevin O'Higgins had presided over seventy-seven official state executions. He also calculated that the battle to enforce the Treaty had cost seven million pounds in the first year and ten million in the second: money the country could ill afford. Article 5 of the Treaty concerned crucial financial relations between Britain and the Irish Free State, and its implementation demanded a solid mandate from the people.

The nation would have little time to lick its wounds. De Valera was right. A new general election would be held as soon as one could be arranged. The date was set for August twenty-seventh.

Mounting an election campaign was difficult for Sinn Féin. The Republicans had been deprived of their most efficient organizers by death or imprisonment. Additionally, the government was making every effort to convince people that a vote for Sinn Féin was a vote to resume the war.

Henry received a hand-carried note from Eamon de Valera: "The bearer of this note can bring you to me. Be certain you are not followed. I have a statement I should like to give to the press."

He found de Valera in a cramped flat over a bicycle shop south of Dublin. Apparently it was his safe house for the day; it bore no sign of permanent occupation. De Valera was accompanied by two silent men in civilian clothing who sat at the back of the room, taking no part in the conversation. Saying nothing. Watching Henry.

"Your friends look as if they don't trust me," Henry commented.

"I trust you," de Valera replied. "That is all that is required." He was not interested in small talk, making it plain that the only purpose of the meeting was to put his statement in Henry's hands.

"It is not the intention of the Republican Government or Army Executive to renew the war in the autumn or after the election," the journalist read. "The war, so far as we are concerned, is finished. Our present purpose is to work through the Sinn Féin organization."[2]

Henry looked up. "How does this affect you personally, sir?"

"I intend to run as the delegate of my party from Clare."

"Does that mean you now accept the legality of the government?"

De Valera's eyes flashed. "It means I continue to deny the right of any foreign authority in Ireland, and refuse to admit that our country may be carved up by any such authority!"

Henry delivered the statement to his press colleagues for publication. Then he wrote his own commentary. "Once Eamon de Valera fixes upon a premise, he will defend it with all the obstinacy of a mathematician defending an irrefutable mathematical point."

Desmond FitzGerald, now minister for external affairs in the Free State government, was quoted as saying, "As long as we are in power de Valera and every other enemy of the country will have to be on the run."[3]

The depleted Sinn Féin Party unanimously endorsed the Long Fellow as its candidate in Clare. Accepting the nomination, he declared, "Our opponents make a mistake if they imagine we are going to remain on the run. If the people of Clare select me as their candidate again I will be with them and nothing but a bullet will stop me."

Ireland was, after all, a small country. Only its moments of highest drama captured international attention. De Valera's words were calculated to contain high drama.

Henry Mooney received a sheaf of cablegrams asking him to cover the Clare election for newspapers abroad.

"I'm not sure if I should, Cap'n," he told his wife. "The baby's due at the end of September, and—"

"Nonsense! I shall have stopped going out soon, but that doesn't mean you must. By all means go to Clare. It will give you a chance to see Ursula, and perhaps Ned."

"Not likely, he's more 'on the run' than Dev. None of his family has heard from him."

"But you do think he's still alive."

Henry stared off into space. "I do think he's still alive. I don't know why I think so, but I do."

IN the meantime there was plenty of other news to cover. In June, James Larkin and his brother Peter announced the formation of the Workers' Union of Ireland. July saw a published estimate of the number of Republican prisoners being held by the Free State: 11,480. That same month, the Appellate Court ordered the release of Nora Connolly O'Brien, James Connolly's daughter, on the grounds that the state of war was over. The Free State government responded by rushing through an Emergency Powers Act allowing them to keep detainees imprisoned indefinitely. It went into effect retroactively.

Henry was furious. "It's imperial arrogance all over again, only worse because it's *us!*"

For publication he was more restrained. "The Free State defends itself in ways reminiscent of the British authority it has replaced. One hopes that when the government feels more secure, it will remember its obligation to justice."

His remarks were published abroad but not in Ireland. Irish newspapers were trying to adjust to changed circumstances. The pro-imperialist *Irish Times* had become the voice of a defeated and somewhat bewildered minority,[4] and even the formerly Republican press was cautious, mindful that the tide had turned. Much of Henry's income depended upon foreign markets now.

On the eighth of August the unarmed Civic Guard was reconstituted under the name Garda Síochána—Guard of the Peace.

"What peace?" Henry wondered aloud. "A civil war never really ends because the combatants remain geographically tied. So the war's fought over and over again in every town and village and pub for as long as they live—or as long as their children carry grudges."

He lay in bed beside Ella, listening to her breathing as she slept. Imagining he could hear the beating of two hearts. One calm and steady. The other as excited as a diver plunging into life.

Chapter Forty-seven

Eᴀᴍᴏɴ de Valera would be running against Eoin MacNeill in Clare. Seán Lester, director of publicity for the government, undertook a campaign to blacken de Valera personally in the minds of the electorate. This would help prepare the public for Dev's being arrested when he surfaced.

To the government's discomfiture, De Valera cooperated by calling for a public rally in Ennis. On the fifteenth of August—the Feast of the Assumption. The day when, according to Catholic doctrine, the Virgin Mary was assumed into heaven body and soul.

"They can't refuse to arrest him," Henry remarked to Matt Nugent, "not after that statement Des made. And when they do, it will make headlines all over the world. The Long Fellow's more of a genius at publicity than Des FitzGerald ever was."

At first Henry planned to go down on the twelfth and spend a few days with the Hallorans, but he kept putting it off. He thought Ella had never been more beautiful. He could not make himself leave her, even for a few days.

Hᴇ awoke before dawn on the morning of the fifteenth. Gave Tilly Burgess detailed instructions she did not need. Changed his shirt twice. Insisted on one more cup of tea.

"If you miss the earliest train," Ella warned him, "you'll miss the rally."

"I'm on my way, Cap'n, don't worry."

A shadow darkened her eyes. "I always worry when you go out that door. You said it yourself—the war isn't really ended."

"It is of course—that was just me trying out the words of an article. I do it all the time. I'll be grand, and back before you know it. You just take care of yourself and our little girl."

Ella's dimples came out like sun after a shower. "How can you be certain it's a girl?"

"I talk to her at night after you're asleep," Henry replied solemnly.

Before he left, he went back into their bedroom and took the pistol from its hiding place at the bottom of a drawer. He thrust it into his pocket without letting Ella see.

PASSENGERS on the westbound train were discussing whether or not de Valera actually would appear at the rally. Most of them were bound for Ennis. Excitement was at fever pitch and rumors flew like bullets. A man who proclaimed to be knowledgeable insisted, "Everyone knows the Long Fellow's going to be assassinated. It's only a matter of time."

Henry hid behind a copy of the *Times*, reading about the new wireless studios recently opened by the British Broadcasting Company in London.

When he reached Ennis he found the town already thronged with spectators who had come from all over the country to witness the anticipated drama. Ursula met him at the station with the pony and trap. Her words tumbled over one another in excitement. "Mr. de Valera's coming here in disguise! He let it be known that he would sail around the south coast, but actually an IRA escort brought him over land. They've promised to be here at two; his secretary's already here. Come on, Uncle Henry! There isn't much time." She lifted the whip and gave the reins an expert twitch. "Gee up, Tad!"

A speakers' platform had been erected in O'Connell Square, where a crowd of dignitaries had gathered in the shadow of the monument to the Liberator. The Irish tricolor fluttered from every flagpole and open window. A local band was playing marches and rebel songs in a vain effort to be heard above the noise of the excited crowd.

Thousands of bodies sweating in the summer heat, acrid, metallic.

HENRY pulled out his watch. He was just saying, "It's two o'clock now, Little Busi—" when a great cry arose from the far side of the square.

A motorcar nosed its way through the crowd and pulled up near the speakers' platform. A tall man in a tweed cap, black overcoat, and plain dark suit emerged, flanked by two Christian Brothers. De Valera had entered town by way of the Kilrush road, somehow avoiding recognition by a military patrol.[1]

As he mounted the steps to the platform he took off the cap and donned a more formal black hat. People wept with joy at the sight of their Chief. A woman rushed forward, saying, "Shake hands, my darling that I suffered so much for!" With a smile, de Valera took her two hands in his own. Then he sat down on one of the chairs provided.

Henry and Ursula had worked their way through the crowd until they were standing close to the platform. De Valera glanced down, saw the journalist, and gave a slight nod of recognition. Henry felt the girl beside him swell with pride.

Tedious introductions and effusive speeches followed. Each local dignitary seized his moment in the sun and relinquished it with reluctance. De Valera waited with his hands on his bony knees. His expression was aloof, curiously withdrawn. When at last his turn came, he was introduced as the president of the Irish Republic to thunderous applause.

De Valera began addressing his audience in Irish, then after a few words changed to English. Waves of emotion shuddered through the throng, ranging from near-religious fervor to barely suppressed antic hilarity.

Suddenly there was a shout from the edge of the Square. "The army's coming!"

The vast audience turned as one and gasped. Free State soldiers accompanied by an armored Whippet and carrying rifles with fixed bayonets approached the platform, firing into the air to drive the crowd back. Their weapons were only loaded with bird shot, but people panicked as several were struck by pellets.

In the confusion on the crowded platform de Valera was knocked down. He scrambled to his feet just as the soldiers vaulted onto the stage beside him. His trousers had been torn by a nail and there was blood on his leg. Men were shouting, cursing. A woman screamed. The crowd was like a wild beast, frightened and furious, explosive as gunpowder.

"We have to get you out of here," Henry said urgently to Ursula.

"I belong here, Uncle Henry—I'm a warrior for the Republic."

"You're a young girl and this is about to get nasty." Ignoring her struggles, he forcibly propelled her away from the platform. He glimpsed Sarsfield and Josephine Maguire a few yards away and shoved Ursula toward them. "Thank God you're here! Would you ever take my niece someplace safe?"

"She'll go home with my wife right now," Sarsfield assured him. "But what about you?"

"Story to cover," Henry said curtly, plunging back toward the speakers' platform.

Soldiers were leading de Valera down the steps. He did not seem to be making any effort to resist, but other men were shouting angry threats at his captors. Henry struggled to get closer. As the crowd surged backward and forward, the weakest and most vulnerable were in danger of being trampled. "Have consideration for the people!" Henry heard de Valera cry to the soldiers.

The frantic crowd became an almost impenetrable barrier. Henry turned sideways and used his shoulder as a battering ram. He burst forward into a cleared space only to find several soldiers busily arresting spectators. Before they could turn to him, he edged back into the crowd and headed in the

opposite direction. Someone elbowed him painfully in the
ribs. When he paused for a moment to catch his breath, he
noticed a narrow laneway between two buildings and stumbled down it. Surprisingly, it was empty.

Henry guessed the soldiers would march their captive to
Home Barracks by way of Jail Street and Station Road.
Through the back laneways of Ennis he hurried to intercept
them. Behind him was the roar of the crowd like a great
baffled beast.

He came out on Station Road in time to see Eamon de
Valera, coatless and hatless, walking briskly forward at the
center of a hollow square. He towered above the soldiers.
There was no chance of speaking to him, of course, but
perhaps once they reached the barracks . . .

In the shadow of a building crouched a man with a rifle.
The oily gleam of the barrel caught Henry's attention as it
swung around to take aim on the officer in charge.

Something snapped in the journalist. *Madman—mad dog!
You should shoot down mad dogs to prevent their doing
more harm.*

Before the sniper could fire, Henry was behind him. Pressing his pistol against the man's neck, he growled, "You may
kill one more Stater, but it won't make any difference to de
Valera, they'll still have him. It will make a difference to
the rest of us, though, because the whole thing will start up
again. I don't want my baby growing up in that kind of
Ireland. Put your rifle down—slow now, and careful—or I'll
shoot you myself. I'm sick of the lot of you."

In one lightning motion the sniper pivoted and straightened up, knocking Henry's pistol hand aside.

The rifle was now aimed at the journalist's heart.

Ned Halloran's green eyes met Henry's across the barrel.

Beyond them Eamon de Valera was marching away to
prison. Neither man noticed.

"I'll shoot you," Ned promised between clenched teeth,
"just like the boys shot Mick Collins."

"Mick was never the enemy. Neither am I, Ned. We both
wanted the same thing you did: the Republic."

"You wanted more than that, you bastard! You wanted

my wife and you took her behind my back!" Ned's finger began to tighten on the trigger.

Henry had always wondered how he would meet his fatal hour when it came. Now he knew. There was no fear, only a great sorrow. "I loved your wife," he said simply. "I wouldn't admit it even to myself, but I loved Síle very much. I never touched her, though. And I never told her how I felt."

The tightening finger paused. "Why not?"

"Because you were my friend."

"Why should I believe you?"

"Because you are my friend."

Henry waited while the green eyes read his soul. Weighed it, measured it.

After an eternity, the barrel of the rifle dropped.

Henry quickly put his pistol back in his pocket. When he thought how close he had come to pulling the trigger, his hands shook. *I could have done it. Sweet Christ, I could have done it.*

He forced his voice to be steady. "Your daughter's with Josephine Maguire, Ned. Why don't you go and collect her now? Take her home to the farm."

"Home to the farm," Ned echoed as if the words had no meaning for him.

"They'll be very glad to see you," Henry urged. "The war's over; you can build a new life."

Ned muttered something.

"Sorry?"

"A baby. You said something about a baby."

Henry grinned in spite of himself. "Ella and I are expecting our first child in October."

Without responding, Ned turned to walk away. Stopped. Stood with his head slumped between his shoulders like a man deep in thought. The moment stretched unbearably. He lifted the rifle again.

Then he tossed it into the ditch beside the road.

"Don't visit the farm anymore," he said without looking around.

"If that's what you want. I'll try to see Dev, then go straight back to Dublin."

Ned turned around then.

Such a little distance separated them: a single long stride or two outstretched arms could have bridged it. Each felt the impulse like an electrical charge running through him.

How simple.

How impossible.

The two men stood looking at one another. Such a little distance separated them.

"Someday I may be able to forgive you," Ned said in a choked voice. "Someday. But not now."

Chapter Forty-eight

September 2, 1923

GOVERNMENT WINS 63 OUT OF 100 SEATS IN
FREE STATE'S FIRST GENERAL ELECTION

September 5, 1923

GERMAN ECONOMIC CRISIS DEEPENS

ADOLF HITLER, LEADER OF NATIONAL
SOCIALIST PARTY, ATTRACTS GREAT CROWDS
AT NUREMBERG

September 10, 1923

IRISH FREE STATE ADMITTED TO LEAGUE OF
NATIONS

BEFORE dawn Ella awakened him with a touch on his arm. "Henry? Dearest?"

Lost in a confused dream of muddy ditches and barking gunfire, he struggled toward her voice. "Wha? Whazzat?"

"The baby, Henry. The baby's coming."

He was instantly awake. "It can't be! The doctor said you had another month."

"He may think so, but the baby doesn't. I've been having

cramps for hours. For a while I thought it was just a stomachache, but . . . here it comes again!" She gasped with sudden pain.

It was Tilly's night off. They were alone in the house. Henry flung himself from the bed and ran out into the passage without stopping for robe and slippers.

When it was installed, the new telephone in the front hall had seemed a wild extravagance, really just a way of showing off for Edwin. Now it was a blessing. Henry stumbled down the stairs in the dark, clutching the banister. At the bottom he turned up the gas jet and snatched the receiver from its cradle. He had to jiggle the phone several times before an operator came on the line. She sounded sleepy.

Henry shouted into the mouthpiece, "We need a motorcab right away, something with good springs! On second thought, get me our doctor first . . . I can't remember his name, damn it! My mind's gone blank . . . Well, yours would too if your wife was having a baby . . . No, of course you don't have a wife. I mean . . . Wait, I have his telephone number right here, it's on the notepad . . . Hold on, I've dropped the damned thing . . ."

He retrieved the pad and read the doctor's number to the operator. While he was waiting for the connection he heard Ella cry out. Dropping the telephone receiver, he ran back up the stairs to her.

A disembodied voice squawked after him.

He found Ella making fretful, ineffectual efforts with the bedclothes. "My water broke." She sounded embarrassed. "I'm sorry, sweetheart, it's such a frightful mess."

"Don't worry about that now. I was just going to telephone the doctor."

Ella reached for his hand. "I should have awakened you sooner, but I didn't want to bother you if it was a false alarm." Her fingers were like ice. "Now I don't think there's time for him to get here."

"You mean you're having it right *now*?" Although in his anxiety Henry could not recall the doctor's name, with dreadful clarity he remembered the man saying to him, "Your wife is narrow in the hips, Mr. Mooney . . . if you take my meaning. It may not be an easy birth. Besides, you've left it a little late, have you not? A woman her age having a first child. We should bring her into hospital for the last couple of weeks."

Ella groaned, caught her breath, groaned again. "Help me," she panted. "Help me."

"What do you want me to do first? Telephone the doctor or change those sheets?"

"There's no time," she said through gritted teeth. "It's happening so fast now. Is it supposed to be so fast? I thought the first labor usually took hours and hours. That's what the doctor said. But it feels like . . . don't leave me, Henry! Promise you won't leave me!"

"I won't leave you." *We need more light in here. Turn up the gas. Fetch some lamps.*

"Did you say something?"

"Talking to myself. It's all right, Cap'n. Everything's going to be all right. I've done this before."

"You've delivered a baby?" she asked incredulously.

Another set of memories flashed across Henry's mental landscape. A shed that smelled of musty straw. A dying mare.

No!

"I have delivered a healthy, living—infant," he assured her, keeping his voice steady. "And I can do it again. You'll both be just fine."

As when he had faced Ned across a rifle barrel, Henry felt a strange calm descend. Like being in the eye of a storm.

ELLA was locked into a pain-filled prison composed of her own body, a cell that allowed her to peer out through the windows of her eyes for brief moments, then closed her in again. In that prison nothing else mattered, nothing but the struggle.

Henry propped pillows behind her and stripped the soiled bedclothes away from her body as best he could. Then he folded a clean blanket and eased it under her hips. "Raise your knees higher," he instructed, "and keep them as far apart as you can."

"I couldn't bring them together if I wanted to. I'm being torn in half, Henry."

"It always feels like that."

"How would you know?" she asked indignantly. "Have you ever had a—" The pain seized her again, swept her away. Her swollen belly heaved. Her sweating face was blotched crimson. Her hair hung in damp strings.

My elegant, fastidious Ella.

Kneeling beside the bed, Henry sketched the sign of the cross over his head and heart. Then he rolled up the sleeves of his flannel nightshirt and set to work delivering his child.

The atmosphere in the bedroom was very heavy. It smelled of flesh and sleep and more fundamental odors. Ella cried out wordlessly in a dreadful rhythm. Her voice was shrill. Almost inhuman.

The pains knotted her and savaged her.

They infuriated Henry.

If she was in hospital they could give her something. Dear Christ, this is barbaric! Suffering like this. Millions of women. Over millions of years. Oh, Cap'n, I'm sorry!

He set his jaw and gave all the help he could. Laboring with her. Reaching into the dark from which all life comes, into which all life goes. The two of them alone in that place.

Alone with pain and fear and hope. No sense of time. No way out but through.

EVENTUALLY someone began pounding on the door below. Henry ignored it. Everything that mattered was already in this room. His hands helping, urging, guiding. The strength in Ella. Her determination to live. To give life.

"Mr. Mooney!" the doctor shouted from the front steps. "The telephone operator alerted me! I've ordered an ambulance if you need one. Can you hear me?"

The pounding on the door went on and on, stopped, resumed. There was a babble of voices on the front steps. Someone began forcing the door.

The sound meant nothing to the man and woman working together in that stuffy bedroom, where the angel of death hovered briefly. Was fiercely rejected. Folded his wings and vanished.

Left the two of them alone.

AND then they were three.

As the child emerged, one of its tiny hands reached out. Grasped Henry's finger. Held on tight.

Source Notes

All sources are listed in the bibliography, p. 509.

CHAPTER TWO

1. *Ireland Since the Rising*, p. 18.
2. *The Irish Republic*, p. 190.

CHAPTER THREE

1. *The Voice of Ireland*, p. 106.
2. *Arthur Griffith and Non-Violent Sinn Féin*, p. ix.
3. *Ireland Since the Rising*, p. 19.
4. *The Irish Republic*, p. 183.
5. Personal letter from Gerald Boland, Second Battalion, to Eileen McCarvill.

CHAPTER FOUR

1. *English Money and Irish Land*, p. 73.
2. *The Irish Republic*, p. 39.
3. *The Irish Republic*, p. 209.

CHAPTER SIX

1. *The Irish Republic*, pp. 210–211.

CHAPTER SEVEN

1. *The Irish Republic*, p. 212.
2. *The Newspaper Book*, p. 133.
3. *The Other Clare*, vol. 13, p. 53.
4. *The Irish Civil War*, p. 98.

CHAPTER EIGHT

1. *Eamon de Valera and the Banner County*, p. 34.
2. *The Irish Republic*, p. 224.
3. *Eamon de Valera and the Banner County*, p. 53.
4. *Eamon de Valera and the Banner County*, p. 57.

CHAPTER NINE

1. *The Newspaper Book*, p. 131.
2. *Potrait of a Revolutionary*, p. 24.
3. *Who's Who in the Irish War of Independence*, p. 68.
4. *Michael Collins: A Biography*, p. 74.
5. *The Irish Republic*, p. 230.

CHAPTER ELEVEN

1. *Michael Collins: A Biography*, p. 64.
2. *Arthur Griffith*, p. 112.
3. *The Irish Republic*, p. 233.

CHAPTER TWELVE

1. *The Shooting of Michael Collins*, p. 27.
2. *De Valera*, p. 99.

3. *Portrait of a Revolutionary*, p. 24.
4. *The Life of John Redmond*, p. 568.

CHAPTER THIRTEEN

1. *The Irish Republic*, p. 237.
2. *The Newspaper Book*, p. 133.
3. *My Fight for Irish Freedom*, p. 29.

CHAPTER FOURTEEN

1. *Michael Collins: The Secret File*, p. 53.
2. *The Irish Republic*, pp. 250–251.
3. *Michael Collins: A Biography*, p. 75.

CHAPTER FIFTEEN

1. *Curious Journey*, p. 117.
2. *Michael Collins: A Biography*, p. 96.

CHAPTER SIXTEEN

1. *The Burning of Bridget Cleary*, pp. 106–108.
2. *The Irish Republic*, p. 254.

CHAPTER SEVENTEEN

1. *The Pity of War*, p. 178.
2. *Lost Dublin*, p. 11.

CHAPTER EIGHTEEN

1. *The Shelbourne*, illustration facing p. 113.
2. *Annals of Dublin*, p. 157.
3. *The Shelbourne* p. 163.

CHAPTER NINETEEN

1. *The Irish Republic*, p. 193.
2. *Big Fellow, Long Fellow*, p. 66.
3. *Dublin as a Work of Art*, p. 153.
4. *The Irish Republic*, p. 276.
5. *De Valera*, p. 130.

CHAPTER TWENTY

1. *The Pity of War*, introduction, p. xxxix.
2. *De Valera*, p. 126.
3. *De Valera*, p. 118.
4. *Big Fellow, Long Fellow*, p. 69.

CHAPTER TWENTY-ONE

1. *The Irish Republic*, p. 284.
2. *De Valera*, p. 133.
3. *De Valera*, p. 144.
4. *The Irish Republic*, p. 299.

CHAPTER TWENTY-TWO

1. *The Irish Republic*, p. 316.
2. *My Fight for Irish Freedom*, p. 82.
3. *Revolutionary Woman*, p. 70.
4. *Irish Bulletin*, March 4, 1920.
5. *De Valera*, p. 149.
6. *Big Fellow, Long Fellow*, p. 93.
7. *The Capuchin Annual, 1970*, p. 510.
8. *The Irish Republic*, p. 327.
9. *Big Fellow, Long Fellow*, p. 92.

CHAPTER TWENTY-THREE

1. *Michael Collins: A Biography*, p. 122.

CHAPTER TWENTY-FOUR

. *The I.R.A. and Its Enemies*, p. 79.
. *The Irish Republic*, p. 444.
. *Limerick, the Rich Land*, p. 61.
. *Days of Fear*, p. 18ff.
. *Big Fellow, Long Fellow*, p. 108.
. *The Capuchin Annual, 1970*, p. 554.
. *The Zeal of the Convert*, p. 173.
. *The Orange Riots*, pp. 31–148.

CHAPTER TWENTY-FIVE

. *The Irish Republic*, p. 356.
. *Guerilla Days in Ireland*, p. 9.
. Radio Telefeis Eireann Archives, direct testimony of Tom Barry.
. *Guerilla Days in Ireland*, p. 1.
. *The I.R.A. and Its Enemies*, p. 79.
. *There Is a Bridge at Bandon*, p. 160.

CHAPTER TWENTY-SIX

. *The Irish Republic*, p. 286.
. *Kevin Barry and His Time*, p. 84.

CHAPTER TWENTY-SEVEN

. *The Black and Tans*, p. 94.
. *The Irish Republic*, p. 389.
. *The Black and Tans*, p. 97.
. *Big Fellow, Long Fellow*, p. 127.
. *Enduring the Most*, p. 195.
. *The Irish Republic*, p. 393.
. *Michael Collins in His Own Words*, p. 2.

CHAPTER TWENTY-EIGHT

1. *The Irish Republic*, p. 396.
2. *Michael Collins*, p. 64.
3. *Michael Collins: A Biography*, p. 160.
4. *Michael Collins: A Biography*, p. 163.
5. *A History of Kilmainham Gaol*, p. 14.
6. *Dublin 1916*, p. 266.

CHAPTER TWENTY-NINE

1. *The Irish Republic*, p. 415.
2. *De Valera*, p. 196.

CHAPTER THIRTY

1. *Irish Bulletin*, vol. 4.
2. *De Valera*, p. 201.
3. *The Capuchin Annual, 1970*, p. 517.
4. *The Irish Republic*, p. 446.
5. *The Irish Republic*, p. 466.
6. *100 Irish Lives*, p. 127.
7. *The Newspaper Book*, p. 143.
8. *The Irish Republic*, p. 472.

CHAPTER THIRTY-ONE

1. *The Capuchin Annual, 1970*, p. 526.
2. *The Irish Republic*, p. 478.
3. *The War in Clare*, p. 104.
4. *Michael Collins: A Biography*, p. 221.

CHAPTER THIRTY-TWO

1. *Michael Collins: A Biography*, p. 226.

CHAPTER THIRTY-THREE

1. *The McGarrity Papers*, p. 109.
2. *Big Fellow, Long Fellow*, p. 193.
3. *Michael Collins in His Own Words*, p. 77.
4. *De Valera*, p. 280.
5. *Modern Ireland 1600–1972*, p. 505.
6. *The Irish Republic*, p. 587.
7. *Arthur Griffith*, p. 227.

CHAPTER THIRTY-FOUR

1. *Michael Collins: A Biography*, p. 274.

CHAPTER THIRTY-FIVE

1. *The Irish Republic*, p. 606.
2. *The Irish Civil War*, p. 9.
3. *Ireland's Civil War*, p. 222.
4. *De Valera*, p. 299.

CHAPTER THIRTY-SEVEN

1. *De Valera*, p. 311.
2. *Potrait of a Revolutionary*, p. 141.
3. *The Irish Republic*, p. 702.
4. *Michael Collins in His Own Words*, p. 35.
5. *The Irish Republic*, p. 694.
6. *The Irish Republic*, p. 705.
7. *Unique Dictator*, p. 197.

CHAPTER THIRTY-EIGHT

1. *Guerilla Days*, p. 179.

CHAPTER THIRTY-NINE

1. *No Other Law*, p. 255.
2. *The Newspaper Book*, p. 164.

CHAPTER FORTY

1. *Oglaigh na h´Eireann—Proclamation*.
2. *Michael Collins: A Biography*, p. 332.
3. *Curious Journey*, p. 340.
4. *De Valera*, p. 324.
5. *The Irish Republic*, p. 785.
6. *The Irish Civil War: An Illustrated History*, p. 71.

CHAPTER FORTY-ONE

1. *The Singing Flame*, p. 123.
2. *Big Fellow, Long Fellow*, p. 312.
3. *Brother Against Brother*, p. 86.
4. *De Valera*, pp. 329–330.

CHAPTER FORTY-TWO

1. *The Irish Civil War* (Coogan & Morrison), p. 207.
2. *Michael Collins in His Own Words*, p. 94.
3. *Harry Boland*, p. 243.
4. *Michael Collins in His Own Words*, p. 94.
5. *Ireland's Civil War*, p. 426.
6. *Michael Collins: The Big Fellow*, p. 240.
7. *Michael Collins: A Biography*, p. 415.
8. *Michael Collins: The Big Fellow*, p. 254.

CHAPTER FORTY-THREE

1. *De Valera*, p. 340.
2. *Richard Mulcahy: A Family Memoir*, p. 196.
3. *No Other Law*, p. 279.

CHAPTER FORTY-FOUR

1. *Civil War in Connacht*, p. 94.
2. *Irish Independent*, December 11, 1922.
3. *Ireland in Quotes*, p. 70.
4. *The Irish Republic*, p. 811.
5. *Ireland in Quotes*, p. 70.

CHAPTER FORTY-FIVE

1. *Report of Commandant Paddy O'Dalaigh, Military Archives, Cathal Brugha Barracks, Dublin.*
2. Personal filmed testimony of Stephen Fuller, from *Ballyseedy*, Radio Telefeis ´Eireann documentary.

CHAPTER FORTY-SIX

1. *Speeches and Statements by Eamon de Valera*, p. 115.
2. *De Valera*, p. 356.
3. *De Valera*, p. 357.
4. *The Irish Times Book of the Century*, p. 144.

CHAPTER FORTY-SEVEN

1. *Eamon de Valera and the Banner County*, p. 187.

Bibliography

Allen, Gregory. *The Garda Siochána*. Dublin: Gill & Macmillan, 1999.

Augusteijn, Joost. *From Public Defiance to Guerrilla Warfare*. Dublin: Irish Academic Press, 1998.

Barry, Tom. *Guerilla Days in Ireland*. Dublin: Irish Press, 1949.

Béaslaí, Piaras. *How It Was Done—IRA Intelligence: Dublin's Fighting Story, 1916–1921*, Dublin: Talbot Press, 1926.

Béaslaí, Piaras. *Michael Collins and the Making of a New Ireland*. Dublin: Phoenix, 1926.

Bence-Jones, Mark. *Twilight of the Ascendancy*. London: Constable, 1987.

Bennett, Richard. *The Black and Tans*. New York: Barnes & Noble, 1995.

Bottigheimer, Karl S. *English Money and Irish Land*. Oxford: Clarendon, 1971.

Bourke, Angela. *The Burning of Bridget Cleary*. London: Pimlico, 1999.

Bowen, Elizabeth. *The Shelbourne*. London: George G. Harrap, 1951.

Boylan, Henry. *A Dictionary of Irish Biography*. Dublin: Gill & Macmillan, 1998.

Breen, Dan. *My Fight for Irish Freedom*. Dublin: Talbot Press, 1924.

Brennan, Michael. *The War in Clare*. Dublin: Irish Academic Press, 1980.

Brennan-Whitmore, W. J. *With the Irish in Frongoch*. Dublin: Talbot Press, 1917.

Brown, Kevin J. *Eamon de Valera and the Banner County*. Dublin: Glendale Press, 1982.

Caulfield, Max. *The Easter Rebellion*. Dublin: Gill & Macmillan, 1963.

Clarke, Austin. *Twice Around the Black Church*. London: Routledge & Kegan Paul, 1962.

Clarke, Kathleen. *Revolutionary Woman: An Autobiography*. Dublin: O'Brien Press, 1991.

Clarke, Thomas J. *Glimpses of an Irish Felon's Prison Life*. Dublin: Maunsel & Roberts, 1922.

Connolly, Colm. *Michael Collins*. London: Weidenfeld & Nicolson, 1998.

Coogan, Tim Pat. *De Valera*. London: Hutchinson, 1993.

Coogan, Tim Pat. *Michael Collins: A Biography*. London: Hutchinson, 1990.

Coogan, Tim Pat, and George Morrison. *The Irish Civil War*. London: Weidenfeld & Nicolson, 1998.

Coogan, Timothy Patrick. *Ireland Since the Rising*. London: Pall Mall Press, 1966.

Costello, Francis J. *Enduring the Most: The Life and Death of Terence MacSwiney*. Dingle: Brandon Book Publishers, 1995.

Costello, Francis, editor. *Michael Collins in His Own Words*. Dublin: Gill & Macmillan, 1997.

Creel, George. *Ireland's Fight for Freedom*. New York: Harper & Brothers, 1919.

Cronin, Seán. *The McGarrity Papers*. Dublin: Anvil Books, 1972.

Czira, Sidney Gifford. *The Years Flew By*. Dublin: Gifford & Craven, 1974.

Davis, Richard. *Arthur Griffith and Non-Violent Sinn Féin*. Dublin: Anvil Books, 1974.

Deasy, Liam. *Brother Against Brother*. Cork: Mercier Press, 1998.

Doherty, Gabriel. *Michael Collins and the Making of the Irish State*. Cork: Mercier Press, 1998.

Doherty, J. E., and D. J. Hickey. *A Chronology of Irish History Since 1500*. Dublin: Gill & Macmillan, 1989.

Dwyer, T. Ryle. *Big Fellow, Long Fellow*. Dublin: Gill & Macmillan, 1998.

English, Richard. *Ernie O'Malley: IRA Intellectual*. Oxford: Oxford University Press, 1998.

Fanning, Ronan, and Michael Kennedy, and Dermot Keogh, and Eunan O'Halpin, editors. *Documents on Irish Foreign Policy*, vol. I, 1919–1922, Dublin: Irish Royal Academy, 1998.

Feehan, John M. *The Shooting of Michael Collins*. Cork: Royal Carbery Books, 1991.

Ferguson, Niall. *The Pity of War*. London: Allen Lane/Penguin Press, 1998.

FitzGerald, Desmond. *The Memoirs of Desmond FitzGerald*. London: Routledge and Kegan Paul, 1968.

Fitzgerald, William G., editor. *The Voice of Ireland*. Dublin: Virtue and Co., 1924.

Fitzgibbon, Constantine. *The Life and Times of Eamon de Valera*. New York: Macmillan, 1973.

Fitzpatrick, David. *Politics and Irish Life, 1913–1921*. Cork: Cork University Press, 1998.

Foster, Roy F. *Modern Ireland, 1600–1972*. London: Allen Lane, 1988.

Gallagher, Frank. *Days of Fear*. London: John Murray, 1928.

Gallagher, Frank. *The Indivisible Island*. London: Victor Gollancz, 1957.

Garvin, Tom. *1922: The Birth of Irish Democracy*. Dublin: Gill & Macmillan, 1996.

Golway, Terry. *Irish Rebel*. New York: St. Martin's Press, 1998.

Gordon, Michael A. *The Orange Riots*. Ithaca, N.Y.: Cornell University Press, 1993.

Gorham, Maurice. *Ireland Yesterday*. London: Batsford, 1985.

Griffith, Kenneth, and Timothy O'Grady. *Curious Journey*. Cork: Mercier Press, 1998.

Gwynn, Denis. *The History of Partition, 1912–1925*. Dublin: Browne & Nolan, 1950.

Gwynn, Denis. *The Life of John Redmond*. London: Jonathan Cape, 1932.

Harkness, D. W. *The Restless Dominion: The Irish Free State and the British Commonwealth of Nations, 1921–31*. New York: New York University Press, 1970.

Hart, Peter. *The I.R.A. and Its Enemies: Violence and Community in Cork, 1916–1923*. Oxford: Oxford University Press, 1998.

Hennessey, Thomas. *Dividing Ireland: World War I and Partition*. London: Routledge, 1998.

Herlihy, Jim. *The Royal Irish Constabulary*. Dublin: Four Courts Press, 1997.

Hickey, D. J., and J. E. Doherty. *A Dictionary of Irish History Since 1800*. Dublin: Gill & Macmillan, 1980.

Hopkinson, Michael. *Green Against Green: The Irish Civil War*. Dublin: Gill & Macmillan, 1988.

Hopkinson, Michael. *The Last Days of Dublin Castle: The Diaries of Mark Sturgis*. Dublin: Irish Academic Press, 1999.

Johnston, Mairin. *Dublin Belles*. Dublin: Attic Press, 1988.

Kearns, Kevin C. *Dublin Street Life and Lore*. Dublin: Gill & Macmillan, 1997.

Kelly, Freida. *A History of Kilmainham Goal*. Cork: Mercier Press, 1993.

Kiely, Benedict. *Counties of Contention*. Cork: Mercier Press, 1945.

Knirck, Jason. *"Ghosts and Realities": Female T.D.s and the Treaty Debate*. New Jersey: Éire-Ireland, published by the Irish American Cultural Institute, 1997–1998.

Laffan, Michael. *The Partition of Ireland*. Dundalk: Dundalgan Press, 1983.

Le Roux, Louis N. *Patrick H. Pearse*. Paris and Dublin: Translated from the French for the Phoenix Publishing Co., n.d.

Lincoln, Colm. *Dublin as a Work of Art*. Dublin: O'Brien Press, 1992.

Lincoln, Colm. *Steps and Steeples: Cork at the Turn of the Century*. Dublin: O'Brien Press, 1980.

Litton, Helen. *The Irish Civil War: An Illustrated History*. Dublin: Wolfhound Press, 1995.

Macardle, Dorothy. *The Irish Republic*. Dublin: Irish Press, 1951.

Macardle, Dorothy. *Tragedies of Kerry, 1922–23*. Dublin: Empton Press, 1930.

McCoole, Sineád. *Guns and Chiffon: Women Revolutionaries, 1916–1923*. Dublin: Government of Ireland Publications Office, 1997.

McDonnell, Kathleen Keyes. *There Is a Bridge at Bandon*. Cork: Mercier Press, 1972.

MacEoin, Gary. *Northern Ireland: Captive of History*. New York: Holt Rinehart Winston, 1974.

MacEoin, Uinseann. *Survivors*. Dublin: Argenta Publications, 1987.

McHugh, Roger. *Dublin 1916*. London: Arlington Books, 1966.

McNiffe, Liam. *A History of the Garda Síochána*. Dublin: Wolfhound Press, 1997.

Macready, General Sir Nevil. *Annals of an Active Life*. London: Hutchinson, 1942.

McRedmond, Louis. *Ireland: The Revolutionary Years*. Dublin: Gill & Macmillan and Radio Telefeis Éireann, 1992.

McRedmond, Louis, editor. *Modern Irish Lives: Dictionary of Twentieth-Century Biography*. Dublin: Gill & Macmillan, 1996.

Maher, Jim. *Harry Boland*. Dublin: Mercier Press, 1998.

Maye, Brian. *Arthur Griffith*. Dublin: Griffith College Publication, 1997.

Mitchell, Arthur, and Padraig O'Snodaugh. *Irish Political Documents, 1916–1949*. Dublin: Irish Academic Press, 1985.

Mitchell, Arthur. *Revolutionary Government in Ireland: Dáil Éireann, 1919–1922*. Dublin: Gill & Macmillan, 1995.

Morrison, George. *The Irish Civil War: An Illustrated History*. Dublin: Gill & Macmillan, 1991.

Moynihan, Maurice. *Speeches and Statements by Eamon de Valera 1917–1973*. Dublin: Gill & Macmillan, 1980.

Mulcahy, Risteárd, *Richard Mulcahy: A Family Memoir*. Dublin: Aurelian Press, 1999.

Murphy, Brian P. *Patrick Pearse and the Lost Republican Ideal*. Dublin: James Duffy, 1981.

Murphy, Jeremiah. *When Youth Was Mine: A Memoir of Kerry 1902–1925*. Dublin: Mentor Press, 1998.

O'Brien, Joseph V. *Dear, Dirty Dublin*. Berkeley: University of California Press, 1982.

O'Broin, Leon. *In Great Haste*. Dublin: Gill & Macmillan, 1983.

O'Buachalla, Séamus, editor. *The Letters of P. H. Pearse*. Buckinghamshire: Colin Smythe, 1980.

O'Clery, Conor. *Ireland in Quotes*. Dublin: O'Brien Press, 1999.

O'Connor, Frank. *The Big Fellow*. London: Thomas Nelson & Sons, 1937.

O'Connor, Kevin. *Ironing the Land*. Dublin: Gill & Macmillan, 1999.

O'Donnell, E. E. *Annals of Dublin*. Dublin: Wolfhound Press, 1987.

O'Donoghue, Florence. *The I.R.B. and the 1916 Rising*. Cork: Mercier Press, 1927.

O'Donoghue, Florence. *No Other Law*. Dublin: Irish Press, 1954.

O'Donovan, Donal. *Kevin Barry and His Time*. Dublin: Glendale Press, 1989.

O'Dulaing, Donncha. *Voices of Ireland*. Dublin: O'Brien Press, 1988.

O'Dwyer, Frederick. *Lost Dublin*. Dublin: Gill & Macmillan, 1985.

O'Farrell, Pádraic. *Who's Who in the Irish War of Independence and Civil War*. Dublin: Lilliput Press, 1997.

O'Gadhra, Nollaig. *Civil War in Connacht, 1922–1923*. Cork: Mercier Press, 1999.

O'Halpin, Eunan. *Defending Ireland*. New York: Oxford University, 1999.

O'Hegarty, Patrick Sarsfield. *The Victory of Sinn Féin*. Dublin: University College Press, 1998.

O'Malley, Ernie. *The Singing Flame*. Dublin: Anvil Books, 1978.

O'Neill, Marie. *Grace Gifford Plunkett*. Dublin: Irish Academic Press, 2000.

Oram, Hugh. *The Newspaper Book*. Dublin: MO Books, 1983.

O'Toole, Fintan. *The Irish Times Book of the Century*. Dublin: Gill & Macmillan, 1999.

Redmond, John, M. P. *The Voice of Ireland* (*Interview*). London: Thomas Nelson & Sons, 1916.

516 Bibliography

Rees, Russell. *Ireland, 1905–25*. Newtownards, Northern Ireland: Colourpoint Books, 1998.

Rose, Richard. *Governing Without Consensus*. Boston: Beacon Press, 1971.

Ryan, Desmond. *Unique Dictator: A Study of Eamon de Valera*. London: Arthur Barker, 1936.

Ryan, Meda. *Michael Collins and the Women in His Life*. Cork: Mercier Press, 1996.

Ryan, Meda. *The Real Chief: The Story of Liam Lynch*. Cork: Mercier Press, 1986.

Ryder, Chris. *The RUC, 1922–1997: A Force Under Fire*. London: Mandarin, 1997.

Saorstát Éireann: Irish Free State Official Handbook. Dublin: Talbot Press, 1932.

Sexton, Seán. *Ireland in Old Photographs*. Boston: Little, Brown, 1994.

Shaw, Desmond. *The Drama of Sinn Féin*. London: Collins, 1923.

Sinn Féin Rebellion Handbook. Dublin: Compiled by the *Weekly Irish Times*, 1917.

Small, Stephen. *An Irish Century, 1845–1945*. Dublin: Roberts Books, 1998.

Spellissy, Séan. *A History of Limerick*. Limerick: Celtic Bookshop, 1998.

Spellissy, Séan. *The Merchants of Ennis*. Clare: Ennis Chamber of Commerce, 1996.

Spellissy, Séan, and John O'Brien. *Limerick, the Rich Land*. Ennis, County Clare: Spellissy/O'Brien Publishers, 1989.

Stewart, A. T. Q., editor. *Michael Collins: The Secret File*. Belfast: Blackstaff Press, 1997.

Taylor, Rex. *Michael Collins: The Big Fellow*. London: Hutchinson, 1958.

The Capuchin Annual. Dublin: 1970.

The Other Clare: Journals of the Shannon Archaeological and Historical Society, Clare.

Twohig, Patrick J. *Blood on the Flag*. Cork: Tower Books, 1996.

Valiulis, Maryann. *Portrait of a Revolutionary: General Richard Mulcahy and the Founding of the Irish Free State*. Dublin: Irish Academic Press, 1992.

Wallace, Martin. *100 Irish Lives*. New Jersey: Barnes & Noble, 1983.

Warner, Philip. *World War I*. London: Cassell Military Classics, 1998.

Wilkinson, Burke. *The Zeal of the Convert*. London: Colin Smythe, 1976.

Williams, W. J. *Report of the Irish White Cross to August 31, 1992*. Dublin: Martin Lester, 1922.

Younger, Calton. *Ireland's Civil War*. London: Fontana, 1979.

ARCHIVES AND UNPUBLISHED PAPERS

Archival material from:
Clare Champion
Cork Examiner
Irish Bulletin, Vols. 1–5, 1919 through 1921
Irish Independent
Irish Press
Irish Times
The Times (London)
Dáil Éireann: Minutes of the Proceedings of the First Parliament of the Republic of Ireland, 1919–1921.
Imperial War Museum, London: Jeudwine Papers.
Military Archives, Cathal Brugha Barracks, Dublin: Material relating to the period 1921–1923.
National Archives, Dublin: RIC Crime Branch Special Papers.
Oglaigh na h-Éireann—Proclamation. Document issued by the Irish Republican Army, dated 28 June 1922.

Personal letter from Gerald Boland, Second Battalion, to Eileen McCarvill (private communication).
Public Record Office, London: Home Office Papers, War Office Papers.
Radio Telefeis Éireann: Sound and Film Archives.

Look for

Lion of Ireland

by Morgan Llywelyn

available in trade paperback
from Tor Books

Now available at your local bookstore!

Chapter One

THE little boy sat on the crown of a rocky hill, his thin arms hugging his scabby knees. He tilted his head back and gazed up into the immense vault of the sky, feeling wonderfully alone.

To the youngest child of a large and brawling family, privacy is a rare thing. Brian always seemed to be walking in someone else's shadow. He had sought this hill because, at the moment, no one else claimed it, and he held his occupancy uncontested.

In a tentative voice he addressed the darkening gray sky. "I am the king," he said, tasting the words. He heard no argument, so he repeated it. Louder. Standing up. "I am the king of all the kings!" he cried, throwing wide his arms to embrace as much as possible of his domain.

THE tireless wind swept across the green land. It came driving inland from the sea, herding a flock of rain clouds before it and releasing them at last above the wooded hills and granite mountains.

Even before the rain fell the air was saturated, heavy and rich with a wetness like the moist breath of babies. Ferns in their dark hollows burned with an emerald flame; the curving flanks of the mountains glistened, polished; the air smelled of life and death and growing things.

Under the cairns and dolmens, within the ruined ring forts and passage graves, deep in the mossy, haunted earth, ghosts stirred. Giants and heroes and cowards slept their thousand year death in the ancient soil and were aware in their powdered bones of the coming of another spring.

BRIGID came to find him, of course. Even the littlest boy had tasks to perform, and Brian was assigned to guard the flock of tame geese that nibbled grass along the banks of the Shannon. Cennedi had no small daughters to be goosegirls.

"Aha, here you are!" Brigid crowed as he came up over the breast of the hill. "Never where you're supposed to be, are you? Your mother's geese could be in a wolf's belly by now for all the good you've been to them." She reached out to pinch his shoulder and give him a shaking, but Brian backed away. He was not about to accept punishment from a girl who was merely the daughter of his father's herdsman.

"The geese are all right," he told her confidently, trying to shade his boyish treble so that she would recognize it as a kingly voice. "I can protect them; I can protect *all* this!" He gestured expansively to indicate his kingdom.

But Brigid was a hard-working girl with chores of her own, resentful at being summoned from them to fetch an errant child, and she had no interest in a little boy's pretend world. She stood before him with her hands on her hips, her tangled chestnut hair whipped about her face by the rising wind. "And how would you be knowing they're all right, when you probably haven't laid eyes on them all afternoon? You come with me right now, and we'll try to get them back to Boruma before this storm blows them away."

She extended a red-knuckled hand to him and, after a brief hesitation, he took it. The two of them started down the hill as the first drops of rain splattered about them. Brigid checked her stride and looked at the little boy.

"And did you come out with no warm clothes? What have you done with your bratt?"

Brian stared blankly up into her stern face, then looked

around him. A few yards distant, crumpled and forgotten,
lay his bratt, the heavy cloak that was a necessity in the
damp climate. Until Brigid mentioned it he had been unaware of the cold, but suddenly the red wool looked inviting.

He retrieved it quickly and handed it to her to pin around
him with the silver brooch that was his only personal wealth.
The wind, which seemed to have been waiting until the child
was snugly wrapped, responded with a rising howl that sent
Brian and Brigid plunging headlong down the slope together, anxious to get the geese to their pen and themselves
under a roof.

They trotted hand in hand through the rain until they
caught up with the scattered flock, grazing in the marshy
grass at the river's edge. Brigid, twice Brian's age and size,
moved after them with the dogged persistence of one who
knows a task will get done somehow. Brian darted about
like quicksilver, second-guessing the nimble geese, turning
and maneuvering them with a skill beyond his years.

To Brigid his antics were annoying; she was afraid he
would scatter the birds and delay them both in the increasingly chill rain. But Brian was not herding geese; in the well-
lit inner landscape of his mind he was a general, marshaling
his troops, wheeling and driving them with the expertise of
a battlefield veteran. His imagination quickly reduced Brigid
to the role of second in command, so that he was angered
when she guided the geese according to some plan of her
own.

"Not that way!" he shouted to her. "Take them up the
path through the trees!" Open country was not safe, his army
could be spotted too easily by enemy scouts!

"And lose half of them in the woods before we get them
home?" Brigid countered indignantly. "Your mother would
have my hide for the pot! Do come along, Brian, and quit
playing around; the both of us will be soaked before we get
these stupid birds penned!"

Actually, Brian was right. The path through the trees was
shorter and more direct, and once the geese were headed
home, their awakening memory of grain was sufficient to
keep them going in the right direction. But Brigid had never
seen them taken by any course but across the meadow, so

that was the way they must go. Flapping her sodden skirt at them, clucking and shooing, she drove them before her as Brian watched in frustration.

"She thinks I don't know anything," he fumed to himself, wiping a lock of dripping red hair from his freckled forehead. "Nobody ever listens to me." He kicked at a small stone that lay invitingly near his foot, then turned to gaze once more at his chosen line of march; he shrugged his shoulders and set off in the wake of Brigid and the flock. "Next time," he promised himself under his breath, "I'll bring them my own way."

The thatched roofs of home glowed golden through the rain. Set in a magnificent grove of oak and pine, Boruma had been built by the princes of the Dal Cais on the ruins of an old ring fort, or *dun*, utilizing its earthen wall and deep ditch as the perimeter of their personal compound. In keeping with his status as tribal king, Cennedi's round timber-and-wattle dwelling was the largest of the buildings. It occupied a central position opposite the gate, surrounded by the homes of his noble kinsmen and domestic buildings and pens for stock. Beyond the wall were the farming lands of the Dal Cais and the cottages of the plowmen. Boruma was—almost—a town, and as large a concentration of people as one could find outside the monasteries and the port cities built by the Norsemen from the distant shores of the place they called Lochlann.

The geese broke into a waddling run as they drew near the gate of the compound. All winter Brian's mother had fattened them in a brush-and-timber pen, feeding them on sprouted grain and bread soaked in barley water. That memory called strongly to them now.

"You feed those birds better than you feed me," Cennedi liked to complain to his wife; but she always had the same smiling answer: "You will get it all eventually, and bad grain and stale bread are much improved by being converted into fat gooseflesh."

"Practical," Cennedi sighed to himself, "she's so practical." Left to his own devices, the chieftain of the tribe was inclined to daydreaming and grandiose visions. It was his wife who saw that nothing was wasted, that food was stored in the souterrains each autumn, and that mattresses were replaced and weapons sharpened in the spring.

Today she was busy in the miller's shed, grinding flour in the communal stone quern. A handsome woman who had not outgrown her beauty, Bebinn looked at the world through calm gray eyes, set in large sockets beneath arching brows. She lifted one feathery brow even higher as the commotion outside announced the arrival of Brian, Brigid, and the geese.

Pouring through the gate, the geese headed straight for their feeding pen, just in time to encounter Cennedi's brace of shaggy wolfhounds returning from some adventure of their own. Forgetting their usual discipline, the dogs flung themselves joyously into the flock, yapping and snapping in mock attack and setting off a cacophony of squawks that brought faces peering from doorways throughout the compound.

Within a matter of moments all was chaos. Bebinn remained at the quern, an amused smile curving her lips. She expected, with justification, that the commotion would become a war and she would be called upon to pacify it.

Soon enough her husband came storming into the miller's hut, waving his fists and complaining bitterly about the amount of peace a man could expect in his own household.

"Your son is out there now, woman, running the feathers off the geese and exciting my hounds so much they'll be no good for hunting for a fortnight! Can't you control that child?"

"I am controlling him," Bebinn responded evenly, not lifting her eyes from her work. "I gave him the job of minding the fowl, to teach him discipline and responsibility."

"Discipline! Responsibility! I tell you, he's out there playing with them, like a wolf harrying lambs! Is that how you want your geese tended?" A massive man with graying hair that had once been the same bright copper as Brian's, Cennedi had a tendency to turn crimson in the face when he was excited. The more he blustered and waved his hands, the calmer his wife became.

"He will always have to make mistakes and suffer for them, if he is to learn," she replied. "If some of the geese are damaged we will cook and eat them, and he shall watch us do it while he goes hungry. And he will learn. But there is nothing to be gained if you go out there yelling and adding to the upset."

"It might not do him any good," Cennedi retorted, "but it will give me a mighty amount of comfort!" He boiled out of the hut, intent on catching his smallest son and rendering him incapable of further mischief.

Bebinn released the handle of the quern and wiped her hands on her skirt. She peered out through the slanting rain, watching as her husband flung himself into the melee. Her eyes were warm with the tolerance of a woman who has borne and raised a dozen sons.

She pulled her shawl over her silver-threaded dark hair and walked briskly across the compound to her house. At the door she turned to look again at the seething mass, to which a new element of confusion had been added as the other Dal Cais menfolk returned from field and pasture. Men were picking their way among flapping geese and darting dogs, and the earth was churned into a sticky sea of mud. The air rang with imaginative profanity.

Bebinn ran her fingers in an unconscious, loving gesture over the elaborately carved doorposts of her home, the gleaming wood polished by her frequent caress. "Come and eat, Cennedi!" she cried between the gusts of wind, her deep voice booming out from her full bosom. "Come and eat, or I shall use it to fatten the hogs in the forest!"

Faces turned toward her, activity lessened for a moment. Satisfied, she went indoors, and soon the cessation of noise from outside assured her the geese had been penned at last. Brian came trudging home, covered with mud, and was followed almost immediately by the vast troop of his brothers returning from the hilly pasturage where they tended the cattle, the "walking gold" of the Dal Cais.

They came in one by one and two by two, tall young men and stripling boys, peeling off their wet bratts and shaking water everywhere as they hung the dripping cloaks close to the fire to dry. They lined up at the hearth, where Bebinn bent over her cauldron, so that each might kiss his mother after his own fashion. Lachtna and Niall and Echtigern

Donncuan, who was to replace Brigid's father one day as chief herdsman. Dermott and Muiredach and Conn the Quarrelsome. Benin and Marcan and Anluan, with his perpetual cough.

Sitting on his little three-legged stool by the fire, reveling in the smells of his mother's cooking, Brian watched the doorway eagerly until Mahon's broad shoulders filled it. He knew that sometime during the evening he could expect a tongue-lashing from his father; but that would be all right, he could bear it, if he could look up and see Mahon's slight smile and subtle wink.

His other brothers did not notice him sitting there in smallness. Even Anluan, nearest him in age, only paid him the attention of sticking out his tongue as he shoved past to salute Bebinn.

Cennedi would not come in to his own hearth and dinner until the men of Boruma were home and the day's business ended. Bebinn believed in discipline and self-restraint for her sons, but she did not expect the impossible; as soon as Mahon arrived she began handing out the crusty loaves of bread, and ladling thick chunks of meat from the pot.

Every edible that came to her hand was simmering in that pot: beef and fowl, with grain and herbs and mushrooms from the woods beyond the compound. Niall had even devised a little tray that his mother could put beneath roasting meat, so that the drippings could be caught and saved for her fragrant stews.

The meal was not a quiet one. Each boy customarily strove to outdo the others in his ability to talk with his mouth full.

"There will be too many cows of breeding age this spring; the red bull can never cover them all."

"Nonsense! You're just saying that because you want to try that gangly brown calf of yours on some of the cows. But he's no good for breeding; you've spoiled him rotten and ruined his temper."

"I have not! I raised him myself because he was orphaned, but I never spoiled him. He's the best young bull we've ever had, and he'll be given the entire herd someday. Just ask Mahon, if you don't believe me!"

The two boys—neither of whom had any say over the policies of breeding—turned to Mahon as the final arbiter of their dispute. Mahon helped himself to a steaming gobbet of meat, chewed it reflectively, winked down the table at Brian, and began wiping out his bowl with his bread.

"It seems to me," he said at last, "that there is something to be said for both bulls. We must observe Liam and our father closely and see what they decide. Perhaps they will use the red one on the majority of the herd, and try the brown on those cows who need more vigor in their calves. But we'll wait and see, and I'm certain we'll all learn something."

The air grew thick with the smell of food, and smoke, and damp clothes drying on warm young bodies. One of the tribeswomen arrived to help Bebinn just as Cennedi himself appeared at last in the doorway, followed by a stooped graybeard wearing a silk-lined bratt.

"Welcome, Fiacaid!" Bebinn hailed the oldster in the nightly ritual. "Will you do us the honor of sharing our evening meal?"

The old man bowed his acceptance and took the seat of honor at Cennedi's right hand, the place that was his from long custom. He was old, and frail, the nobly sculptured bones of his face hidden behind a network of lines like the creases in parchment, yellow and dead. Only his bright eyes were alive, glittering wetly beneath his tangled brows. The years of his maturity had been given in service to the Dal Cais as their *seanchai*, their historian and storyteller, and on a night such as this he often congratulated himself for having a talent that earned him a place at the table and a dry bed.

Bebinn selected the choicest contents of the pot for his bowl, and poured his mead herself, rather than entrust it to the serving woman.

"Will he tell a tale tonight?" the woman asked eagerly, almost treading on Bebinn's heels.

"How can I tell? The physician lives with your family, does he not? And does he set a broken bone every night, or brew a potion at each meal? It is the business of the tribe to care for the members of the *filidh*, the artists and physicians, the poets and harpers and students of the law, and in return for that they share their talents with us when they are needed. It is not my place to tell the *seanchai* that one of his stories is wanted tonight, Maire. Nor is it yours."

The woman snapped her lips shut and returned to her chores, but she frequently rolled her eyes toward Fiacaid, alert to the possibilities of his magic. If he began to talk she would abandon her tasks and run to the other cottages with the news, that all who could crowd into Cennedi's house might come and listen to the legends of their people.

So it happened this night. The old man finally pushed his bowl away and wiped at his stained beard with a square of linen. He tilted his head back to gaze at the underside of the thatch, listening to the rain on the thick straw. He smiled.

"It is a fine night," he announced in a deep and musical voice.

A little sigh of pleasure went up into the smoky air. Bowls were pushed back, hands folded.

"A fine night," Cennedi echoed, taking up the thread of tradition.

"It's a fine night," many voices repeated.

"Rain is good for the memory," intoned Fiacaid. "When there is rain on the roof and meat in the belly, it is time to look over our shoulders and remember."

"We will remember," chanted his audience. The *seanchai* had educated all of Cennedi's tribe; they knew the litany by heart. Since the days of Saint Patrick and before, even to the misty dawn of their race, the chieftains of the island's numerous tribes had vied with one another to possess the most gifted and knowledgeable *seanchaithe*. Fiacaid was a great prize, as Cennedi often reminded his family when he felt their whispering and under-the-table pranks jeopardized their ability to learn from the story-teller's words.

"As you all remember," Fiacaid began, "our last discussion was about the invasions of Ireland in ancient times. Long before history was written down, this land was settled by the descendants of Nemed. They were attacked by the Fomorians, a race of sea pirates from Africa. These Fomorians were great warriors and conquered the land, but some of the Nemedians escaped. Of these, some made their way to distant Greece.

"There they were enslaved by the Greeks and called Firbolgs, a term given them because they were made to carry leathern bags filled with earth to enrich the rocky Greek hillsides. After a long bondage some of them fled from Greece and made their way back to Ireland, armed with Greek weapons and knowledge of warfare.

"They overran the Fomorians, defeating them by stealth and treachery, fighting in hidden places, and always attacking by night. The victorious Firbolgs partitioned the land into those five sections we know today as Ulster, Leinster, Munster, Connacht, and Meath.

"But the Firbolgs were a dark and contentious people, never at peace with themselves, loving argument and discord." The *seanchai's* voice dropped to a lower tone to indicate the sinister nature of his subjects, and Niall kicked Conn under the table and hissed at him, "You're a Firbolg!"

"I am not!" Conn cried, punching his brother in the arm. There was a general shushing and scowling, but Fiacaid merely smiled.

"No, boyo, you are not a Firbolg. It is true that many of their blood are still in our land, stirring up trouble; every gossip and liar, every sneak and thief and hater of music may well be a descendant of the Firbolgs. But the sons of Cennedi are of another tribe, and we will learn of them in good time."

"What happened to the Firbolgs?" Echtigern wanted to know.

"Yes, well. The Firbolgs were a doomed race, as the night is doomed by the coming of the day. Although they built many forts and thought themselves supreme, their time was growing short. From a distant place—some say the islands to the north—came the next of the invaders, a bright and magical people known as the Tuatha de Danann, the people of the goddess Dana. They were highly skilled in the arts of Druidry, and could call the wind by whistling for it, or make barren cattle conceive."

Fiacaid leaned forward, and all his listeners leaned toward him in response. "From their city of Falias they brought the Stone of Fal, which shrieks aloud when the lawful Ard Ri is named king of all kings at Tara." His audience exchanged glances and knowledgeable nods.

"From Gorias they brought with them the Spear of Lugh, which insures victory in battle. Out of the city of Findias came the Sword of Nuada, the most deadly and irresistible of weapons; it belonged to the king of the Tuatha de Danann and never left his hand, even sharing his bed at night.

"And with them from the city of Murias they brought Dagda's Cauldron; no one who ate from it was ever left unsatisfied."

Bebinn's eyes brightened at the mention of such a cooking pot. *Just the thing for the mother of twelve sons*, she said to herself wistfully. *Is there a chance, I wonder, that the thing still exists?*

"Did they fight with the Sword and the Spear?" asked Dermott, leaning forward so eagerly that he spilled Donncuan's unfinished cup of mead and was smartly cuffed on the ear for it.

"Ah, yes," Fiacaid assured him. "People who think they have superior weapons always find reasons to test them." Once Fiacaid had enjoyed the thrill of battle with all the gusto of the would-be warrior relegated to watch from the sidelines—members of the *filidh* being exempt from fighting by reason of their superior and valuable education. But now the chill of winter lingered in his bones through the summertime as well, and the glories of warfare had turned to ashes in the memory of a man who had seen too many friends die.

Yet as he looked down the table and saw the eager faces turned to his, the old intoxication came as a faint echo in his thinning blood. The heady wine of storytelling, the addiction to the shape and color of words, the desire to pass on his own enthusiasms—it was sweet to yield and feel himself grow young again, telling the tale as it was told to him in his childhood.

"Oh, they were a beautiful people, the people of Dana!" He raised his head so that his old eyes seemed to look beyond the crowded room, into a past clearer to his vision than the present. "Their king was Nuada, the perfect and fearless, who towered above the lowly Firbolg as the oak above the alder."

Brian looked across at Mahon and felt in his heart that King Nuada must have looked very much like that. Fair of hair and broad of brow, Mahon was even taller than his father, a handsome young giant indeed. To Brian, he was the image of a hero-king.

"The Tuatha de Danann met the Firbolgs in battle on the Plain of Moytura. They came with a blowing of horns, and a shining mist all around them like dust from the stars, and the grass bent down beneath their feet in homage. The battle lasted four days and four nights, and the brilliance of the Tuatha de Danann stayed the darkness so that the Firbolgs could not attack by stealth, as was their custom. They had to stand and fight, face to face, and by the fourth sunrise even the birds and insects had fled the place, so terrible was the fighting.

"Then it was that the two kings, Nuada the Perfect and Eochai of the Firbolgs, met in single combat to put an end to the slaughter. The Light against the Darkness."

Brian saw Mahon standing tall and proud, his invincible sword in his hand, slashing at the evil king who crouched and slavered at his feet.

"While time stopped and the very land held its breath, the two champions fought in that place. They fought in skill and in silence, with only the hissing of their breath about them, and at last Nuada gained the advantage and killed Eochai!" Fiacaid's voice rose, filling the room with triumph. "The Tuatha de Danann were victorious, and the time of the Dark People was over!"

The inheld excitement of the listeners poured out in a great sigh of pleasure.

"But wait!" An anxious expression crossed the old man's face, and he held up his hand to show that his audience must not rejoice too soon. "During that final contest Nuada, great warrior though he was, suffered a fearful wound."

Brian's eyes darted to Mahon again, and the little boy was reassured to see his brother sitting whole and well.

"Nuada's hand was cut from his wrist by the dying blow of the Firbolg king. Thus he became imperfect, ineligible to rule under the laws of his people. He was forced to abdicate, and tragic days followed for the People of Light."

Fiacaid's skill was not limited to the extent of his knowledge or the richness of his voice; he also knew when to stop. "The rest of the history of the Tuatha de Danann must wait for another time," he announced firmly. "My eyes are burning with want of sleep; I will go to my bed now and refresh myself."

"No! Please . . . just a little more!"

Fiacaid shook his head. "Not tonight. But soon I shall tell you of Nuada and the Silver Hand, of Second Moytura, of the destruction of the monster Balor of the Baleful Eye, and"—his voice trailed away, leaving an aching emptiness in the room—"and many other things," he finished brightly. "But that will be another day. I bid you all God's peace this night."

He wrapped his bratt around him with a dramatic flourish and left the table. The others reluctantly shook off his spell and busied themselves with their own pursuits. Only Brian sat, quiet and dazzled, still seeing wonders.